Point of Honour

Madeleine E. Robins

A Tom Doherty Associates Book
New York

This is a work of fiction. All the characters and events portrayed in this book are either products of the author's imagination or are used fictitiously.

POINT OF HONOUR

Edited bt Patrick Nielsen Hayden

A Tor Book
Published by Tom Doherty Associates, LLC
175 Fifth Avenue
New York, NY 10010

www.tor.com

Tor® is a registered trademark of Tom Doherty Associates, LLC.

ISBN 0-812-57049-9
EAN 978-0812-57049-6

Library of Congress Catalog Card Number: 2002045486

First edition: May 2003
First mass market edition: May 2005

Printed in the United States of America

0   9   8   7   6   5   4   3   2   1

on the hob. "Wouldn't you rather take your dinner from there?"

Miss Tolerance reached to ruffle the fair hair of her guest. He was young and open-faced, with a square jaw, broad mouth, blunt nose, and good-natured brown eyes, dressed in buckskin breeches and a finely made linen shirt. His shoes and stockings, Miss Tolerance saw now, were drying before the fire.

"Go out into *that* for a plate of ham and peas? Bread and butter will do me well enough. But why aren't you taking your dinner in the house?"

Matt stretched and made a face. "It's my evening off, and Holyfield is there. He will not take no for an answer, and I haven't the energy to defend myself from him tonight."

"Defend? I thought Holyfield was one of your favored patrons." Miss Tolerance took bread and cheese from the cupboard and cut a healthy slice of each.

"One of the wealthiest, and he's not a bad fellow." Matt shrugged. "Money is money, but before God, Sarah, as we don't rest even upon the Sabbath day, I've a right to an evening of rest"—he descended into the dense accents of the Eastside stews—"and I ain't spending mine on the likes of milord Holyhell." His normal voice, and the genteel accents Mrs. Brereton required of her workers, returned. "But the marquess has no interest in you, so why not delight your aunt and join her for supper?"

"I'd hardly do her credit, looking like a drowned rat. And I'd rather not encounter any of my aunt's clientele this evening."

"For cause?"

"I'm sick of the lot of them. I finished a bit of business early this morning, made my report tonight, and it has given me a roaring distaste for men of a certain class. Is that the paper? Be quiet for a few minutes and let me read."

Miss Tolerance took the cup of tea which Matt handed her and sat in an armchair convenient to the fire so that she could prop her feet up on the fender. Then she took up the week's issue of the *Gazette*. Passing lightly over the society notes, she

skipped the foreign news entirely and turned to the Dueling Notices for the previous month:

By the sword, fatally: Peter, Lord Henly
By shot, fatally: Mr. David Pankin
By shot, wounded: Sir Vandam Godalming
By shot, fatally: Mr. Wallace Strachey . . .

Below each listing was a brief descriptive paragraph of the
meeting, and in some cases, its putative cause.

"Henly's got himself killed, Matt," Miss Tolerance observed
coolly. "The *Gazette* is not specific upon the point, but I suspect
it was a quarrel with Jennaroe over Harriet Delamour."

Matt *tsk*ed and bit into an apple. "Little Carrie will be deso-
lated by the news."

"Was he one of hers?" Miss Tolerance asked.

Matt nodded. "I ought not to say; you know how Mrs. B dislikes us to gossip. Any other notables on the list?"

"Peters winged Godalming and their seconds considered the
matter concluded. Lazenby cried off the meeting, pleading a
stomach disorder—that won't gain him much with Fitch—"

"Lord Fitch?" Matt scoffed. "Whatever could Dennis Fitch
find to quarrel with Frederick Lazenby about?"

Miss Tolerance raised one eyebrow quizzingly. "What do gentlemen with more money than sense generally quarrel about?
Women, horses, money, cards—the list is endless. Perhaps they
fought about you, for all I know. I'm only surprised that Lazenby
allowed himself to be cozened into a meeting with a man who
is a renowned shot." She returned her attention to the paper,
noting the names of two more former clients among the deceased. "Damn, what a plague of killing. Matt, toss me my
counts-book, it's just there by your lazy head."

Matt reached around behind him, rummaging blindly among
the pile of books and papers on the shelf above the settle. "Is
this it, Sarey?" In response to Miss Tolerance's nod, he tossed
the book to her, pages fluttering. She caught it deftly, one-

handed. "What's the matter? Checking to see if one of the dear departed had settled his shot?" He grinned.

"It's all well for you to laugh, parasite. So long as there's a market for your talents, you'll never go hungry. Some of us must needs make a living elsewhere," Miss Tolerance said without rancor. "Well, Millward paid his account. In gold, too."

"Such a handsome way to meet one's obligations. Who's the other corpse?" Matt pitched his apple core past Miss Tolerance's knee and into the fire.

"Sir Evan Trecan; wrote a draft on his bank, which the bank has so far declined to honor. Damn, damn, damn."

Matt rolled over onto his stomach and set his chin on his fists. "How does a lowly woman of business dun a member of Parliament—a *dead* member of Parliament?"

Miss Tolerance sighed gustily. "I shall write a note to his estate. Although if Sir Evan's pockets were as deeply to let as I believe them to have been, his agents will likely laugh at it. At least someone will derive some amusement from the matter. Damn, there's paper and ink spent, probably to no account."

For several minutes, as Miss Tolerance scratched earnestly at her paper, there was no other sound but that of the fire. At last she looked up and cocked an eyebrow. "How does my aunt's business tonight?"

"Brisk, my dear, brisk. Something about a thunderstorm seems to bring out the rake in any number of our notable citizens."

"I don't suppose Horace Maugham has come by this evening?"

"That bore? He rarely comes to us—I think he prefers a lower class of pleasure, and I'm not what he fancies," Matt said airily.

"I didn't expect it, merely wondered. I finished Mrs. Maugham's business this morning and gave her the damning evidence tonight as she was dressing for Almack's." She smiled mirthlessly. "It will doubtless be all over town tomorrow, for it's as Mrs. Maugham suspected, only less savory. Her husband keeps a pair of girls—little more than children—in a cottage near Riversend, on his wife's money."

"Lower class and younger, then." Matt nodded.

"Sisters, not above thirteen. And Mrs. Maugham's thoughts will be all for punishing her husband—she'll bring him to heel, and the children will be cast aside."

"Enough to give you a jaundiced view of marriage," Matt said. "How lucky we are to have avoided it."

Miss Tolerance frowned for a moment, then went back to the paper, turning the page from the Dueling Notices to the city news. "The Queen Regent and her doctors report that the King's health remains good, despite his infirmity—is madness an infirmity, then, like gout?"

"I've heard the Queen will not be left alone with her husband for fear that he will ravish her. At her age?" Matt sounded delighted by the thought. "Marriage is overrated."

Miss Tolerance did not rise to the bait. "The Queen Regent has canceled Thursday's Drawing Room owing to a slight indisposition," she read. "Lady Julia Geddes has moved the venue for her ball to Versellion House, owing to a recent infestation of ladybugs in her own establishment. And hear this! Fevier is running in the by-election for a seat in the House, with Versellion's support. Montroy means to oppose him, and in that I suspect the delicate hand of Lord Balobridge. What great boards these kingmakers play upon! And the vote in the House regarding the question of support for Viscount Wellington's Spanish campaign was tabled for more debate—again. By the time the House votes support for Wellington, the war will be five years over, and Bonaparte long in his grave. The price of corn has risen again. And— dear me: a Mr. James Mondulac was beaten last night as he left his club—Tarsio's, as it happens—and sustained considerable injury. What was that about, I wonder? I believe I shall take my lunch at Tarsio's tomorrow, and nose about to satisfy my vulgar curiosity. If anyone wishes to discuss business, they are more likely to search for me there than here."

"A very respectable ambience that is, Sarey." Matt shook his head.

"Unlike the refined precincts of my aunt's brothel?"

"The membership of Tarsio's is . . . variable. At your aunt's, you know the quality of the help"—Matt sketched a bow—"and you know the clientele is impeccable."

"Whereas I collect, the women at Tarsio's are in the main players, poets, and adventuresses. *Entirely* unlike myself." Miss Tolerance favored her friend with a tight smile. "There are not so many places in London that a ruined woman may comfortably frequent, Matt. There's no reason for your snobbery. Not everyone can be a whore at Brereton's, and it's hardly fair to hold it against Tarsio's that they admit all sorts of people."

"And if I declared you an honorary doxy?" Matt grinned.

Miss Tolerance's expression was carefully neutral, her tone cool. "I should die a pauper, and little honor in that. Now"—she had noted the hour on the pocket watch that rested on her mantel, and roused herself from the firelit comfort of her chair—"I will send you out into the night. I've been abroad since dawn tracking Mrs. Maugham's wayward husband. I need to sleep."

Matt grimaced, took up his boots in one hand and a large, rectangular rain shield in the other. "You're certain you wouldn't prefer I stay? I'm little good to you as a man, but I'm far more agreeable than a copper bedwarmer." He grinned as if he knew what the answer would be.

"Cat! You would do anything to avoid going out in the rain again, wouldn't you? Go!" Miss Tolerance gave him a gentle shove in the direction of the door but did not wait to see him go out into the night. She took up her candle and went upstairs to her chamber.

By the light of the one candle, she brushed her long hair and braided it, exchanged dressing gown for nightshift, and climbed into her bed. While the cottage she let from Mrs. Brereton was rustic in its appointments, the bed was, like all those in the house itself, broad and lushly comfortable. With a small fire in the grate to take the chill out of the air, she would shortly be delightfully warm and sleepy. Except that, as sometimes happened when an assignment was completed, Miss Tolerance found that she could not sleep at all.

At last, irritated, she relit her candle, propped herself on one elbow, and took up Mainley's *Art of the Small-Sword*. She had read it often before and found it a remarkably soporific work, but should its tranquilizing power fail to lull her to sleep, she reasoned, at least it would reinforce her training. She read until the candle guttered and the book fell from her fingers, but still did not sleep. The best she could manage to do was to lie listening to the thrum of raindrops on the roof and the tap of rain on the window, the small, sharp crackling of the fire, and the slow, even sound of her own breath.

Miss Tolerance woke the next morning to find the sun well advanced in a blue sky; only the gutters, still clogged with leaves, and her greatcoat, still smelling of damp wool and gunpowder, put the lie to the sunshine. She took her time in rising, calling across to Mrs. Brereton's kitchen for hot water, and bathing the last memory of sodden chill from her muscles. Then, with no assignment before her and the pleasant memory of Mrs. Maugham's account, paid in full, to comfort her, Miss Tolerance dressed for the day. As she did not anticipate any activity more taxing than luncheon or a game of whist, she allowed herself the vanity of going out in her new blue morning dress and ivory straw bonnet. She braided her hair, put it up in a coil on her head, and at last took up her gloves, half jacket, and reticule and left the house for Tarsio's Club, in Henry Street.

Making her way through the street past fruitmongers and a clutch of climbing-boys engaged in vociferous argument, Miss Tolerance felt the air sliding around her, warm, thick, humid; the hot breeze which blew from the river did nothing to improve matters. A few tendrils of her dark hair escaped their confinement and curled damply at the nape of her neck; her gloves felt too small and very sticky. She began to think with anticipation of a glass of punch in the cool white confines of Tarsio's Conversation Room.

The footman at Tarsio's, who was an old acquaintance of Miss Tolerance's, greeted her with a mixture of familiarity and respect, hoped that he found her in good health, and regretted that no messages were waiting her.

"I hear there was trouble a few nights ago, Steen," Miss Tolerance observed.

Steen nodded. He was assumed, professionally, to be above gossip, but Miss Tolerance had more than once slid him a coin across a tavern table to acquire some choice bit of information. He had learned to speak freely to her, and was not infrequently the source of new business. "An ugly business, miss," he said now. Several members were crossing the hall to the Billiard Room.

Miss Tolerance waited until the hall was again clear, then asked, "Did it happen close to the club?"

Steen looked mildly affronted. "Would I have let a gentleman of this club be beaten in my sight, miss? It were around the corner, on King Street. By the time we heard the commotion and Corton and I run around to see what was afoot, Mr. Mondulac was lying on the ground and all I saw of his attackers was the soles of their boots."

"More than one of them, then."

"Yes, miss. Might happen there was three of 'em, though I'm sure I couldn't say for sure."

"Ah, well. Thank you, Steen. Oh." Miss Tolerance took a coin from her reticule to press into the footman's hand. "Should Mr. Mondulac be curious as to who his assailants were and wish to pursue the matter, you will stand my friend, will you not?"

Steen permitted himself to smile. "I will, miss." He pocketed the coin.

From the hallway, Miss Tolerance repaired to the Ladies' Salon, where a collation had been arranged on the sideboard in lieu of the more formal noontime meal which was commonly served in the Men's Dining Chamber.

In the Salon there were perhaps a dozen women of all conditions of respectability, Tarsio's one criterion for its female members being that they were sufficiently funded to afford the yearly fee and commons. A recent and notorious author was listening with sympathy to the narrative of a woman Miss Tolerance recognized as the mistress of a well-placed peer; with each nod of comprehension or empathy, the author's highly ornamented bonnet shook violently, with a rustling that could be heard throughout the room. A young opera dancer whose rapid rise had been recently matched by a precipitous fall from public favor entertained three dewy, blinking young men, chatting vivaciously; she was shopping for a protector so blatantly that Miss Tolerance was surprised she had not been politely ushered out. Despite a liberal attitude toward its members, Tarsio's Club did have some standards to uphold.

There were several women seated together at a table enjoying a quiet game of cards; Miss Tolerance nodded to the group but took a seat by herself near the window, drew a journal from the table nearest her chair, rethought the notion of punch, and ordered a pot of tea. She then settled in, intending nothing more than to spend the afternoon reading and dozing, like any of her counterparts in the Men's Reading Room. As she read, however, she listened; before her tea had arrived, she had learned that it was indeed a dispute over the favors of that same Harriet Delamour, who now sat across the room choosing from among her three suitors, that had led to the untimely demise of Lord Henly; that there was a new shipment in of gold-shot silk at the docks; and that at any moment an Oxford scholar could expect to be sanctioned by the archbishop on suspicion of popery. No immediately profitable intelligence, Miss Tolerance thought, but less interesting news had proved valuable before.

After a time she put her feet up on a footstool, folded the journal in her lap and crossed her hands over it, and stared out the window. The affair of Mrs. Maugham had been accomplished with a little less simplicity than she had led Matt to believe; she had left her rooms on Mrs. Maugham's business nearer midnight than dawn, and the dissipations of the night, which had included being chased along a narrow footpath at the riverside by one of Mr. Maugham's lackeys, had taken their toll of her. It was very pleasant to sit in a sunny window and think of nothing for an hour.

"Miss Tolerance?"

As she disliked to be taken unawares, Miss Tolerance did not move her gaze. She gave a small nod and said, "I am she, sir."

"Madam?" From the sound of it, her interlocutor was not sure that Miss Tolerance was, in fact, awake.

"I am still she, sir. How may I assist you?"

"I am Trux. You have heard my name before?"

Miss Tolerance turned from the window and smiled. "Your name is known in the circles I frequent, my lord." That, she thought, was a nice turn of phrase. He could believe she meant the gentry or the criminal classes, as he pleased.

Trux flushed, bobbing his chin slightly, as if his neckcloth were too tight. Miss Tolerance motioned toward a chair, and observed him as he settled into it. He was stocky, not above medium height, and the fine-knit fabric of his breeches strained across heavy thighs as he sat. His clothes were of excellent quality, but his blue coat was just a shade too bright in hue, the buttons a quarter inch too wide, and his neckcloth was tied poorly in too elaborate a knot. He wore his dark hair cut fashionably short, in a style that made the worst of his features: small, peering eyes, ears that jutted from the side of his head, and jowls already too heavy for a young man's face—she did not judge him to be much above twenty-five. Youth and money, Miss Tolerance thought, but decidedly no taste.

"Miss Tolerance," Trux said. "I understand that you undertake, from time to time, small tasks. . . ."

"I do, sir."

"Tasks of a private nature. . . ." He paused as if to convey a sense of delicacy.

"I try to keep all my business private, sir. It is not always possible, but I undertake that no disclosure will come from me."

"Rather from the sight of Hermione Maugham throwing a cup of Almack's lemonade into her husband's face?"

Miss Tolerance cocked an eyebrow. "Did she so? Lord Trux,

I can but complete my client's assignment. What happens after, I cannot control."

Trux paused to consider this, then nodded. "Reasonable, I suppose. I will be brief, Miss Tolerance. I act as the agent of another, who has requested that I find, or cause to be found, an article of his which is missing." Trux raised his lace-edged handkerchief and delicately blotted the sweat on his upper lip. As he did so, Miss Tolerance noted the dark circles under his arms where the sweat was already soaking through his coat.

"And was this article stolen from your . . . patron?" Miss Tolerance paused meaningfully. She had seen all too many people who pretended the work they required was not to be done for themselves.

Trux frowned and shook his head. "It was not stolen, no. The article in question—"

"Which is?"

"A fan, Miss Tolerance. A very old, antique fan, an heirloom of my friend's family which he rashly gave away as a token . . . a token of . . . that is, he was young—"

Miss Tolerance nodded. "It is not an original story, my lord. A young man is smitten with a young lady, and gives to her as a token of his affection some item which he ought to have left home in its drawer. These tokens are more usually jeweled necklaces or brooches that the young man has no right to pledge, but I suppose an antique fan is as good a gift as any other."

"The fan was his to give," Trux said defensively.

"Well, then, what is to prevent him from going to the lady now and asking for its return?"

"The situation is a delicate one."

"Is this a sort of delicacy I should understand, so as not to bruise its tender flesh?" Miss Tolerance asked dryly. "I frequently find that the more particulars I am acquainted with, the more delicately I can perform my task."

"I'm afraid the particulars are not within my power to give, Miss Tolerance." Trux looked smugly pleased to be able to deny her something. "I can tell you only that the fan is delicately made, of ostrich skin painted with a copy of an Italian landscape, stretched upon golden sticks that are studded with rubies and brilliants. The lady we believe to be in possession of the fan is—" Trux stopped. "But you have not yet agreed to undertake the commission."

"Very true, my lord. I would be happy to perform this small task for you. I must warn you, however, that as I am a woman alone in the world, I must charge a good fee for my work."

"We are prepared to pay." Trux paused; she watched as he did a sum in his head, saw his cheek twitch in displeasure, then watched him, as she fancied, revise the sum. "We offer you two guineas for recovery of the fan. Plus expenses," he added kindly, as if offering her a special treat.

Miss Tolerance did a calculation of her own, guessing what Trux's original sum was to have been. "Obviously your patron little understands the nature or the expenses of work such as mine, my lord. I regret to inform you that the cost for such an errand would be three guineas a day, in addition to any reasonable expenses I should incur. I will, of course, produce a written summary of such expenses when the commission is completed."

Trux frowned. "That's a great deal of money. We could as easily hire a Bow Street man—"

"It is a delicate commission, sir? Finesse is expensive."

He shrugged and nodded. "As you say. The woman to whom you should apply for the fan—"

"Can I expect that she will simply release it to me?" Miss Tolerance asked in surprise. "Then I truly do not see why you or your patron could not save yourselves some money, hire a chair, visit the lady in person, and have the matter done with."

"We do not expect that she will part with it without remuneration," Lord Trux said stiffly. "You may offer her up to five hundred pounds. If she requires more than that, you will kindly let me know by directing a note to my attention at my club, Boodle's. I will let you know how to proceed."

Miss Tolerance nodded. On the table at her side, the cup and the teapot stood, both quite cold. She raised two fingers quietly to summon a waiter, and gestured to summon a fresh pot of tea. "Shall I ask for another cup, my lord?"

Trux shook his head. "My business is almost concluded. The lady to whom you must apply is Mrs. Deborah Cunning. Her last address, so far as my friend knows, was Richmond."

"And how long ago was that?" Miss Tolerance asked. Trux did not answer. She sighed. "I see. Is that another of those delicate details about which I must not inquire? You tie my hands, my lord, and make my task doubly difficult."

Trux stood. "From what I have heard of you, Miss Tolerance, I do not believe that a little difficulty will keep you from earning your fee."

Miss Tolerance rose likewise. "It is kind in you to say so, my lord. May I ask from whom you heard of me?"

"Your name is known in the circles I frequent, ma'am." Trux tilted his chin up slightly, with the air of one conferring a killing blow.

Miss Tolerance laughed, a full, delighted sound that rang through the hush of the room. The heads of the card players, of Harriet Delamour and her followers, turned toward the unexpected sound; Lord Trux looked embarrassed and angry.

"Very good, my lord. Well, I shall send reports of my progress to you at Boodle's. If the task is as simple as you seem to believe, it should be concluded before too long." She extended her hand.

Lord Trux took it, but looked uncertain whether to bow over it or shake it as he might have a man's. Miss Tolerance decided the matter by shaking his hand and withdrawing her own. He turned to go, then turned back again. His eyes gleamed with malice.

"I must say, Miss Tolerance, you seem a very genteel sort of woman. I cannot understand how a lady of good family, no matter what her past, could arrive at such a pass, and in such a position, as yours."

Miss Tolerance smiled. "Society offers a woman like myself very few choices, my lord. Some become whores, some madams or hatmakers. I became an investigative agent. In the end it is all the same: a woman who can fall no farther has little choice but to go into business for herself."

"I see," said Lord Trux, who clearly did not see at all. He bowed, bade her good afternoon, and left.

Two

Miss Tolerance dined at Mrs. Brereton's house that evening. Her aunt's parlor was a handsome room at the back of the house on the second floor. The drapes were blue and a soft gold; the furniture was in the sleek style favored by the first Empress of France and her court, although with a good deal less gilding. Several well-chosen pieces of statuary in the Grecian style framed the window that looked onto the rear garden; the roof of Miss Tolerance's cottage was barely visible through the trees. The effect overall was of restful quiet, and of a good deal of money spent to excellent effect.

Mrs. Brereton was at her desk when Miss Tolerance arrived, attending to a stack of invoices and her counts-book, with her pen moving smoothly across her paper. Mrs. Brereton's hair was dark, short-cropped and pomaded in the style of the day, and becomingly threaded with silver. Despite her years and the silver in her hair, her profile was as firm as Miss Tolerance's own; her dark, intelligent eyes and full mouth gave the impression of a far younger woman. She was tall, like her niece, and had been a slender girl. Now her figure was beginning to thicken, but a clever dressmaker and good carriage gave the impression of slimness still. Unlike most women of her calling, she did not paint her face, but let her well-tended complexion and hair give the lie to her years. "Artifice cheapens," she told the women in her employ. About her neck she wore a necklace of pearls which contributed to the youthful impression she made. Mrs. Brereton's jewels were always entirely real, and of excellent quality.

Miss Tolerance took a chair by the fireplace and waited in silence until the scratch of pen upon paper should stop.

At last, Mrs. Brereton looked up from her work. "Good evening, my dear." She presented her cheek for her niece's kiss.

"Good evening, Aunt. Fretting over money again?"

"Paying bills. What this house uses in sea sponges and siliphum seed, not to say wax candles and laundering soap, is scandalous." Mrs. Brereton spoke lightly.

"At least you may comfort yourself that the price of sea sponges and vinegar is less than for the fostering of bastard children, ma'am. And given the throng of custom I see coming and going, I cannot believe that money is a concern for you."

Mrs. Brereton closed her books and capped the inkwell. "Don't be foolish: money is always a concern. I need not only pay my bills and deal straightly with my staff, but save against my retirement. There is no such thing as too high a profit, Sarah."

"I will remember that, Aunt," Miss Tolerance said.

Her aunt sniffed and changed the subject. "Well! I hear that you have pitched the Maugham household into a mighty state of confusion."

Miss Tolerance shook her head. "Not I. I merely confirmed for Mrs. Maugham what she already suspected. I would rather say that Mr. Maugham was responsible for the turmoil in his home."

"Perhaps, my dear. But if you had not uncovered his secrets—"

"Someone else would have done so, or he would have revealed them himself. Mrs. Maugham is not the sort of woman to suspect and sit meekly by."

"No, from what I hear of the matter, she is not. Well, may I assume she paid well for your work? That is, of course, the main thing," Mrs. Brereton said comfortably. "And I don't suppose Hermione Maugham will go so far as to kill her husband, so you really needn't have a qualm, need you, my dear?" She reached gracefully for a handbell, then rose to lead her niece to a table with covers for two elegantly laid.

Miss Tolerance frowned. "I'm less concerned for Mr. Maugham than for the girls he was keeping. I doubt he'll spare a thought for them."

"Oh, they will doubtless find some other keeper." Mrs. Brereton appeared unconcerned.

"They might starve instead."

"If they have had the enterprise to find a keeper once, I don't doubt they shall find another," Mrs. Brereton said. "And here is Cole with our dinner, so neither one of *us* shall starve tonight."

Acknowledging to herself that to debate her aunt on female enterprise was useless, Miss Tolerance turned her attention to the dinner laid before her. As they ate, Mrs. Brereton regaled her niece with bits of gossip which had come to her ears in the last few days, and Miss Tolerance obliged with information her aunt might find useful or entertaining—most particularly with word of the gold-shot silk she had heard of that day.

"Do you know which warehouse it was to go to?" Mrs. Brereton asked.

"If you like, I can inquire."

Mrs. Brereton nodded. "Chloe has been receiving Sir Randal Pre of late, and frequently. He's not the most pleasant of her visitors, but it is profitable business, and she deserves a reward. A new dress would do nicely."

"What about Sir Randal is so difficult that it calls for shot silk?" Miss Tolerance asked.

Mrs. Brereton raised one expressive eyebrow. "You know I cannot tell you that, Sarah. I sell discretion—"

"As much as flesh. So I have heard you say before. I was merely curious as to what makes one man an agreeable patron, and another a problem."

"Manners and madness, as much as anything else. Gentlemen who go beyond what is permitted—"

Now Miss Tolerance raised an eyebrow. "Beyond what is permitted? I thought that anything was permitted, so long as your *staff* was willing."

Mrs. Brereton ignored her niece's satiric tone. "A gentleman who cannot manage his passions when he is in his cups; a gentleman who not only plays at brutality, but indulges his tastes with someone who is reluctant; a gentleman—well, there are tastes to which we do not cater, as you well know."

"Goats, I suppose. Or swans?" Miss Tolerance's tone was deceptively mild. "And where does Sir Randal Pre fit into this moral continuum?"

Mrs. Brereton refused to be drawn. "Why, my dear, I've already said I will not discuss particulars. Even with you, whom I trust implicitly."

Miss Tolerance laughed. "Gods, Aunt, don't trust me, for heaven's sake. My livelihood depends too much upon learning things which others would keep hidden."

"Just so," Mrs. Brereton agreed mildly. For a time the two women applied themselves to their dinner, going from pork roasted with apples and prunes to a course of savories, and thence to fruit and tea, which they took at table.

"So, Sarah, how does your business?" Mrs. Brereton asked at length.

Miss Tolerance sighed. When her aunt asked this question, it was inevitably followed by a predictable set of further questions. "It does well enough, Aunt Thea. Some pay their bills, some don't, but on the whole I am able to earn my keep, which is all I require."

"Have you no aspirations beyond that?" That was question the first.

"Not really, Aunt. I am not a burden to anyone, I meet my

obligations, I have a new dress"—she smoothed her hand over the rosy sarcenet of her skirt—"and new boots. I save against the day when I cannot play these games any longer. What other aspirations need I have?"

"But surely you work very hard for very little money?" That was question the second.

"Hard enough, Aunt. But I enjoy it. I was always happy to poke into corners when I was a child; this work suits me."

"It's dangerous, Sarah. And unfeminine. *Why* won't you come to work for me?" That was question the third, and the heart of the matter.

Miss Tolerance looked bland. "Why, Aunt, have you a commission for me? It would be my pleasure to help you."

Mrs. Brereton fixed her niece with the same look which she used to put riotous lordlings in their place. "Don't willfully misunderstand me. Why won't you work for me, Sarah? You would earn far more money, make connections that would see you through your life, and at the end I could make you a partner in the business. You'd be a great help to me, you know. The running of this establishment is not a simple matter. You would be far more comfortable—and you could even keep the little guest house for your own, if you like, to safeguard your privacy."

Miss Tolerance shook her head. "Aunt, your offer is very kind, but I haven't the temperament to be a whore."

"And what temperament is that?" Mrs. Brereton asked coolly.

Miss Tolerance smiled. "The temperament to be accommodating—or to feign it. I'm far too prickly. I've had but one lover, I'm more widow than courtesan, and I'm eight-and-twenty. Surely that's too old to appeal to most of your clientele."

"Lisette and Marianne are almost thirty. Chloe is six-and-twenty. *I* still entertain a caller or two. You have looks and you have character—"

"Character? Is that a trait much admired in a courtesan?"

Mrs. Brereton frowned. "It is in a good establishment, among a decent clientele. There have been inquiries, you know. Your story is not unknown."

Miss Tolerance had been engaged in peeling a pear. She gave the work her whole attention for several minutes, as she attempted to master the feelings which rose in her breast. "I am sure my story is not unknown, ma'am. A young woman of good family does not elope from the schoolroom in the middle of the night—and reappear in London almost a dozen years later—without it causing some gossip. But I took a new name and I've done what I could to keep the talk quiet—"

"Did you think it would soften your father's heart toward you?"

"Father's heart? Good God, no!" Miss Tolerance was startled into a laugh. "I hope I am not so foolish or so sentimental! My father made it plain that any affection he had had for me—not much, I think—was lost forever when I eloped. But I had hoped that my mother would suffer no further hurt than she had already. Aunt, this is ground we have trod before. I wish you will not ask me again. I love you, and admire what you have built here, but I've no ambition to be any part of it."

Mrs. Brereton sipped her tea with a look of one much resigned, and said no more.

After a time, Miss Tolerance spoke again. "Aunt, do you know a woman named Deb Cunning?"

Mrs. Brereton began to gesture in the negative, then stopped. "Deb Cunning? I—no, I do remember something. A very pretty girl from the—the country somewhere, just barely a gentleman's family. Gently reared, too gently to be really successful, those nagging, shabby-genteel scruples can freeze a whore's best instincts. But she was pretty, very pretty, which served her well enough for a few years. Is she part of some business of yours?"

"You know I cannot tell you that. Discretion is part of the service *I* provide, no less than it is for you. I was hoping you could tell me what became of her, though."

"Became of her?" Mrs. Brereton laughed. "Sarah, that sour reformer Colquhoun said there are fifty thousand whores in London. Do you expect me to know them all?"

"I believe he included in that figure the women who only

prostituted themselves casually. The figure for professed courtesans must be rather lower. You remember nothing?"

"I cannot recall—but when I consider it, that surprises me. I always thought Mrs. Cunning would bring herself, or the people around her, to grief."

"Really? The woman you describe? A sweet, pretty innocent?"

"Sarah, you're no fool. It cannot have escaped your notice that certain naïfs attract disaster as candles attract moths—by their very naïveté. I always took Deb Cunning for one of those. What *did* become of her? Did she learn common sense?"

Miss Tolerance smiled. "I was hoping you could tell me, Aunt."

"Of course you were," Mrs. Brereton said tartly. "Let me think. The last I recall—she had lost her protector and taken rooms in some dreary suburb. Leyton, Hornsey, something like that."

"Richmond?"

"Perhaps. No, she did live in Richmond, but that was when she was younger, with a well-set-up protector. After they parted, she was kept by a man who moved her north of the city. I think it was Leyton. She had one or two other lovers after that, I think, but I suspect she fell upon the sort of hard times which force one to juggle three or four lovers just to make ends meet—all the while pretending to each that he is the only. I cannot imagine she came to a good end, but if she died spectacularly, I would surely have heard of it."

"So the last you know of her, she was in Leyton."

"I think so. It was a long time ago, Sarah—you would still be in the cradle."

"In the cradle? Really." Miss Tolerance offered her aunt a slice of pear. "Well, if I discover what became of Mrs. Cunning and I may do it without breaching my client's privacy, I will certainly share the story with you."

"I can ask no more." Mrs. Brereton dabbed pear juice carefully from the corner of her mouth.

"Now, Aunt," Miss Tolerance said, with the air of someone

conferring a special treat, "you must tell me what you think of this by-election. Will Montjoy take the seat, do you think?"

They began to talk of politics, one of Mrs. Brereton's passions, until they were interrupted by Mrs. Brereton's dresser, in haste and much distressed.

"Madam." Frost's voice quavered. "Miss Chloe is having a problem with her gentleman."

Mrs. Brereton stood at once. "Something that Keefe cannot handle?" Keefe was the chiefest of Mrs. Brereton's footmen, a massive Irishman with a sweet smile and three years of pugilistic training under the master boxer Cribb. He had been hired specifically to deal with customers unruly or in their cups.

"Keefe can't—madam, Sir Randal's drawn *steel*—"

"Pre. I ought to have known. Has he hurt Chloe?"

Frost shook her head. "Not yet, ma'am."

Miss Tolerance had already risen to her feet. "Which room?"

"Sarah, you can't—"

Miss Tolerance paused at the door. "Don't be stupid, Aunt. Of course I can."

Mrs. Brereton's voice followed her niece out of the room. "But your dress—"

Frost ran up the stairs, with Miss Tolerance close behind. There was no question as to which room, since half the staff (and their customers) were clustered around the open door. Marianne, a plump woman in daffodil sprigged-muslin, was silently watching the scene in the boudoir beyond, clutching the arm of her client, an elderly dandy in a coat of blue superfine with buttons the size of saucers. Miss Tolerance noted the smallsword that hung from his left hip, pushed past him with a murmured "Your pardon, sir," and drew the sword in one smooth motion, her back to the room all the while.

"I say," the man protested. He was fat, tightly corseted, and his stays creaked in unison with Marianne's murmured, "Hush!" Despite his protest, his eyes were all for the scene in the room. "What do you—"

"Your pardon, sir, but I must try to help my friend," Miss

Tolerance murmured. She took the smallsword in her left hand, hidden in the folds of her dress, and turned to survey Chloe's dilemma.

The room itself was quiet—all Miss Tolerance heard were Sir Randal Pre's labored breathing and Chloe's quieter, shuddering breath, broken once or twice by a sob. Sir Randal stood over the whore with a smallsword in his hand, the forte pressed to her throat edgewise, as if it were a carving knife. He wore no coat, his waistcoat hung open, and his neckcloth lay crumpled on the floor. Chloe sat pressed against the foot of the bed, straining away from the steel at her throat. Her dress was torn off one shoulder, leaving one breast bared; a trickle of blood from a cut on her neck was staining the lace and muslin of her gown, and Sir Randal's left hand was tangled up in Chloe's fair hair, holding her head back, forcing her to look up at him.

Miss Tolerance strove to recall what she knew of Sir Randal Pre: from the West, country-bred, not above thirty. He looked full of himself and full of wine, a bad combination. Mrs. Brereton had hinted that he was difficult, but not how, so she would have to take action and hope, for Chloe's sake, that it was right.

She relaxed her posture slightly, cocking her left hip out; she raised one hand to her bodice and pulled it down so that her breasts were more clearly visible; when she spoke, it was in a soft Somerset burr that turned her esses into zees. "What'z zis, then, loove?" She took two steps into the room—not so close as to move Sir Randal into action, but near enough to make herself a part of his tableau.

Sir Randal looked up from Chloe, surprised. He was panting hard and, Miss Tolerance noted, he was aroused. "The bitch bit me!" he snarled.

Miss Tolerance smiled. "Did she, loove? There's some as likes a bite from time to time—don't you?" She took another step, raised her right hand to her mouth, and mimed nibbling along the length of the finger. Her smile grew broader. Behind her, she heard her aunt's murmured warning; she clasped the hidden smallsword more tightly in her left hand.

For a moment Sir Randal was distracted by Miss Tolerance's question. The sword in his own hand dropped an inch or two away from Chloe's neck.

"Or are you the sort as likes to do the biting?" Miss Tolerance asked. She locked eyes with Sir Randal for a moment and took another step forward. "Reckon a gentleman strong as you'd have to be gentle with a girl like me." She nipped her lower lip between her teeth for the briefest moment, then released it to smile again. "Happen a gentleman would have to show a girl like me how he likes to be bitten. Then there'd be no need of steel." She ran her fingers along her throat and downward, and stopped with her hand cupped around her own breast, as if offering it to him. "Happen a gentleman has steel enough of his own, see?"

Sir Randal loosed his hand from Chloe's hair, and her head fell back against the footboard of the bed. He still held the sword at Chloe's throat, his hand wobbling up and down. *Drunk as a lord,* Miss Tolerance thought disgustedly. *Stupid, vain, and drunk.* She smiled more broadly. There were now only six or seven paces between them.

"Old Chloe, there, she needs eddicatin'," Miss Tolerance went on. She kept her voice low and her tone even. "Happen maybe you and me could teach her something. She's not a bad sort, old Chloe. So if you show me what you like, see, I can tell her—or show her, if that's to your liking. If you like to watch." She closed the distance by another step. Sir Randal dropped the blade from Chloe's throat and turned more toward Miss Tolerance. Behind him, quietly, Chloe began to edge away.

"What would we teach her?" Sir Randal asked. His voice was hoarse.

"Whatever you like, sweet." Miss Tolerance kept the West Country vowels in her diction. "Whatever you desire." She hit the last word with clownish emphasis; she was only a pace or two away now.

Behind him, Chloe moaned softly. Her dress was trapped under Sir Randal's heel. Distracted, he started to turn back to her, his hand tightening on the hilt of his sword. Miss Tolerance abandoned subtlety.

"Never mind her!" she said sharply, closed the distance between them with a step, and reached with her right hand to run her fingers along his neck. Sir Randal's mouth opened wetly.

Blessing the man who'd taught her, Miss Tolerance brought the sword in her left hand up between them, knocked his sword from his hand, and circled her blade up to rest against his throat; her right hand was tangled in his hair, holding his head still. "Never mind her," she said again in her own right voice. "You've more than enough trouble with me, haven't you, sir?"

Without taking her eyes from Sir Randal's face, Miss Tolerance called back, "Keefe? Would you take custody of Sir Randal, please? I think he's ready to leave."

The footman was at her side at once, locking Sir Randal's arms behind his back. Another footman gathered up the man's coat, neckcloth, and smallsword. Miss Tolerance stepped away and bowed to her opponent.

"In future, sir, if you have a complaint, I suggest you take it up with the management before trying to resolve it yourself."

Pre stared at her in befuddled stupefaction. Then the fury he had felt at Chloe was back, redoubled. "Whore!" he roared. "Trollop! Harlot! Damned bitch!"

Miss Tolerance smiled again. "That last, very probably, sir. For the former, you'll have to look elsewhere. I doubt you'll be admitted to Mrs. Brereton's again. Good night, sir."

Keefe wrestled Pre out the door, past the few servants, employees, and patrons still clustered there, and toward the stairs. Mrs. Brereton took charge, dispatching them to their duties or their pleasures, then joined Chloe on the rumpled bed, speaking soothingly and dabbing with gauze at the cut on the side of her neck. The woman wept fiercely for a few moments, then less and less. Mrs. Brereton, still with her arm about Chloe's shoulders, turned to her niece.

"I understand the imposture as one of my girls, Sarah. But

was it necessary to sound so provincial and underbred? As if I would ever have a woman in my establishment with vowels like those!"

"I was once told that if you could speak to a man in the same accents he heard from his wet-nurse, it unmanned him, made him more susceptible. A nice trick, don't you think?"

"When it works," Mrs. Brereton said grudgingly.

"And so it did. I never disdain an advantage, Aunt."

"And who was the author of this sage advice?"

"Charles Connell, Aunt. Reaching from the grave to assist me. Chloe, how are you?" Miss Tolerance turned the topic.

Chloe had begun to hiccup through her tears. "Better now, thank you. It's really only a scratch. Thank you, Sarah. I truly thought he was going to kill mè."

Mrs. Brereton shook her head. "Nonsense. You don't think I would have permitted that? Still, it was very quick-witted of you, Sarah. I'm glad to see your fencing master taught you something."

Chloe nodded. "Yes, yes, thank you, Sarah."

Miss Tolerance had opened her mouth to respond to her aunt's jibe, then shut it again firmly. Peace was worth more than a truth her aunt would not listen to.

"If you don't mind, Aunt, I think I've had enough excitement for one evening. If you can manage without me," she said dryly, "I am going home, and to bed. Tomorrow I'm for Leyton and my mystery woman."

Mrs. Brereton nodded absently to her niece and returned her attention to Chloe's wound; a damaged worker would not draw in custom.

At the door to the room, Miss Tolerance returned the small-sword to the fat gentleman. "Thank you, sir. I apologize for the imposition, but the need was—"

The fat man, red-faced and creaking still, kept his arm about Marianne's shoulders, but his admiration was all for Miss Tolerance. "Not at all. A pleasure—no, a privilege to have been of assistance."

"That was finely done, Miss Sarah," Marianne said firmly. She looked sidewise at her elderly beau, obviously amused at his outbreak of hero worship. "Chloe might have died but for you."

"Nonsense. You heard Mrs. Brereton. She would not have permitted any harm to come to Chloe. I simply moved matters along a bit."

"But are you new, my dear?" the fat man asked. His gaze had drifted past Miss Tolerance's face and settled predictably upon her décolleté. *God preserve me*, Miss Tolerance thought.

"I'm only a visitor, sir, as you yourself are." Let him make what he would of that. Miss Tolerance bade him and Marianne good evening, then stopped in her aunt's parlor to gather her hat and cloak. Matt Etan was waiting for her.

"Nicely done, Sarey!" he said, grinning. "You were the perfect Covent Garden strumpet. Is that what you think of us all?" He followed her down the hall to the back stairs.

Miss Tolerance shook her head tiredly. "Not in the least. But I did not think Sir Randal would respond to anything but the broadest impersonation of a slut. So I played a Covent Garden strumpet. I'm glad you enjoyed it."

"Damme, yes, it was magnificent. Of course, when Chloe remembers that you called her *old Chloe* not once but several times, she'll forget her gratitude and want your head."

"Fine, she is welcome to it. But first I want some sleep. Unless you're planning to follow me over to the little house, say good night now."

"I've a guest coming shortly, else I'd walk you safe to your door as a gentleman ought. Good night, Sarah."

Her response was lost in the night air in the garden. Miss Tolerance crossed the shadowy darkness, following the flagstone path beneath her slippers by feel rather than sight, and was glad to reach her little house. Once inside, she pulled off the rose-colored dress, took up the ewer of water that stood near the fire, and washed herself all over, briskly, as if she could scrub away the imposture as well as the dirt of the day. Finally, wrapped in her dressing gown, she sat on the settle before the fire and dozed off, dreaming, as she often did, of her ruin.

Three

*E*arly in her career, Miss Tolerance had discovered the difficulties attending travel for a young woman of independent mind and investigative turn. She kept no maid to lend her countenance on her rambles about the city—such a thing would have been absurd—and she had not the funds to maintain her own carriage, nor even a horse and groom. Hired carriages and hackneys she resorted to rather more often than she liked; they were expensive, frequently ill-kept and foul-smelling, and by their nature required the inclusion of other persons in business meant to be confined strictly to herself. Often she hired a hack and rode by herself, but this caused its own problems. A respectable young woman riding unaccompanied through the streets or parks was subject to the grossest sort of insult—such solo rides were the favored way for the better class of courtesan to attract custom. Thus, Miss Tolerance often found it convenient to affect man's dress when she had a need to travel beyond walking distance. This was not a wholly satisfactory solution, as even in breeches and coat, her femininity could be discerned by the observant. Still, it had been her experience that most people in London were too bound in their own lives to notice much about her. Where the eye saw breeches and top boots, the mind of London's citizenry thought *man* and troubled her not. For those who looked further, the sight of the sword at her hip and a crop in her hand tended to dissuade all but the most vulgar from an approach. If she did not relish the occasional comment, she had long ago accepted that her status made remarks inevitable.

The sun sparkled in the garden that morning, having somehow outrun the perpetual coal haze of London, but no breeze moved the trees. It looked to be hot and humid. Miss Tolerance had, the night before, asked Keefe to arrange for the hire of a hack. As she was tying her neckcloth, Keefe announced that the horse had been brought round and was waiting in the mews. She coiled her braided hair on top of her head, pinned it rigorously there, took up her hat and the Gunnard greatcoat, and made her way back to the stables, where Mrs. Brereton's groom was holding an even-tempered gray. With thanks, Miss Tolerance mounted the hack and turned it toward Leyton. This early the streets were busy with tradesmen and merchants; a miscellany of small, dirty boys swept the mud and dung from the crossings, teased the flower girls, and chased each other under the wheels of the traffic. Miss Tolerance enjoyed riding through the city at this hour. Polite society was, most of it, still at home in bed, and the people she encountered went about their business as she went about hers.

She knew several public houses in Leyton, and headed first to the Silent Man. She had great faith in the tavern as a source of useful neighborhood information. Unfortunately, she arrived early enough so that the regular tapster was still abed. Miss Tolerance ordered a pot of coffee and a bread roll and sat in a corner under a window to break her fast. When she had dispatched the coffee, she cast about for a paper to read, but found none. After an hour, the tapster was still asleep. She paid her shot, told the girl who took the coins that she would return, and made her way to the Queen's Arms, several streets away. There the barman poured coffee for her and, at her invitation, for himself as well.

"*Retired ladies?*" he asked, in response to her query. "Ladies of a certain sort, you mean to say?" He made a point of looking Miss Tolerance up and down; she did not flinch. "There used to be a regular nest of 'em, Walthamstow way. Every lordling with two farthings settled his mistress out there, away from the noise of London—and the shops, too. Not many of 'em stayed, though. Too quiet for them, after the years of excitement."

Miss Tolerance nodded sympathetically. "This would be a retired woman," she said. "Her name was Mrs. Cunning."

The barman shook his head. "You'd know the way of that, miss. Woman takes one name for her . . . well, her business, then goes back to her family name when she retires. Or takes Smith, or Brown, something unremarkable, like."

Miss Tolerance, who had not been born to the name she used, nodded. "Is there anywhere that such a . . . nest . . . of retired ladies might be settled?" she asked.

The barman shook his head. "The ones I know of, the older ones, tend to keep to themselves, miss. The younger ones that're still in keeping, they like to live close to each other, share the gossip, like. The old ones has mostly a powerful hankering after respectability, if you know what I mean. Most of 'em pretends as if they'd never heard of the others. You might talk to a couple of the younger ones hereabout. They're fine for gossip, I imagine."

He offered, once Miss Tolerance had slid a few shillings across his polished oak bar, the name and direction of several of the "younger ones." He and Miss Tolerance parted on an exchange of mutual cordialities, and he returned to polishing his taps.

It took Miss Tolerance some time to locate the first of the addresses to which the barman had directed her. She found, at last, a cottage somewhat larger than her own house, set close among other houses on a pretty road. When she knocked at the door, a girl in a cap and apron answered. She was pretty until she smiled and displayed several teeth missing or darkened with decay, and her accent marked her for a Kentish farm girl. Still, she was well trained enough to make no comment at the strange figure Miss Tolerance presented; she took Miss Tolerance's card in to her mistress directly.

A moment later she was back. "Ma'am says she'll see you, Miss. May I take your hat?" She showed Miss Tolerance down a dark hallway into a pretty, fussy room at the back of the house, where a woman some years older than Miss Tolerance was drinking chocolate and leafing through an old number of the *Belle Assemblée*. She was plump and agreeable-looking, with short, curling hair a nearly natural shade of yellow, and rosy cheeks that owed considerable to art rather than nature.

"Mrs. Cockbun? I am Sarah Tolerance."

"Why, yes." Mrs. Cockbun had a high voice, pinched, affected vowels, and a slight lisp. "Did dear Wolfie send you?"

Miss Tolerance paused to think. Who was Wolfie? Presumably Mrs. Cockbun's patron, but beyond that? He might be Wolvingham, or Henry Wolfe, or any one of the Woolfe family, or anyone else, for that matter. Clearly she could not claim that Wolfie had sent her. "It's kind of you to see me, ma'am. Actually, I've come to ask a favor of you."

Mrs. Cockbun tittered. It was an annoying sound. "Oh, don't call me *ma'am*, my dear! We're nearly of an age, I might be your sister." She looked meaningfully at Miss Tolerance's breeches and riding coat, as if to remind Miss Tolerance that they were both of the sorority of the Fallen, just in case her visitor planned to give herself any airs.

"Mrs. Cockbun, then. I was told you might know of a lady who lives, or lived, in this neighborhood. Of course, she came here some years ago, and you are probably too young to recall her. . . ." Miss Tolerance let the implied compliment sink in and was pleased to see Mrs. Cockbun dimple up, her suspicions allayed for the moment.

"Well, my dear, you never know what *I* might know. People tell me things, you know, dear. I'm told I have a sympathetic manner."

Miss Tolerance smiled sympathetically herself. Mrs. Cockbun rang for more chocolate. "You'll take a cup, won't you? How lovely! It isn't often I have morning visitors; Wolfie comes rather less than he used to, you know, what with the property to manage and his family responsibilities." Miss Tolerance detested chocolate; she took the cup from her hostess and smiled. "Now, my dear, who is it you're seeking?"

"A lady by the name of Deborah Cunning, ma—Mrs. Cockbun. I'm told that she retired to this area some years ago." It occurred to Miss Tolerance that she had not provided herself with a story of why she was seeking Mrs. Cunning. Fortunately, Mrs. Cockbun did not seem concerned to protect another woman's privacy.

"Cunning? Well, of course, my dear, she's never using *that* name in retirement, is she? Hmmmm. When would she have come here?"

Miss Tolerance felt again the irritation of an artisan who has not the proper tools to complete her work. "I cannot say for certain, ma—Mrs. Cockbun. Only that it would have been a least ten years ago, perhaps as many as twenty."

"Ah, well, you see, I was a child then! I hadn't even made my Wolfie's acquaintance, and was living in the city."

Miss Tolerance asked if perhaps Mrs. Cunning might have been in the neighborhood when her hostess arrived there. Mrs. Cockbun was unhelpful.

"You see, dearie, once a woman loses the protection of a gentleman, she tends to live retired, like, and keep to herself. Perhaps that old woman down by the river would know."

"Old woman?"

Mrs. Cockbun sniffed. Beside her, a dog, which Miss Tolerance had previously mistaken for a beribboned pillow, stirred and sneezed.

"Bless you, Pierrot!" She pronounced the name Pee-rote. "Oh, yes, Mrs. James or Johnson or Williams, something like that. Lives in a cottage down by the river. Poor as a church mouse, as I understand, without a farthing to bless herself with. If she's still alive. She's terribly old and feeble, my dear." She smoothed the silk of her dress again, quite content with her own relative youth and energy. "Now, tell me, my dear, why are you looking for this Mrs. Cunning? What call has a girl your—our age to be searching out an old whore?"

Miss Tolerance looked at the cup in her hands with studied intensity. "She is my aunt, ma'am—Mrs. Cockbun. I find myself . . . as you see me, ma'am. Cast out by my family and seeking the only relative who will not turn me from her door. I am in hopes she will counsel me on what to do, since—" Miss Tolerance could be pardonably proud of the manufactured choke in her voice. Miss Cockbun nodded sympathetically; the lappets of her lace cap bobbed.

"You see, I knew there was a story to it. A proper lady of your age would be long married and running after a brood of dear little children. You are a pretty thing, dearie, if you didn't do yourself up in breeches like that. If you're looking for advice on finding a protector, I could give it to you as easy as your auntie." The courtesan smiled. Was she imagining Miss Tolerance as her first whore, the foundation of a modest house of joy?

Miss Tolerance gave no sign of her distaste for this idea. "You're very kind, ma'am," she said. "Perhaps another time I will come and ask your advice. But now—I really feel my place is with my aunt, ma'am. Perhaps she needs me."

Mrs. Cockbun's smile faded. "Well, I made the offer," she said.

"Indeed, ma'am, you did." Miss Tolerance took up her hat. "I will inquire of the elderly woman by the river, ma'am. And I thank you so very much for your help and your hospitality."

"Oh, must you go?" Mrs. Cockbun grasped Miss Tolerance's arm to stop her; her grip was surprisingly strong. For a moment Miss Tolerance wondered if she actually meant to keep her there, if there was a confederate waiting to bind her and 'press her into one of the lowest sort of stews. But no; another look at Mrs. Cockbun and Miss Tolerance saw writ plainly on her face the woman's terror of another day spent waiting for her protector, without the benefit of resources, imagination, or industry to enliven the wait. "Have another cup of chocolate," Mrs. Cockbun urged.

Miss Tolerance patted the hand that grasped her arm as if to remind the older woman that it was there. The hand released, and Miss Tolerance stepped away, taking up her hat and seating it firmly upon her head.

"I must not take up more of your time, ma'am. But I thank you again—and give you good morning." She bowed—curtseys go ill with breeches and a riding coat—and made for the door. Mrs. Cockbun fed a biscuit to her dog disconsolately.

"The old lady by the river" was not a useful address, but Miss Tolerance had in her mind the sort of establishment which might be kept by an impecunious retired courtesan. She turned her hired hack toward the River Lea and rode along its length, surveying the cottages there. From the stench that rose up from that side of the road, it was clear that the sewers and drains of Leyton emptied into the Lea; in the late morning sun, the stench was appalling. The houses across the road were, in the main, nicely kept up, with flowers or blooming trees framing them. Those on the river side were more tumbledown, as if their owners could not be bothered in making the exterior of the house give the lie to the turmoil of the interior. Clearly the differences of class and money were at work in which side of the road one might occupy.

For no reason clearly defined except that it seemed the right sort of place, Miss Tolerance stopped her hack in front of a tiny, painfully well-kept cottage at the farthest reach of the town on the river side. The building had been whitewashed sometime in the past, although close inspection suggested that the whitewash had not been applied in a year or more; there were banks of small pink flowers around the door, and a bell of polished brass hung by the door. As she stepped closer, the smell of the river in the heat grew stronger. Miss Tolerance's stomach rebelled when she thought of living in such a dwelling.

She tapped the bell very gently. A sweet note rang out. After a few moments, a face peered out at her from the window, and then the door was opened. The woman who stood there barely came up to Miss Tolerance's breast, a tiny, wizened creature whose monkeyish face was surrounded by a frilled lace cap tied beneath her chin. Her clothes, Miss Tolerance noted, were like the house: neatly cared for but showing signs of age and a stringent budget. If this lady was Mrs. Cunning, she thought, it should be an easy thing to exchange five hundred pounds for the fan—but this lady looked too aged to have been anyone's mistress in the last ten years, or even twenty.

"Yes?" The woman raised her eyebrows inquiringly but reserved her smile.

"Good afternoon, ma'am. I am sorry to disturb you, but I am looking for . . ." Miss Tolerance paused. She could hardly say "a friend" or "my aunt," if this woman was the person she sought, but if the woman now went by some name other than Cunning, she did not want to annoy her by using her *nom d'amour*. She would have to chance it, she thought. "I am looking for Mrs. Cunning."

"Are you, then?" The old woman cocked her head to one side and looked Miss Tolerance in the eye. As if satisfied with what she saw, she opened the door wider. "Well, you had best come in." The woman stood aside and Miss Tolerance entered the house, ducking her head to pass beneath the low-set lintel. Her hostess led her from a dark, close hallway into a tiny, cramped sitting room that faced onto the street. The room's only light came from the sunshine which poured in through the window, softened by dusty gauze drapes. The furniture was dark and shabby-looking, and most surfaces were covered by bundles of papers tied with ribbon, bowls of dried flowers, sturdy candles studded with dried flowers, or large dozing cats. The room was stifling and smelled of lavender, cat, and the barely masked stench of the river. Miss Tolerance was hard-pressed not to sneeze.

"What is your business with Mrs. Cunning?" the old woman asked. She sounded genuinely curious, without judgment.

"I've been sent to find her on a matter of business."

The old woman leaned forward and took Miss Tolerance's hand in one of hers; it was cold and papery to the touch. "My dear," she noted, very kindly, as if striving to avoid offending her guest. "My dear, young ladies do not ride about in breeches on matters of business."

Miss Tolerance blinked. What was she to say to this? "Perhaps young ladies do not, ma'am," she agreed at last, laying slight emphasis on *ladies*. "But I do. And I have been asked to seek out Mrs. Cunning."

The old woman took up a decanter and poured some thick, syrupy stuff, so dark it was almost black, into two highly polished wineglasses. She handed one to Miss Tolerance. "Please take a little of my cordial, my dear. I make it myself, and it's a specific against the summer fever. We see a great deal of it, living here by the river."

Mute, Miss Tolerance took the wine. It tasted of plums.

"I blame the Queen for it," the woman said. "And those stupid men in Parliament who gave her guardianship over the poor mad King. It would have been far more suitable to have one of the Princes as regent. When I was a girl, young women did not ride about in breeches and the world was a better place for it. Ever since the Queen became Regent, people have come to believe a woman may be licensed to do anything. Even a girl who's ruined ought to have some standards, to my way of thinking." She paused and looked kindly at her guest. "I'm sorry, my dear, but I'm old, and shall speak my mind. You would be happier with a husband and a clutch of children, I don't doubt, instead of riding about the countryside in that style."

"Perhaps you're right, ma'am," Miss Tolerance said slowly. "But that was not one of the choices open to me, and I preferred this to my other alternatives."

"To be a whore?" The old woman smiled charmingly. "Nothing so wrong with that, my dear. Earned my keep that way for a score of years, and kept myself in a feminine way. If you'll forgive my saying so," she added kindly.

"Oh, certainly, ma'am," Miss Tolerance said. The room was

very hot, and the smell of cat, river, and lavender seemed to increase with each passing moment. "Might I know, ma'am, to whom I have the pleasure of speaking?"

The old woman giggled. "Mrs. Smith, dear. You'll find we're all Mrs. Smith when we reach a certain age. Most of us that survive, anyway. Mrs. Charlotte Smith. And your name?"

Miss Tolerance told her. Mrs. Smith giggled again. "Tolerance? What was you thinking, dear, to take a name like that? As well to name yourself Dishrag or Wholesome!" She shook her head in dismay. "Tolerance!"

"Tolerance, ma'am. Don't you think it suits me?"

Mrs. Smith *tsk*ed mildly. "Gracious, perhaps it does. Well, my dear, who was it you said you was looking for?"

"Mrs. Deborah Cunning, ma'am."

The old woman's eyes narrowed for a moment, reflectively. Then she smiled, nodding her head. Curls of white hair had been stuck to her withered cheeks with pomade or perspiration, making her look rather like a painted doll.

"Deborah Cunning. Gracious, I haven't heard that name in a brace of years. A pretty girl, but didn't wear well, that one. When she quit the game, I thought she'd go back to the village she come from, but it seems she didn't manage her money well—so few do, dear—and couldn't afford to set herself up in comfort. She did very nice embroidery, though. Perhaps one of the milliners or dressmakers on Bond Street would know of her?"

"But not as Mrs. Cunning, ma'am?" Miss Tolerance prompted.

Mrs. Smith laughed. "Oh, dear me, no. Not as Mrs. Cunning. Let me see, did she style herself as Smith or Jones?" She reflected, and Miss Tolerance took another sip of the syrupy wine. It left a musty taste in her mouth. "Carter, I think. Or Cook. Cook. Mrs. Deborah Cook. Took to wearing black, as though she were in mourning for her last keeper, though given how he left her situated, he must have been a monstrous unpleasant man. Well, they all are, soon or late. Monstrous *and* unpleasant!" She laughed again, a coarse, knowing sound that came oddly from her monkeyish face. "Oh, now I've shocked you. Well, I know more of the matter than you do, dear, I'm sure. Think your man wasn't unpleasant, don't you?"

Miss Tolerance shook her head. "Nor monstrous, ma'am." The smells of the room were combining with the wine to make her feel queasy. She found she was jiggling the handle of her riding crop nervously and put the thing aside.

Mrs. Smith snorted. "Then you didn't have him long, did you? What, did he seduce you and run away?"

This was treading close to territory Miss Tolerance preferred not to discuss. "Perhaps it was I seduced him, ma'am," she said lightly. "I *am* the sort of woman who rides about in breeches, after all."

Rather than be offended, Mrs. Smith cackled. "Well, you're not mawkish, I'll give you that. Now, have you the information you came for, Miss Wholesome-Tolerance? I hope you will not think me rude if I cut your visit short, but I'm an old woman and my cordial makes me a bit drowsy. Come, I'll see you out."

But Miss Tolerance was on her feet, assuring her hostess that there was no need for her to rise. She thanked the old woman and made for the door, almost knocking over a deep bowl filled with dried lavender, verbena, and other tiny white flowers in her haste to leave. Outside, she stood blinking in the doorway for a moment, breathing deeply of the fresher air. Her horse was patiently cropping the heads from the flowers by the gate, and she led the gray to the end of the street before mounting, hoping to settle her stomach. Then she rode back to the Queen's Arms and bespoke two baskets, each containing a ham, a wheel of cheese, and a bottle of wine, to be sent to Mrs. Cockbun and Mrs. Smith, with her compliments. Lord Trux would stand the bill; information, as she had told him, always had a price.

I t was midafternoon when Miss Tolerance arrived back in Manchester Square. She returned the horse to Mrs. Brereton's groom and went at once to her cottage to wash away the dust of the road, and to change into a walking dress and half-boots.

With the idea of stopping into some of the shops in Bond Street, she inquired in the House if any of the ladies there had need of ribbons, gloves, or other necessities. Chloe not only declared a pressing need for a new handkerchief, but proposed that they go together. This had not been Miss Tolerance's intention, since the harlot would bring not only herself but, in keeping with Mrs. Brereton's immutable rule, a maid as chaperone, but she could not escape from the excursion without awkwardness, particularly when Chloe was still regarding her in the light of hero for her rescue of the night before.

"I had wanted to tell you again how very grateful I am—" Chloe began when they were out-of-doors and walking toward Bond Street.

"There's really no need. Mrs. Brereton was right; she would never have allowed you to come to harm under her roof. I grant it was unpleasant—"

Chloe gave a hard little laugh. She was slight, with very large, nearsighted brown eyes and soft curling yellow hair, which made her look quite defenseless. That look, Miss Tolerance believed, was one of her stocks in trade, and the reason why men such as Sir Randal Pre preferred Chloe's company to that of others in Mrs. Brereton's employ.

"He would have killed me," she said with breathless certainty.

Miss Tolerance shook her head. "Not then," she said. "Not when he thought he had the power. His sort don't kill until they think they're losing their power."

"Well, if you don't want my thanks . . ." Chloe pursed her mouth unpleasantly.

"It was a pleasure to help you and my aunt," Miss Tolerance said lightly. "Now, is there a particular shop you wanted to visit?"

Chloe, it seemed, was unbiased. She liked all the shops, and liked to linger, touching the fabrics and having sharp little discussions of price with the assistants. She bought nothing, but seemed ready at any moment to buy a great deal, so she was assiduously attended to in each store. If the modistes and their assistants knew that Chloe was a member of Mrs. Brereton's establishment, they gave no sign, nor did they indicate any distaste for her custom. The other patrons of the stores, in blissful ignorance of the figures of sin who moved among them, did not withdraw, either; so all parties were happy. It was, Miss Tolerance reflected, as close as she could come to reclaiming her own birthright and status.

It was difficult to ask questions with Chloe at her side and other customers vying for the attention of the attendants. Still, in a quiet moment a murmured question, always accompanied with a coin, could be answered before Chloe began another query about the price of jaconet muslin. At the first three shops, the assistants reluctantly confirmed that they had no knowledge of an embroiderer named Mrs. Cook or Carter. At the fourth, the description was recognized, but the young woman could not supply her direction. Miss Tolerance quietly passed along her card, and several more coins, in the hope that Mrs. Carter-Cook's address could be discovered and a note sent to apprise her of it. She bought a pair of gloves, too, and a matching yellow ribbon, hoping that would dispose the shop's owner kindly toward the shopgirl.

Miss Tolerance and Chloe, with the maid, Annie, trailing just behind, returned to their stroll along Bond Street. Chloe insisted on reviewing Miss Tolerance's purchases, and informed her she could have gotten the same gloves cheaper elsewhere.

"Then why shop on Bond Street?" Miss Tolerance asked mildly.

"You find out what's the mode on Bond Street, then buy it cheaper somewhere else. Your aunt taught me that." Chloe looked mildly surprised that Mrs. Brereton had not imparted similar wisdom to her niece—in fact she had, but Miss Tolerance was not about to explain the reasons for that day's purchases. She was distracted from any response by the sight of Lord Trux, walking up the street with the air of a beau of fashion who need not discuss anything with the great world. He was, as he had been the day she met him at Tarsio's, expensively dressed in a

coat of fine wool, green this time, with biscuit-colored breeches
and handsomely polished boots, yet the result was not elegance
but strain. Trux seemed happily unaware of how poorly his
clothes became him; just as well for a man who clearly gave his
tailor full rein to indulge in the excesses of fashion as they occurred.

Miss Tolerance watched the man's face, looking for a clue. If
they met, should she acknowledge the acquaintance or not? Trux
solved the problem for her by changing his direction quite suddenly, waiting while a ragged, nimble boy swept the street before he crossed it. Following his course, Miss Tolerance's eye was
drawn to a knot of men on the far side of Bond Street. She
stopped, on the pretext of examining the contents of her pocketbook, to see who her client was meeting. There was nothing
about the men themselves that attracted her eye; from their
dress, they were all well-to-do, but not members of the Dandy
set. The oldest one, indeed, wore the skirted coat of the last century and affected an ebony stick upon which he leaned lightly.
What drew Miss Tolerance's particular attention was the sense
of confrontation emanating from the group. Even from across
the street it was plain that the brown-haired man in the brown
coat and Hessian boots was in a rage, and that rage was focused
entirely upon the taller man in dark blue. If the object of this
fury returned the feeling, he gave no sign of it; his expression
was bland, only one raised eyebrow suggesting he might dislike
taking part in such a scene. Miss Tolerance was seized with a fit
of curiosity and taking Chloe's arm, urged her across the street
to examine half-boots in a window there.

As they crossed the street, Miss Tolerance kept her glance
away from the group of men; when they reached the other side,
she steered Chloe to a shopfront half a dozen paces from them,
where she could hear some part of the conversation, and watch
it all in reflection in the shop's glassed front. Lord Trux, Miss
Tolerance noted, now stood at the elbow of the man in the blue
coat as if to lend him countenance, although the man in blue did
not seem to require such support.

"Have you spoken with him?" the elderly man was asking. In contrast to the anger of the man in brown, the old man seemed as calm as the younger, and taller, man in blue. "I think you'll find the Prince's enthusiasm for your party has waned with maturity." His tone was smooth and pleasant, sailing upon the tension between them. When the man in blue answered, his tone was just as untroubled.

"I never thought an interest in the opposition was the exclusive province of the young, sir. My father remained an active and convinced Whig until his death, and he was a good friend of the Prince's."

"*Your father*—" The man in brown spoke as if the words were an oath.

In the glass before her, Miss Tolerance saw the elderly man put a restraining hand on his companion's elbow. "Your father, Versellion, had the sorry luck to be raised as a Whig, which His Highness was not. As we grow older, common sense—"

The man in brown interrupted furiously. "You think to turn matters to your own advantage! You scheme to get power just as your father did, your lies—"

The elderly gentleman again put his hand on the sleeve of the man in brown, this time with more force. "Henry," he said mildly. "Unless you wish to find your name in the dueling column of the *Gazette*, I counsel you to keep your conversation civil."

The man in brown shrugged the older man's hand away with little grace. "The devil with civil conversation! You heard him baiting me—"

"I heard accusations, falsehood, slander!" This was Trux, sputtering in outrage.

Now it was the turn of the man in blue to restrain his companion. "Let him say what he likes, Trux. It hardly matters; he knows where the truth lies, although he does not care to speak it. What the Prince believes or does not believe, we shall see, if this matter goes on for long. I, for one, do not intend to bandy it further upon the open street. My lord—" The man in blue bowed to the old man. "Cousin"—a bow to the man in brown. "Come, Trux," the man in blue said, rather like one who was calling a dog to heel.

Trux and the man in blue wheeled about and were suddenly facing Miss Tolerance, who turned her face slightly away and continued her examination of the half-boots in the shop window. It seemed to Miss Tolerance that as the men passed her, Lord Trux's step faltered, but then he went on. After a moment or so longer—the half-boots really were quite elegant and wholly impractical, pale blue kid painted with delicate forget-me-nots at the ankle—Miss Tolerance suggested to Chloe that they start back to Manchester Square.

"You don't wish to try the boots?" Chloe asked.

Miss Tolerance shook her head. "What was it you suggested? Find what you like in Bond Street and buy somewhere cheaper?"

Chloe agreed, but appeared disappointed to have had her shopping excursion ended so soon. "As *you've* found what you wanted, I suppose we might as well go home," she said disagreeably. The walk back to Manchester Square seemed a long one.

M iss Tolerance made a quiet supper of bread and cheese and an apple, writing a few notes to herself on the matter of Lord Trux's investigation. Briefly she considered going to Tarsio's for a while. In fact, she was tired, and her interviews with Mrs. Cockbun and Mrs. Smith had left her dissatisfied and unquiet. She put the kettle on the hob and was warming the teapot when one of the footmen from the House came with a summons.

"A man has called for you, miss."

"Called for me at my aunt's house? Did he give a name?"

The footman presented a card. Written on it in a small, spidery hand was the name *Trux.*

Miss Tolerance sighed. "Oh, lord. Bring him here, please, Cole."

Given the choice of entertaining a client in her own unimpressive dwelling or in the midst of her aunt's clientele, she had no hesitation in having Trux join her. Still, she preferred to keep her home hers; she kept her membership at Tarsio's particularly for interviews with clients.

In a few minutes Cole reappeared and bowed Lord Trux into Miss Tolerance's cottage. She had a pot of tea brewing, and two cups warming. She did not believe that Lord Trux would require tea, from the look of him. The high color on his face was not a product of the firelight, she thought, but of some sudden choler. Evidently Cole thought so, too, for he lingered at the door of the cottage as if unsure whether it was safe to leave Miss Tolerance with the gentleman.

"Thank you, Cole," she said pleasantly. "My lord, I had not expected to see you this evening. Will you take a dish of tea with me?"

Trux faltered. He was clearly expecting his anger to oppress her. "I have not come for tea," he said.

"No, of course not. But will you take some regardless?"

He shook his head. His face grew redder. "I must know—" It seemed his words were being pushed out of him with great pressure. "Were you *following* me this afternoon?"

Miss Tolerance permitted her eyes to open in a cartoon of dismay. "Following you, sir? Our paths crossed in Bond Street, but I would never embarrass a client by seeming to know him in public."

"But were you following me?" Trux shouted, then seemed a little abashed by the sound he made in her quiet cottage.

"Of course not, my lord." It was near enough the truth, Miss Tolerance reckoned. "Why would I do that?"

The question apparently confounded Trux. "Well, then, perhaps you can tell me if you have made any progress on my . . ." He paused as if the proper word eluded him.

"The matter of the fan? I have made good progress, I think, sir. I spent the morning interviewing women who might have reason to know Mrs. Cunning, and this afternoon pursuing more information, based on what I had learned in Leyton."

"Leyton!" The ruddy color returned to Trux's face. "I told you Richmond!"

Miss Tolerance poured a cup of tea for herself. "Indeed, she may be in Richmond, but my information is that she was removed from Richmond and set up in Leyton some years ago. So Leyton is where I went."

"To get information?"

"Yes, sir. And I did obtain some useful news which I put to good use this afternoon."

"In Bond Street?" Lord Trux seemed determined to find some fault with her, Miss Tolerance reflected. "If you were not following me in Bond Street, then you were shopping! You had a *parcel*!"

Miss Tolerance was hard put not to laugh. "Can I not persuade you to take some tea, my lord? I think you will find it soothing." She poured out another cup and set it down upon the settle, and nodded toward it as if to invite her guest to take his ease. Reluctantly Trux sat down. He looked at the tea in his cup as if it were a substance entirely foreign to him.

"Now, sir," Miss Tolerance said firmly. "You must understand something about the work that I do. It is often necessary, for that very discretion which you desired, for me to appear to be doing one thing when I am, in fact, doing something else. I appeared to be shopping this afternoon—I bought a pair of gloves to lend veracity to my imposture. But in fact I was interviewing shopgirls about the possible whereabouts of your Mrs. Cunning."

"By God, how am I to judge the truth of that?" Trux sputtered. "You can say whatever you like and charge me three guineas a day for nothing. For gloves!"

"You will not be charged for the gloves, sir. I intend to keep them for myself. Now, my lord: I must operate my investigation in the way that seems best to me. I am not a common thief-taker; you came to me, I had supposed, because I have some experience in such matters. If you cannot have faith that I know my business and am working to do your will in the swiftest manner I can, then we had best part company at once, and I will send you a report and a bill for my services to this date." She smiled sweetly at him.

Lord Trux looked deflated. His lower lip drooped and his brows knit together fiercely. "There has been progress?" he urged.

Miss Tolerance nodded. "Indeed, my lord, given how little information you gave me to work with, and how much of that was flawed, the progress has been considerable." She indicated the pile of notes by her hand. "Would you like a written report?"

"No." He seemed suddenly to recollect where he was. "I had thought you lived in Mrs. Brereton's establishment," he said. "Surely this is not very comfortable."

"It does me well enough. More tea, sir?"

Trux shook his head. "No," he said almost sadly. "I must go. I have a dinner to attend, and I must be shaved and dressed." He looked around him as he turned toward the door. "It's such a small little place," he said peevishly. "You *cannot* be comfortable here."

"Ah, but I've only myself to worry about. I really am far more comfortable here than I would be at Mrs. Brereton's. Now, may I bid you good evening?"

Miss Tolerance stood in the door of the house, watching as Trux crossed the garden to the back of Mrs. Brereton's, where she was sure Cole was waiting to show him to the street.

"Well," she murmured. She turned back into her house and settled herself by the fire again, musing. "Well. A fan missing these twenty years is, overnight, the subject of some anxiety to its owner. My dear Lord Trux!" She clicked her tongue thoughtfully. "What have you neglected to tell me about your Italian fan?"

Four

Miss Tolerance dreamt she was in Amsterdam, fencing in the *salle des armes*. The dream was a sum of many sensations: sweat beading between her breasts and on the nape of her neck; the damp cling of linen across her back; the protest of muscles as the sword drill went on and on. The high-vaulted ceiling of the *salle* echoed the bite of boot heel against wooden floor as she advanced, thrusting to head, to wrist, to hip, to shoulder, and around again; then retreated, parrying in *quarte*, in *tierce*, in *prime*, and *sixte*. There were the smells of sweat, worn leather, and burning torches, and beneath them the pleasant memories of straw and horse dung: the *salle* had once been a stable.

Gradually, without words, Sarah and Connell shifted from drill to sparring, caught up in the exchange of blows, as if each cut expressed a feeling that could be expressed no other way. The torchlight flicked and danced, and they moved in and out of the shadows as they traversed the room, so focused on each other's faces that Sarah felt she would fall into her teacher's dark eyes. Still they fought on.

At last she caught Connell's blade on the forte of her own and pressed in, *corps à corps*, until their faces were only inches apart. Their arms, and their swords, were caught between their close-pressed bodies, and Sarah felt the hard, rapid beat of his heart against her forearm. He was tall; she had to tilt her head up to look into his eyes, which met her own, steady and unsmiling. His breath came as raggedly as her own, and smelled sweetly of fennel seed. Sarah flushed with heat and exertion. Her lips trembled. He bent his head as if to kiss her, and she awoke.

Her heart was still pounding, and the bedclothes were tangled and damp as if she had fenced among them. She lay in the dark, waiting for her pulse to slow, letting the heat and the pain of memory seep from her. At last she lit the candle at her bedside and took up *Art of the Small Sword*, but tonight even Mainley's dry prose could not soothe her. She was still awake at dawn, staring at the book's pages without seeing them.

I n the morning Miss Tolerance turned her cottage inside out looking for her riding crop. She was very soon satisfied that the crop was not there, and a few minutes' reflection convinced her that she had left it in Leyton the day before, most probably in Mrs. Smith's musty, odorous parlor. It would have been a simple thing to forget the matter and buy a new crop, but Miss Tolerance was fond of this particular one; she liked the balance, and knew several neat defensive tricks calculated to its weight. That the crop was one of the few possessions remaining to her that had once belonged to her seducer, the fencing master Charles Connell, was of course incidental to the necessity to retrieve it. Swearing at her stupidity, Miss Tolerance went round to the mews to arrange for the hire of a horse for another day. She would retrieve the crop from Mrs. Smith that morning and hope that when she returned to Manchester Square, there would be news of Mrs. Cunning's whereabouts awaiting her.

She made the trip as quickly as she could. As she rode up the quiet lane toward Mrs. Smith's house, the greasy smell of the river again rose up to assault her. Not for the first time, Miss Tolerance thanked God for her own small, snug establishment, so insulated from the worst of London's smells and sights. She dismounted and tied her horse, and knocked upon Mrs. Smith's door.

After a few moments of knocking, Miss Tolerance was forced to the conclusion that the old woman was not at home. She only hesitated a moment before trying the door—she had no desire to ride out to Leyton yet again on this errand, and after all, she had only come for her own property—which yielded at once to her touch. Again Miss Tolerance found herself in the dark, dusty box of a hallway. To the smells of cat, river, and dried flowers, the scents of burnt bread and meat had been added, and something else, a faint smell Miss Tolerance could only identify as an old lady's scent. She wrinkled her nose and entered the parlor to retrieve her crop.

She found it lying where she had left it, on the cushion of the sofa she had occupied the day before. Mrs. Smith's body half covered it. She was dead; her eyes and mouth were wide open as if in surprise or outrage. She lay on her side, one hand outstretched, her temple crushed against the carved wooden arm of the sofa. Blood from her temple had flowed down the arm of the sofa onto the seat cushion and left a sticky, half-dried puddle. There was blood, too, on the white-work embroidery of her cap that had been knocked askew and bunched under her head. On the old woman's cheek, Miss Tolerance noted, there was a dark, plummy bruise. A lamp and several candles had been knocked to the floor, and at least one bowl of dried flowers upended. In the scattering of lavender and verbena across the floor and rug, she saw cat prints, and the print of a man's boot.

Miss Tolerance swore.

She had seen death before, been its cause, even. But she did not like finding the corpse of an elderly woman who had apparently died by violence; a blow to the face that had sent her crashing into the knobby arm of the sofa. The bruise was full and purple; Miss Tolerance surmised that the old woman had taken some little while to die. Had she been conscious? Afraid? Miss Tolerance shivered at the thought.

After a moment, the hardheaded concerns of commerce asserted themselves. Miss Tolerance considered what to do, and in the end decided there was no point in becoming further involved in Mrs. Smith's tragedy. Leaving matters as they were was cowardly, but reporting the death would inevitably lead to interviews with the authorities, perhaps even the magistrates of Bow Street. (Miss Tolerance had made it a practice to steer clear of the Bow Street Runners, feeling that contact with the civil investigative force would only draw attention to herself which was professionally and personally unwelcome.) Much better, if possible, to retreat immediately. Someone else would find Mrs. Smith before long, surely. Gingerly, Miss Tolerance drew the crop from under the old woman's body, tucked it under her arm, and left the room.

She was untying her horse when she realized she was being observed. Across the lane, standing on the lawn of a pretty brick house, a small child was watching curiously; behind her a woman stood, eyeing Miss Tolerance with familiar hostility. The woman was several years older than Miss Tolerance, heavyset and in the dove gray of half mourning. The child was no more than four or five, and fidgeted with a hoop and stick as she watched. Their silent observation forced Miss Tolerance to change her plans. Better to report Mrs. Smith's death than be remembered later as the person who had not reported it but had departed under suspicious circumstances.

"I beg your pardon, ma'am. Can you direct me to the justice of the peace or magistrate?" Miss Tolerance called.

The woman frowned. "Why do you need one?" Her accent was genteel. A navy widow, perhaps, Miss Tolerance thought. There had been enough battles in the endless war with Bonaparte's forces to widow half the nation. This woman clearly did not approve of young women who traveled about the countryside in breeches any more than her neighbor had.

"Mrs. Smith—" Miss Tolerance stopped, not wanting to voice her suspicions before the child. "I'm afraid Mrs. Smith has died." She gave the woman a look as full of meaning as she dared. The woman drew back, eyes wide, and turned to the child.

"Anne, you go inside. *Now*, if you please."

The child went reluctantly, gawking at Miss Tolerance. When she was gone, the woman turned back. "You're one of her sort," she stated.

Miss Tolerance bit back her first denial. "I am not—what she was."

"Then what are you doing here? Like *that*?" the woman asked.

Miss Tolerance felt the threads of her patience fraying badly. "I am looking for direction to the magistrate," she said again. "It is my belief that Mrs. Smith died by force, sometime last night or early this morning. A report must be made. Perhaps you would prefer to send a servant to inform the authorities, ma'am?"

The woman took another step back, as if violence might be contagious, and appeared to consider what was to be done and whether her own involvement was necessary. "Robbery?" she asked.

"I honestly could not tell you, madam. Which is why I would appreciate it if you could direct me to the justice or magistrate."

The woman turned back to the house. Miss Tolerance watched her in the doorway in brief conversation with a maidservant. Then the maid came out and directed Miss Tolerance to the justice of the peace. The woman herself had gone into the house without another word.

The justice of the peace was a heavy, dull-eyed gentleman farmer with no other apparent business than to sit at a desk surrounded by numbers of the sporting gazettes. The books that lined the wall behind him were all on agriculture; Miss Tolerance wondered if he had read them, or merely kept them there to give himself the appearance of industry. The house was a stolid cube in the middle of a cropped lawn; the office a small, chilly chamber with a desk, the bookshelf, an undusted globe, and an inkstand. The justice listened to Miss Tolerance's tale without enthusiasm, his eyes trained on the front of her double-breasted riding coat as if trying to imagine what it concealed and thus to reassure himself of her gender. At last, after Miss Tolerance had finished speaking and the room had been silent for several minutes, Mr. Gilkes heaved himself from his chair and demanded that she return to the house with him.

There was, of course, nothing to be done for it. Damning the whole business, Miss Tolerance went.

They found the house as Miss Tolerance had left it. Now that the shock of finding the body had abated somewhat, her curiosity was strongly in play. Mr. Gilkes made disapproving noises at the sight of Mrs. Smith's body while Miss Tolerance looked into the other room on that floor: a kitchen, which overlooked the river. On the table she found the basket she had sent from the Queen's Arms, with the cheese and the bottle of wine still in it. A loaf of bread had been cut in two, and Miss Tolerance found the charred remains of one half fallen from the fender onto the hearth, with a blackened slice of ham next to it. The ham itself lay on the floor, scarred with the small, dainty marks of cat teeth and cat claws. There was barely anything else in the larder: several bottles of Mrs. Smith's dreadful cordial, a few eggs in a rush basket, and a packet of tea leaves. As she turned to leave, Miss Tolerance saw the card she had given the innkeeper with her own name and Mrs. Smith's direction on it. She pocketed it and returned to the hallway.

She had her foot on the first step of the narrow stairway when the justice emerged from the sitting room. He held his handkerchief to his nose, which gave him the look of a mourner, and he had clearly had his fill. "Tragic, tragic," he said in monotone. "But we can do no good here. I'll have the parish clerk arrange a funeral."

Miss Tolerance gestured toward the staircase. "Perhaps we should look abovestairs?"

Mr. Gilkes frowned heavily. "For God's sake, Miss—" he faltered over her name. "You're in the presence of death! Show a little respect."

"I meant no disrespect at all, sir. But I was hoping—"

"Whatever your hopes were, the old woman's death has put paid to them neatly, eh? There's nothing more for you here."

"Perhaps not, sir. Will I be needed for the inquest?"

He looked past Miss Tolerance to the door, clearly wishing he were on its other side.

"Will not the coroner have to rule upon the death?" Miss Tolerance persisted. "She was clearly struck down."

"I see no evidence of that."

"The bruise on her face. She was struck down and left to die."

"She could have got that bruise at any time. All that concerns us is that she fell and hit her head." He frowned. "She was old, these things happen. I consider it death by misadventure, with nothing suspicious about it. There is no need for the coroner to put himself to the trouble of saying so. A sad business, but consider her life, ma'am. Consider her life. Surely such an end was inevitable." The justice looked meaningfully at Miss Tolerance, as if prophesying just such an end for her. He clearly hoped not to pursue the matter himself and saw no profit in encouraging Miss Tolerance to do so. It seemed that a small consideration such as his obligation under law meant little to him, and he could conceive of no reason other than money for Miss Tolerance to care. Miss Tolerance had not wanted to become involved. She should be blessing this imbecile for his lack of interest, but Mrs. Smith's eager, monkeyish face played in her memory and she found herself reluctant to let the matter go.

Mr. Gilkes firmly led Miss Tolerance out of the house. He promised again to have the parish clerk see to a funeral. There were, he was certain, no relatives who would wish to be privy to the arrangements. There was no reason for Miss Tolerance to stay in Leyton, he thanked her very much for her attention, but strongly recommended that she be on her way.

Had it not been for the justice's utter lack of imagination and drive, she might have suspected him of some suspicious motive in suppressing inquiry into the death. However, it was plain to her that the inconvenience, and a squeamish dislike of what Mrs. Smith had once been, had ruled Mr. Gilkes's decision. With little choice, Miss Tolerance mounted her horse and started back to Manchester Square. There was nothing she could do for Mrs. Smith; although Miss Tolerance doubted that Gilkes would put himself to the trouble of seeking out Mrs. Smith's true name and family, she was equally persuaded that any family Mrs. Smith owned would prefer not to hear of her death from another Fallen Woman. Common sense dictated that she return to London and the matter of the Italian fan, and yet she was unable to erase from her memory the image of Mrs. Smith, sprawled without dignity across her sofa, reaching out for help.

Why would anyone offer violence to an elderly female of decayed morals, long retired from her profession and living in pressed circumstances? The motive had surely not been robbery, at least not by any common thief. The foot that had ground the lavender into the rug had not worn a heavy workman's boot but a narrow, more fashionable one, perhaps one made for riding. A gentleman's footwear. And the state of the parlor spoke to her of sudden rage, not the planned cruelty of a burglar. As her horse jogged along the lanes, Miss Tolerance returned again and again to a single conviction: that her own visit to Mrs. Smith had somehow precipitated the old woman's death. Almost, Miss Tolerance turned the horse back to Leyton to ask at the Queen's Arms if anyone had inquired as to her own movements the day before. But there was the matter of the damned fan to be resolved, and seeking Mrs. Smith's killer would not pay her rent.

W hen Miss Tolerance returned to Manchester Square, it was a little after three. She handed the horse to her aunt's groom to be returned to the stables from which it had been hired, and retired to her cottage to think. The day was nearly gone; she could not in justice charge Lord Trux the entire day's fee, but perhaps she could salvage some little part of it in considering the next steps to be taken in the matter of the Italian fan. Her luck appeared to turn, for she had not been home for above half an hour when Cole arrived with a letter which had been that moment delivered to her—and a look betokening a burden of gossip.

"What's the matter, Cole? You look . . ." She searched for the correct word. "Full of news." Miss Tolerance took the letter from him, and looked at it briefly: not inscribed in a hand familiar to her. "I wish no more than you to breech my aunt's promise of discretion to her clients, but if you can say—"

Cole shook his head. "Ain't one of the clients, miss. Not the meat of it, anyway. But one of 'em—I shan't say which, it's as much as my job's worth—he says . . . it's the Queen Regent, miss."

Miss Tolerance raised her eyebrows. "Take me with you, Cole. *Queen Charlotte* is one of my aunt's clients?"

The footman blanched. "God save me, no, miss." He appeared to boggle at the thought for a moment, as Miss Tolerance did herself. "No, miss. Only that one of the gentlemen told—and was overheard, and the maid—" The footman grew more and more confounded, trying to authenticate the story without implicating anyone in the house.

"I need not hear who overheard what, or told whom. But what is this news of yours?"

"The Queen's took sick, miss. Might be like to dying, an apoplexy, Lor—the gentleman said. He'd been up all night at Kew Palace, and ridden back at dawn to meet at Whitehall—then come here for a bit, for the release, if you take my meaning."

"I do, thank you." Miss Tolerance let out a long, low whistle. "If the Queen Regent dies, it'll be a nasty scrum, won't it? Old Mad George may live on for another twenty years while his sons scramble to rule the country." She shook her head. "Well, we must pray for her recovery. There's certainly nothing you or I

can cure ourselves. Thank you, Cole." She smiled in dismissal
and the footman bowed himself out the door. Miss Tolerance's
ruminations on the subject lasted only a few moments more, long
enough to wonder whether the "Lord" was of the royal party or
opposition. The political maneuverings of the Whig and Tory
factions and their puppet princes might bring her business in the
future, but for the moment her concern must be for Lord Trux
and his fan.

She opened the letter and found it was, as she had hoped,
from one of the shop clerks she had spoken to the day before.

> *I believe the person your seeking goes now by the name of Cook,
> not Carter. Mrs. Cook lives in considable reduced circumstances,
> and sends the broidery she does for us from Greenwich, by a mes-
> senger comes from an inn there, the Great Charlote. I have reason
> to believe she is the person you axed after. One of the clerks has
> been here for five-and-twenty years says Mrs. Cook was once a
> patron of our establishment in her better days, and a notable
> Beauty.*
>
> > *Hoping this will be sufficient, I remain, etc.*

Miss Tolerance sighed. It would have been pleasant to discover that Mrs. Cunning, now Mrs. Cook, lived close enough by
that she would not need to hire another hack. It would have
been pleasanter still to discover that Mrs. Cook was absolutely
Mrs. Cunning and no other, before she went through the trouble
and expense of the ride. She looked at the clock and decided that
by the time she had procured another horse and ridden out to
Greenwich, it would be early evening—not the best time to be
in an unfamiliar town looking for an unknown woman, particularly as Greenwich, home to the Royal Naval College, was often
thick with seamen home on leave and ripe for the happy prank
of chasing down an unaccompanied woman.

Regretfully, Miss Tolerance decided the day must be written
off. In the wake of her brief interview with Lord Trux the night
before, she was more than a little conscious of the fact that this

day had yielded nothing remarkable in the way of progress. Still, there were sometimes such days; tomorrow would doubtless be better.

Miss Tolerance took up her writing desk, sharpened her pen, and put out a few sheets of paper. She wrote a series of notes. First, to the stables asking them to arrange the hire of another horse for the morning. Next, a reply to the shop clerk who had so obligingly provided Mrs. Cunning's whereabouts, sending her thanks and a half-crown note. And finally, a note to Lord Trux detailing what she had accomplished. He had not asked for a report, but she felt the better for providing it.

In a few minutes she gathered up her notes and walked them across to Mrs. Brereton's, where Cole undertook to have them delivered. Then she went upstairs to call upon her aunt. Mrs. Brereton was in conference with her cook regarding the evening's refreshments. She nodded cordially to Miss Tolerance, finished with the cook, and offered her a glass of wine.

"Well, my love, what do you make of our news from White-hall?" Mrs. Brereton asked. It seemed there would be no escape from politics that afternoon.

"Which news is that, ma'am?" Miss Tolerance asked blandly, not wishing to implicate Cole in the one great sin of the establishment: gossip. However, Mrs. Brereton, an ardent supporter of the Whig party for many years, appeared to find the news too important to pretend ignorance.

"You mean no one has told you? A visitor this morning has given out that the Queen Regent had an apoplectic stroke four days ago, and her life was quite despaired of."

"It is no longer so?" Miss Tolerance asked.

"They do not fear her immediate death. But I believe she is quite feeble, partly paralyzed. No official word has gone out, even the opposition papers are mute upon the subject—the government trying to avoid a panic, most like. But I imagine the Tories are all in a twist! If she cannot carry on the business of government, a new regent will have to be found, and whoever it is might well call for a new government."

"Which would mean, perhaps, a shift in power. But since Mr. Fox's death, who have the Whigs to lead a government? There does not seem to be a clear leader—"

"Grenville, I suppose," Mrs. Brereton said thoughtfully. "Or Lamb or Versellion, although neither has held a cabinet post yet. Versellion was too new to his title the last time his party held government—"

"And Mr. Fox was still alive and in control of the party."

"And his rivalry with the old Lord Versellion was well known. But Fox is dead," Mrs. Brereton said sadly. In her youth she had traded considerably more than kisses for votes in support of her political idol. "The real problem is who would be regent."

"Would it not have to be the Duke of Clarence?" Miss Tolerance asked. She did not share her aunt's passion for politics, but it was impossible not to be concerned with the succession to the throne itself. "Since York died, and the Prince of Wales was removed from the succession—"

"But Clarence's liaison with Mrs. Jordan will be a problem for those who don't fancy his handful of bastard FitzClarences. As for Wales—at least he married his widow and has legitimate heirs, which is more than can be said for Clarence or Kent! There's been more than one resolution raised in Parliament to restore Wales to the succession."

"And he was a friend of Fox's and said to favor the Whigs, which would suit your purposes admirably," Miss Tolerance said teasingly.

Mrs. Brereton refused to be drawn. "The Whigs' purposes."

"So I apprehend that the author of this tale, whoever he is, is not of the opposition party? I wonder that you admit such persons to your house, Aunt."

"Don't be stupid, Sarah," Mrs. Brereton said comfortably. "A Tory's coin is as good as anyone's."

"And some Tories are better than others. I imagine a good deal of them are richer than Croesus."

Five

The carriage was well sprung and handsomely outfitted, the footmen and driver polite, well trained, and closemouthed. Miss Tolerance attempted several times to ask where she was being delivered; the best she got was a terse "I regret, miss, I cannot say," from the footman who had brought the note to the house. Nor would the attendents say who had sent the carriage for her. Still, whoever had done so had provided for her comfort: There were pillows and rugs in the carriage to make her ride more comfortable—at the sight of them, Miss Tolerance grinned to herself, for whoever had obscured the crest on the doors of the carriage had not thought to remove the crests visible on each of the lap rugs and pillows. These gave her a new, and quite intriguing, notion of where she was going and with whom she would meet. Greatly relieved in her mind, Miss Tolerance sat back to look through the half-curtained window, considering how to play out this latest hand in the game of the fan.

The carriage rattled first south, along Hyde Park, then westward through the suburbs. Miss Tolerance reflected briefly on the possibility of highwaymen, but was not much concerned; there had been a considerable reduction in such crimes in recent years, and even were the carriage stopped, she did not doubt the footmen were well armed. They rode for considerably more than an hour. By the time the carriage turned onto a graveled drive, the sun was long gone, and Miss Tolerance could see nothing more than the circles of light cast by the coach lamps. She listened to the spit of gravel under the wheels for a good quarter mile, at which point the carriage came to a stop before a large residence, well lit by flambeaux. The footman leapt down and handed Miss Tolerance from the carriage.

She was met at the door by a manservant who attempted to overawe her, looking down his nose at her (and her breeches, boots, and riding coat) as if the sight pained him. He frowned in clear disapproval as he bowed her into a small room and closed the door firmly behind her. Miss Tolerance had an unpleasant sense of imprisonment, for the room was not above twelve paces square, paneled in dark wood that made the space seem smaller even than it was. It was furnished with one large chair and one very small table, opposite which a coat of arms had been carved into the dark paneling. Miss Tolerance sat down to wait and whiled the time parsing the Latin motto under the crest of a crouching lion crowned with flames: *impavidus fiducia.*

When the door swung open again some minutes later, a different man stood before her. Miss Tolerance was not altogether surprised to find that he was one of the men she had observed on the street with Trux the day before: the man in blue. As she had noted then, he was tall, although perhaps not so tall as the small room made him seem.

"Did they put you in here? I must apologize, Miss Tolerance. If you will have the goodness to join me in a more comfortable room?" Her rescuer's tone was entirely pleasant, but he did not stop to see if Miss Tolerance would follow; he turned and led the way across the hall to a much larger room, furnished in a more modern style and lit with branches of candles. "Won't you be seated? Good. And take some refreshment with me?" He waved a hand at a row of decanters. "There is sherry here. Or I can have tea brought, if you prefer."

Miss Tolerance sat and crossed her legs. It was high time, she thought, to take some control of the situation. "Is that whiskey in the third decanter, sir?"

"It is."

"I would take a dram of it," she said pleasantly. "If you would join me."

Her host smiled. "I would be pleased."

He was tall, as she had observed, and only a few years beyond thirty. His dark hair was untouched by gray, close-cropped as if to suppress unruliness. His eyes, Miss Tolerance thought, were his best feature, large and well set, and a dark brown. His face was handsome, but not distractingly so. He wore his excellent clothes casually, as if they were a matter of no importance, and his boots—despite the hour, he had not yet changed to evening dress—were well made and beautifully kept. Miss Tolerance's impression was of wealth, style, and intelligence.

"There." He handed her a glass of tawny liquor. She sipped at it, rolling the whiskey on her tongue.

"Whiskey is not usually a lady's drink," he noted.

Miss Tolerance smiled politely. "If I were a usual sort of lady, I would hardly be here."

"Perhaps so. But I cannot imagine you as a usual sort of lady under any circumstances, Miss Tolerance." He bowed and smiled, making it a compliment, and Miss Tolerance added charm to her list of the gentleman's qualities. Considerable charm, which he was not above using for his own ends. She returned his smile.

"Now." Her host took a chair near her own. "Having brought you out here, I must make myself known to you. I am Versellion." He did not pretend she would not recognize the name.

"I had surmised it, my lord," Miss Tolerance said.

"Had you?" He raised one eyebrow. "May I ask how?"

"If you truly wish to keep your guests in the dark about your identity, don't send a carriage for them with crested cushions."

She smiled and took another sip from her glass. "But perhaps you were not so much interested in baffling me as in confusing observers as to the origin and destination of your coach. The point on which I am not entirely clear is the reason for your flattering summons. I was promised information which would be useful to me."

"And you shall have it. Prudence is all very well, but it was becoming apparent to me that my wish for discretion was hampering you in the inquiry you are conducting on my behalf."

Miss Tolerance tilted her head. "*Your* behalf, sir? Which inquiry is that?"

"The matter of the Italian fan you are reclaiming for me."

"*If* I were undertaking such a thing, sir," Miss Tolerance said carefully, "I regret that it would not be on your behalf."

The gentleman nodded. "Your discretion is everything I would wish it, Miss Tolerance, but I assure you: you undertook to act for Lord Trux, who was acting as my agent."

"If that is the case, then this will be the first time someone has come to me with a job to undertake for a *friend* where such a friend actually existed! I hope you will not take it amiss, my lord, if I ask if you have any proof that you, and not Lord Trux, are the person with whom I should discuss this matter?"

"I can show you this." Versellion handed her a slip of paper. "And for the rest, I will tell you some things which Trux, I believe, has not. I believe the information will make more sense of your task, and that must be my best proof of who I am."

Miss Tolerance opened the paper, apparently written to Versellion by Trux: it contained the details of the inquiry Miss Tolerance had related to Trux the evening before. She returned it to Versellion.

"The matter of the fan may be one of some delicacy, and arose at a point when Lord Trux was pressing for a way to be of service to me. Lord Trux," Versellion said dryly, "wishes very much to be of assistance to me."

"How very agreeable that must be," Miss Tolerance said in the same tone.

Versellion laughed. He had a very flattering manner, Miss Tolerance thought, unsettled. One who fell under his gaze might feel as though she were the only person in the world. "Trux has his uses," he was saying now. "But to the subject of the fan, Miss Tolerance, it *is* a matter—"

"Of some delicacy," Miss Tolerance finished. What could there be about this fan that the Earl of Versellion would set such an inquiry in motion? He was head of one of the most politically inclined Whig families, the target of matrimonial gambits by mothers and marriageable daughters, a man of power and wealth, singularly blessed by fortune. Even if an ancient courtesan chose to publish memoirs which named him as one of her lovers—but that was not the case, or did not fit the facts she knew—what damage could seriously be done him?

"Whatever delicacy you require, my lord, the inquiry will go more smoothly if you are candid with me."

Versellion frowned. "I have every intention—"

Miss Tolerance shook her head. "You, or rather Lord Trux, have given a story which is false upon its face. I shall be hard-pressed to help you unless you deal straight with me. I was told that the fan was given to Mrs. Cunning by her lover, and it was strongly implied that *you* were that lover."

"And?"

"Whatever habits of secrecy politics has bred in you, sir, I hope you will abandon them with me. I may have left my school-room under unorthodox circumstances, but I learnt to add. Everything I have learned suggests that Mrs. Cunning retired from her profession almost twenty years ago, and nowhere has it been suggested to me that her last lover was a boy of—you would have been, what? thirteen? fifteen? If you were not the last of her lovers, that would make you younger still at the time. Whatever her morals, I cannot quite believe that Mrs. Cunning would have taken a nine- or ten-year-old boy into her bed. May I presume that it was not you, but your father who had the honor to be Mrs. Cunning's lover?"

For a moment she believed the earl would dissemble; then he

laughed. "My God, Miss Tolerance, you must forgive me. Trux suggested the story, but I should have realized from your reputation that it was ill-considered. You are right, of course."

"If you do not deal straight with me, sir, it will only take me longer to decipher the truth. Had I not been able to find several persons who remembered Mrs. Cunning, I might have been looking for a woman far younger and in different circumstances."

Versellion downed the remainder of his whiskey in a quick toss and stood up, pacing rapidly across the room. "I see that now. But I collect you have found Mrs. Cunning?"

"I have a good idea where I might find her, sir, but I cannot be certain until I have interviewed her. I can tell you that from what I understand, the lady is poor and lives upon the proceeds of her needle."

Versellion looked bewildered. "Her needle?"

"She does piecework embroidery. She may, as well, have an annuity, or she might have sold off her jewelry—"

"Has she sold the fan?"

Miss Tolerance shook her head. "I cannot know that until I speak with her, sir. And I remind you that at this point, all I have is a woman I *believe* to be Mrs. Cunning. I will know more tomorrow. But my lord, you brought me here with a promise of information which would assist me in your commission. Did you merely intend to identify yourself as my client, or was there some other matter you wished to share with me?"

Versellion turned his glass between his fingers, seeming to examine the amber crawl of whiskey as it splashed along the side of the glass and dripped downward. At last he smiled slightly and looked up at Miss Tolerance.

"You must forgive me. Sometimes I am too much a politician. We are not a breed known for its candor, and I cannot help but weigh what I tell you—"

"My lord, if you do not feel secure in my discretion—" Miss Tolerance started.

He waved the protest aside. "I was told that I could place

complete reliance in you," he said "But I cannot help but weigh what you would need to know to accomplish my commission against—"

"What you would prefer not become a public matter?" Miss Tolerance finished for him. She was becoming impatient, and thought her impatience might have a salutary effect upon the discussion. "My lord, as you have seen, I will reason my way around the problem. But you will make it easier for me—and less costly for you—if you are candid. I have questions to ask."

Versellion nodded and fixed her with that potent gaze. "Perhaps that is where we should start, Miss Tolerance. With your questions."

Nettled, Miss Tolerance returned his look evenly. "In that case, my lord, I wonder why retrieving this fan is of such importance to you?"

Versellion frowned. "The sentimental meaning of—"

Miss Tolerance shook her head emphatically. "Politics being such a sentimental business? That will not do, my lord. If the fan was given to Mrs. Cunning by your father, it has been in her hands for most of your life. Why is its retrieval suddenly so important?"

"My father's reputation—" Versellion began again.

"*Stop, please.*" Her tone would have done credit to a nursery maid. "You have done me the honor of saying I am astute and it is no good to lie to me, but then you continue to tell tales. Your family is wealthy, you are a member of the House of Lords and a fixture in your party. What kind of warmed-over trouble could your father's liaison with an unimportant *fille de joi* cause you now?"

"*I don't know.*" From his tone it was clear that Versellion's patience, no less than her own, was being tried. More quietly, he went on. "Miss Tolerance, you are right in that I do not believe Mrs. Cunning or her liaison with my father to be important. It is the fan itself which I must reclaim. I had rather not say why unless you particularly require it."

Miss Tolerance shrugged. "My lord, I have no personal curiosity about the fan. My only concern is to accomplish the assignment with which you have honored me. However, I must point out that if the reason you wish to recover the fan is material to its discovery, you will only render my task more difficult and more costly." She rose, went to the table which held the decanters, and poured a little more into her glass, waiting for his reaction. She was not unaware that she had taken a great risk; one does not lightly upbraid the wealthy and powerful, and despite his charm and apparent affability, she doubted Versellion liked her polite unwillingness to accept false coin for the truth.

She became aware of the ticking of an ormolu clock upon the mantel, and the disturbance of the curtains by an evening breeze. At last Versellion spoke again.

"I owe you an apology, Miss Tolerance. Telling politic half-truths is a difficult habit to break, as you see. I should not be surprised at your acuity; everything I have heard of you should have prepared me for it."

"I am acute enough, sir, to realize that that is the second— no, it is the third time you have referred to what *you* have heard of *me*. Are you trying to intimidate me with the wealth of your intelligence about me? I assure you, if you have a question, you have only to ask."

Versellion smiled pleasantly. "I know only what I have been told, Miss Tolerance. You are the daughter of Sir William Brereton, you were raped by your brother's tutor and turned from the door of your father's home, and you live in a brothel run by Mrs. Dorothea Brereton, one of the few . . . professional . . . women of her generation with whom it seems my father did not have a liaison. I would be curious to know how you hit upon your unorthodox profession, Miss Tolerance."

He had rattled off his account of her life coolly, apparently without malice, but Miss Tolerance suspected there was in it an attempt to regain the upper hand. She laughed lightly.

"What a Covent Garden melodrama you've been fed, my

lord!" It cost her something to be so blithe, but her expression was one of genteel amusement.

"Were my informants wrong?" Versellion frowned. "A politician lives by information."

"As does an agent of inquiry, sir; the exact point I was trying to make earlier." Miss Tolerance drained the last of the whiskey from her glass and set it down firmly upon the table. She took her seat again. Her tone was as cool as his own; she had no intention of letting her past be used as a lever against her. "Your information is what the world might believe, but you should always look closer than that."

"What would I find upon closer examination?" Versellion asked. He seemed genuinely curious, as if she had at last won him from his careful political manner.

"I was not raped, nor was my seducer my brother's tutor. He was a fencing master, with whom I fled to the continent and lived quite happily for some years. If you seek the origin of my unorthodox profession, my lord, you must find it there."

"With your seducer?"

"With what I learned from him. When I saw the things he could do with a sword, I wanted to learn. And he taught me."

"Too well, by the sound of it," Versellion said.

"In my line of work, one cannot be too well trained in the uses of the smallsword." Miss Tolerance shook her head as if to clear it. "Sir, if you are satisfied as to my pedigree, I have one more question. You wish the return of the fan for its own sake, correct? If it has so valuable a character, is there any likelihood that someone else is pursuing it as well?"

He shook his head. "I cannot imagine it, Miss Tolerance." His expression indicated that he could imagine it, but rather hoped not.

Miss Tolerance smiled. "Then, my lord, if you have no more information to share with me, perhaps I may be returned to London?"

Versellion rose. "But you have not answered *my* question, Miss Tolerance."

Miss Tolerance tilted her head to one side. "Have I not, sir? Please remind me: what was the question?"

"How you came to do the work you do."

Again, she smiled. "What else was I to do, sir? Acting as an agent of inquiry seemed to draw upon the skills I had. I was an inquiring child and have grown into an inquiring woman—with a facility for swordplay and a familiarity with Society. Now, sir, I have my notes to write up and some other work to do. If I may ask to be excused?"

Versellion nodded. "I will have the carriage brought round immediately—unless I can persuade you to take your supper with me?" Miss Tolerance shook her head. "Very well. I thank you for making the journey to see me, Miss Tolerance. It has been unexpectedly pleasant. I shall be in Town for the next week or so if you have need to reach me."

During the ride back to Manchester Square, Miss Tolerance amused herself by considering what she thought of Edward Folle, Earl of Versellion. He was attractive, certainly. Among tonnish mothers looking to marry their daughters well, he was likely the great catch of the season: wealthy, highborn, good-looking, and with good address. His lack of candor did not weigh overmuch with her; if there was anything that her profession had taught her, it was that everyone had secrets to keep. So long as Versellion's secrets did not keep her from doing her job, Miss Tolerance could control her curiosity. Still, as she had told the earl, she was of an inquiring disposition.

The whiskey had left her pleasantly relaxed. She closed her eyes and fell into a doze which was not interrupted until the brougham moved into the more heavily trafficked streets of London itself. The carriage drew up in Manchester Square and the footman was immediately at the door, ready to hand her out and escort her into Mrs. Brereton's. Miss Tolerance, loath to deal with the noise and bustle of the brothel, waved away his arm, thanked him, and pressed a coin into his gloved hand with instructions that he and the driver should drink her health with it.

Then she turned away from the door of her aunt's establishment toward the private gate on Spanish Place.

It was a clear night, and the sound of music which emanated from Mrs. Brereton's house was agreeably subdued. Lights from the Square spilled irregularly onto Spanish Place; it was shadowy but not completely dark. She was thus able to make out the forms of two men waiting by the private gate in the garden wall. The gate was difficult to find in the dark; they could only have been stationed there to wait for her by someone who knew there was a gate there to find. Miss Tolerance drew her sword without haste, held it low, and continued forward.

The first of the men moved toward her; in his hand she saw a glint of steel. Any hope that these were friendly visitors was banished.

"You'll be Miss Tolerance?" he asked. He must have been forewarned, as the sight of a woman in breeches did not confuse him. Miss Tolerance's first thought was that Sir Randal Pre must have hired the men to pay her in kind for his humiliation the other night. "You're to come with me," the man said.

She shook her head. "I'm afraid that will not be possible, sir. The hour is late and I am very tired. Excuse me." She took another step.

The man raised his sword and pointed it at her midsection as he might have a pistol. *Not a swordsman,* she thought. *He expects the mere sight of the sword will reduce me to tears.* Tired as she was, Miss Tolerance had no patience now for bullying at swordpoint. Perhaps she could chase them off.

She raised her own sword, stepped in to engage his, corkscrewed the point in, and swept her hilt upward, neatly knocking his sword into the air. She caught it in her left hand and tossed it over the wall into her aunt's garden.

"Christ!" the man growled. "Jack! Take the bitch—but be quiet, and don't kill her. That's orders." He waved his accomplice forward.

Miss Tolerance stepped fast, kicking hard at the first man's groin, and watched him drop. "Pardon," she breathed as she turned to meet the second man.

The accomplice gave a cry of outrage and moved in, sword drawn. This one had obviously trained with the smallsword. For a minute or so Miss Tolerance was busily engaged, and the sweet chime of sword against sword rang out in the street, not loud enough to bring people from the Square or from the houses with a face on Spanish Place. There would be no rescue, so it was time to bring the encounter to a close.

The man thrust to her shoulder; she beat his point away and returned the thrust, pinking his left arm. Her tip almost became fouled in the sleeve of his coat, but she pulled back, retreated a step, watching to see if the wound would make him stop. He followed after her, angry enough to thrust for her heart and be damned to his orders to keep her alive.

"Your teacher surely told you to keep your point up!" She parried the thrust. "If you don't"—she slipped her hilt along the length of his blade, driving his arm up, sword still clutched in his hand—"you will find your blade is very easily captured!"

She dropped her hand and drove the hilt of her sword down just above the man's temple. A nasty blow; he would have hell's own headache in the morning. He staggered back, tripped over the body of his partner, who still lay moaning on the cobblestones, and fell hard.

Miss Tolerance took up the second man's sword, pitched it across the street and into the shrubs that guarded the house there; in the dark, it would take some time to find them. She turned back again and stood over her attackers, thinking what to do next. She did not particularly want to turn the miscreants over to the inquiries of the Watch, and certainly she had no desire to kill them.

The problem was solved, for the moment at least, by the appearance of a closed coach which turned the corner onto Spanish Place and bore down on Miss Tolerance and the two men. She sheathed her weapon and watched as the two men staggered to their feet and across the street out of the path of the carriage.

"You may tell whoever gave you your orders that I respond much more helpfully to a civil request," she called. "Good evening."

She did not turn away, however, but stood with her back against the ivied wall of her aunt's property, watching as her attackers limped up the street to Manchester Square. It occurred to her to follow them to the corner and enter at Mrs. Brereton's brightly lit and well-attended front door, where any second attempt by these footpads (or any others) would be easily repulsed. But a tug at the gate suggested that the garden was still secure, and thus her little cottage would be as well. And with a good deal to consider, Miss Tolerance found herself loath to be caught up in the society of the brothel tonight.

After another glance around her, she unlocked the gate, entered, locked it again, and stood listening. She thought she heard, over the festive noise issuing from her aunt's parlors, a shouted inquiry to her attackers. Was it the Watch, wondering what these two were doing in the Square at this hour, or their employer asking after their success? She was gambling that the two men would not want to tell anyone in authority what they had been about, or that they had been beaten by a woman with a sword. When the shouting ceased, Miss Tolerance turned toward her little house.

It was dark; perhaps it had been a busy night at Mrs. Brereton's, for usually one of the servants found time to come and light a lamp for her if she was out. The unaccustomed darkness gave Miss Tolerance enough of a qualm that she drew her sword again, just in case, and entered her cottage prepared to find an intruder. There was none. Feeling a trifle foolish, she stirred up the coals in the banked fire and lit a candle at the hearth. Within a few minutes she had made herself comfortable and snug: her boots off, her dressing gown on, her hair loosed and falling down her back, and a plate of bread and meat beside her. She sat with a child's slate at her hand and a piece of chalk, making idle notes as she thought.

Who had sent her attackers? The first names which occurred

to her, Sir Randal Pre and Mr. Horace Maugham, she dismissed almost at once. She suspected that Maugham, at least, would be kept mighty close to home by his wife for a time; his wife had brought her considerable fortune to the marriage, and the money had been tied up so efficiently that the improvident Mr. Maugham could not afford to anger his wife overmuch. Sir Randal might have the wherewithal Mr. Maugham lacked, but she did not imagine he would have stressed to his minions that she was not to be killed—quite the opposite, in fact. There were a few subjects of past queries who might have been pleased to hear of her death, but none of them could she imagine conniving at it.

She was left with an unsubstantiated, but powerful, suspicion that the attack had something to do with Lord Versellion's fan.

When the matter was combined with the fact of Mrs. Smith's death, Miss Tolerance could not help but believe that there was far more to the fan and its history than the Earl of Versellion was willing to admit. Perhaps more than he knew. And more hazard to herself, too.

Something else occurred to her, a very disturbing thought. It was commonly believed that she lived in Mrs. Brereton's house; who would know that she did not, or that she usually did not go through the house in order to reach her own cottage? Who would know how to find the door in the ivied wall? Who would know she had gone abroad tonight?

Only some member of Mrs. Brereton's household.

It was a cold notion to take to bed. Miss Tolerance wiped the slate clean, finished her tea, and, before falling into her bed, checked her pistols and put them on the table by her bed.

Six

When she came downstairs the next morning, Miss Tolerance found a small pile of the previous day's correspondence which had been left upon her doorstep by one of Mrs. Brereton's servants. She made a pot of tea, cut herself a piece of bread, and nibbled on the crust while she shuffled through the letters. London's haze had lifted from the precincts of Mayfair, and the glittering light of morning was tinted spring-green by the trees that gathered closely around the cottage. The breeze combed through the ivy on the brick of Mrs. Brereton's house across the garden with a pleasing low rustle. The scent of wood smoke and black tea filled the small sitting room of the cottage comfortably. In such delightful surroundings, it was hard for Miss Tolerance to give credit to her suspicions of the night before.

The men who had accosted her on the street were somehow attached to the matter of Lord Versellion's fan—Miss Tolerance was inclined to trust her intuition upon this point. Her best defense was to conclude the investigation as soon as she might.

The bells of All Souls tolled in the distance; Miss Tolerance realized with chagrin that it was Sunday, and to accomplish what she planned, she would miss services—not for the first time in the pursuit of a client's goal. *Next Sunday for my soul*, she muttered, *today for Greenwich, and the lady formerly known as Mrs. Cunning.* Miss Tolerance was about to go across to the house to ask Cole to hire a hack for her, but a thought stopped her. If someone at Mrs. Brereton's had given information about her movements to the men who had attacked her, then it was better that she keep her movements to herself. She would go directly to the stable herself to find the hack.

She would have enjoyed, on such a morning, time to linger over her breakfast. Instead, she went rapidly through her mail: a dunning note for her new boots; a bank draft from a client— Miss Tolerance pressed the paper to her lips in thanksgiving, as she had despaired of seeing a penny from that quarter; a note from a haberdasher advising her of the location of the striped silk she had sought out on her aunt's behalf; and a note from the secretary to the Viscount Balobridge:

> Lord Balobridge presents his compliments, and requests the honor of a meeting with Miss Tolerance, on a matter of potential benefit to both parties. If Miss Tolerance will name a place and time that is convenient to her, Lord Balobridge will be pleased to make himself available.

Discreet, yet intriguing. "How sudden is my popularity with the peerage," she murmured. Miss Tolerance considered the note as she dressed. Balobridge, like Versellion, was rich, well known, and highly political, an elder in Tory politics, one of the Queen's circle of advisors. If he had need of her services and she could assist him to his satisfaction, it was likely to be a very good thing for herself and her purse. But the timing of this summons was intriguing. Balobridge was one of Versellion's political rivals, and the coming of this note, on the heels of the attack she had suffered the night before, made her wonder. What had she told her attackers? That she responded better to a civil invitation than to force? This—she looked again at the note lying on the table—this was a very civil invitation indeed.

She finished tying her neckcloth, drank the last of her tea, wrote out a reply to Balobridge, and let the ink dry while she pulled on her boots and coat. Then she sealed the note and tucked it into her pocket, banked the fire, and for the first time since she had taken up residence in Mrs. Brereton's guest cottage, locked the door behind her as she left.

As she had decided, reluctantly, that she could not trust even her favorites among Mrs. Brereton's servants, Miss Tolerance delivered her reply to Lord Balobridge's house, pressing it into the hand of a footman who clearly did not often encounter females in masculine dress. Then she turned her hired mount toward the river, crossed at Tower Bridge, and proceeded to Greenwich, inquiring there for the inn called the Great Charlotte.

She found it at last, after some difficulty. Because the Royal Naval College was located there, Greenwich was acrawl with officers and sailors, most of whom could not be counted upon to give reliable directions, and a number of whom were piqued by Miss Tolerance's appearance in breeches and riding boots and made every effort to follow along with her, plaguing her with noisy admiration. At last, however, she was directed to a street not far from the Royal Observatory, where she found the inn. Contrary to its name, the Great Charlotte was a small establishment, shabbily genteel in its trappings, and with no particular pretensions to affluence. Mrs. Cook's name was immediately recognized by the maid who opened the door.

"I don't know if she's awake yet, sir—I mean . . ." The girl looked around her in confusion, and Miss Tolerance gathered that Fallen Women in the bloom of youth were not a daily occurrence here. *I must be careful not to give Mrs. Cook's past away, if she has succeeded in disguising it,* Miss Tolerance thought.

"Do you mean that Mrs. Cook lives here?" she asked. She had

imagined that the woman merely used the inn as a dropping-off place; it was unexpected luck to find her actually in residence.

The girl was nodding. "I could go up and see if she's to home for you," she offered. Her slight emphasis on the last word made it clear the girl considered that very unlikely. Miss Tolerance took her to be fifteen or sixteen years of age, and perhaps the daughter of the owner. Her accent was rather purer than might be expected of a tavern maid east of London, and her dress was made up modestly, nearly to her throat.

Miss Tolerance nodded and dropped a penny into the girl's hand. "If you would tell her that I have been sent on a matter of business, and it may mean a sum of money for her?"

The girl's eye brightened, and her caution was replaced with a cordiality which told Miss Tolerance a good deal about Mrs. Cook's financial situation. "I'll tell her this minute, si—ma'am. If you'd like to sit in the parlor?" The girl opened a door to a small chamber and waved Miss Tolerance in. A little time later she reappeared, smiling.

"Mrs. Cook's compliments, and would you be able to come up to her rooms, ma'am?" She gestured toward the stairs. "She's none so spry these days, and it'd be a kindness, like. Second floor, first on the left, if you don't mind seeing yourself. I hear someone in the coffee room and—"

"I perfectly understand." Miss Tolerance pressed another coin into her hand.

She climbed the two flights up and found the door without trouble. She knocked and was bade to enter by a pleasant, low voice.

Rooms was a charitable word for the chamber in which she found herself. In reality, Mrs. Cook's suite was made up of one small room, with an even smaller alcove at the rear in which Miss Tolerance could see a clothespress and a small bed. The furniture crowded into the room; shabby, but the wood was polished and the whole rendered cozy with pillows and shawls probably made by the occupant herself.

"Please come in," Mrs. Cook urged. "I am very sorry not to

greet you by name, but Nancy forgot to tell it to me. She's a good child, but forgetful."

"The fault is mine, Mrs. Cook. I don't believe I told the girl my name. I am Sarah Tolerance, at your service. It is very kind of you to see me all unknown." Miss Tolerance stepped into the room, taking in the pleasant clutter of fabric and pattern books, with Mrs. Cook at its center. She was settled in a broad old armchair and surrounded by four embroidery frames, each with a piece of work in progress; she had another frame in her lap. The woman was enormously fat, with a heart-shaped, pretty face framed by a highly ruffled cap. Her hair, a soft, fading brown, curled in a fringe above her brow. Her dress was of a style and fabric that had been popular some years before, and she wore two shawls over her meaty shoulders. Her swollen feet had been squeezed into old leather slippers; as Miss Tolerance came closer, the older woman tucked them under the sofa as best she could, as if she were ashamed of their shabbiness. But her smile was charming, and from it and the low, sweet tones of her voice, Miss Tolerance thought she could understand the reasons for Mrs. Cunning's early success.

"By your name and your dress, I take you for a member of"—Mrs. Cook paused delicately—"that *interesting* sisterhood to which I once belonged."

"In a sense, ma'am. In fact, I am here on behalf of a gentleman who believes that you may be in possession of something he wishes to purchase."

Mrs. Cook seemed genuinely surprised. She looked around the room as if to remind herself of its contents, then shook her head. "As you see, Miss Tolerance, I live quite inexpensively; money is always scarce. I cannot imagine what I could possess—"

"A keepsake," Miss Tolerance interrupted. "A token given to you many years ago by a connection of yours; his son now wishes to regain it, as it has some familial value, and he is willing to pay handsomely for it."

The older woman's shoulders slumped slightly. "I do not

think . . ." She paused as if the admission were painful to her. "I sold so much of what I was given when I was young, to buy the annuity that supports me now. My dear Miss Tolerance . . . if one who is considerably older may presume to offer you advice, do not squander your money, for when you are no longer young and handsome . . . this is a hard world, Miss Tolerance. It forces you to make choices you would not like to make, to make associations unpleasant to you, to do things—" She turned her face to the room's single window and was silent for several moments.

At last Miss Tolerance put her hand on the older woman's shoulder. "I thank you for your advice, Mrs. Cook. You need have no fear for me, however—"

Mrs. Cook turned back to her emphatically. "No, you must believe that even you may be overtaken by—"

"I beg your pardon, ma'am," Miss Tolerance interrupted. "I have not made my situation clear. I am indeed—that is, while I lost my virtue some years ago, I did not adopt the profession from which you have retired."

Mrs. Cook looked puzzled. "I do not understand. I thought you said the son of one of my lovers had sent you?"

"So he did, ma'am. But I am his agent, nothing more."

"You are his agent but not his mistress?" Now the older woman seemed troubled, as if the fact that a woman might lose her reputation and yet maintain her autonomy confused her.

"May I sit down, ma'am?" Miss Tolerance asked. Mrs. Cook nodded and motioned to a chair. "I have fashioned an odd career for myself; I solve puzzles, unravel little mysteries, and find things out for the people who honor me with their patronage."

Mrs. Cook drew back. "You are a *spy*? Has this thing you wish to purchase to do with the war with France?" Her eyes went round with shocked disapproval; her unlined, fleshy face quivered with outrage.

For the love of heaven, Miss Tolerance thought wearily. "I am no spy, ma'am. Not in the way you mean. My patrons are most likely to be ladies who wish to find out if their husbands are spending their jointures on light-o'-loves, grandfathers who need to learn whether their dissolute grandsons are incorrigible wast-rels or merely sowing wild oats, or men who need to learn if their stewards are cheating them."

"Are you a lady thief-taker, then?" Mrs. Cook asked. She ap-peared determined to fit Miss Tolerance's calling into a form recognizable to herself, even one outmoded by several decades. Miss Tolerance was hard put not to smile at the notion of a lady thief-taker, like something out of a broadside ballad.

"I don't think of myself as a thief-taker, ma'am, although on occasion I have caught a thief when my client required it. I call myself an agent of inquiry. And sometimes I find things for per-sons who do not wish to be seen making inquiries themselves."

"Then 'tis not political, what you do?" Mrs. Cook considered for a moment. Her posture had relaxed, but there was still a furrow between her brows. "I am sorry, Miss Tolerance. Living in a naval town, where everyone seems to be a sailor, or to have a brother or son who is a sailor, the war, and fear of spies, is perhaps more present with us than it is in London."

In her turn, Miss Tolerance apologized. "I should perhaps have explained the capacity in which I am visiting more clearly, ma'am. Although you see it is not easily explained! But I promise you on my honor that the object I am seeking has no connection to the war."

The older woman nodded. "I thank you for your assurance, Miss Tolerance. Now." She looked around her as if hoping to find something she knew would not be there. "I regret I cannot offer you refreshment, my dear, but I am afraid . . . I keep no wine, you see, having too great a weakness for it myself. And I would ring for tea, but it is near the end of the quarter, and . . ."

She was so obviously eager to make amends for her suspi-cions with hospitality that Miss Tolerance's heart went out to her.

"Mrs. Cook, if you will allow me to call the maid up and order refreshments—I assure you, the expense will be borne by my client, who can well afford to indulge two ladies in a light nun-cheon." She made sure to speak confidingly, as if buying cakes and tea were a slightly wicked dissipation. The gesture worked. The older woman sat back and smiled.

"If you will ring the bell for Nancy, then? It is there, by your hand. I do not move about as well as I was used to once. I am sadly dropsical, as you see." She held out her pudgy, swollen fingers for her visitor's inspection. Miss Tolerance rang the bell sharply, hoping that the girl in the coffee room would actually hear it. "Now, Miss Tolerance, perhaps you can tell me which of my former connections has sent you to me, and what he is seeking?"

"Yes, ma'am. May I first ascertain that in your youth your professional name was Deb Cunning?"

Mrs. Cook looked embarrassed, but nodded.

"Well, then. I have been sent by the Earl of Versellion, who hopes to regain a fan that his father gave to you some twenty years or so ago."

"Oh, longer than that, my dear. It was . . ." Mrs. Cook's expression became at once pleased and dreamy. "It was in '85, for my twenty-first birthday. I had not thought of that fan in an age! Such a pretty thing, gold sticks and silk painted with an Italian landscape, cypress trees, you know, and a jewel set in each stick. It was the last thing he gave me, and I kept it—"

"You have it now?"

"Oh, mercy, I don't know! I sold so much over the years. I cannot be sure if I sold the fan when I sold my rings and the other pretties. Ah, but here is Nancy."

Indeed, the door had opened, and the girl whose acquaintance Miss Tolerance had made downstairs stood waiting.

"Nancy, we would like tea and currant cakes, if Mrs. Mardle has made any this morning? Thank you. And if you would ask Mr. Mardle for the box he keeps for me downstairs? Yes, dear, bring it along, if you please."

When the girl had gone again, Mrs. Cook asked, as delicately as possible, what sort of remuneration Lord Versellion was offering for the fan, should she still have it. Miss Tolerance was torn between the impulse to promise the entire five hundred pounds she had been authorized to spend, and a more hard-headed sense that her patron would be appreciative if she was able to bring Mrs. Cook to settle for less.

"How much would you expect to receive for it?"

Mrs. Cook flushed. "I do not know its worth, really," she said. "And were I not in such reduced circumstances, Miss Tolerance, I should happily return it to Versellion without requesting payment. As it is . . . do you think he might pay fifty pounds?"

If Mrs. Cook was serious, Miss Tolerance understood her aunt's comments about the woman's improvidence. Certainly she was no adventuress.

"I think Versellion can be brought to part with such a sum," she agreed.

The look of pleasure on the older woman's face was almost childlike. "Then you must have five pounds for yourself!" she insisted. "What wealth! I can have a new dress, and slippers, and pay my shot here without waiting for the payment of my annuity, and have money for vails. I shall ask the bookseller to order a copy of *The Curse of Kehama*!"

Miss Tolerance thanked her hostess for the offer, but assured her that she would be more than adequately compensated by the earl for her exertions. Privily she resolved to get at least two hundred pounds for Mrs. Cook if she could. There was remarkable charm in spending someone else's money.

Until Nancy reappeared with a tray and a dusty locked box, Mrs. Cook kept up a happy monologue upon the subject of what she might buy or do with her potential wealth. When the maid arrived at the door, she immediately stopped speaking except to thank the girl. The box was settled upon the arm of Mrs. Cook's armchair; the tray, with a pot of tea, a plate of currant cakes, and a small bowl of jam upon it, was settled on the footstool nearest Miss Tolerance's chair, and she poured out tea as Mrs. Cook fumbled in her pocket for the key to the box.

It was opened to reveal several packets of papers, all of them covered with the same loose, ornamented schoolgirl hand and tied together inelegantly with bits of twine: not love letters, cer-

tainly. Beneath those packets, two more packets of letters, these
tied up more romantically with ribbon, each of them subscribed
in handwriting more masculine. Below those, a necklace of amber beads, a brooch of brilliants, a fan—but quite an ordinary
one with wooden sticks, covered in white lace.

Mrs. Cook surveyed the contents sadly. "*That* fan came from
Johnny—my first, you know. I had misremembered it as Versellion's fan, I suppose. It would have been so very nice to have
a little nest egg." She looked up at Miss Tolerance. "But I have
had tea upon the strength of your kind visit, and that was a treat
I did not expect." She lifted up the bits of trumpery jewelry and
revealed another pile of papers, unbound and shuffled together
every which way. "Oh! Would it be of any value to you to know
to whom I sold the fan?" she asked. "I might still have the re-
ceipt."

Miss Tolerance, who had taken the loss of her only material
lead to the fan with as much composure as she could, released
the breath she had been holding. "It would be of great help to
me, and it would give me great pleasure to pass along a small
gratuity in exchange."

Mrs. Cook smiled and took up the pile of papers at the bottom
of the box, rifling through them, murmuring to herself as one,
then another of them called up memories for her. "Ah, I had not
thought of that bracelet for years! And the locket! And . . ." Then
she came upon a slip of paper which she silently proffered to
Miss Tolerance.

There was a date seventeen years in the past.

> *Sold to Mr. Humphrey Blackbottle, one pr. emerald earbobs,*
> *2nd qual. One garnet brooch. One fan, gld sticks w brilliants.*
> *One pr. gold and jet earbobs . . .*

"Who was Mr. Humphrey Blackbottle?" Miss Tolerance
asked. It saddened her to note how little money Mrs. Cook had
realized by the sale of her treasures.

Mrs. Cook sighed. "A jumped-up tradesman, quite well-to-do. He bought great quantities of jewelry, but never anything very fine and never anything from a jeweler. He fancied himself a very sharp fellow, as I recall, but as you see, he thought the diamonds on the sticks of the fan were mere brilliants."

"Do you recall what trade he followed?"

"I believe . . ." Mrs. Cook made a moue of concentration. "No, I can recall nothing helpful. The whole matter was handled by the landlord of the rooms I had then, who undertook to sell my jewels for me as a favor. I know Mr. Blackbottle's name seemed familiar to me at the time, but to be frank, I cannot recall why."

It was clearly useless to press further. Miss Tolerance smiled at her hostess. "It makes no mind, ma'am. I thank you very much for your help, and I shall see that you are rewarded for it. Now, I have taken a good deal of your time." She rose. "Will you pardon me? The sooner I can locate Mr. Blackbottle, the sooner you and I will both receive our rewards."

Mrs. Cook put an anxious hand on her visitor's sleeve. "But—I hate to ask it, but you will see to the matter of the tea, Miss Tolerance? It is quite beyond me at this present moment."

Miss Tolerance took up her hat, nodding. "I promise it," she said kindly.

Only later did it occur to her to wonder how often, and with what expectation of fulfillment, Mrs. Cook had heard those words.

After an uneventful ride back to London, Miss Tolerance returned her horse to the stables. It was nearly two o'clock, and she had no time to change to more feminine attire before she walked to Henry Street for her next appointment. At the door of Tarsio's Club, Steen greeted her with a look of significance.

"I'm that glad to see you, miss. You've a visitor in the Conversation Room. An important one—Mr. Jenkins is beside hisself to have such a personage in the house."

Miss Tolerance could easily imagine the pleasure of Mr. Jenkins, the club's perpetually beleaguered owner.

"I trust any refreshments Lord Balobridge ordered have been billed to my account," she said mildly, and offered Steen her hat. She stopped before a mirror to smooth her hair, then proceeded up to the Conversation Room on the first floor. It was a smaller chamber than the Ladies' Salon, paneled with wood and therefore darker. Despite the warmth of the day, a fire had been lit, and a large chair was drawn before it. At the sound of Miss Tolerance's footfall, the chair's occupant rose and turned to greet her. He was a wiry, elderly man in a long black coat in the old skirted style; he was old-fashioned enough not only to wear a wig, but powder upon it. He was no taller than Miss Tolerance, with a long face, a long nose, and a long upper lip that made him look rather doggish. His expression of amiable, slightly foolish pleasure was belied, she thought, by the shrewdness of his eyes. Miss Tolerance was interested to note that he was the third of the crowd of men she had seen Lord Trux join on Bond Street two days before. Very curious.

"My Lord Balobridge?" Miss Tolerance bowed.

Lord Balobridge bowed also—a courtesy hardly owed to her station by his, which gave her a good impression of his manners. "Miss Tolerance? I am delighted to meet you."

Miss Tolerance took the chair opposite Balobridge's. She waited until he had settled himself again in his own seat, leaning heavily upon a handsome ivory-headed cane.

"I apologize for my tardiness, my lord, and my apparel." Miss Tolerance raised a finger to summon the waiter who hovered in the back of the room, obviously under orders from Mr. Jenkins to see that their distinguished visitor lacked for nothing. "My earlier appointment kept me longer than I had expected, and left me no time to change my dress."

Balobridge shook his head. "You must not apologize to me, my dear child—you will not mind that I call you so? I am old enough to be your grandsire, after all. I have been very comfortable: I had this excellent fire to warm my old bones, and a cup of good tea as well."

The waiter appeared at her side; Miss Tolerance requested another cup and a fresh pot of tea. When both had been procured and the waiter had again retired across the room, she asked politely to what she owed the honor of his summons.

"Directly to the point, I see!" he crowed as if her question gave him pleasure. "I can tell it will be a pleasant thing to deal with you, Miss Tolerance. Well, now. I understand that you are involved in an inquiry for a certain person?" He laid coy emphasis on the last two words, and waggled his heavy eyebrows.

"I am usually involved in an inquiry for some person or other, my lord. To whom do you refer?"

The eyebrows knit. "Ah, I would prefer not to engage in particularities just yet, my dear girl. Let us speak hypothetically. You understand what I mean by that?"

Miss Tolerance spoke coolly. "You mean, let us speak in such a way that if I am later asked about this conversation, I cannot swear that you meant what you obviously hope to make me understand that you mean, my lord."

Balobridge cackled. "How rarely one meets with a woman who has a sense of humor! Very good, my child, I see we understand each other. Now, hypothetically, if you were involved in discovering the whereabouts of a certain item, and someone were to offer you a considerable compensation to have that article diverted into his own hands, rather than those of your patron, what would your answer be?"

Rather than look at her now, Balobridge took a gold-and-enamel snuffbox out of his pocket and proceeded to serve himself a pinch of the stuff, finishing by dabbing carefully at his nose with a neat linen handkerchief. He left a spill of snuff down the front of his buff waistcoat. Miss Tolerance waited until he had finished the performance before she replied.

"My lord, I would be delighted to oblige you—hypothetically—but for one consideration. A person in my profession has little to recommend her if her patrons cannot rely upon her discretion and integrity. If I did what you suggested and my client learned of it, I very much doubt that I should ever get another client again. I have lost my reputation as a woman, sir. I have no particular hankering to lose my professional reputation as well."

Balobridge nodded sympathetically. "I understand entirely, my dear. Unfortunately, this is a matter upon which I might not be able to indulge your scruples. I might be brought—oh, very reluctantly indeed—to persuade Bow Street that the matter of the death of an old woman in Leyton ought, really, to be investigated."

"I wish you would, sir," Miss Tolerance said firmly, giving no indication of her surprise. "Nothing would please me better. I tried to persuade Mr. Gilkes, the justice to whom I reported Mrs. Smith's death, to bring the matter to the Coroner's Court." *How did Balobridge come to know of the matter?* Miss Tolerance wondered. *And does he realize how much he reveals by speaking of it?*

"Ah, did you so?" Balobridge turned his teacup around and around on its saucer, seemingly fascinated by it. "The Runners might not believe that was anything but a ruse, my dear." Despite the foolishness of his expression, Miss Tolerance could not doubt the steeliness of the viscount's intent.

"They might not," she agreed. "But I believe I can establish that I was not responsible for her death." Miss Tolerance smiled. The conversation was taking on the character of a fencing match, a milieu in which she showed her best. " 'Twould be an inconvenience to me at best. Certainly not a fatal one."

Balobridge smiled. "How would you accomplish it, my dear?"

"Surely it would be unwise of me to tell you, sir. For all we are speaking hypothetically, a woman must not give away all her stratagems."

If Miss Tolerance's unwillingness to cooperate bothered him, Lord Balobridge gave no indication of it. He tilted his head back, tapping lightly on his lips with the fingers of his right hand, regarding her from lidded eyes. His expression was quizzical. At last, he folded his fingers into a fist and rested his chin upon it, still regarding her calmly.

"This is a very anxious time for our nation, Miss Tolerance," he said. "The opposition hopes to appease Bonaparte and withdraw from the war; the peasantry here is being stirred up by poets and madmen, and at the highest level of the nation, there are matters afoot which threaten our very way of life."

"How very vague these threats are! I am not political by nature, but if pressed, I must say that I have more sympathy for the peasants—and the poets and madmen—than you would probably find comfortable."

"But surely to a woman of good family—"

"Which is what I no longer am—"

"The principles learned at your mother's knee?" Balobridge leaned forward insinuatingly. "A sense of the fitness of things, the proper way of life? This stays with you for life, my dear, regardless of less savory experience."

Miss Tolerance smiled. "The principles I learnt were at my nursemaid's knee, sir, and perhaps from the grooms in my father's stables. My 'way of life,' as you put it, is far closer to theirs than to your own. Now, as to the great matters you mention, you will have to be more explicit for me to feel myself concerned in them."

"To do that, I must place myself fully in your confidence, Miss Tolerance, and beyond the precincts of the hypothetical."

"And you are not prepared to do that just yet, I believe."

"I fear that I cannot, while you are in the pay of the opposition." Lord Balobridge took a long, noisy sip of his tea. Miss Tolerance poured more into her own cup and, upon his gesture, filled his cup as well. It was a shame that the viscount wanted something from her that she could not perform; she believed she would have enjoyed working for the old man.

He took one more sip from his cup, then set it down and

regarded her seriously. "Miss Tolerance, I understand from my discussion with Mr. Gilkes that he was far from satisfied in the matter of the death of Mrs. Smith."

Miss Tolerance permitted herself an expression of polite disbelief. "The justice? Indeed, he must have revised his opinion after I spoke to him; he could not, then, wait to rid himself of the matter, and more or less threatened me with sanction should I press him upon it. I apprehend that it was your discussion woke in him this great dissatisfaction?"

Lord Balobridge nodded solemnly. "I urged Mr. Gilkes to keep the matter quiet, as a favor to Sir Adam Brereton."

Miss Tolerance blinked. "*My brother?* Is he in some wise concerned with Mrs. Smith's death?"

"He knows nothing of Mrs. Smith, I believe, but I cannot think he will wish to have his sister dragged through the ignominy of a public investigation into her activities," Balobridge said smoothly.

Miss Tolerance laughed so loudly that the waiter at the end of the room started from his doze. "Adam would not care if I were hung at Newgate, my lord. I was declared dead to my family long ago. My brother might not thank you, were such an investigation to occur, but that would simply be for fear of damage to his *amour-propre*. Sentiment is not my family's besetting sin."

"Perhaps not, Miss Tolerance. But as you say, the sullying of his own name—"

"My lord, I hope you will spare yourself concern on that head. I took my present name to spare my family, who on their part cast me off without a second thought. My parents are dead; I do not consider that I owe anyone—save my aunt, who did extend a familial hand to me—anything. More tea, my lord?"

Balobridge shook his head. "I am afraid I shall not be able to stay much longer, Miss Tolerance."

"I am sad to hear it, my lord. I have enjoyed your visit. Oh . . ." Miss Tolerance paused for effect. "May I inquire after the gentlemen you sent to summon me last night, sir?"

He looked at her impassively. "Gentlemen?"

"Perhaps I use the term too broadly. The men with swords, who accosted me outside Mrs. Brereton's."

He did not scruple to deny it. Balobridge chuckled and shook his head. "Ran home with their tails between their legs, Miss Tolerance. You used them mighty hard, from what they told me. But how did you know that they were my emissaries?"

"Propinquity suggests it, sir: an attack last night, followed by an invitation this morning. Of course, I did not know for certain until now. May I presume that someone in my aunt's house is in your employ as well?"

This time Balobridge was not to be caught. He assumed an expression of saintly innocence as he assured her he knew nothing of what she was saying. "You are a redoubtable woman, Miss Tolerance. It would grieve me to cause you distress."

Miss Tolerance smiled. "Then, by all means, my lord, please do not do so. If I cannot be of use to you in this matter, it may well be that someday I will be of assistance in some other."

Balobridge shook his head. "It must be this matter and no other, my dear. I must have the fan—" He stopped himself. "I must have the item we were discussing, must see it, at least, before your client does. Would your scruples permit that?"

She shook her head. "I am afraid they would not, my lord."

The viscount rose, a sober expression on his long, doggish face. "I hope your refusal will not push me to more desperate measures, Miss Tolerance."

She refused to rise to the bait. "Why, I hope so too, my lord." She rose and offered her hand. "Thank you for the honor of your confidence."

He looked surprised. "You will not apprise your client of this conversation?"

"Ought I to? It was hypothetical, was it not?"

The viscount raised her hand to his lips and kissed it. "I see that despite your condition, Miss Tolerance, you are a lady still."

She found herself unexpectedly moved, but felt it unwise, with this very shrewd man, to let him know it. "Merely a businesswoman, sir."

Balobridge bowed and turned on his heel. The toadying waiter at the door bowed and followed him, and Miss Tolerance returned to her seat to finish up the tea in her pot.

Seven

The name Blackbottle was not unknown to Miss Tolerance, but she did not immediately place it—and its owner—in its proper context. After meeting with Lord Balobridge, she had returned to her house to find Matt Etan waiting glumly by the door. It was late afternoon; the sun was yet high enough to wash Mrs. Brereton's garden with red-gold light, but Miss Tolerance's cottage stood in the shadow of the garden wall. It, and her visitor, looked gray and chilly.

"It's locked!" he said irritably. "You've never locked the door before, Sarey! What's amiss?"

Miss Tolerance had a brief impulse to tell Matt her suspicion of a spy in Mrs. Brereton's household, but the habit of discretion won over. "I'm trying to stop the wholesale plunder of my larder, parasite."

"Locked your door against *me*?" He looked, if anything, more dejected. "I come seeking a friend and this is what I find: a locked door, a nipfarthing lack of hospitality—"

"Stop, I pray you." The door swung over and Miss Tolerance

waved Matt through it. "When you have the whole of my aunt's establishment—and kitchens—in which to seek friendship, why come to me? Has something driven you from my aunt's house? Have you no custom this evening?"

He shook his head. "None so far. I'm unwanted. If this keeps up, your aunt will decide she cannot afford to keep me—"

"Unlikely. At worst, she'll keep you as an ornament to the establishment. You're such a pretty fellow." In fact, the gray and purple shadows that filled the cottage did not become him; he appeared haggard and ghostly. Miss Tolerance hurried to light a lamp.

"I shall wind up in the stews in Cheapside, drinking Blue Ruin, my looks quite destroyed," he continued, as if she had not spoken. "In the end I'll probably hang myself with my last remaining silk stocking and be buried at the crossroads." He dropped onto the settle in a theatrical attitude of dejection.

Miss Tolerance laughed.

"Idiot! With your turn for drama, you should be in Covent Garden rehearsing with Mrs. Jordan. I'll wager you anything you like that within an hour someone from my aunt's will be here to announce that you've a visitor. Or more than one. And if you have no taste for gin now, why would you start? Furthermore, you have far too much *amour-propre* to allow yourself to be disfigured by hanging. Your face would turn purple, your eyes swell up, and I understand that at the moment of death—"

"For God's sake, enough! I know hangings—used to be as good as a festival day where I came from. You're right, I won't hang myself. As for the rest . . . what would you wager? I'm feeling forlorn tonight. Perhaps a wager will cheer me up."

"A pair of silk stockings against . . ." She thought for a moment. "A favor. I may have need of someone to run an errand for me in the course of this current business."

"Nothing more intimate than running an errand?" He feigned disappointment. "I'll do it, though it's a grossly unfavorable wager; for what your aunt gets for an hour of my time . . ." He settled onto the bench by the fireplace, poking desultorily at the coals until the fire lit, then put the kettle on. Miss Tolerance, in the meanwhile, had taken up her writing desk and was reviewing notes she had made.

"You're muttering to yourself, Sarey. What is fretting you?" He stretched one arm across to her, plucked the penknife from the writing desk, and began to clean his nails with it.

Miss Tolerance shook her head. "You know I cannot tell you."

"Spoilsport. You could let me know in the most general way. You've talked about your cases before."

It was on the tip of Miss Tolerance's tongue to note that this was the first time she had ever suspicioned betrayal from within her aunt's household. She bit hard on the sentiment and said mildly, "It is only a puzzle I must unravel, nothing more. I'm on the track of what appears to be an unexceptionable object, only it seems that several people are in pursuit of that same prize. I should like to know why."

"D'you need to know?"

"To find the prize? I don't think so. But to play the game that seems to be springing up around the prize, I may." She looked down at the papers on her desk quizzically, then drew a fresh sheet of paper, inked her pen, and began to write a report for Versellion. For some little while the room was silent except for the pleasant sounds of pen scratching on paper, and cups and kettle rattling as Matt made tea for them both. Miss Tolerance had finished the note and was blotting it when someone knocked at the door.

"Come," Matt called out before Miss Tolerance could say anything.

Cole entered with a summons for Matt: a Mr. Blethersfield was inquiring for him.

"Ah, dear David!" Matt said with unfeigned affection. "I am saved from Blackbottle's for one more day." He rose at once from the settle.

Miss Tolerance looked up sharply. "What did you say?"

Matt grinned. "You won your bet, Sarey. I owe you an hour of my time, although I'm sure I could think of a better way to

while it than on *errands*." He waggled his eyebrows at her meaningfully.

"Be serious, Matt. What did you just say?"

"That I was saved from the Cheapside stews once again. Mr.
Blethersfield wants me, your aunt will continue to employ me,
and I needn't consider taking sailors at—"

"Blackbottle! Good God, of course I knew the name." She
locked the note in her desk, thinking to send it later, and rose
up. "Go along, Matt. Don't keep your *beau ami* waiting. I have
just recalled some business I must attend to." She took up her
hat, coat, and sword, pushed her friend out the door before her,
and locked it up again. Then, following Matt into her aunt's
establishment, she desired Cole to fetch a hackney for her. The
address she gave was Bow Lane, Cheapside. Cole raised an eyebrow but said nothing.

P assing through the airy avenues of Mayfair, where the last
blush of sunset cast rosy light on the faces of the great
houses, Miss Tolerance watched as the streets became progres-
sively darker, narrower, and meaner. The driver pointed the carriage toward Covent Garden (doubtless to avoid the dangerous
neighborhood of Seven Dials, some streets to the north). The
Garden was bright enough: the theaters and opera waited to be
filled, and a well-behaved throng of farmers turning homeward
from the market crossed paths with flower girls and prostitutes
awaiting the arrival of the night's audiences, and beggars preparing their piteous lies for the benefit of the soft-hearted. But
as the hackney crossed Drury Lane and continued east toward
the city, the character of the neighborhood around them changed
swiftly. Now and again the driver was forced to pull up to let a
knot of people brawl across the thoroughfare; voices grew
louder, more quarrelsome. Past the counting houses and courts
of the city, still busy at this hour, then through the august shadows of St. Paul's, they continued until the hackney drew up on
Cheapside, at the entrance to Bow Lane.

Miss Tolerance was no stranger to these streets, yet she found them uncongenial. She took comfort in the sword at her side and the small pistol, primed and ready, in the pocket of her Gunnard coat. The driver was duly paid and sped away. Miss Tolerance turned to view the narrow, ancient lane, off of which struck even narrower, less savory alleys. The homely smell of horse piss and manure mingled with the smells of sweat and of the effluvia of slops jars in the gutter, and wafts of hops and gin which issued from the open doors of the public houses.

Miss Tolerance asked the first person she saw—a woman much younger on close inspection than her dress implied—the way to Blackbottle's establishment. In the dusk and shadows of Bow Lane, the girl clearly saw only Miss Tolerance's clothes and not the woman who wore them: she offered to supply "the gentleman" with anything that Blackbottle's could provide, at half the cost.

Miss Tolerance politely refused the offer; her business was with Blackbottle himself and no other.

The girl grimaced. The lace on her bodice was shoddy stuff, grimy and torn, and the spray of flowers in her bonnet was sadly worn. Her face and the expanse of flesh revealed by her décolleté had been washed, but her neck was grimy and there was dirt under her fingernails. She took a step closer, moving in a cloud of gin.

"You don't want to go messin' with Blackbottle's, darling," she told Miss Tolerance in slurred northern tones. "All them girls got the pox, and likely Blackbottle with 'em. I never heard he fancies boys, but you're a pretty one. . . ." She reached a hand toward the front of Miss Tolerance's trousers, obviously hoping to distract her from her purpose. Then she reared back.

"Christ! What *are* you?"

Miss Tolerance pushed the groping hand aside. "If you could show me the way, I can give you a shilling,"

After a beat of hesitation, the hand stretched out again, palm up this time, to receive the offered tip. "Zis somethin' new at Blackbottle's, then? Girls tarted up to look like boys?" She closed her fist around the coin Miss Tolerance gave her and turned on her heel, steps still wobbly with gin, but all the seductive purpose gone from her movements.

"I don't work for Blackbottle," Miss Tolerance told her, picking her way around the trash and dung that littered the street. "I need to talk to him."

"Talk!" The girl laughed. "They do precious little talking there, my girl. You'll need that pigsticker ere you're done!" She stopped abruptly before an undistinguished door. "Zis'll be it, then." She backed away and Miss Tolerance looked up to see a big man framed against the light from the house.

"That you, Callie?" he asked, not unkindly, but with a tone of warning. "Better clear out before Mrs. Virtue hears you're out here."

"I'm going, Joe, I'm going. Brung you a caller, 'z all." The girl smiled again. "Good luck, dearie. Come tell me how you fare." She turned away and in a moment was lost to sight in the darkness of the street. Miss Tolerance turned back to the man in the doorway and asked to see Mr. Blackbottle. What it had taken the departed Callie several minutes to realize, Joe apprehended at once.

"What, you come looking for work tricked out like that? Mr. Blackbottle won't have none of that in this house, no more will Mrs. Virtue. Side of which, Mr. Blackbottle don't hire hisself, he leaves that to Mrs. Virtue—"

"Who is the manager of the establishment, I take it?" Miss Tolerance used her quietest, most polite tone, as if she were speaking to a clerk in a circulating library. "I am not here looking for work. Nor am I looking for . . . companionship," she added, as Joe opened his mouth to speak. "I merely need to speak to Mr. Blackbottle on a matter of business. You may tell him that there is the chance of an easy profit in it for him. But I must speak to him and no other."

The doorkeeper nodded, thought it over, then paused to greet and admit a heavyset man with a kerchief tied under his ear, who shouldered past Miss Tolerance with the assurance of a longtime customer. Joe turned to follow the customer, closing the door firmly in Miss Tolerance's face with one growled word: "Wait."

It took a good ten minutes for the doorkeeper to reappear. Miss Tolerance was joined several times by men of differing quality and degrees of inebriation, all desiring admission to the house and none discerning enough to discover Miss Tolerance's gender. When Joe did return, he admitted the men, who could be seen disappearing into a room to the right of the stairway. The doorman turned to Miss Tolerance, his brows drawn up in a frown.

"You wait there," he said grudgingly, indicating with a nod of his head the chamber into which the others had vanished. This proved to be a small salon ringed around with chairs and sofas, on which sat a number of women, waiting. Despite the garish use of rouge and powder, and clothes which varied from full dress to little more than corset and garters, the waiting whores put Miss Tolerance strongly in mind of those young women at parties who, blessed with a squint, a stammer, or a lack of dowry, sat waiting hopelessly to dance. The men who had entered before her chose their partners and left with them. The remaining women stared at Miss Tolerance, murmured among themselves, tittered, and ignored her. They had no occupation other than waiting. Each time the front door opened, each one looked up hopefully; when one man familiar to all entered the room, they greeted him effusively as an old friend. On his part, the man crooked at finger at one of the girls and started up the stairs without waiting to see if she followed.

After another ten minutes or more, Joe the doorman reappeared and muttered that the lady was to proceed to the room at the top of the stairs. Out of habit, much as she did at her aunt's house, Miss Tolerance moved through Blackbottle's establishment with her eyes down, seemingly unaware of her surroundings. Still, by the time she gained the first floor, she was convinced that this brothel was like most others of its kind: most of the doors were ajar, the smell of sex was pervasive, and cries of manufactured passion mingled with the howl of a dog on the street. A woman laughed loudly on the floor above, and a man growled an unintelligible command.

At the top of the stairs Miss Tolerance knocked on the door and entered a room filled with the superficial trappings of luxury, startling after the sordid appearance of the ground floor. There were many candles in branches around the room, hangings of a rich, dark red, a Turkish carpet, and a sofa and chairs in the Egyptian style lately in vogue. A second glance showed Miss Tolerance that the carpet was grimy, the hangings of insubstantial material, and the gilded furniture cheaply made. The scent of rose attar hung on the air, mingled with another smell, sweet and familiar, which Miss Tolerance did not immediately place.

"How may I help you?"

The voice was low-pitched, beautiful, with a musical trace of foreign accent. The English, though very formal, was quite correct. Miss Tolerance turned to see its owner.

"Mrs. Virtue? I was hoping to speak to Mr. Blackbottle."

"So Joe told me. You will sit down, perhaps, and take some refreshment?"

The woman at first gave the impression that she was much the same in age as Miss Tolerance. She was tall, fleshy, and well-corseted; her red hair was piled atop her head in a tousled but pleasing arrangement that suggested she had lately arisen from a couch of pleasure. Her robe was made of velvet in a tawny shade of gold, an unusual color that conferred an air of the exotic. But like the room, a second glance undid the impression of the first: Miss Tolerance realized that the woman was probably her senior by a score of years, although a good deal of skill had gone into disguising the fact. She looked, certainly, far superior to her surroundings, and Miss Tolerance found herself wondering how this woman had come to be the mistress of so disreputable an establishment.

"You're very kind, ma'am," Miss Tolerance said. She avoided the first chair offered, which had one leg askew and looked ready to fall under its own weight, took the second, and settled gingerly into it.

"I fear that some of my chairs show their age, as you see," Mrs. Virtue said. "You will drink some wine?" Her smile was warm and just slightly curious. Her teeth were even and very white.

Miss Tolerance refused the wine. She did not wish to linger here, nor did she wholly trust the wine in an establishment like this to be undrugged. "I do not mean to take up your time, ma'am. I am in hopes to locate Mr. Blackbottle on a matter of business—"

"For which you come armed. I will need some reassurance, before I send you on to my employer, that I am not sending him an assassin." Mrs. Virtue smiled and poured a glass of wine for herself.

"Assassin?" Miss Tolerance blinked, startled by the thought. "Is Mr. Blackbottle likely to be assassinated, ma'am?"

"Probably not—but then, the appearance of a woman in men's clothes, armed, at the door, is not so likely, either, is it?"

"Mrs. Virtue, my weapons are merely prudent for a woman like myself in a neighborhood to which she is a stranger and which is, if you will pardon me, not of the best. I am the agent of a gentleman who wishes to reclaim an item sold to Mr. Blackbottle many years ago: the bauble has sentimental value to his family. Far from wishing your employer harm, I have it in my power to reward him generously for return of the item."

"But you cannot tell me what the item is?"

"No, ma'am, I cannot. My client's privacy—"

"A delicate thing, I'm sure." Mrs. Virtue's smile was faintly malicious. "Well, I must tell you that my employer's privacy is also delicate." The smile became a grin. "And I must think twice about letting a woman in trousers force herself upon his notice after telling me a story of the cock and the bull and *her client.* Even if the lady is one of great virtue." She inclined her head with mock graciousness, and her red curls bobbed.

"You have nothing to fear from me, ma'am. My virtue is exactly what you think it, but my profession is different from yours, and I have no ambition to change it. I am precisely what I say: the agent of a man who wishes to buy something Mr. Blackbottle may possess."

"And you are not going to run Sir Humphrey through with that sword, or entice him to hire you—you're not one to whore yourself, you'd want the running of an establishment, I think. But you wish only to find a piece of jewelry, a bauble." Mrs. Virtue drained the wine from her glass and set it down without taking her eyes from her visitor's face.

Miss Tolerance nodded. The room was very close, and the longer she sat there, the more the unpleasant whorehouse smells became evident to her, despite the scenting of this room. She wanted to leave, but could not in good conscience without pressing a little further.

"I would certainly make your assistance worth the time it took, ma'am." She met Mrs. Virtue's gaze with one of cool politeness.

The mention of money banished any apprehension Mrs. Virtue had had for her employer's privacy or safety. She turned, poured another glass of wine, and drank deeply. Refreshed, she smiled. "One cannot be too careful." The musical inflection of her words seemed stronger now. "It is hard to be sure who is to be trusted and who not."

As if to illustrate the point, Mrs. Virtue's words were interrupted by an uproar from a room upstairs: a woman's scream, of pain or terror Miss Tolerance could not tell, and a man's voice swearing. The scream brought Miss Tolerance to her feet, hand on the hilt of her sword, but Mrs. Virtue did not stir from her chair. The tumult continued above their heads, joined by the sound of boots upon the uncarpeted stairway.

"Miss . . . I forget the name? Sit, I beg. Your concern does you credit, but Joseph will have matters in hand in a moment."

And in fact, the screaming and the swearing had stopped, although Miss Tolerance thought she could hear weeping now. She sat again.

"Mrs. Virtue, may I have Mr. Blackbottle's direction?" She slid her hand into her coat to remove her pocketbook, and drew a five-pound note from it. "I hope this will be an adequate expression of my gratitude for your assistance?"

Mrs. Virtue took the note and examined it. "You know, there was a time when I would have given this as vails to my maid. But life, it changes, yes?" She tilted her head and regarded Miss Tolerance with some curiosity. "You truly are not this client's mistress? You will come to it, soon or late."

Miss Tolerance shook her head. "I believe not, ma'am. Now, Mr. Blackbottle?"

Mrs. Virtue folded the note and pushed it into a pocket at the waist of her velvet gown. "You will probably find him in one of the houses across the river. He has several. Try Butler's Wharf or Clink Street," she suggested. "If you do not find him there . . ." She shrugged matter-of-factly. "He does not tell me where he goes with his girls. Try the Wharf first." She smiled and stood, clearly dismissing her visitor.

With a silent prayer of thanksgiving, Miss Tolerance took her leave.

Smoky and fetid as the air outside the brothel was, there was at least some hint of breeze on the street. It was a relief after half an hour spent in Mrs. Virtue's boudoir. Miss Tolerance took off walking purposefully up Bow Lane to Cheapside, where she found a hackney carriage. If the driver she found was dismayed at being ordered across the river to Butler's Wharf, he did not show it, but shrugged and urged his horses in the direction of London Bridge.

It was close to midnight when the hackney finally drew up near the Wharf. Miss Tolerance paid the driver and stepped out, mindful of what she might encounter in the unswept street. The buildings surrounding were either shuttered and silent or brightly lit and filled with merriment. The people she passed were either drunk or plying their trade, or in some cases both. The whores on the street corner, once they realized she did not mean new custom for them, refused to talk to her. Even the offer of half a crown left them unmoved. "I'd as soon direct you to hell as Blackbottle's," one spat, by which Miss Tolerance understood that a trade war of sorts was in process between themselves and Blackbottle's establishment. A few feet down the street, in the doorway of a darkened house, she met with a man sitting, legs spread before him, gazing mournfully at the shattered remains of a square blue-glass bottle, from which the contents—certainly gin, by the smell of the man himself—had spilled.

"It broke," he said sadly. He repeated this observation several times, as if to test its validity; he seemed likely to slide sideways with one more repetition.

Miss Tolerance took him firmly by the shoulder.

"Sixpence for you if you can tell me which way to Blackbottle's, my man," she said. She held the coin before his eyes, which lit with the glow of salvation.

"Third on the left, with the music. Doorman's a little feller name Horkin', don't take no nonsense." The drunkard made a swipe at the coin and missed. Miss Tolerance pressed it into his hand with a word of thanks and left him.

If Mr. Horking would take no nonsense, he was yet quite businesslike about taking the coins Miss Tolerance pressed upon him inquiring for Mr. Blackbottle, and directed her to yet another of the brothels owned by that gentleman, the one on Clink Street, directly back in the direction from which her hackney had come. Since no carriages appeared, Miss Tolerance sighed and began to walk west. Here and there a streetwalker offered dreary pleasure, and a few times Miss Tolerance was aware that she was being appraised by those who make their living at the cudgel's tip. At those moments she folded the tail of her coat so it more prominently displayed her sword, and walked on.

The brothel at Clink Street was identical in all but architectural detail to the two she had already visited, including the women waiting for custom, and a large and surly doorman eager to be paid for his assistance. Again, Mr. Blackbottle was not there, nor did the woman in charge, a Mrs. Bottom, offer any suggestions for Miss Tolerance's further inquiry. The hour was now very late—or very early, depending upon one's point of view—and Miss Tolerance's step was dispirited as she left. The doorman, however, was waiting for her just outside the house as she was leaving.

"Hssst, sir!" He stood in the boarded and darkened doorway of the next building, almost invisible in the inky darkness of the street. "Mrs. Bottom give you what you wanted, sir?" The man grinned broadly.

"No, I'm afraid not," Miss Tolerance replied gruffly. If the doorman was cup-shot enough to believe her a man, that was all to her good. "Have you any information which would help me find Mr. Blackbottle?"

"If'n you got more coin to spread about for it." The man was not merely half drunk; Miss Tolerance recognized the tone of voice peculiar to a large man who believes he is about to take advantage of a slighter one.

"I might have, at that," she agreed, slipping her hand into a pocket of her Gunnard coat. Her fingers closed around the hilt of a small dagger which she kept for those situations in which there was too little space for swordplay and no time to prime a pistol. "Mr. Blackbottle's address?"

"Ah, fuck old Blackballs," the big man said. "And fuck you, too. Gimme the coin or you'll not make it home to your mama, boy." He threw one arm around Miss Tolerance's shoulder and made to pull her backward into the door with him. The shock of grasping the evidence that the man he was robbing was in fact a woman set him off balance. Miss Tolerance ducked under the slack arm, drove one knee upward into the man's gut, then grabbed his forelock in her left hand as he doubled over, and forced his head up. The dagger she pressed against his throat.

"If would have been far more profitable for you to have given me the answer at once, you know. Now, do you know where Mr. Blackbottle is to be found?" She spoke through clenched teeth.

"Christ! Christ, all right! He's in the next street but one, a set a rooms he's got there with one of the girls. Heeble Lane, third floor. Christ, you bitch, let go!"

Miss Tolerance, not wishing to be attacked again, led the doorman back to the brothel, opened the door, and shoved him in. "Keep him still a few moments, he's had a shock," she called to the first whore who peered around the door sill of the saloon. She tossed a few coins after and shut the door. As she walked to Heeble Lane, she kept her hand on the hilt of her sword in readiness, but there was no further attack.

Heeble Lane, was little better than an alley, so short that there were only three houses on each side of the thoroughfare, so narrow that even in full daylight it was doubtful that the sun ever reached the faces of those structures. Only one building—the centermost on the eastern side—boasted a doorway that let onto the lane itself. With a little inward trepidation, Miss Tolerance entered the unlit hallway and, in near pitch-darkness, found and climbed the stairs to the third floor.

Her discomfort at the necessity of making her way blind through unfamiliar and possibly dangerous territory lent a particular authority to the knocks she rained upon the door. Almost immediately a sullen glow appeared at the bottom of the door, indicating that a light had been lit within. A moment later the door opened a few inches and a dark-haired woman in a rose-colored gown looked out. She was considerably the worse for drink—rum, by the smell.

"I swear to you, Taffy, if it's about that old—" Realizing the person who stood in the hallway was not Taffy, the woman broke off, blinked, and asked, "Who are you?"

"I'm seeking Humphrey Blackbottle on a matter of business," Miss Tolerance said calmly, as if it were not close to two o'clock in the morning. The fact that the woman, for all her bleariness, was fully dressed and gave no indication of having been asleep secured Miss Tolerance in the thought that she had come during business hours. "Would you be so kind as to tell him that I am here?"

The woman blinked again and took a step backward, less to

signify an invitation to enter than because she was extremely unsteady on her feet.

"Will you be a-listenin' to that!" she announced to no one in particular. "Will I be so kind?" She regarded Miss Tolerance with an owlish stare. "Christ, you a new girl from one of the other houses? Don't know your face. Sir Humphrey is busy at the moment, as you might say." But she took a further step back, allowing Miss Tolerance to enter. The room was small, lit only by a lamp that stood near to the woman's hand, and by the far brighter light that squeezed through the slightly opened doorway on its opposite side. The groans issuing therefrom, and the considerable disorder of her hostess's gown, gave Miss Tolerance a pretty fair idea of Mr. Blackbottle's occupation.

"I can wait until he's at liberty," she said coolly.

The woman burst into a peal of laughter, closed the door to the hallway, and turned to go back to the inner chamber. "Can you, then? I'll leave you the lamp." She drew her skirts in and disappeared into the other room, closing the door behind her firmly.

It occurred to Miss Tolerance as she waited that she was within sight of the end of her commission for Lord Versellion, and that she still did not understand the meaning of the fan or what made it an object of such interest to her client and to Lord Balobridge. It should not have concerned her—she would, after all, be paid whether she understood or no—but there was also the matter of the late Mrs. Smith, whose murder would quite likely never be resolved. She sighed, and in the dim light tried to make out the time on her watch. Nearly half-past two. She dozed.

"Gawd, she's still here!"

Miss Tolerance opened her eyes and was greeted by the sight of a woman, fair-haired and wearing a gauzy dressing gown, peering from the doorway.

"Is Mr. Blackbottle ready to see me?" Miss Tolerance asked collectedly.

The girl giggled, then opened the door and swept a deep

curtsy to the visitor. "Oh, do pray enter!" she said broadly. The effect was rather spoiled by the way she teetered in rising. Miss Tolerance thanked her and walked past. The scene which met her eyes looked like nothing so much as a satirical etching on the horrors of debauchery: everything was in disarray, from the sheets and hangings on the bed at the rear of the room to the woman who slept heavily in the midst of them, her bodice unlaced and her breasts bared. In the fore of the room, a man in a violet silk dressing gown lounged in a deep chair, one leg raised as if to ease the effects of gout. He was picking idly at his teeth with a gold-handled toothpick; a tankard lay close to hand and the remains of a chicken just beyond.

"Mr. Humphrey Blackbottle?" she inquired.

"You may call me Sir Humphrey," he informed her kindly. "All the pretty girls do. Sit down, my love, and tell me what I can do for you." He looked at her appraisingly, as if she were a bit of bloodstock on view at Tattersall's horse sales, and waved her to a chair. He drank deeply from the tankard, put it down with an emphatic bang, and smiled broadly.

Miss Tolerance restrained the impulse to query him regarding his self-appointed baronetcy, and said mildly, "I am sorry to call so late, sir, but it took me some time to find you."

"Fanny sent word someone was desirous of finding me, my dear. What I don't understand is how you did, seeing as I hadn't given word that I was willing to be found." His accent was broadly northern, with the superficial tones of one who has moved in genteel society. If he was displeased with his staff, he did not seem inclined to extend that displeasure to Miss Tolerance.

"Your staff was not particularly forthcoming," she agreed. "However, the doorman at your Clink Street establishment extended himself a little further, with sufficient prodding."

Sir Humphrey grinned. His teeth were blackened and gummy, by far the most revolting thing Miss Tolerance had seen that evening. "Tried to bully you, did he? And you took him with that pigsticker?" He gestured toward Miss Tolerance's sword.

"You apprehend perfectly, sir. But I promise you, I *am* here on business. If you can help me, it will be well worth your time."

"So I hear. Fanny told me you was looking for something, but cut up stiff and wouldn't tell her what."

"Fanny?" Miss Tolerance asked.

"Mrs. Virtue, runs my house in Cheapside."

"Of course. Well, sir, I have been commissioned by a patron—I need not tell his name—who wishes to reclaim a gift that was given to a woman some twenty years ago. It was a decorated fan, gold sticks and brilliants, and painted silk. You bought it, I believe, from Mrs. Deb Cunning—"

"There's a name I've not thought of for dogs' years!" Blackbottle sucked on his teeth reminiscently. "She's one as has gone respectable, that's sure as eggs. She was the type for it, couldn't sell her little treasures direct, had to have some fellow do it for her. A fan, d'you say?" He took another draft from his tankard, then waved it imperiously until the fair-haired woman took it off to refill it. "Gold sticks and brilliants, and stretched-out looking trees. I remember it."

Elation and disbelief clashed within Miss Tolerance. "After nigh on twenty years, sir? Truly?"

Blackbottle stared over the rim of his tankard at her. "I remember every damned thing I spend a farthing on, girl! I couldn't have reached my current lofty position"—he waved the tankard in a broad circle, indicating the slovenly room; a good deal of wine sloshed out and spattered the table and his dressing gown—"if I didn't keep a tight rein on my money!"

"I'm sure, sir," Miss Tolerance said. "But as to the fan?"

"You'd as well to have told Fanny the whole tale, girl. All your chasing about has been for nowt. I gave the thing to her, years ago."

Miss Tolerance felt a wave of exhaustion sweep over her, but she forced a bright smile. "Well, sir, I thank you for your help.

At what hour do you think I might call upon her again?"

Sir Humphrey guffawed. "You know your way around right enough, don't you, sweet? Unless you're planning to go there now, I'd not show my face in that house again until late in the afternoon. Fan don't go to sleep much before dawn. But I've been forgetting my manners. Will you take a little wine with me?" This as the fair-haired girl advanced again to refill his tankard.

"You're very kind," Miss Tolerance said. "But I won't take your time further. Thank you very much for your assistance, sir. If I might . . ." She slipped her hand into her pocket to take up her pocketbook. "I should like to buy you a bottle to drink my health." She put a few coins on the table—she was not about to pay the man more.

But Sir Humphrey slid the coins back to her. "No need for that among friends, my love. P'raps someday I shall need a favor of you, eh?"

Miss Tolerance was unwilling even to play at indebtedness to a whoremaster of such longevity and reputation as Humphrey Blackbottle. "Sir, I insist," she said gently. "If not for you, then perhaps your friends will be so kind as to drink my health? If you ever have need of my services, we can, of course, discuss the matter."

Blackbottle did not seem to be offended by her refusal. He smiled appreciatively and slid the coins into his pocket. "You're a knowing one, you are, my darling."

Miss Tolerance agreed that she was, and took her leave.

T he sun was almost up, a dirty glow that barely cut through an unseasonable fog, when she arrived back in Manchester Square. She was so tired that she did not bother to walk round to her own entry, but knocked at the door of her aunt's establishment and, when admitted, went straight through to the kitchens. The cook was working dough into floury rolls for the oven; a scullerier was setting chocolate pots on trays; and she found Matt Etan slouched in front of the fire, drinking tea.

"Lord, Sarey, where have you been?" he drawled. "Your coat is all a-mud."

"Is it?" She shrugged out of the Gunnard coat and examined the back, which was indeed badly spattered. She dropped it on the table.

"Leave it there, I'll take it up with mine and have Perry clean it for you," Matt offered.

Miss Tolerance smiled wearily. She would have enough to attend to when she woke. Then a thought occurred to her.

"Matt, may I call in our wager?"

"What, at this hour?"

"I really think so." Miss Tolerance sat down at the table, took up a pencil, and began scribbling out a note. In two minutes she had finished, sealed it, and told him to whose hand it should be delivered.

Matt grinned and agreed to undertake the commission. "But why not give it to Cole or Keefe?" he asked.

"I will tell you about that once this business is concluded. My God, I'm tired." She yawned broadly. "Good night, parasite, and thank you."

"Good morning, Sarey. I'll see you when you wake." He put the note in his pocket, threw her coat over his arm, and sauntered off, whistling.

Eight

In the light of late afternoon, the precincts of Bow Lane were perhaps less threatening, but no less squalid, than they had appeared the night before. Miss Tolerance, rising very late after her night abroad, had made it her first order of business to revisit Mrs. Fanny Virtue and inquire for the Italian fan. As she walked down Bow Lane toward the narrow alley wherein Blackbottle's Cheapside establishment was situated, she regretted that she had not taken the time to stop at Mrs. Brereton's and reclaim her Gunnard coat from Matt's valet: the sky threatened rain. Miss Tolerance thought philosophically that if this visit yielded the fan, she would hire a hackney to return to Manchester Square, make up a final report—with a reckoning of expenses—for Lord Versellion, and ask to meet with him at his earliest convenience. He would be primed for good news; the note she had sent with Matt desiring a meeting had been optimistic as well as discreet. There had been no reply waiting when she woke; perhaps when she returned from Cheapside, there would be one, appointing a time and place to conclude their business.

With an unhappy glance at the brassy, unpromising sky, Miss Tolerance turned into the alley and in another few steps was at the door of Blackbottle's establishment. The door was again opened by the hulking doorman; his ears and nose by daylight clearly bore the marks of one who has been a member of the pugilistic fraternity. Miss Tolerance recalled that his name was Joe, and greeted him by it.

"Come back again, 'ave ye?" He did not seem unpleased to see her, and admitted her immediately to the house; something that might have been a grin creased his unshaven cheeks.

"I have," Miss Tolerance agreed. "Has Mrs. Virtue risen yet?"

"Still a-takin' of her chocolate, an not ezzac'ly dressed for visitors." His tone told Miss Tolerance that he considered the drinking of chocolate while abed a silly affectation, but also that he was proud to belong to an establishment prosperous enough to indulge the abbess's affectations.

Miss Tolerance pressed a half crown into Joe's hand. "Perhaps someone could inquire if I might have a word?"

Without turning, Joe gestured behind his back and called out, "Becky! Go see!" A woman from the salon—tired and creased in a white muslin gown most likely intended to create an impression of despoilable innocence—rose and trudged heavily up the stairs toward Mrs. Virtue's rooms. Joe hurried her on with a casual slap at the woman's posterior; she gave a titter by rote but did not look back.

After a few minutes the woman returned and jerked her head toward the stairs. "She sez yer t'coom on ooop," the whore murmured, and went back to her seat in the salon.

Joe grinned again and stood aside. Miss Tolerance suspected he would like to make the same gallant gesture to her as he had made to his messenger a few minutes before. She gave him a level glance; he raised one eyebrow, his grin widened, and he retired to the doorway again. Miss Tolerance continued up the stairs unmolested.

Like the streets outside her door, daylight deprived Mrs. Virtue of a good measure of her mystery. Miss Tolerance found the madam reclining on a divan, propped upon a pile of somewhat grubby pillows and wearing a frowzy negligee of copper-colored satin. The flame-colored hair was largely concealed under a highly ornamented cap, tied rakishly with a bow under one ear; the exquisitely applied maquillage that had passed in candlelight for a fine complexion was blurred and faded.

"You come back to us, Miss Tolerance? Did you not find Sir Humphrey? And will you take a cup of chocolate?" Mrs. Virtue's accent was more apparent this morning—foreign, but neither French nor Dutch, the two languages best known to Miss Tolerance. The woman waved at an old-fashioned Sevres chocolate service on the table nearest her elbow, and despite her dislike of the stuff, Miss Tolerance accepted a cup of chocolate as a useful prop for her negotiation.

"I did find Sir Humphrey, ma'am, but he directed me to you again." She sipped the chocolate and was surprised to find it heavily sugared and far more palatable than the usual bitter brew.

Mrs. Virtue's sculpted eyebrow rose. "Sir Humphrey directed you to me? Then perhaps I will now know what it is, this object you are seeking?"

"Sir Humphrey informed me that he had given the object—a fan with gold sticks and a painted scene upon ostrich skin—to you some years ago."

Mrs. Virtue made no pretense of consulting her memory. "He did," she agreed. "A very pretty thing. Is that what your employer wanted?"

"Do you have it, ma'am?" Miss Tolerance asked neutrally.

"I have all the gifts that were ever given to me, my dear. They are for the security of my old age. So," she said briskly, "what is the worth of this fan to your employer?"

Miss Tolerance recognized the opening gambit of a seasoned negotiator. She smiled. "If it is the object I seek, what would be an acceptable price?"

Mrs. Virtue laughed. "As much as possible, my dear! I collect that a thousand is probably too much?" She did not wait for her guest to agree, but began to reason aloud in a singsong voice. "If he is paying you to find the fan, then it is of more than common interest to him. Which means it might be of more than common interest to other parties as well—although one must wonder why. It is a pretty thing, but not out-of-reason expensive. Say a hundred pounds for the thing itself. But of course, I have kept it safe all these years, and that must be worth something."

Miss Tolerance smiled politely.

"Ah, I hate to place a value upon sentiment, do not you, Miss Tolerance? But I think—perhaps your employer would pay as much as four hundred?"

Miss Tolerance made a great show of considering the figure. "I think," she said slowly, as if the matter required some stretch of the imagination, "I think that with persuasion, his generosity can be brought to extend that far."

Mrs. Virtue nodded and put her chocolate cup down. "Well, then it seems we are both fortunate today." She rose from the bed—uncorseted, her body strained at the seams of the satin negligee, but the effect was less of blowzy overripeness than of comfortable sensuality—and disappeared through a door behind the divan. She came back a few moments later with a fan and handed it to Miss Tolerance.

"You will wish to assure yourself it is the fan you seek, yes?"

Miss Tolerance opened the fan and turned it over in her hands—gold sticks, tiny rubies and diamonds at intervals along their length; a landscape of cypress trees, sheep, and distant mountains against a cerulean sky painted upon the ostrich skin of the fan—a relic of the last century, rather dry and in need of oiling. Everything just as Trux had told her.

"All is in order?" Mrs. Virtue asked. She held her hand out for the fan.

"It does indeed appear to be the item I am seeking." Miss Tolerance kept the fan, turning it over and over as if she were still examining it.

"I presume you did not come here with four hundred pounds in your pocket," Mrs. Virtue said. She took the fan from Miss

Tolerance's hand and smiled. "When I have the money, I will be happy to release it to you."

"I can probably bring you the cash this evening, once I speak with my employer. I would, of course, prefer to take the fan with me—it will certainly make a better argument for disbursing the full amount that you require."

Mrs. Virtue laughed. "The best argument for that is that I will not release the fan for any less than four hundred pounds. Indeed, if there is some difficulty about the price, I can easily sell the fan to the next person who seeks it. It matters nothing to me whose money I take."

"Is someone else seeking it?" Miss Tolerance asked blandly. "I don't recall having said so." In fact, the memory of Lord Balobridge's insistent interest in the fan, and her suspicion that the viscount had a spy in her aunt's house, made her determined to bring the fan away with her now. "I should like to present my client with his prize this evening, ma'am. Is there no way I can persuade you to let me take it?"

"If I am to trust a woman I have never seen before, an oh-so-respectable woman in breeches who wanders the night doing errands for anonymous gentlemen . . . I really think I must require an additional sum. As . . . what is the word? As security of my cooperation. Five hundred, total?" Mrs. Virtue held the fan just out of Miss Tolerance's reach, as if she were teasing a child.

Miss Tolerance swore a silent oath, but her own smile did not waver. "Is a few hours' patience worth one hundred pounds?" she asked mildly.

"I became more sentimental when I held the fan in my hands. And as I say, there is a risk that I will never hear from you—or your employer."

Miss Tolerance silently weighed her own series of risks and rewards, and at last made an offer to Mrs. Virtue. "If I can be certain that you will not have another burst of sentimentality before I return with your money, I can offer you my own note as security. For four hundred and fifty."

The old courtesan laughed. "*Your* note? Has an *agent* like yourself the wherewithal to offer such a sum?"

Miss Tolerance rose from her chair. "You are not the only one who saves against the rigors of old age, ma'am. If you have pen and paper to hand, the matter is resolved in just a few minutes."

Mrs. Virtue regarded her visitor for a few moments, then nodded. "You do not do this easily, whatever you say. Which makes me believe the money is there, and you could lose it. Very well. Four hundred and fifty. How soon can your note be redeemed with cash?"

Miss Tolerance scrawled the required note and tucked the fan into the pocket of her waistcoat, offering her hope that she could return that evening with the funds to redeem the vowel. With thanks, she excused herself and made her way downstairs; as she left the house, it began to rain. She hired a hackney and settled back to enjoy a pleasant sense of accomplishment, only slightly marred by anxiety at the risk she had taken in leaving her note with Mrs. Virtue.

S he found Mrs. Brereton's establishment in a state of uproar. She had gone first to her own house in hopes of finding a note from Versellion; finding none, she turned to the big house, intending to retrieve her coat and ask Matt if he had been given a message of any sort. Instead, she was met at the kitchen door by the scullery maid, who burst into tears at the sight of her—by the evidence of her red-rimmed eyes, not the first she had shed—and ran past her into the garden. The cook, her own face drawn and tight, said nothing, only nodded Miss Tolerance through the green baize door to the public rooms.

Mrs. Brereton herself stood in the middle of the hall, seemingly frozen to that spot. Several of the ladies of the house lined the gallery of the upper stairway. All showed signs of tears or vaporish hysteria.

Miss Tolerance went at once to her aunt's side. "My God, what's amiss?"

Mrs. Brereton turned to her niece with a blank, stark expression. "Matt's dead," she said simply.

Miss Tolerance was conscious of a buzzing in her ears, and the sensation that her knees might suddenly refuse to bear her weight. It took her several long moments to make sense of her aunt's next words.

"They're bringing his—they're bringing him back to us. I've had Keefe—Keefe is—he cleared the salon for him. I shall have to ask Mr. Hallet at All Soul's about burial. . . ." Her voice trailed off as the front door of the house opened and Keefe, together with Cole and two men Miss Tolerance did not know, silently carried a litter into the house. The corpse had been covered with a rough blanket.

"What happened?" Miss Tolerance asked. Neither she nor her aunt seemed able to tear their gazes away from the door of the salon.

"He went out this morning," Mrs. Brereton said. "Early, on some errand of his own. From what the Watch said, he was set upon, robbed, and left for dead—" Mrs. Brereton broke off, watching as Keefe paid the porters with a few coins and a murmured word of thanks. "We shall have to dress the body—he was so vain, he would hate to appear in anything shabby."

From a great distance, Miss Tolerance heard herself asking calm, quite rational questions. "Where was he set upon? Does the Watch have any idea who attacked him?" With her aunt following, she went into the salon to view the body.

When she pulled the blanket off the corpse, Miss Tolerance drew a sharp breath. Mrs. Brereton reached out a hand to comfort and steady her niece, quite misunderstanding what had caused the reaction. The facts were bad enough: Matt had been beaten brutally, then slashed across the throat and left to bleed to death. His clothes were stiff with blood, his handsome, boyish face misshapen, and his hands, when she inspected them, were crossed with cuts, as if he had held them before his face, unable to defend himself in any other way.

He was wearing her own dark green Gunnard greatcoat.

"We shall be closed tonight," Mrs. Brereton was instructing Keefe. "Sarah?" She had turned back to her niece. "What are you doing?"

Miss Tolerance paused in the process of going through all of Matt's pockets. "I have a great deal of work to do, Aunt. Not least is to find out who wanted Matt dead."

"Wanted him dead? My dear child, it was footpads, a robbery—"

Miss Tolerance shook her head. "I don't believe so, Aunt. Look: he still has his pocketbook, and that vulgar gold ring he so delighted in. What footpad would have missed taking them? And he was wearing my coat—the idiot!—and he was about my errand. I think he was mistaken for me, and I intend to know by whom, and why." She stepped back into the room and embraced Mrs. Brereton. "I should be of no use to you here. When the . . . arrangements . . . are made, please let me know."

For the first time in all the years her niece had known her, Mrs. Brereton looked her age. "Sarah, you're not leaving?"

"Aunt, I must," Miss Tolerance said firmly.

"Then be careful, Sarah. Please."

Miss Tolerance smiled grimly. "I'm less decorative than Matt, but far better able to care for myself. I'll find who did this, Aunt, I promise."

Not until she had attained the privacy of a hackney and given the driver directions did Miss Tolerance give vent to her feelings in tears, and even that very natural reaction was brief. Her grief at Matt's death was consumed by rage—at Matt, for borrowing her coat unasked; at herself, for believing, despite her conversation with Lord Balobridge, that no danger could attach to being her messenger; and at whoever had been the agent of Matt's death. Miss Tolerance had long ago schooled herself to keep anger under rein; Charles Connell had taught her that such emotion was useful only as a fuel for action—not as its substitute. Still, she was grateful for the opportunity to master her emotions in private before arriving at her destination.

She presented herself at Versellion House, only to be informed that his lordship was expected to return to Richmond that evening. Miss Tolerance thanked the footman civilly, walked back to her stables, and hired again the patient horse which had been her companion so often recently. It was coming on dark, and despite the best efforts of the horse patrols on the highways to London, some risk attached to riding unaccompanied out to Richmond; she did not accomplish the ride at a full gallop, but caution and the tumult of her emotions made her set a brisk pace. She arrived at the house before the earl did.

The butler, summoned to deal with the scandalous female waiting in the same tiny withdrawing room to which she had been shown on her last visit, recognized her at once, made her comfortable, and brought a tray of port and biscuits, which masculine refreshment he clearly believed matched her attire.

It was nearly an hour before she heard Versellion's voice in the hallway, and the butler murmuring to him urgently. A few moments later the earl himself appeared, smiling cordially. He wore a rain-spattered greatcoat, and his hat was still tucked under his arm.

"My dear Miss Tolerance, had I known that you were here, I would assuredly have cut my business short." He stripped off his gloves, shrugged off the coat, and handed them and his hat to the butler, who hovered behind him. "Can I persuade you to take some refreshment with me? And can I hope," he continued, as the butler bore away his belongings, "that you have news?"

Miss Tolerance had had some time to compose herself, and to decide what she wished to say, and to ask of her client.

"I do have news, sir. Several sorts. I have secured the fan for you, although its release will require a payment of four hundred and fifty pounds—I gave my own note in order to take it away with me."

Versellion instantly understood the import of the statement.

"You have only to tell me to whom the payment must be made and I will have it delivered, and your note returned to you." He held out his hand as if to receive the fan.

"Thank you, sir. But before I can give you your property, I would like the answer to some questions."

Versellion's eyes narrowed. "From our earlier interview, Miss Tolerance, I had taken you for a woman of some integrity. Must I revise my view? Do you now intend blackmail?"

Miss Tolerance met his glare with her own unbending look. "My lord, did you receive a note from me this morning?"

"A note? No. I've been in Town the last day or so. If something was sent here—"

"It was sent to your house in St. James's Square. There is no possibility that a note might have been delivered without being shown to you?"

"None," he said firmly. "My staff know me too well to believe I would tolerate such a thing. Miss Tolerance, take me with you. Explain what this is all about, and what it has to do with my fan."

"A friend of mine was killed this morning—apparently before he could deliver the note to you. As the note was not upon his person when he was discovered, I must assume he was killed for the note itself—the murderer took nothing else. And I suspect he was mistaken for me—I was attacked the other night when I returned from my visit to you here. You will understand that the fan's significance has become a matter of pressing concern to me." She was very pleased that her voice betrayed nothing of her fury.

On his part, Versellion sat across from her, the suspicion quite gone from his countenance. "My God, Miss Tolerance, are you certain that your friend's death has something to do with your business for me?"

"Given the circumstances, what else am I to think?"

"What did the note say? Could the thieves have learned anything from it?"

Miss Tolerance smiled without humor. "My fee includes discretion. I put no particulars in the note, only that I desired a meeting and hoped to bring your matter to a conclusion within the day. Matt died for *nothing*." She leaned forward and rubbed her hands over her face, suddenly exhausted.

He put a hand on her shoulder. "You are tired and distressed. And hungry, I think. Will you not let me help? First, let me discharge the debt you incurred in my name, so that you needn't be distracted from your purpose." He rang, and the butler appeared. A few brief instructions and the man reappeared with a strongbox. Versellion counted out in bills and coin the full amount of the debt, made a package of it, and asked Miss Tolerance to address it.

"Have Leeward deliver this, and see that he does not return without the note Miss Tolerance left on my behalf. Tell him not to wear livery, take the black carriage, and that I'll expect him back in the morning." Versellion spoke with the easy authority of rank, and a note of sympathy for the sorts of distractions Leeward might discover in Cheapside. "When that's been accomplished, lay a cover for Miss Tolerance at dinner."

"I cannot dine with you," Miss Tolerance protested. "It would do you no credit, and would delay my inquiries. I am in deadly earnest, sir. I need to know what this fan is and why several people are so eager to claim it. Two people are dead—"

"Two! Dear God, who is the other?"

"An elderly woman in Leyton who helped me discover Mrs. Cunning's whereabouts. She was bludgeoned to death, sir, hot upon my heels. So you will understand why I must know what the significance of the fan is. It touches upon my honor and my safety."

"Miss Tolerance, I give you my word. The fan is significant only to me and my family." His voice was as steady as the dark gaze which transfixed her; had he been perhaps a little less open, she would have trusted him more. As it was, Miss Tolerance recalled Lord Balobridge, and reminded herself that both these men were politicians, bred to persuade.

"Have you a contentious family, my lord?" she asked in the

same even, sincere, and reasonable tones he had employed. "Is there no one of them that has reason to want the fan? I should hate to think you are telling me less than the full sum of the truth."

"You are asking if I lie?" The earl's countenance did not change, but his tone became pointedly formal. Miss Tolerance took this to mean she had scored a point. She prepared herself for the possibility that Versellion would shortly have thrown her out of the house. After a long moment, the tension she read in his face eased; he appeared to come to some decision.

"Miss Tolerance, I have perhaps gone about this business in the wrong way, but it touches upon my family honor, and upon public matters I had as lief keep quiet. I still do not believe that anyone in my family could be responsible for the dreadful events you mention—your friend's death and the death of that poor woman. But . . . I have still your promise of discretion?"

Miss Tolerance assured him that he did. Versellion rose and began to pace up and down the length of the small room.

"These are perilous times, Miss Tolerance. Perhaps more so than you are aware. The war drags on, the effect on the economy is catastrophic, it would take so little—" He held up a hand as if to forestall interruption. "I am not preparing an oration, I promise. But there are events—"

"My lord, you are the second person in as many days to lecture me on the perils of our times. I understand it to mean you have no intention of telling me what I need to know. And as far as the events to which you allude—I assume you mean the Queen's illness?—unless you are prepared to tell me what your fan can possibly have to do with the matter, I am not prepared to be put off by their mention."

"What have you heard of the Queen's illness?"

"Very little, in fact, sir. Only that she was ill—an apoplectic stroke, I believe. And nothing since that time."

He sighed. "I suppose it was inevitable that it would get out. But not yet, damn it. Miss Tolerance, I will be as forthcoming as I can, but I pray you will tell no one what I tell you. The Queen's life is despaired of; if she lives, she will not be fit to rule. The King is old, blind, fitfully foolish. There will have to be another Regent chosen, and it's a matter of some moment to my party and the Tories as to whom that will be. I spent the morning canvassing for votes, and this afternoon at Carlton House talking to His Highness—"

"Wales? But his marriage removed him from the succession."

"It did." Versellion sat again, speaking as if he were rehearsing his thoughts aloud: upon the Duke of York's death, the Duke of Clarence became heir apparent. But Clarence, quarreling often with the Queen Regent, had been wholly compromised by his mistress; he had ten bastard children and not one legitimate heir. By comparison, Wales, a widower with two legitimate children whose greatest crime had been to marry a Catholic widow, and whose worst excesses had been curbed by his late wife, was a far more savory choice. Both parties were in a race to secure the Prince's assurance of support—the Tories because they were in power, the Whigs because they were not. The Whigs were able to pursue the Prince with reminders of his old support for their ideals, and his friendship with Charles Fox. "But many of my party are for ending the war; the Prince stands with his mother in this, that Bonaparte must be stopped. As it happens, so do I."

"As it happens, so do I," Miss Tolerance agreed. "But the fan, sir?"

"If Wales sides with my party and we are able to return him to the succession and make him Regent, it is almost a certainty that I will take the ministry. I do not doubt that the Tories would like to discredit me and leave my party with no one whose war aims are sympathetic with the Prince's."

"And the fan? How could a thing which has been boxed away for twenty years cause your party trouble? I was approached by someone—of the opposition—who was uncommonly interested in the fan."

"Was it my cousin Henry?" Versellion asked.

"Folle?" Miss Tolerance asked blankly, nearly startled into disclosure. "No, it—it was not Sir Henry Folle, sir."

"And you will not say who?" Versellion asked.

At this interesting moment the butler entered. A messenger had arrived from the city. Versellion made no show of disinterest; he snatched the note from the proffered tray, broke the seal, and read it forthwith.

"Things move apace. His Highness has asked me to return to talk again. Miss Tolerance, I pray you a thousand pardons, but I must go back to London at once. Before I take my leave, may I have the fan?" He held out his hand. "I know we have a further reckoning, you and I. Perhaps tomorrow you can bring me an accounting of your expenses and I can discharge them, and your fee? And I promise, I will answer any other questions you care to put to me at that time."

Trumped by the Prince of Wales, Miss Tolerance knew better than to resist. She took the fan from her pocket and placed it in Versellion's outstretched hand. He looked at it for a long moment, then put it in his own pocket and looked out the window.

"The rain has stopped, I see, and there is half a moon. I have ridden to Town in worse circumstances. If you mean to return to Town tonight, Miss Tolerance, I would be happy for your company—but I intend to keep a stiff pace."

Miss Tolerance dreaded the likely atmosphere of Mrs. Brereton's establishment, but she was no more eager to stay in the guise of a man at some inferior country inn. She thanked the earl for his suggestion.

Night had fallen, and while it was not very late and there was still some traffic upon the Richmond road, there were stretches where it was only the two of them, riding side by side at a brisk canter. If Miss Tolerance had hoped for further conversation about the fan and its seekers, she was disappointed. The speed with which they rode precluded discussion. As Miss Tolerance was unaccustomed to riding with speed over such ground, she soon found her attention required to guide her horse through the shadows and past the holes that peppered the road. Versellion sat his own mount with the air of one familiar and comfortable with the route. Thus, between Miss Tolerance's attention to the road and Lord Versellion's familiarity, neither one was prepared when a man stepped into the road with pistols raised.

The highwayman had timed his appearance to a nicety, giving them no time to turn aside. As the riders came to a halt, two more men scrambled up the embankment toward them. These carried no pistols, but both had swords drawn. One of them stepped up to Versellion, the other to Miss Tolerance, with their hands held out for the reins.

Miss Tolerance spoke quietly. "Please don't take the horse, sir. 'Tisn't mine, and I cannot afford to pay the owner for it." She tried to sound like a nervous schoolboy, and the dark aided her imposture.

The man with the pistols turned his eye to Miss Tolerance. "You may ride on if you like, boy—we've no quarrel with you. But if you go, you ride like hell and don't look back. It's as easy to kill two as one." He approached Versellion and put his hand up, apparently to take the valuables he was about to demand. Then, startlingly, he grabbed the earl's coat and pulled him off the saddle and onto the grassy verge. The man slapped at Versellion's horse and watched it canter off. "Ride like hell, boy," he said again.

"Like hell," Miss Tolerance agreed, and kicked out with one foot. The toe of her boot caught the man nearest her neatly under the chin, depriving him of breath as he was thrown backward and down the embankment. She did not stop to see whether he was conscious or no; Versellion, on the ground, was grappling with the man with the pistol as the other man stood dumbly there, apparently stunned into immobility by what he found himself part of. Miss Tolerance drew her sword and swept the pommel, backhanded, into the back of his head. The man dropped heavily, raising a cloud of dust in the moonlight.

Versellion was on one knee, wrestling for possession of the pistol. His opponent was distracted when his companion fell to the road, and Versellion took advantage of the moment to grab the pistol and toss it to the side of the road, where it released its charge—by some miracle not into any of them upon the road.

For a moment it seemed as if matters were in hand, and Miss Tolerance advanced to assist the earl with his attacker. But then she was grabbed from behind, her arms pinned behind her: the man she had knocked down the embankment had returned to the fray. Unaided, Versellion continued to fight, so closely positioned to the man that neither he nor his attacker could draw their swords. Their fight was an ugly thing of tumbling blows.

In Miss Tolerance's ear she heard her assailant's growl, "Christ, Jerry, finish it! There's no money if he lives. I'll do for the boy." The man tightened his grip with one hand, reaching, Miss Tolerance assumed, for a knife with the other. Uninterested in having her throat slit, Miss Tolerance brought her boot heel down hard on her attacker's instep. The man loosed his hold just enough so that she could pull free. As she turned, she took up the sword she had dropped when she was captured, but in that moment the man had recovered himself and taken up his own sword. Hoping that Versellion could fend for himself while she dispatched her foe, Miss Tolerance engaged her attacker. For the next few minutes she was very busy; her opponent attacked with a savage slash to her shoulder, then attempted to drive her backward with a rain of cuts. He had the advantage in weight, Miss Tolerance in speed and training. Still, it took several minutes for her to land a deep cut on his left arm.

Versellion, who had broken away from his opponent and taken up the pistol, now moved to Miss Tolerance's side.

"Give it up, boys," he advised the highwaymen breathlessly. "You'll get nothing from us tonight."

The wounded man looked as though these were words he might heed, but the other, Jerry, spat at Versellion's feet. "The charge is gone. Might as well aim your boot at me, Your Lordship." Animated by the thought, the wounded man lunged past Miss Tolerance, aiming to run Versellion through. With no time for a neater job, she beat his sword away and drove her own into his side. The man folded over at once. Miss Tolerance had to brace her foot against his leg to pull her blade free again.

When she turned back, the leader, Jerry, had leapt down the embankment, abandoning his companions cold-bloodedly.

Miss Tolerance surveyed the scene before her: one man crumpled at her feet, alive but badly bloodied, and another man still lying in the dust where her blow had put him. Her own horse still stood placidly in the midst of what a moment before had been a battleground, and Versellion's mount some hundred feet along the road, cropping grass upon the verge.

"It seems I am in your debt again, Miss Tolerance," the earl said. His breath still came raggedly, and even in the moonlight she could tell that his color was high. Miss Tolerance suspected that he had enjoyed the fight.

"A pleasure to have been of service, my lord," Miss Tolerance said lightly. "If you will take my advice, we will not linger here. It might put you in further danger."

"Further danger? Surely we won't encounter two sets of highwaymen in an evening."

"Not highwaymen, sir." Miss Tolerance looped the reins to her own horse around one wrist and led it down the road, directing the earl to follow and collect his own mount. "Did any of them ask for your purse, your watch? Surely you heard what the leader said?"

Versellion shook his head and admitted he had given more attention to the pistol than the man holding it.

"First the man told me to run and not look back, for they had no quarrel with me. Then he said they could as easily kill two as one. Do you not infer from that that their task was a specific one: to kill you?"

The earl blinked. "Perhaps one of them had a grudge—"

" 'There's no money in it if he lives,' " Miss Tolerance quoted. "These men held no grudge, sir. They were paid to kill you. I wonder how they knew where to find you."

The earl and Miss Tolerance stood beside their horses now. A groan from down the road where their assailants still lay reminded Miss Tolerance that this was not the place to linger, and they mounted their horses and turned toward London again. "We can send aid back to them from the next inn," Versellion suggested.

Miss Tolerance nodded, but her mind was busy with thoughts she suspected her companion would find unwelcome. At last she asked, "Do you think it is wise to return to London tonight, sir?"

"Wise? The Prince has desired to see me. As matters stand, I cannot refuse such a command."

"I see." Miss Tolerance thought for a moment. "Who would know you had been summoned to London?"

"My people at Richmond who knew I was returning to the City. The man who wrote the note. Perhaps the courier who brought it. His Highness, of course."

"I think we can leave the Prince out of our calculations for the moment," Miss Tolerance said. "Are you sure of your people, sir?"

"Sure?" Versellion, accustomed to political intrigue, paused to consider the idea that one of his servants might be in the pay of an enemy. "What you suggest . . . I pay my servants well enough that they should be able to resist bribes, Miss Tolerance."

"There are, of course, other motives for betrayal than money," Miss Tolerance suggested. But she could see the earl was unwilling to consider such a thing. She tried another tack. "If I may ask, sir—please remember my discretion in this matter is complete—what did the note you received say?"

The earl smiled. "I trust you, Miss Tolerance. But the note said very little, simply that His Royal Highness wanted to talk and desired my return to London."

"In those words, sir?"

"Exactly?" Versellion shook his head. "I believe the words were, 'He needs to speak again, this evening.' "

"And that was sufficient to bring you back from Richmond?" Miss Tolerance's eyebrows rose. "No specifics, no names, no—"

"Miss Tolerance, at this moment there is only one He in the kingdom: Wales. This is, as I said earlier, a dangerous time. Specifics and names are the things one strives not to put in such a missive."

"But you are sure who sent it."

"His secretary, I assume," Versellion said blankly. "Who else would do so?"

Miss Tolerance felt a moment of fulminating outrage. "There was no crest on the paper? No seal? No signature? Nothing to suggest that the message was not a joke on the part of your bootblack, but from the household of the Prince of—"

Versellion held up his hand. "Please, Miss Tolerance, I admit I did not think to look for a seal—"

Miss Tolerance nodded without satisfaction. "You cannot be certain of your servants, you do not know for a surety from whom the message came or whether it truly was a summons from His Highness, and we do not know how many accomplices our friend with the pistols may have waiting on the road to London. I don't think you should continue onward."

"I must go. I was summoned—"

"By someone who may or may not have been speaking for Wales. Was that message in the character of every other message you have received from Carlton House?"

"There have not been so many that . . ." Versellion stopped and considered. At last he whistled a long, low note. "Damn. Damn it, you're right. It was only the urgency of the summons that kept me from questioning it. I rode straight into a trap."

"I very much fear that you did, sir. You should not go forward to London. And I misdoubt that a return to Richmond is a good idea, either."

"Well, then, where the devil can I go?" The earl was beginning to assume the familiar aspect of a much-tried man. "If I cannot decide whom to trust, I cannot think of a place to go."

Miss Tolerance stood in her stirrups, surveying the night-shadowed landscape to the north. "Perhaps, my lord, you need, then, to go to a place away from your usual haunts, where you are unknown." She turned back to the earl. "I believe I may have a solution—a place where no one would think to look for you."

Nine

The Briary Arms was located northwest of London by some twenty miles, at an inconvenient distance from the Birmingham road. It was a hostelry as undistinguished as its name, little more than a public house with a few tiny rooms upstairs; the village of which the inn formed the center was no more than a tidy cluster of cottages and an old graystone church. An hour past midnight, a half-moon provided the only illumination on fields, hedges, and cottages along the road; in the village itself, no single light burned. It was just so that Miss Tolerance had last seen the town, on the occasion of her elopement. Riding through the moon-frozen landscape, she was filled with gladness and a sudden strong wish to hear news of all her old friends. The only part of the town which did not beckon to her was the manor itself, which she associated only with acrimony and banishment. In all the years, she had never come back, never intended to come back. Until this night. After all, no one would think to find the Earl of Versellion in Briarton. And no one who knew her would ever imagine Miss Tolerance returning there of her own will.

The landlord of the Briary Arms had stumbled downstairs in response to her merciless knocking, his musket clutched in one hand and his nightcap hanging well off the back of his head. It had taken him more than a moment to understand who the insistent fellow at his doorway really was—then Miss Tolerance had been pulled inside, examined, and embraced with exclamations of delight which lasted until the innkeeper realized what Miss Tolerance was asking.

"Miss Sarah, 'f it were up to me, I'd give my own chamber to you," the man protested. "But your brother holds my lease, and his orders—and your dad's before him—was plain. If he found I'd been harborin' of you . . ." There was no need to finish the sentence.

Miss Tolerance was dismayed. At some point after her father had declared her dead, she had ceased to consider what effect her obstinate hold on corporeal health might have had—or the irritation the villagers' substantial affection for her might have caused him. As she had never seriously considered returning to Briarton, it had never occurred to her that her father—and her brother—would have dragged their stubborn vengefulness out for a full dozen years. She could well appreciate the landlord's precarious situation: whatever his pleasure in welcoming her back, she could not force the man to endanger his livelihood. Still, mindful of the hour and of the fact that Versellion was waiting in the yard with their horses, she pressed on. "One night, Thomas? Surely my brother will not know—"

"He'll know, Miss Sarah. If I let you stay, my wife will have to know of it, and she'll want to see how you are after all these years. Once that's done, she'll tell Mary Lewes and Mrs. Cropsey at the house, and Nurse Bolton and old Peter, just to set their hearts at ease, you know. Before you can pour water, it'd be all over, and I out of the house."

Laid out so baldly, Miss Tolerance could not but admit the truth of the matter. "But Thomas, we're sorely tired. Is there a house, a barn, even, where I might safely look for shelter for the night? I can pay."

Apparently relieved that his visitor was amenable to common sense, the landlord considered. At last, and reluctantly, he told her he could think of nothing, for every location nearby which might have afforded suitable shelter was either owned by Sir Adam Brereton or held by someone to whom his disfavor would be cataclysmic. "I'd try the Birmingham road, Miss Sarah. Sorry I am to send you back that way."

Miss Tolerance clasped the landlord's hand. "Thank you, Thomas. I'm sorry to have put you in any difficulty. And sometime, when you think it safe, will you give my love to Nurse, and Peter and Mrs. Cropsey and the rest? And Mrs. Thomas, of course? Tell them I am well and . . . they need have no fear for me."

"I will at that, miss. But now—"

She nodded. "I know. Go!"

She joined Versellion in the shadow of the stable, mounted quickly, and turned her horse. Once they were out of the yard, she whispered, "We must go on."

"No room?" Versellion asked.

"The intervention of melodrama: Briarton would have been a perfect hiding place except that my brother has enjoined his tenants from giving me shelter."

She could not see the earl's expression, but his voice was very dry. "Your brother is an aficionado of melodrama?"

"I had never credited him with so much imagination. One learns."

"Then let us go back to the Birmingham road and put up at an inn there." It was not the first time that evening that Versellion had suggested such a thing. Miss Tolerance renewed her objections.

"I cannot advise it, Versellion. The chance that you might be found—"

"Do you seriously propose that whoever sent those brawlers after me could trace us here?"

"It is unlikely they would look in a town this size and off the main roads. That is why I proposed we come here. But on a well-traveled posting road—"

"If I use a name other than my own? Miss Tolerance, I believe it's worth the risk to have some supper and sleep in a real bed."

Miss Tolerance kept her voice low. The clear, soft night air was peculiarly carrying, and she had no wish to wake the occupants of the cottages they passed.

"My lord, you are a well-known political figure. Despite the country air, some of these people do read the London papers, some might have heard you speak on some occasion. There is a chance your face might be known. You are riding a remarkably handsome horse from your well-known stable, and ostlers who take no notice of a face will recognize a horse like that. It would be the work of a few moments for someone seeking us to describe both the horse and the rider, and you would be under attack again."

"It seems to me that with sufficient money, a landlord's discretion could be bought," Versellion said.

"And with sufficient money, a searcher could buy it back again," Miss Tolerance parried. But her resolve was weakening. It was late, and fatigue born of grief, too little sleep, and several sorts of exertion was telling upon her. The notion of a bed and a bite to eat was very attractive.

"If we don't go to a posting inn, but one of the smaller hostelries—Miss Tolerance, you look to be weaving in your saddle. I must insist. You will scarcely be able to help me if you are exhausted." Without looking to see if she followed, Versellion turned his horse east, toward the post road. After a moment, Miss Tolerance followed suit.

She hoped he was right. It was she who had insisted upon removing the earl from the vicinity of London. The entire night, when they slowed to a pace which allowed conversation, Versellion had argued against the flight. He disliked to leave Town in the midst of a negotiation with the Prince; surely he could be adequately guarded in his own home; was not Miss Tolerance refining too much upon an incident which might well turn out to be casual robbery?

" 'There's no money if he lives,' " Miss Tolerance had quoted. "Your absence, even in the midst of negotiations with Wales, will doubtless serve your party and the nation better than your death." She had no objection in principle to his returning to London, but did not believe it could be safely accomplished that night. "In the morning, when we can hire a chaise and outriders, you might return safely. But for the moment, I beg you will believe that your life is in jeopardy."

She could not be sure that Versellion was not humoring her, as a healthy man with a sniffle might humor the cosseting of his doctor. Still, he rode along beside her, at an hour and under conditions which surely must have him questioning his sanity.

In a little less than an hour they had crossed the Birmingham road and were riding west, in search of an inn at which the Earl of Versellion would be unknown, and in which the sheets were likely to be aired and free of vermin. At last Versellion turned into the yard of a moderate hostelry and dismounted. After a moment, as a groggy ostler was taking the reins of his horse, Miss Tolerance dismounted as well. She insisted that the earl stay outside while she bespoke rooms; she wanted to check the safety of the inn, and she did not believe Versellion truly understood that the peril he faced might be immune to the remedies of money and position.

The landlady took Miss Tolerance as she presented herself—as a young man—and was ready enough to provide a room. But only one. The inn was near full, and not even the promise of a substantial tip could change that fact. Lucky, indeed, that the gentlemen did not have to bed with strangers, the woman said irritably. If the young gentleman and his uncle could not manage to share, they had as well take their custom elsewhere and let a respectable woman go back to her bed. Unwilling to make herself and her client more conspicuous by departing, Miss Tolerance took the room. She fetched in her "uncle," who had been cooling his heels in the inn yard, and they were escorted to a small chamber which faced the rear of the building.

"I have given our name as Watson," Miss Tolerance murmured under cover of the landlady's mutterings about gentry who arrived in the deep of night. "I am your nephew Samuel."

Versellion nodded and together they went in and up to the room.

"Well, Sam, I think this will do," Versellion said. He asked the landlady if her kindness would extend to a bite of supper, and while she offered nothing more than a plate of bread and cheese, her tone was less aggrieved, and she asked if the gentlemen required brandy-and-water or small beer to take with it.

Climbing the steps in the rear of the parade, Miss Tolerance was aware that the silence between herself and her client had changed from that of pleasant companionability to something more awkward. It occurred to her now that her situation could easily become intolerably difficult. She wondered if similar thoughts had occurred to the earl.

She and Versellion were bound by ties of commerce only, and yet the earl knew her history—or at least that part of her history which included her ruin. He might easily assume that she had had and continued to have a string of lovers stretching back a decade, and he might decide it was only reasonable to make himself part of that company. Without recourse to vanity, Miss Tolerance sensed that the earl found her attractive. If he chose to presume upon her history and make advances to her, the choices open to her were few and unpleasant. A Fallen Woman who defended herself against rape would find few sympathizers—particularly if her attacker was rich, titled, powerful, and handsome.

Of course—the landlady had taken a great ring of keys from her apron and was unlocking the door of a room at the far end of the hallway, facing the rear of the inn—of course, Versellion might not want anything more than a solitary bed for the night. If she spoke to forestall his advances, she risked giving her employer a disgust of her manners and a very poor idea of her intellect. Miss Tolerance found she was loath to do that. She balled her hands in the pockets of her coat and frowned.

When the door closed upon the landlady, who had gone to fetch the bread and cheese, the earl raised the candle she had left behind high and inspected the room. There was a bed, a chair and a stool, a cupboard, and a small table which held basin and ewer and a chamber pot below. A small window stood open to the moonlight and a light breeze.

The landlady returned with the trencher, said good night, and bustled away. In silence the earl cut some bread and cheese while Miss Tolerance shot the bolt on the door. When he handed her the trencher, she took some cheese, but between exhaustion and tension, she had very little stomach for it. They ate in silence, looking neither at each other nor the room, but at the fine view of moonlit fields and the back of the stables.

"I will sleep in the chair," the earl said at last.

Miss Tolerance had been about to make a similar offer. " 'Tis kind of you to offer, my lord, but I can take the chair. Were I a male retainer, you would have taken the bed as a matter of course. You need not scruple—"

"What an autocrat you think me!" To Miss Tolerance's relief, he did not seem offended. "I would at least have offered to toss a coin for the bed, or shared it, as our landlady intended. That is clearly not suitable. Now, if you will not let me treat you with the courtesy to which your gender and station entitle you, permit me to observe that you saved my life this evening. It makes sense that I would wish my protector to be well rested in case I have further need of her aid." Versellion paused. "You will meet with no ill treatment at my hands."

Miss Tolerance heard this frank acknowledgment of her predicament with powerful relief. She looked out the window, tears starting in her eyes, and fought to control her voice. After a moment she said briskly, "My *station* does not generally entitle me to such courtesies, but there is sense in what you say, and great kindness, for which I thank you. May I suggest, however, that I am more accustomed to sleeping in hardship than you?"

"Miss Tolerance, one night of privation will not unman me, I promise you." He smiled at her. "We are both tired. Please. If you will not honor a civil request, I shall have to order you as your employer."

"My client, sir." Miss Tolerance smiled. "Well, if you mean to do this, I think you will be more comfortable on the floor. Sufficient padding"—she opened the cupboard, which proved to be stocked with several blankets—"should make you an agreeable couch."

Working together, they made up a rough bed upon the floor. As soon as the work was done, however, the awkwardness descended upon them again. Finally Miss Tolerance sat on the bed and removed her boots and coat. Clad in shirt, waistcoat, and breeches, she stretched out upon the bed and made a show of closing her eyes.

"Good night, sir," she murmured.

He returned the salutation. She heard rustling as he settled into his bed. He blew out the candle and the room was instantly shadowed.

Miss Tolerance was on the verge of sleep when she heard Versellion mutter, "Damn!"

"Are you uncomfortable, sir? I will be happy to change with you," she told him.

"Stay where you are, Miss Tolerance. I'm only damning my own stupidity. I had meant to examine the fan, but I've blown out the candle and have no fire to light it again."

"In the morning, sir," Miss Tolerance suggested. She turned on one side and closed her eyes. As sleep took her, she was wondering how they would manage the use of the chamber pot come morning.

M iss Tolerance slept poorly. Exhausted though she was, the unaccustomed noises of another person in the room troubled her sleep, and her anxiety that they might be pursued made it impossible for her to fully relax. Sounds of an arrival in the inn yard, an hour or so after dawn, brought her fully awake. Her hair had come unpinned as she slept; she wound the braid up again and pinned it in place, pulled on her boots, and crept from the room to stand in the shadow of the door at the top of the stairs. One look was sufficient to assure her that the man speaking in indistinct tones to the landlady was Jerry, the attacker who had fled the scene of their fight the night before.

She returned to the room, shot the bolt on the door, and knelt to shake the earl awake. "Versellion!"

His hand came up to cover hers. His eyes opened.

"We're discovered. We'd best run now, if we can. God knows what story your friend from last night has told our hostess." She pulled her hand away and stood.

"My friend from—" Comprehension drove the sleep from Versellion's eyes. "They found us here? My God! And my apologies, Miss Tolerance. I did not take your warning seriously enough." He had his boots on and picked up his coat.

Miss Tolerance had her hand upon the door, hoping to discover a back stairway that would take them to the kitchen and thence to the back gardens. The sound of heavy footfall on the landing, and the landlady's expostulations, decided her against it. She took up her coat, went to the window, and looked out hurriedly. There was a dormer just to the right below them, and the stable at a few yards' distance from that. With luck they could drop to the dormer roof, slide down far enough to jump to the ground, and take their horses from the stable.

She turned around to find Versellion leaving coins on the table. "To settle the shot," he explained. "Are we climbing down?" He did not seem dismayed by the idea.

"I think we—"

She was interrupted by a hard knocking on the door. Miss Tolerance took up her sword in its hanger, slung the whole over her shoulder, and motioned Versellion to the window. To his credit, he went through without a murmur, dropped lightly onto the dormer, and was on the ground before Miss Tolerance was out the window herself. She dropped to the earth just beside him and they ran for the stables. Above them, continued knocking persuaded her that their departure had not yet been discovered. At the door of the stable, Miss Tolerance crept around the sill, letting her eyes adjust to the dim light.

As she expected, another man was guarding their horses, a short, blocky fellow. She did not recognize him from the attack the night before; there was a chance he was merely a stableboy. She could not afford to assume so, however. She moved forward in the shadows until she was behind the man, and in one movement she had his arm doubled behind him and her pocketknife at his throat.

To her captive she murmured, "Be silent and I shan't hurt you. Move, and . . ." She did not finish, letting the man's imagination provide a suitable admonition. "Sir," she called, as loudly as she dared. Versellion appeared at once. "That rope, if you please? Thank you. Now, our horses."

As Miss Tolerance tied the man and gagged him with her own handkerchief, Versellion saddled the horses, brought them to the stable door, and mounted his own.

A crash, and the landlady's scream of outrage, suggested that their tracker had at last broken into their lately vacated room. Leaving the guard on his knees amid the straw, Miss Tolerance swung up on her horse; at her nod, Versellion crashed through the stable door into the yard, and thence to the road. Miss Tolerance was directly behind him. There were several shouts of "Stop!" but Versellion set a racing pace. He led them down the road for a quarter mile and then, after a bend which blocked them from the view of any pursuer, took off over a field toward the cover of a wood ahead of them.

They rode hard for a good half hour. At last, Versellion slowed his mount to a walk.

"Do you think we're followed?"

Miss Tolerance shook her head. "I think they will have tried, but—no. I do wish I'd had the presence of mind to loose the other horses in the stable. That would have made us certain of it."

The earl grinned. "I seem destined to adventure in your company, Miss Tolerance." More soberly he added, "This would not have been necessary had I trusted your instincts a little further."

There was no need for Miss Tolerance to agree. "I think we might stop a few minutes now and rest the horses."

They found a clearing and tethered their horses to crop the grass. Miss Tolerance sat under a tree and took off her hat to wipe her brow. Her braid, unpinned again, fell heavily across her shoulder. As she undid the braid and combed her fingers through her hair, she became aware that Versellion was watching her.

"The perils of hard riding," she said briefly. Quickly she braided her hair and pinned it thoroughly.

Versellion smiled. "You should find more occasions to wear your hair down, Miss Tolerance. It suits you."

Miss Tolerance flushed. Versellion did not appear to notice her discomfort, for he had taken the long-sought fan from his pocket and opened it in the sunlight. He turned it this way and that, opening and closing it, holding it flat before his eyes and sighting down its length as he might down the barrel of a hunting rifle. It was a pretty toy, Miss Tolerance reflected, but there was nothing about it to indicate why two people had lost their lives for its sake.

Miss Tolerance cleared her throat. "My lord?"

Versellion looked up, blinking in the sunlight.

"The question I asked you last night grows hourly more pressing."

Versellion seemed lost. "Take me with you, Miss Tolerance. Which question?"

"Why people have died for this fan. Do you know?"

He shook his head. "The longer I examine it, the less I understand." He handed the fan to her. Miss Tolerance turned it over in her hands as he had done; the rounded end-sticks were warm from the sun and the touch of Versellion's fingers.

"Perhaps if you tell me why you sought the fan so anxiously?" she suggested.

Versellion did not answer at once; Miss Tolerance suspected

he was trying to judge how little information he could give without appearing to evade the question.

"I will find it out," she told him. "But by that time you may be dead, or your careful secret may have become common gossip."

"Are you so certain the cause of all this uproar is the fan?" he countered. He looked away from her, across the clearing. He had taken up his hat in both hands and ran the brim between thumb and forefinger, smoothing the surface of the felt. "I have political enemies—"

Miss Tolerance cut him off. "Do you see any benefit to your political enemies in the death of an elderly woman in Leyton, or of my friend who was carrying a note to you? Those events seem uniquely tied to the fan. In the usual way of business, I would ask no questions; your secrets are your own. But now I cannot afford such nicety. Nor can you. Why did you want to retrieve the fan?"

Versellion continued to toy with his hat brim. "I presume when I say that my mother bade me do it, that will not satisfy you? She did. On her deathbed. I had never heard of the fan until two years ago when my mother became ill. For a time the doctors were hopeful of the outcome, but she began at last to fail. When she was certain that her illness was fatal, she told me—urgently—that I must find the Italian fan, that all would be ruined if . . ."

"If?"

"If my cousin found it first. What do you know of my family, Miss Tolerance?"

"Political. Wealthy. Whigs—your father was part of the Devonshire set, wasn't he?"

"He was. Politics is a kind of mania in my family, Miss Tolerance. My grandfather Folle raised his sons to political power as a farmer might raise his sons to the plow. Unfortunately, in my father's generation the politics of the family interfered with politics of the nation. My father and my uncle quarreled—my uncle envied my father the title and property, and my father, I believe, could not bear that his brother did not follow meekly where he led. I often thought my father valued me chiefly because as his heir, I kept Uncle William from—" He broke off. "This must sound remarkably trivial to you."

"The rivalries of families are rarely trivial," Miss Tolerance said blandly. "I presume the fan comes into this at some point?"

"I believe so. There was a schism in the family—my uncle William was of great assistance to the Crown when the King went mad in '88, and when Queen Charlotte was made Regent, she created him baronet in his own right, and he tucked himself into the Crown party with a vengeance. My grandfather never spoke to him again; my father barely did."

"May I infer that the baronetcy did not slake your uncle's thirst for position?"

"It seemed rather to inflame it. The bitterness between my father and my uncle grew so profound my mother feared it might lead to a duel. It did not, but my cousin and I were raised to hate each other like—"

"Capulets and Montagues?" Miss Tolerance asked dryly.

"Precisely. Of the two of us, Cousin Henry was the apter pupil. It is not enough that our politics still divide us; he hates me as deeply as his father could have wished, and I believe he would stop at nothing to see me ruined."

"And your mother did not wish him to have . . ." She held up the fan. "This?"

"What she said was not very lucid. My mother was in great pain, and the doctor had been giving her steady doses of laudanum. All I could make out was that the fan held some sort of secret that could bring ruin upon my family. She raved on about the fan. And Deb Cunning. She was quite . . . bitter about Mrs. Cunning."

"I see. And no one had ever mentioned the fan before?"

"My father died in '05 without mentioning the fan or potential ruin, or anything but his hope that Fox would return to the ministry again." The earl's tone was dry. Miss Tolerance suspected there had been little love lost between him and his late father.

"What I know is what my mother told me. And frankly, for a time I did not think about it. But when the Queen was stricken—this is a time when the opposition could become a force. I had to be sure there was no way my cousin could harm my party—"

"Or your own chances?"

He looked at her, a little nettled by her cynicism, Miss Tolerance thought.

"Or my own chances," he agreed. "And why not? I have worked for this, I have great hopes for reform, for— No, I will not make a speech to you, Miss Tolerance. In your work you must encounter in good measure the hunger and hardship this war has caused, and . . ."

Miss Tolerance did not listen too closely. The earl had been raised to politics, and it would not do to believe a client too wholeheartedly, particularly a client as elusive, and attractive, as the Earl of Versellion.

This cynical thought was broken by the sensation of a pin-prick. Her finger had caught on a tiny bit of raised gold chasing on one of the fan's end-sticks. She tried to push the wire down; it would not go. She looked more closely and an exclamation of surprise escaped her lips.

The protruding wire was part of a minute catch, so tiny she would have taken it for an imperfection of the design. When she inserted her thumbnail in the catch, the top of the rounded end-stick opened, revealing a space no more than half an inch across and less than a quarter inch wide. A slip of paper was folded inside it. Using her thumbnail again, Miss Tolerance pried at the paper until she could prise it out of its concealment. Without looking at the contents, she handed it to Versellion. "Perhaps this will make all clear, sir."

Ten

The earl unfolded the paper gingerly. It was a flimsy sheet, written and cross-written in a tight, florid script. There was no crest or other identifier, but the paper was still white, the ink unfaded. Versellion smoothed the paper between his fingers, flattened it on his knee, and tried to read it. After a moment he shook his head, clearly frustrated.

"The damned thing's written in Italian!"

"Italian?"

He nodded. "I believe so. I read French and Latin, but all I know is singers' Italian." He stared at the paper for several minutes, then shook his head. "I cannot make head or tails of its meaning—especially with the lines so tightly compacted. It seems to be about cookery."

"Cookery?" Miss Tolerance held out her hand. "May I, sir?" She studied the edges of the paper on both sides, seeking the beginning of the document. "Ah, see. *'Caro frate mio . . .'* it appears to be a letter from someone to his brother. Have you an Italian connection in your family, Versellion?"

Versellion shook his head.

"What made you think of cookery, sir? Oh, I see. '*Pisi verde*': green peas. And vines? Perhaps it is not cookery but gardening." Miss Tolerance folded the paper and returned it to Versellion. Surely there was no recipe so powerful it would threaten one of the greatest families in England. She wondered if the late Lady Versellion might, under the influence of drugs, have confabulated the entire story. But if the whole matter was a wild-goose chase—why would anyone know? Why kill Matt or Mrs. Smith, or make an attempt upon Versellion's life? "We cannot decipher this without help, which we will not find sitting here, sir. And we have rested long enough, I think." She got to her feet and reached around the earl to untangle her horse's rein from the branch to which she had tied it. At once Versellion was at her side and offered his hand to help her into the saddle.

"Where shall we go?" Versellion threw her up into the saddle and moved to mount his own horse.

Miss Tolerance thought. "I am convinced that the smaller roads are where your safety best lies. But we need to find a town large enough to support a bookshop."

"A bookshop?"

"We need an Italian lexicon, my lord. That is, I presume you would prefer we try to decipher the note ourselves, rather than taking it to a third party who could read it for us. Good. Then let us start westerly and see what we can find."

The last firm notion of their bearings Miss Tolerance had was in Briarton the night before. Since that time they had ridden— she imagined a map in her head—east and south, to find the inn they had slept at, then farther west to elude their pursuers. To say they were somewhere west of London was to include a singularly vast territory.

"Maidenhead and Reading should both be to the south of us," Versellion volunteered at last. "Either is large enough to contain a bookshop. I recall one in Reading—"

"As well attach a fox's brush to your hat, my lord, and loose the hounds, as to send you to a place where you are known."

"Then why can we not simply return to London?"

"I don't advise it until we have hired a bodyguard to bring you back to the city—and stay with you until you have hired another to keep with you there. Someone has killed to gain the fan, and twice attempted your life, and until we know for certain that no one in your establishment in London or your house in Richmond is part of that plot, I cannot advise you to go either where."

"Then I'll go stay with friends," Versellion suggested.

"Which friends? Are you sure of them all? Even more, are you sure we could get to them unharmed? We do not know how many people are pursuing you, but if they found us on the Birmingham road, with no particular reason to believe that we had gone west rather than south or east, it suggests that whoever is behind this had men out on all the post roads."

"Then let us hire a bodyguard at once. You cannot possibly understand how important it is that I return to London; the future of my party, of the nation, my own future—"

"Your own future is very much the point, sir," Miss Tolerance said.

Versellion glared at Miss Tolerance. She kept her gaze steady and abruptly he shook his head as if to clear it. "I was trying to bully you. I'm sorry." He held out his hand to her. "Forgive my temper."

Miss Tolerance clasped Versellion's hand and shook it, businesslike. "There is nothing to forgive, sir." They sat handfast for a moment. Then, with a feeling of some reluctance, Miss Tolerance released her hand and set her heels to her horse's sides. They rode west.

I n the end, Miss Tolerance left the Earl of Versellion in a field a few miles outside of Reading, well back from the roadside by a stand of trees. He gave her money to purchase an Italian lexicon and to retain the services of an outrider, if she could. It was close to noon, and both of them were hungry; Miss Tolerance promised to find provisions as well. Before she left him, she gave the earl her pocketknife. Versellion turned it over in his hand thoughtfully.

"Is this for self-defense, or that I might take my own life if the enemy surrounds me?" he asked dryly.

Miss Tolerance blinked. "I had thought, sir, that you might do some whittling. There's not much else I can suggest by way of amusement."

As she rode away, a backward look showed her the Earl of Versellion sitting with a small apple branch in one hand and the knife in the other, considering.

June was not the high season in Reading, nor was it market day. The streets were not crowded, which made it easier for Miss Tolerance to watch for persons she could identify as dangerous, but also meant she stood out as a stranger. She left her horse stabled at a public house on the western end of the town and walked on, looking for a cook shop, a bookshop, and a inn large enough so that she might hire a chaise, horses, and a bodyguard. She spied such an establishment upon the main street and turned toward it, then stopped. Coming out of the inn was the man she had left tied up in the stable some hours before. He was in close discussion with a large, villainous-looking fellow, both looking away from Miss Tolerance.

She sank back into a side street with her heart beating so loudly she was surprised that in itself did not give the alarum. Thinking rapidly, she slouched into the back streets of the town. The sight of a used-clothes shop inspired her: she sold her coat and bought another of longer cut, in a drab brown wool, and a pair of gray breeches and a sagging felt hat. Upon a moment's thought, she bought a coat for Versellion as well, of dark red wool, and an old-fashioned tricorne hat with one side fallen. Wearing her new coat, she immediately felt better, less obvious. It had occurred to her to buy a dress, for her pursuers would be expecting two men, not a man and a woman; but there was the problem of riding pillion. Miss Tolerance balked. Now her objective was to get food and leave Reading undetected. She had forgotten the lexicon until she passed a tiny, shabby bookstore which, from the character of the books it sold, was clearly kept for the governesses and tutors in the households that surrounded the town. There she found an Italian lexicon and a good deal of dust; bought the one, sneezed at the other, and skulked back to the public house where she had stabled her horse.

It was still there. From the house, she bespoke a basket with a half ham, a cheese, some chicken and fruit, a loaf of bread, and a jug of ale. It was hurriedly assembled; at the last minute, making free with Versellion's funds, she bought a small bottle of brandy and the London papers.

There was no sign that she had been seen or followed, but Miss Tolerance took a long route to return to Versellion. By the time she reached the orchard, the afternoon was well advanced, and Miss Tolerance was aware of an unladylike appetite. Between hunger and the intelligence that men were still actively in pursuit, she was uncommonly eager to find the earl and assure herself of his safety. She marked all the landmarks leading to the tree under which she had left him. She saw his horse tethered by a distant hedge and dozing over the lush grass there. What she saw no sign of was the Earl of Versellion himself.

Miss Tolerance swore and urged her horse forward. There were no signs of a struggle. If Versellion had gone, he had left willingly. But why not take his horse? A sensation of panic-flush swept over her. Under the tree she stopped. There was a pile of wood shavings at the base of the tree, and she realized with a pang that Versellion had been whittling. It was a substantial collection of shavings, made over some time: the earl could not have been gone from the clearing for long. Perplexed, Miss Tolerance removed her hat, wiped the perspiration from her forehead with the rough sleeve of her new coat, and regretted her own lighter coat of blue superfine wool, now hanging from a peg in Reading.

"The devil! You changed your coat!"

Miss Tolerance spun around, seeking the source of Versellion's voice, but saw nothing behind her, nothing to the left or right or anywhere in the broad expanse of meadow that stretched before her. She looked up and thought she could see, through the thickly leafed branches of the tree, a dark shape.

"Climbing trees, my lord?" She swung down from the saddle, tethered her horse to a tree nearby, and returned to watch as Versellion came down through the branches. "You gave me a moment's pause, sir."

The earl dusted bits of twig and leaf from his coat. "No more than you gave me, Miss Tolerance. I looked up from that profitable occupation to which you urged me"—he took a newly made wooden peg from his pocket—"to see an unfamiliar rider approaching. I judged it would be prudent to make myself disappear as completely as possible."

Miss Tolerance took from her saddlebag the parcel which contained the book and newspapers she had procured. "Very neat, sir. Had I not had cause to look for you here, I would never have stopped—although you did leave some evidence of your presence." She toed the pile of wood shavings.

Versellion grinned. "I'm new to your game, Miss Tolerance. Next time I shall make sure to take my evidence with me."

"God willing there shall be no next time," she said, and took the basket down from her saddle. "I waited nuncheon for you, sir. I presume you have an appetite?"

"My God, yes!"

They sat in the lee of the tree, and no one who had not known they were there could have expected to find them. Versellion laid out the food and Miss Tolerance explained the reason for her change of coat.

"They were in Reading? But how in God's name could they know we would go west?" Versellion asked at last.

Miss Tolerance had already given the matter some thought. "I wonder if your enemy has not sent out people in all directions, and having found us this morning near the Birmingham road, blanketed the countryside north and west of London? If that is so, your enemy has a good supply of money and men at his disposal. I doubt he will give up easily. Who wants you dead so powerfully, Versellion?"

In silence he considered the question, but found no answer. "Although I tell you, if I do not return to London soon, I had as well be dead as far as my prospects and my party's are concerned."

"I understand that—but you must agree that hiring a chaise and outriders will certainly not be possible in Reading. We shall have to go farther afield."

They made inroads on the meal spread on oiled cloth, drinking in turn from the jug of ale that sat between them. At last Miss Tolerance wrapped the remains of the meal for later consumption. By the sun's height she reckoned it was about four o'clock. They could count on a little more than four hours more of useful light.

"I think we had best find a place to stay the night, sir. We can continue riding on, north or west, and hope to find an inn so small our pursuers will miss it, or we can look for rougher shelter. I would prefer to ride a little farther from Reading, having seen your attackers there."

"I am sure you will not want to put up at a posting inn, and any inn small enough for you to endorse as safe will likely be as rough as sleeping in a stable," Versellion said dryly. "I think, in fact, I should rather prefer a well-kept barn."

"I believe," Miss Tolerance said slowly, "that you are beginning to enjoy yourself, sir."

"I lead a sedate life, Miss Tolerance, and this sort of adventuring is novel to me. Climbing trees and jumping out of windows? Learning rustic skills like whittling? And fresh air is beneficial to the health, is it not? But I think," he added, "that we must find someplace secure to sleep tonight. I worry for my protector; she looks tired."

"She is tired, sir," Miss Tolerance allowed, and put the parcels back in her saddlebag. Versellion's solicitousness was at once welcome and distasteful to her; she did not like to expose any weakness, even fatigue, but the fact was that she had not slept the night through in several days, and she knew the strain was telling upon her. "Shall we ride west, then?"

They scattered the wood shavings and the crumbs from their meal and mounted their horses, riding at a fair pace, seeking a shelter which would combine the virtues of solitude and solidity. An hour or so before sunset they found their haven, a small cottage that had been abandoned and was now, apparently, used to store hay. The cottage was dry, despite the rains of the last week, with a tiny hearth at the back, framed in stone. The windows were cut high in the walls, meant to admit daylight, not permit observation, and the door was the only way in. Miss Tolerance pronounced herself satisfied, and gathered tinder for a fire.

With the cottage ordered for occupation, Versellion took up the lexicon and the Italian letter and sat down by the door to catch the last daylight. Miss Tolerance sat on the opposite side of the door and produced from her wallet the stub of a pencil; as the earl dictated, she wrote down words on the margins of the newspaper, not trying to make sense of what they meant when strung together. An hour later Miss Tolerance blinked hard. Between fatigue and fading light, the words she wrote were blurring before her.

"My eyes hurt," she said irritably. "And to tell truth, I cannot make heads or tails of what this means. Could it be writ in code?" She yawned hugely and handed the paper over to Versellion.

The earl examined the paper while Miss Tolerance looked out at the twilit fields. For some time she let the noises and smells of the evening wash over her and thought of very little. If she stayed like this, she would shortly fall asleep.

"It is no use," Versellion said at last. He held the newspaper before him and was turning it to read the transcriptions and notes which she had made. "Even if I could find every word in the dictionary, I can't be certain we'd have the meaning of the thing. I must have help." He sounded thoroughly discouraged.

Miss Tolerance rose from her place, found her saddlebag, and produced the brandy.

"I judged we might need this for the medicinal raising of spirits, my lord."

Versellion put the paper down. "A very good notion." He took a long draught and made a face. "And very bad brandy." He took another draught and bowed to Miss Tolerance: "To my protector!"

Miss Tolerance acknowledged the toast with an incline of her head and took the bottle herself. "To our puzzle," she said. "Perhaps it is time to light the fire."

As she set to the task, she asked the earl where he thought he might find help in translating the letter. The earl did not answer. He was bent over the newspaper, poring over it by the last bit of light. When Miss Tolerance repeated her question, he waved one hand at her as if to gain quiet for concentration.

"What were the names we found in the letter?" he asked at last.

The fire was lit. Miss Tolerance took up the letter and held it up. "Miracoli. DiPassi. Hawley. Grudden, Hanschen, Cole, Ippolito . . ."

"Spell Hawley," Versellion demanded. She did so, and the earl made a noise of triumph. "I believe, then, that Mr. Hawley might be—or know—*nostra collega di Oxford*. See there." He poked at a paragraph of type.

Suddenly fully awake, Miss Tolerance took the newspaper and read the item. A small group of scholars at Oxford had been censured for correspondence with Catholic scholars in Italy and Germany, and investigation into possible charges of treason were being discussed.

"There's nothing new in this, sir. I read a similar notice last week. The war has the whole nation looking under covers for spies."

"But look at the names, Miss Tolerance." Versellion leaned

close to point out the one name that had caught his attention. "Charles Hawley, lecturer of B—— College, Oxford. He stands to lose his post if he cannot defend himself."

Miss Tolerance shook her head. "I am plainly too tired to understand what this means to *us*. Even were this letter part of that correspondence which has come under investigation—what on earth does this have to do with your family? How came such a letter to be in a fan kept by an old Cheapside abbess? God, I cannot think!"

Versellion drew back, contrite. "You should sleep. In the morning we will both reason better." He made to assist her up, but Miss Tolerance waved him away and retreated to a corner of the cottage where the straw was thick. She pulled off her boots, lay down with her coat to cover her, and shouldered her way into the straw until she was comfortable. She murmured good night to her companion and within moments was asleep.

She woke, suddenly, in the middle of the night. She could not tell what had wakened her, and lay still for a time, listening in the darkness. At last she rose up, bootless, and went to the door. The fields and trees that lay beyond were only shadows silvered by the moon. Under one tree their horses drowsed silently. Miss Tolerance looked one way, the other, saw nothing moving, and slumped against the doorframe.

Versellion spoke out of the darkness behind her. "*En garde*, even in your sleep? Your fencing master taught you well."

She nodded. "Yes, sir, he did."

Versellion emerged from the shadows of the cottage and joined her, looking out over the fields. He leaned in a posture mirroring hers against the far side of the door. "Surely fencing was an odd sort of pastime for a schoolgirl. Ought you not to have been making samplers and learning to play the pianoforte?"

"I did those things, too. But I badly wanted for active occupation. I was permitted to ride—sedately, with a groom at my side. I was permitted to walk—sedately, with my governess. I could stitch, and read sermons to my grandmother, and write letters, and practice upon the pianoforte."

"It sounds dreary."

Miss Tolerance laughed. "It was dreary. When I first saw Connell demonstrating a *pasado*, I was seized with such a . . . I hardly know what to call it. Longing, I suppose. To move that way, to have that freedom and that power. I took to the lessons at once."

"And the preceptor soon after?" Versellion asked dryly.

"It was not a difficult step to go from loving the exercise to loving the preceptor, no. But Connell was hardly a hero from a romance; he was portly and rather shy, except when he had a sword in his hand. It was certainly not his intent to seduce me."

"Then what was his intent?"

"To serve out his six months teaching my brother, then to find another position, and so on and on until he had the money to open a small *salle* in London. Our elopement ruined him, in a sense, as well as me."

"If it was not his intent, how did you come to—"

"Elope? Have you ever fenced with a person of the opposite sex, my lord? The focus and the exertion can be . . . stimulating."

Versellion appeared to consider the idea. "And so you eloped."

"Not at first, no. But later . . . we were not left much choice in the matter," Miss Tolerance said. "When we were discovered, my father went into a frenzy of high Gothic rage, threatened to turn me out on the highway in my shift! He challenged Connell—and a duel between them would have led inevitably to my father's death and Connell's exile. So we ran away."

Versellion had been studying the moonlight. Now he turned his gaze back to Miss Tolerance. "But if your father was prone to—what did you call it? high Gothic rage?—how came you to be studying fencing? Surely your he—"

Miss Tolerance sighed. "It was done in secret. My brother detested fencing, so we worked out a trade: I would take his lessons and he would do my mathematics."

"My God, you *were* young." Versellion appeared to muse over this for a time. "Where did you go?"

"We feared pursuit if we went to Scotland. We went to the continent."

"The hazard of that—in what year?"

"Ninety-nine. sir. We went over in the trail of the English forces to the lowlands, and stayed behind when General Brune chased them out. The French forces were everywhere, trailing havoc in their wake—and we took advantage of the chaos and hid ourselves in it. I traveled as Connell's nephew, we taught fence, and finally opened a *salle* in Amsterdam."

"His nephew?"

"I wanted to fence, sir, and neither of us wanted the *salle* to have the reputation of a brothel."

"And the man never married you?"

Miss Tolerance shook her head.

"He had a wife?" Miss Tolerance thought she heard disapproval in the earl's tone.

"Oh, far worse than that, sir," she drawled. "Connell was Catholic, and we could not agree *how* to marry. I was very young, and disliked the idea of a civil wedding—and I fear I was determined that he should love me enough to marry as *I* wished. By the time I had stopped refining upon it, we had been together for so long the ceremony seemed unnecessary, even dangerous—how could I change from a boy to a wife overnight? Perhaps my father was right and I am like my aunt, with no discernible morality."

"Your father," Versellion said crisply, "was an ass."

"Well, yes. But that does not mean he was wrong. I made my bed very thoroughly, and now . . ." She stirred up the crushed grass at her feet. "Now I am lying upon it. And very dusty it is, too."

The earl smiled. For a few minutes the only sound to be heard was the breeze riffling the grasses.

"If your father could not see the honor in you, he *was* an ass,"

Versellion said at last. He took a step toward Miss Tolerance. In the silvered light, his face was ghostly; he examined her closely, and she was aware of his unghostly height and warmth.

"Not everyone reckons as you do, sir," Miss Tolerance said. She looked up at his face, reading what was there to be seen. "My lord, this has been an extraordinary day; I beg you will not confuse the excitement of our situation with any other kind of—"

Versellion took her hand and studied it, tracing the veins under his thumb. "Miss Tolerance, I assure you I am well able to distinguish the excitement of the day from any other sort. My admiration for you did not begin this morning—or last night."

Her heart beat so strongly that Miss Tolerance was sure the strokes must be audible to Versellion; he must be able to feel them in the hand he held, and only moonlight hid the flush that warmed her cheeks. She drew her hand from Versellion's grasp with some reluctance. "My lord, this is not wise. Your assailants—"

"Are miles away. Look." He gestured toward the moonlit fields. "Not a cutthroat in sight. Miss Tolerance, if your feelings are not in sympathy with mine, I will say nothing more than to beg your pardon for my impertinence. But I thought you were not wholly insensible—"

Miss Tolerance shook her head. "Not insensible, sir, no." Feelings she had believed lost, or buried across the Channel in a pauper's grave in Amsterdam, wakened. She shivered.

"Come back inside. The moonlight makes shadows and ghosts; you will catch chill. Please—I beg your pardon, but I have forgot, what is your Christian name?" His voice was almost a whisper.

"Sarah, sir." She said it firmly, not certain what she would do.

"Sarah. Come back inside with me, Sarah."

He held out his hand but did not touch her. The space between them was filled with heat, the lack of contact more persuasive than an embrace.

With the feeling that she was jumping from a very high place into a pool of darkness so inky she could not predict if she would swim or drown, Miss Tolerance took the hand he offered and followed Versellion back into the cottage.

Eleven

Miss Tolerance awakened to find herself in an embrace of the sort which had been foreign to her since the death of Charles Connell, and lay for some time cherishing the sensation. They were face-to-face; Versellion's arm lay light across her hip, his face pillowed upon her hair (which, she was shortly to discover, pinned her to their rustic bed), and the warmth of his body communicated itself to her own. Her arm stretched under her head like a pillow, then arched around Versellion's head, with the fingers lightly brushing his dark hair. Straw prickled beneath her hip, and a single shaft of bright morning light danced across the blanket which covered their closely joined bodies. The mingled smells of straw, dust, and Versellion's skin caught her with such force that her eyes closed of their own accord.

"Sarah?" Versellion murmured. She let her eyes open and found the earl looking at her. "Good morning." He moved his face closer and brushed a kiss upon her eyebrow.

Miss Tolerance ran her fingertips up the arm that lay across her hip, over his shoulder, and spread them through his hair before she moved to kiss his lips. "Good morning," she said at last. Their faces were now very close together, their eyes darting from mouth to chin to eyes and back to mouth again, as if each of them were committing the other to memory.

"Ought we to rise?" Versellion asked. He made no move to do so.

Miss Tolerance shook her head slightly. "Wait a moment. When we rise, we go back to Miss Tolerance and the Earl of Versellion. I become your protector again, and you my client. Let us just . . . tarry . . . for a moment." Her hand loosed itself from his hair and moved down across his back.

Versellion slid his hand around the swell of her hip and drew her toward him. "By all means," he murmured. "Let us tarry."

The sun was high when they started for Oxford. Versellion had carried the argument; even with the lexicon, he did not think they could reliably translate the Italian letter on their own, and Oxford was the nearest place outside of London where they were likely to find a disinterested scholar fluent in Italian. It was also, Miss Tolerance warned, a place where so notable a person as the Earl of Versellion might well be recognized.

"Then we use my notoriety as a shield," Versellion suggested. "In daylight, in a populous town where I am likely to be recognized, will it not be more difficult to attack us?"

He had donned the rustic clothes Miss Tolerance had purchased for him in Reading, and sat now, with his back against the cottage wall, observing Miss Tolerance as she combed her fingers through the tangled mass of her dark hair and attempted to pick the hay straws from it. She was very aware of his gaze, but strove to adopt again the professional composure which had previously characterized their relationship.

"That would work if we were amidst a crowd where everyone knew you, Versellion—say, on the floor of Parliament, or in an Almack's cotillion. But in Oxford, all it requires is one person who recognizes you amidst a great crowd of people who do not, telling a man who is hunting you, and we'd have all your pursuers fall upon us in a quiet alleyway."

"You must see I cannot spend my life in hiding—particularly not now, when the political situation is so unresolved. Why cannot we take up one of these searchers and ask him who has sent him to find me? I dislike running. It smacks of cowardice."

Miss Tolerance finished braiding her hair and wound it upon her head again.

"Common sense. Connell taught me to keep my feelings in check when I fought—and never to attack an opponent of whom I knew nothing, unless I had no alternative. If I had accosted one of our pursuers in Reading yesterday, what do you imagine would have been the result? He might have had a friend—or two friends or five-and-twenty—in the next street, ready to come to his aid and kill me. I might have got some little information from him and then, scrupling to kill him where he stood, let him go . . . so that he could follow me here to you. The minute we tip our hand to the opposition, let whomever set the hounds upon your trail know where you are, your peril increases tenfold. Where's the sense in that?"

She took up her saddlebag, packed the Italian lexicon in it, and turned to survey the area for any other trace of their tenancy. Versellion stood and approached her, smiling.

"What do I need to fear with my protector near me?" His tone made an endearment of the title.

Having satisfied herself that they had left nothing behind, Miss Tolerance sidestepped the earl's approach. "Your protector can only do so much, sir. I cannot catch a bullet, for one thing. No, I see the logic of Oxford, Versellion. I just hope we can go as quietly as possible, at least until I can hire assistance."

The earl bowed. "I will be guided by you in all things." But he stepped directly into her path and drew her into a light embrace. "Don't scold me, Sarah. I only wished to kiss you good morning."

Miss Tolerance permitted the embrace, but with an air which said quite clearly that the kiss was meant to seal all further endearments away until a later time.

T hey rode without much conversation; the journey was not a long one. By early afternoon they had arrived on the outskirts of town and found rooms in an inn in the shadow of St. Clement's Church, across the Magdalen Bridge. At Miss Tolerance's insistence, Versellion stayed at the inn while she went out into the city to find an Italian scholar. As she had never been in Oxford before, she expected that this would be a task which consumed her for several hours: one could not, after all, stand on street corners crying out for a scholar as if one were hawking strawberries or cockles. Versellion, who had spent a year at Oxford without emerging with anything so undignified as a degree, told her to inquire first at the coffeehouse on Queen Street and, if she had no joy there, at the Bear, in Alfred Street. She left him ordering a vast dinner, his manner very much at odds with the broken-down coat he wore.

As the university was nearing the end of Trinity term, the streets teemed with young men, most gowned and with the heavy, anxious look of students facing examination. Miss Tolerance began to wish she had kept her good coat and breeches—a common laborer such as she looked had less chance of disappearing in a crowd like this. There was no point in repining; better to suit her words—and accent—to the clothes she wore. The host of the Queen Street coffeehouse, however, displayed no democratic sympathies; he was plainly prejudiced against Miss Tolerance by her plebeian look.

"What's the like of you want with a don?" he growled.

Miss Tolerance had thoughtfully provided herself with a story. "I've a letter from a—a signorina in Italy. My brother's gone to fight for the Queen, and not a word have we had till now, when I get a letter from this . . ." She paused as if remembering. "This Constanzia, naming my brother. But I can't make heads nor tails of it. I'd pay one of them teachers to read it to me."

The man shook his head. "Not my job to remember who tutors in what," he said, and turned his back on her.

Miss Tolerance bit down on her frustration, finished her coffee, and took herself off to the Bear, where she was pleased to find a far more egalitarian spirit. The barman clearly noted her gender and, as clearly, decided it was none of his business; for the price of a pint of bitter for each of them, he regaled Miss Tolerance with his opinions on which starving tutor to approach first. After discarding this one, then that one, for reasons no clearer than *"He* won't do, will he?" the barman at last offered Miss Tolerance the name and direction of a tutor named Deale who roomed in Leckford Road. Having provided this information, the barman went on to explain Mr. Deale's situation, antecedents, and family troubles. Apparently the tutor, when in funds, spent his coin at the Bear.

At last, with thanks, Miss Tolerance escaped this torrent of information and left the Bear. At the inn she found Versellion in the private parlor he had engaged. He had bathed and changed into his own clothes, which made her more conscious of her own grime. The earl greeted her with the news that he had ordered venison and squab for their dinner. "I am tired of bread and cheese. But you! What news have you?"

"I've a name and direction of someone. I thought I would stop here and send a note; better if he call here as soon as possible. You will want to be there when the letter is read, and I prefer for your safety that you not go much abroad while we are here."

"Invite him to dine?" Versellion suggested.

Miss Tolerance grinned. "If Deale's as poor as the barman at the Bear suggested, I imagine venison and squab will be a considerable enticement."

Versellion smiled. "By all means, let us entice him. Although . . ." He paused thoughtfully. "I had had a foolish notion of entertaining you alone; a decent meal, a decent bed . . . But you are right, we should speak to this fellow as soon as possible. We will have time."

Miss Tolerance, touched and discomfited, said only, "I shall write to him, then. Dinner is ordered for what hour? Good. And then perhaps I will order hot water brought up for myself. Oh, good God—" A thought had occurred to her with some force. "At dinner I shall have to play a different role—or wear my hat throughout the meal. Or cut my hair short."

"I should dislike to see you cut your hair," Versellion said.

"But think how remarkable our visitor must find a man with hair to his waist. The shears are the most efficient solution." Versellion began to protest, but she waved a hand to silence him. "Failing the shears, I must find myself a dress in which to greet our Mr. Deale." Versellion rendered the decision more complex by coming up behind her, so close that she could feel his breath on the nape of her neck.

"Please do not cut your hair," he said. "Buy a dress, buy whatever you have need of. I have sufficient funds, and you must not scruple to permit me to pay for clothes which you have sold upon my business."

Moved far beyond what was comfortable, Miss Tolerance stepped aside.

"I hope I shall not regret this new facet of our relationship, my lord. I seem to have difficulty putting common sense before sentiment. Very well, I shall go out again and find a dress at the secondhand shops. When I make up the reckoning for my services, we can settle the matter."

A letter bidding Mr. Matthew Deale to dine at seven o'clock, when a proposition to his advantage would be broached, was written and dispatched. Miss Tolerance went out, returned half an hour later with a bundle under one arm, and retired to their room for her toilette. Versellion stayed closeted in the parlor, desiring the innkeeper to bring him all the London papers he could part with.

At a few minutes before seven, Miss Tolerance joined the earl in the parlor. A table had been laid with covers for three, and several bottles of claret stood on the sideboard. Miss Tolerance wore a dress of light blue muslin, only a year or so out of fashion, and a handsome cashmere shawl, only slightly stained upon one edge. She looked rather like a governess: not in the first bloom of fashion, but not wholly removed from it.

Their guest arrived almost on her heels. One of the maids showed him in, announced him with a roll of the eyes which clearly said that his was a type with which she was all too familiar, and closed the door. Matthew Deale advanced into the room, looking around him as if he had fallen into an unexpected dream. He was a tall, thin man with the marks of poverty heavy upon him: his coat and stockings both showed signs of discreet darns, his chin was patchily shaven, and his hair rather too long. His skin had the pasty, unhealthy look common to persons who are too much indoors and too little in the habit of eating decent food. Hunger, curiosity, and the stink of anxiety clung to him like smoke, and so Miss Tolerance was the more surprised and impressed that the man was clearly making every effort to be cordial and gentlemanly.

"My name is Deale," he said. "May I have the honor to know from whom this kind invitation came?"

Versellion stood and bowed; Miss Tolerance curtsied. "I am Mr. Small and this is Miss Little," Versellion said. He had not prepared Miss Tolerance for her new name; she cast an appreciative look at him. "I hope you are hungry. We have a decent meal laid on."

It was to the credit of all three parties that there was no indecent rush to table. For some time they concentrated on the excellent food before them: turbot served in a sauce of cream and leeks with a remove of fresh beans; a squab pasty; and a loin of venison, dressed with dried fruit and Madeira and served with removes of salsify and parsnips. For the first time in days, Miss Tolerance was conscious of that sense of well-being which comes of being pleasantly overfed. Mr. Deale, on the other hand, ate politely and steadily, as one might who was determined to consume as much as he decently could against a later hungry time. A bottle of claret was emptied, another begun.

At last, with a wistful look at the emptied dishes upon the sideboard, Mr. Deale turned to his host. "You have fed me royally, Mr. Small. May I know how I can return your generosity?"

Versellion drew the Italian letter from his pocket. "You may, Mr. Deale. I have a letter here, writ in Italian, I believe. I must have it translated, as accurately as possible, tonight. For that service I am prepared to pay handsomely. It was represented to us that you might be the man to do it."

Deale smiled and extended his hand to take the letter, but Versellion shook his head. "This commission is of necessity a most private one. I must ask first for your word that you will not communicate what you learn here tonight to anyone."

It was to his credit, Miss Tolerance thought, that Mr. Deale did not immediately give his word and snatch the paper from Versellion's hand. Poor as he was, Mr. Deale was obviously neither a knave nor an idiot. "May I have your assurance in return, Mr. Small, that the letter will not contain anything of a treasonous or dangerous nature?"

Versellion was no less thoughtful in his reply. "As I do not know what the damned letter says, sir, I cannot promise that. I can promise you that if the contents of the letter require action to safeguard the peace of the country, I shall make sure such action is taken."

Deale considered for a moment. "And my fee for the task, sir?"

"Will ten pounds be sufficient?"

The tutor nodded, apparently rendered speechless by such a sum. When he found his voice again, he asked if he might be permitted to see the letter now. Versellion handed it to him; Miss Tolerance fetched a writing table, sharpened the pen, and announced that she was ready to take down the translation if Mr. Deale would be so kind as to begin. Deale examined the letter for some time without speaking.

"Sir," he said at last. "Are you truly unaware of what this letter says?"

Versellion nodded.

Deale pulled at his chin with one long-fingered hand. He twitched his mouth and knit his eyebrows. "It appears to be . . .

that is, I should dislike to be the agent whereby a colleague came to harm, and this—"

"For God's sake, man, let me know what the letter says. I have no more interest than you in bringing any of your colleagues to harm, but I must have the text of the letter. If you will be so kind?"

Frowning, Mr. Deale began to dictate.

"My dear Friar—"

"Friar?" Miss Tolerance exclaimed. "Not brother?"

"*Frate.* Friar. If I may continue?"

More than an hour passed before Deale and his auditors were satisfied with the translation. A great deal of perplexity had been aroused by the contents, but Mr. Deale assured them that the translation was as accurate as he could make it. Miss Tolerance read back the whole of the letter's text one more time.

"*My dear Friar—*

"*Thank you for your interesting letter of the seventeenth. The program of breeding laid out by our colleagues in England and Germany is not so far advanced as your own, and I hear with great pleasure of the advances in fertilization. Especially in England, where the support of the Crown for agricultural sciences withered with the old King's intellect (was there ever a sadder day for science than that when the Queen was made Regent?), such researches have become the province of a few aristocratic dilettantes who have no idea of the exchange of ideas that rigorous science demands. I only regret that the nature of the European situation precludes my journeying to see the results of our joint work.*

"*I rejoice to learn that the peas have not only reproduced to the sixth generation, but have done so in ways that begin to be predictable. I have written to Grudden and Hanschen to share your news, and learn from them that their own experiments— conducted also with peas, so as to provide useful comparison to your own data—are proceeding. They were at first unconvinced that the safeguards you have undertaken to ensure purity of fertilization were necessary, but I believe the arguments of DiPassi and myself convinced them. They have noticed, in particular, a distinct predictability in the height of the vines, which trait they have now reproduced in three generations. Writing to our colleague in Oxford, I have suggested that he may wish to focus upon that trait at this present, but Hawley, whose enthusiasms you will recall, argue that the color of the flower produced is at least as useful a datum as that of height! Cole and I have agreed that there is no point in arguing the matter for now.*

"Cole and I are also concerned that we do not dismiss from our minds the fate of traits in plants that we do not desire. We must ask ourselves which such traits sustain themselves despite cross-pollination; at what generation a given trait is reliably expressed or suppressed; and if it is possible to cause that suppressed trait to reemerge in some later generation. Patience, indeed, must be our watchword.

"One last note: Miracoli has conceived the notion that our results, when final, might be applied scientifically to all sorts of species. Programs of animal breeding might benefit from an extrapolation of our research. It might even, one day, be possible to predict whether the union of a given man and woman would be more likely to yield children fair-haired or dark, blue-eyed or brown. That, of course, is to tread into the province of the Divine, which action, despite our Differences upon that subject, we will agree must be taken with the humblest respect. That being said, is not the scientific vista before us magnificent?

"I remain, dear Ippolito, your servant —D"

When finished, Miss Tolerance folded the translation and looked up to find Mr. Deale regarding Versellion with some perplexity.

"May I inquire if you are an agent of the government, Mr. Small, or part of Hawley's group?" he asked.

Versellion shook his head. "Neither, sir. Why should you think it?"

Miss Tolerance, who had put these new pieces of the puzzle together over the course of the evening, looked up from the paper. "It seems we have stumbled upon a piece of that proscribed correspondence that has occasioned so much attention in London. This Mr. Hawley, whose name you noted in the newspaper yesterday—"

Deale interrupted. "I have met Hawley on one or two occasions here. He's one of the old fellows, a history scholar with no more idea of treason than a baby. He has two enthusiasms—the Punic Wars and agriculture—but I think he's as loyal an Englishman as you'll find anywhere. If there is anything sinister about this correspondence, I'm certain you'll find Mr. Hawley is an innocent dupe."

"I am sure you are correct," Versellion said gravely. His mind seemed already to have moved to another subject entirely. He took out his pocketbook and extracted several notes from it, which he exchanged for the letter Mr. Deale was holding. "Sir, I thank you for your help, and I remind you that you have given your word that the contents of this letter will remain our secret."

"You have my word, sir. I should hate to think that I have caused trouble for Mr. Hawley—"

"Not from me, Mr. Deale," Versellion assured him. "I heard nothing in the letter to indicate that Mr. Hawley or his colleagues are a threat to England's security—and if it's writ in code, it's the damnedest cipher I ever encountered. May I offer you more wine? No? Then perhaps we may bid you good evening, sir."

Mr. Deale appeared much relieved by this abrupt dismissal. He made his bow to Miss Tolerance, exchanged nods with Versellion, and backed out of the room as if leaving an audience with the Queen. The door closed behind him and Versellion dropped his head into his hands.

"Peas. Vines. A whole page double-written about peas and how tall they grow. Great scientific vistas?" His shoulders began to shake with laughter which seemed composed, to Miss Tolerance's ear, of anger, frustration, and genuine amusement.

She let him laugh himself out, then handed him a glass of wine.

"I think," she said carefully, "that several important questions have escaped your notice, sir. This business with Hawley and his correspondents is fairly recent; according to the papers, it cannot have been going on for much more than two years—three at most. How comes this letter of recent vintage to be in a fan your father gave Mrs. Cunning a near score of years ago?"

Versellion, who had been examining the surface of the wine in his glass, looked up sharply.

"The fan you bought is not the one I seek!"

"Perhaps, sir, although it matches the description and appears to have the right pedigree. Mrs. Cunning could identify it positively for us. But perhaps the fan was not so buried away as Mrs. Virtue gave me to understand—in which case the message you are seeking might have been replaced with this letter."

Versellion drew a long breath and sank back in his chair. "And we have been chasing geese all over Oxfordshire. Another reason we must return to London. I did not have the time to tell you before Deale arrived." He got up and fetched the *Times*, which had been left on a chair by the sideboard. "Look at this."

Miss Tolerance followed his finger to a brief item. The Queen had been taken ill; reports from Kew Palace were guarded. The wishes and prayers of an anxious nation were with Her Majesty at this most distressing time, and so on.

"This is hardly news to you, sir," Miss Tolerance said.

"It is not the news, it is the matter of where I find it. The *Times* is the Crown's paper, the most likely to dismiss any rumor of the Queen's illness until the matter is so grave that the outcome is not in doubt. If the *Times* says she is ill, the inference is clear: she will not recover."

"You cannot know that."

"I certainly cannot know that here, Sarah. I *must* return to

London tomorrow. Take what precautions you like, hire a battalion of Hussars or let us return to the city with a company of trained bears. But I return to London tomorrow, if I have to take the stagecoach."

Miss Tolerance looked at her companion mildly. "Have you ever ridden a public coach, sir? It would be an education for you."

He glared at her.

She sighed. "I do not think a battalion of Hussars will be necessary, Versellion. I will hire bodyguards in the morning—the only reason I did not today was because—"

"Our whole attention was on translating the damned letter. You're right." He sat down again. "Perhaps there was never anything to this damned fan, perhaps it was some sort of fever dream of my mother's."

"That is possible. But do not forget that two people have died in this matter, one of them my friend. Pursuit of the fan is important in some way, and we will discover why." She gathered up the sheets she had covered with her transcription of the letter. "Are you tired, sir?"

Versellion looked at Miss Tolerance and appeared to read something in her face of which she herself had been unaware. "Not in the least," he said, and smiled.

It was not in Miss Tolerance's heart to deny that smile. "Then let's to bed," she said.

The next morning was foggy and cold. Miss Tolerance quitted her bed with considerable reluctance and took herself to the Mitre, the coaching inn on High Street where a chaise and four might be bespoken. For just a moment, as she stood by the bed waiting for Versellion to empty the contents of his pocketbook into her hands to defray the cost of the hire, she shivered. How like a scene of prostitution this might seem: herself, at dawn's breaking, hand extended to take her lover's money. The reality, she assured herself, was of course different. Still, the thought was as oppressive as the day itself.

Chaise and horses arranged for, Miss Tolerance entered into a far more delicate negotiation with the landlord of the Mitre to suggest, or provide, a burly, trustworthy, and closemouthed man to ride beside the driver. "My uncle's of a nervous temperament," she explained. "And deadly afraid of highwaymen." The amount she offered was sufficient to acquire a bodyguard of considerable short-term loyalty, as well as the landlord's convenient amnesia regarding the arrangement. Pleased with her work, Miss Tolerance turned east along High Street to return to the inn for breakfast.

They left the inn within a quarter of eight by St. Clement's bells. Versellion was once again in the sorry secondhand coat and hat she had procured for him. He had arranged to stable their horses until a groom could be sent to collect them, so they had very little to carry with them on their brief walk to the Mitre. They crossed the Magdalen Bridge, the Cherwell flowing beneath almost invisible in the fog, and up Bridge Street, past the great arched entrance to the Physick Garden on their left.

"Good God, Versellion! What the devil are you doing here?" The words seemed to emerge from the fog itself, somewhere within the garden gate. Miss Tolerance spun to face the sound, hand on the hilt of her sword, with the earl only a step or so behind her.

"Trux? I might ask the same of you." Versellion stepped from behind Miss Tolerance.

Lord Trux stepped out of the thinning fog, a smile on his lips. "My dear fellow, half of London is wondering where you are!" He extended his hand, clapped an arm around Versellion's shoulder, withdrew it fastidiously upon contact with the greasy wool of the secondhand coat, and drew the earl into eager discussion.

"My lord, must you do this now, in the middle of the street?" Miss Tolerance muttered.

At the same moment, Trux pressed again, "What are you doing in Oxford? And in that coat!"

Versellion lied smoothly. "I had some business with my old college—and my own coat was ruined by a serving wench with a bottle of claret. But what of you, George? How do matters stand—" He left off meaningfully, as if Trux must know precisely of what he inquired.

"My lord," Miss Tolerance said more urgently.

"The chaise will wait for us," he said over his shoulder. "I want to know—"

"Take a turn with me, Versellion. I'll tell you all that I know!" Trux had Versellion's elbow and was steering him into the Physick Garden.

"My lord, this is not wise," Miss Tolerance said.

Versellion was already entering the gate with Trux at his side, their heads bent together. Damning men and politics equally, Miss Tolerance followed. There must be roses somewhere, she thought, as the smell of them when they entered the garden was quite powerful. She could not, however, see beyond five or six feet.

When the first man stepped out of the fog, she was not surprised.

Swearing under her breath, Miss Tolerance stepped forward, drawing her sword, to stand between Versellion and the newcomer. Another man appeared just beyond the first.

Lord Trux, who had been a few steps ahead of Versellion in their progress into the garden, stumbled backward with a screech, reaching out in panic to grab the earl's arm, as if he would thrust the earl forward in his own place. Versellion shook his arm to dislodge Trux, who clung stubbornly; as Trux thrashed, the first of the attackers moved to the right around Miss Tolerance and swung a cudgel at Trux, catching him a glancing blow on the head. Trux loosed his hold on Versellion and crumpled to the ground, moaning. Freed of Trux's grasp, Versellion drew his sword. Miss Tolerance stepped in again; she had time to note that they appeared to be armed with nothing more than cudgels, no swords and no pistols. Still, a well-aimed blow might break her small sword in two. She waited *en garde*.

The forward of the two, who wore a red kerchief around his neck and a villainous black hat that obscured his face, took a step forward and swung at her. Miss Tolerance dodged the blow, bringing her point up to pink the man on the forearm. The cut did not stop him; he swung again, she dodged again, a much nearer blow. Again she cut the man, this time on the shoulder, the cut deeper than the last. He stepped back for a moment.

The other man had been eyeing Versellion, or rather his blade, without advancing. Now he stepped forward and swung his cudgel at Miss Tolerance. With a murmured prayer for luck, she stepped in under the blow, grabbed the man's neckcloth in her left hand, and brought the hilt of her sword up in a blow to the chin that stunned him. She turned to find that Versellion was advancing on their first assailant, sword drawn.

Red Kerchief feinted back a step, then took his cudgel in his left hand and swung it at Versellion. The earl dodged the blow— or would have, but Trux, who had half raised himself, one arm across his bruised face, reached out blindly and grabbed the earl's left arm, knocking his balance awry. The blow missed dashing Versellion's brains out, but it caught his shoulder and he went down at once.

Before Red Kerchief could deliver another blow, Miss Tolerance stepped in with a thrust to the man's thigh. She felt the meaty impact—this was no neat pink but a full thrust—and she felt the muscle grip at the steel of her sword when she pulled it out. The man did not fall to the ground, but hunched, bloody and panting, against the wall of the garden.

Miss Tolerance took her kerchief from her pocket and handed it to the man.

"Stanch the bleeding," she said curtly.

The man took the cloth and pressed it against the wound on

his leg, shuddering as he did so. The smaller cuts on his forearm and shoulder still bled as well. Miss Tolerance did not judge them likely to be fatal; she lifted the point of her sword up to flick the hat off the man's face so that she could observe it. It was not familiar to her, but the look in her opponent's eyes—of pain at war with rapid thought—was.

"Who hired you to set on us?" she asked.

Behind her, Trux was still moaning. To her left she could just see Versellion rise to sitting, his right hand on his left shoulder as if to reassure himself that the damage was no worse than it was.

Red Kerchief lowered his eyes. "No one hired us. Looking for a purse or two is all."

Miss Tolerance brought the tip of her blade to Red Kerchief's ear. "Who hired you?" she said again.

Eyes flickering from Miss Tolerance to Versellion to his companion, the tough said, "Man at the tavern. Said 'f we saw a pair answering your description, we was to take you."

"What was this man's name?"

Red Kerchief shrugged. "Dun't know. Some swell, high in the instep, couldn't hardly bear the smell of the likes of us. Money was good, though: promised two guineas, gave us half a crown on account."

Miss Tolerance stepped back and sheathed her sword. "I'm sure your half crown will go some way to paying a surgeon to patch up your wounds." She backed away from the man and assured herself of the unconsciousness of his companion. "When your friend wakes, he will gladly help you home, I'm sure."

Versellion had risen to his feet, pale and unsteady. Trux was still seated on the ground, one hand to his head, moaning loudly.

"We'd best get out of here—we're in no condition to take on a further gang," Miss Tolerance murmured. She moved to take Versellion's good arm. "Can you walk? How are you?"

"Nothing broken, I believe, but I'm damned dizzy." As Miss

Tolerance took a step toward the garden gate, he added, "We cannot leave Trux here. I can manage. Help him."

Miss Tolerance bit down on several comments. Her objective now must be to get her charge as quickly as possible to the Mitre, then into their carriage for London. There was no point in arguing. She bent solicitously over Trux, assisted him to stand—no mean feat, as the man was heavy, ungainly, and completely uncooperative. By some effort the three of them left the Physick Garden and proceeded along to High Street, thence to the Mitre. Such passersby as observed them most often looked away again, either too absorbed in their own abstracted thoughts to be concerned, or unwilling to engage so disreputable a party as theirs appeared to be. At the Mitre, Miss Tolerance put Trux in the care of the landlord, explaining that he'd been set upon by footpads and advising the immediate application of a beefsteak to the rapidly developing bruise on the side of his face. That done, she was introduced to the bodyguard she had hired, a satisfactorily large and humorless man who swung himself up beside the driver of their chaise. She and Versellion climbed into the chaise and at last were on their way to London.

O nce the chaise was under way, Miss Tolerance helped Versellion to remove his coat, and probed his injury with fingers as gentle as the jolting of the carriage would permit.

"Nothing broken," she confirmed. "You will have a nasty bruise in a few hours, and for some days it will hurt a good deal."

Versellion smiled wearily. "It has already begun. At least I have you to minister to me. Poor Trux, left to the gentle mercies of the innkeeper at the Mitre! You were rather brusque with him, don't you think? Trux has never claimed to be a man of action, after all."

Miss Tolerance regarded the earl with curiosity. "I should think he had had enough action for one day. Did you truly not see—" She stopped, looking at him.

"Not see what?"

"That Trux engineered the whole attack?"

Versellion stared at her. The carriage hit a rut and he clenched his teeth on a gasp of pain.

Twelve

There was a silence in which Miss Tolerance assumed Versellion was seeking to subdue both the pain in his shoulder and the shock of his associate's betrayal. At last he inquired how she had reached her conclusion.

Miss Tolerance said quietly, "This is unpleasant for you. I know you reposed some trust in Trux. But consider." She ticked her points off on her fingers. "First: Did he say why he was in Oxford, and how he happened to be lurking at the gateway to the Physick Garden precisely at the right moment to encounter you? Leaving aside the question of how he came to be in Oxford, Lord Trux does not strike me as a man in the habit of early rising—it was not yet eight in the morning when he found us. Second: Why insist that you take a stroll in the garden on a cold, foggy morning, rather than inviting you to take a cup of coffee or a mug of ale in some public house? Or is Lord Trux so avid a horticulturist that even the dreariness of the morning could not deter him from walking in the garden?"

"Do you imagine that your tale is improved by sarcasm?" Versellion asked.

"Forgive me." Her tone was as cool as his. "Very well, then. The third point: When the attack came, Trux thrashed and kept you from drawing your blade. His clumsiness was deliberate and well timed."

"You're mistaken. I told you, Trux is not a man of action." The earl's voice was emotionless.

"I think you wrong him. That was a performance worthy of Covent Garden. No, Versellion, let me finish. Fourth point, and the last: The only moment of genuine terror I saw on Trux's face this morning was when the fight was finished and I was talking to the man in the red kerchief. When I asked who had paid for the attack, Red Kerchief's eyes went to you, to me, to his accomplice—everywhere but to Trux. That made me look at Trux; he was regarding the tough with complete dread, which I take to mean that he was afraid the man would give him up to us."

Miss Tolerance leaned back against the seat and stared out the window, meaning to give Versellion a few minutes to consider the charges she had made against his ally. But when he spoke, it was to challenge her.

"What would Trux gain by betraying me?"

"You told me once that Trux wished very much to be of service to you. Perhaps he did not feel adequately rewarded by your patronage. Perhaps someone else made him an offer that was richer than yours."

"Damn it, this game is not played for money—"

Miss Tolerance lost all patience. She leaned forward and said with fierce slowness, "Because money is not what motivates *you*, don't make the imbecile mistake of believing that all men must be motivated as you are. I have told you: this is not a game. I lost a friend on your business, and I don't know how I shall count that when we settle our accounts. Your life is in danger. Even now. Does the pain in your shoulder tell you nothing about the seriousness of your opponents' intent? God protect me from men who think their positions exempt them from danger!"

She turned away, closing her eyes, and leaned back into the inadequately upholstered seat. The carriage rattled on through the foggy countryside, and some of the chill outside seemed to leak inside. The silence between them lasted perhaps a quarter hour. When Versellion spoke, it was in tones of quiet inquiry.

"I cannot believe Trux is behind everything. The attack in Richmond? The men at the inn?"

Miss Tolerance turned back to her companion. "As for that, I agree. If you will forgive me, Lord Trux may be a good cat's-paw, but he's no schemer. The subtleties of this plot are not of his authorship."

"I had come to the same conclusion," Versellion said. "And now he knows we are on to him."

"Does he? Lord Trux's vanity is considerable. He may convince himself that he has played a deep hand and that we have no idea of his involvement. You'll note that I did my best to see him taken care of—and damned awkward it was, too. It never hurts to have one's opponents underestimate the extent of your information."

"Do you think Trux's master will be likewise deluded?" Versellion sounded very tired. Miss Tolerance was suddenly sorry for her earlier impatience.

"I think that he will at least have room for doubt, whoever he is. When we are returned to London, I will do my best to find out. Now, my lord, you must rest awhile. Here: you may lean your head on my shoulder. Good. Now close your eyes—"

"Edward," he prompted.

"Close your eyes, Edward," she said, sounding less like a lover than the stern overseer of a nursery, but she raised her hand to stroke his forehead and brush the thick, dark hair away from his brow. "Close your eyes, my dear, and rest awhile," she said softly. She listened as his breathing slowed into sleep, and turned her eyes unseeing to the landscape outside the carriage window, thinking.

R ain fell off and on throughout the day, and by the time they reached London, it was nearly dark. The chaise rattled along through patches of fog, and as the ruts of country roads gave way to the regular jolt of paving stones, the sounds and smells of London grew more insistent. Miss Tolerance had slept awhile herself, with Versellion's head still pillowed on her shoulder. Now she was awake, her eyes closed, listening to the quarrels and cries in the street.

"We're nearly at Versellion House," the earl said quietly. "You will come in, I hope. My aunt Julia may be about, preparing for the ball she is hosting here, but we may easily elude her—"

Miss Tolerance shook her head. It was a question which had featured large in her meditations. "Only so long as it will take us to settle accounts, my lord."

Versellion paused as if to fully parse what she had said. "Certainly. We may do so at once," he said stiffly.

Gently, Miss Tolerance said, "We are in London again, sir. I must keep our business on a businesslike footing. I regret that I will not be able to offer up a full accounting of expenses incurred in your behalf until tomorrow, but as I have accomplished the task I undertook—"

"You require payment. I see. Then you will not pursue the matter of the fan any further for me?"

"As far as you like. You have only to ask. The terms are the same as before."

Versellion looked out the window onto the rainy street. "This is cold, Sarah."

Miss Tolerance shook her head. "Cold, sir? No, it is merely common sense. My position does not permit me to allow sentiment to interfere with business. I hope you will not take it amiss."

The carriage jolted over broken cobblestones.

"You must think very little of me," he said.

"If I thought little of you, sir, I would not have become your lover."

"Well." Versellion sat back against the cushions. "Come in and I will pay your wage. I would like to engage you again to settle the matter of the fan for once and all. Find out if what we hold is the true fan, and what mystery it holds. I should not mind knowing," he added more lightly, "how my fan is tangled up with this circle of obscure treasonous horticulturists that has exercised the government so."

The carriage halted before Versellion House and the guard Miss Tolerance had engaged, soaking wet but impassive, stood at the door to usher his charge into the house.

"One more word, Versellion. The minute we leave this carriage, you will be pulled into the thick of your politics, so I remind you now. Hire bodyguards. Extend the hire of this poor fellow waiting here, or hire others of your own choosing, or I will find men for you—but make sure you are protected at all times. Everywhere. I am in deadly earnest about this, and so should you be."

"Why cannot you be—"

"You have just hired me to uncover the secret of the fan. I cannot do so while protecting you. Please, Versellion."

The earl nodded. "As you say. You think I should keep this fellow on?" He nodded at the man standing outside the door. The rain was falling harder still.

"I think he should be allowed a change of clothes and a cup of soup before you speak to him about it," Miss Tolerance said, and opened the carriage door.

Half an hour later, with a draft for the first sennight of her employment in her pocketbook, Miss Tolerance took her leave of Versellion. It appeared, from his demeanor, that the earl had believed she would yield to his persuasions and stay, even become a fixture in his household. Miss Tolerance had resolutely refused his hospitality.

"I have business to see to, my lord."

"Return tonight. No? Tomorrow, then."

Again she shook her head, although it cost her some little effort to refuse him. "I cannot say when, sir. I'll be about your business. If you need me, you can reach me at my aunt's establishment. But have a care with any message you send; I'm not certain there is not someone there in the pay of your enemies."

"You must bring me reports, then. Daily." He smiled. "*Detailed* reports."

"I cannot direct my inquiries from your bed, Edward." She smiled to take the barb from the words. "I shall be around and about in London for the next few days, I imagine."

"Do you mean to consult Mrs. Cunning? You will need this." Versellion drew the fan from his pocket and held it out to her. Miss Tolerance examined it for a moment, then slid the fan into her own pocket.

"Versellion, until I have some report to make to you, please be careful whom you trust."

Versellion took the hand she offered and turned it palm up, to his lips. "I place my trust in you alone," he promised, folding her fingers as if to hold the kiss in its place. She put her hand in her pocket, sketched him a bow, and left.

The rain had stopped. Miss Tolerance walked to Manchester Square.

Her little cottage, empty for only three days, was musty and cold. Miss Tolerance lit a fire and changed at last from the secondhand clothes she had bought in Reading into a round gown and kid slippers. Across the garden the lights of Mrs. Brereton's establishment glowed, warm and attractive in the drear of the night. Mourning for Matt, she thought, had not been permitted to interfere with business for long. She found herself reluctant to go across to the big house, but common sense—a wish to see if any mail had arrived, and a sudden powerful longing for her dinner—made her throw on a cloak and cross the garden.

She was greeted as a prodigal returned. First the cook, seeing her in the kitchen doorway, threw her ladle into the soup and bustled forward as if she would gather Miss Tolerance to her substantial breast. The woman simultaneously scolded her for making them all worry, and promised her the best of a fine supper. Keefe, who encountered her as she passed through the pantry, was less demonstrative, but admitted that he was relieved to see her returned. " 'Tain't no secret we was all a mite concerned, miss, the house already in mourning and all. And in the usual course of things, you give word when you plan to be away. All well, miss?"

Miss Tolerance, who was not accustomed to the notion that her whereabouts mattered to anyone but herself, assured him that all was very well. "I'm sorry to have worried anyone, Keefe. Is my aunt here?"

She was directed to Mrs. Brereton's private parlor and found her aunt seated before the mirror and applying a last delicate touch of rouge. Mrs. Brereton broke her habitual attitude of calm upon the sight of her niece, cast down the hare's foot, and rose to greet her.

"Sarah, my dear child! Where have you been? First, Matt dies, then you *disappear* for days on end. Can you not conceive of how worried we have been? And now—I've a guest coming for a *souper intime*. But will you stay and take a glass of wine?"

"Happily, Aunt Thea. I am heartily sorry to have caused such concern. How does business?"

Mrs. Brereton frowned. "Don't change the subject. Where in heaven's name have you been?" It was difficult to discern, from her tone and manner, whether Mrs. Brereton was the more relieved to see her niece safely home, or angered by her disappearance.

"I was in the country, Aunt. Following an investigation."

"You missed Matt's funeral," Mrs. Brereton said. Angry, Miss Tolerance thought. "I would have thought you would be particularly keen to attend."

"Keener to catch his killer. I did want very much to be there, Aunt. How was it?" She noted now that on the sleeve of her garnet-red dress, Mrs. Brereton wore a narrow black mourning ribbon.

Mrs. Brereton smiled. "The funeral was small but handsome. All Souls Chapel and everything Matt might have wished. None of his particular favorites came, of course, but Matt had many friends in the profession. Afterward we had a gathering here, and a cold collation, and many tears were shed quite honestly, since there was none but each other for the girls to impress. We missed you." Mrs. Brereton handed her niece a glass of Madeira. "And you were pursuing his killer?"

"I believe I was, ma'am. Did my absence cause comment?"

"A little. Some of the girls were surprised, as you and Matt had been such friends. There had been some speculation that you and he . . ." Mrs. Brereton paused delicately.

Miss Tolerance choked on her Madeira. "You should know better, Aunt. Lovers? Not unless I had learned to shave." She took another sip of wine. "What word of your political pursuits? I saw notice in the *Times* of the Queen's illness—"

"No one cares for the Queen now," Mrs. Brereton said. "It's all the Princes—Clarence and Kent and Wales—and which is most like to be named Regent in her stead. I have heard that the Queen would not hear Clarence's name spoken in the last few years—he has been heard too often criticizing her—and there is such a stink that attaches to his name on Mrs. Jordan's account. Kent's military history is so sad no one seriously believes he will be made Regent. Wales is really the most savory of the elder Princes: he merely wed a Catholic, and she had the kindness to reform him and die, removing herself as an obstacle and transforming him into an object of sympathy."

"Remarkably thoughtful of her," Miss Tolerance agreed.

"The parties are all in disarray. Lord Balobridge sent an emissary to Wales—by report—who utterly bungled the conversation. The Whigs should have jumped upon the occasion, but their best man has disappeared and no one else is so close in Wales's favor. It's catch as catch can. Every politico is trying to drop a persuasive word in the Prince's ear."

Miss Tolerance trod gently. "So the Crown party has irritated the Crown, and the opposition—lost an entire Whig? One would have thought they were too large to misplace."

Mrs. Brereton laughed, but her niece detected a speculative look in her eye. "The Whig in question being a strapping fellow,

I— Yes?" The last was directed to Keefe, who had appeared at the door. There was a murmured conference between them, and Keefe withdrew.

Mrs. Brereton set her glass down. "My supper guest has arrived, and I must say goodbye for now." She offered Sarah her cheek to kiss. "I am glad to see you home safe, dear child. Are you done now with the business that took you out of Town?"

"I hardly know how to answer you. One bit of business has led to another and another, which I think may lead me to Matt's killer. I shall be in and out for the next few days, I think, but I will call on you when I can."

With a smile that nearly masked her urgency, Mrs. Brereton brought her niece to her dressing room, which let onto the back stairs. "You will not mind, my dear?" she said, and watched until Miss Tolerance started down. From this urgency Miss Tolerance surmised the visitor was of considerable rank, or at least a man with considerable money to spend.

She went down to inquire with Cole for her mail.

Three bills, a new, and very welcome, bank draft from the estate of the late Sir Evan Trecan—not the full amount due, but above half, which was more than she ever expected to see on that particular account—and one item of personal correspondence. This Miss Tolerance took to a quiet spot just outside the kitchen to read. Its author stated that he was investigating the death of a Mrs. Smith of Leyton, and desired to speak with Miss Tolerance at her earliest convenience. It was signed Sir Walter Mandif.

Miss Tolerance regarded this letter with resignation. Balobridge had apparently made good on his threat and raked up the matter of Mrs. Smith. She did not anticipate a meeting with Sir Walter with any eagerness, but ignoring such a summons was not to be thought of. She wrote offering to call upon Sir Walter at his earliest convenience, went to the blue room, where the usual informal dinner had been spread for the house's patrons and employees, and collected a plate of food—she did not much notice what she took—which she carried back to her cottage.

The fire had taken the chill from the air. She had brought the new number of the *Gazette* with her and turned, as always, to the Dueling Notices, gratified to find that none of the recently deceased owed her money. Miss Tolerance ate her supper, drank a glass of wine, and went to bed, noting that since she had slept there last, it had become unaccountably large and empty.

Miss Tolerance was finishing her breakfast when Keefe brought word that she had visitors: two men from Bow Street, and a magistrate, whose card he delivered to her. Sir Walter Mandif had evidently been unwilling to wait until she should call upon him. Considering the matter, Miss Tolerance decided that Mrs. Brereton's establishment was not the proper venue for such a meeting, and requested Keefe to show her visitors to the little house. It was the work of a moment to tidy the room; when the three men appeared, she was just sitting down again, settling the skirts of her blue morning dress around her.

The Bow Street agents came in with the bluff certainty of men who expect their office will inspire dread. They were dressed alike in rusty black with the red waistcoats common to all Runners; the two waistcoats were different shades of red, one a bright yellowish vermilion, the other a dark scarlet. The kerchiefs tied about their necks were alike in their grubbiness; they might once have been white, but would surely never be so again; and the soles of their boots were caked with mud which flaked off upon the new-swept floor. They gave their names as Penryn and Hook, and took positions, one to the left of the door and the other to the right, as if to forestall any attempts at escape.

"Good morning, gentlemen. May I offer you tea?" Miss Tolerance asked politely.

The Runners exchanged a look; this was clearly not the expected reaction to their presence. The third man, who stood in the doorway surveying the room, spoke for the three of them.

"It is kind of you to offer, Miss Tolerance, but I doubt we shall be here long enough to require it." His voice was dry.

She had somehow expected, from his name and position, that Sir Walter Mandif would be bluff, red-cheeked, and beefy, with a booming voice and an impatient eye. The man who had entered behind the Runners was slightly built, not above medium height, with light hair brushed back from a high forehead in defiance of the current style, and a long nose which emphasized the length of his face. His demeanor was unexceptionable, his dress gentlemanly but not exquisite, and his gaze shrewd.

He bowed. Miss Tolerance curtsied and begged him and his companions to sit. These preliminaries observed, Sir Walter spread the tails of his coat and sat upon the settle. The Runners continued to stand, frowning down at her.

"You are inquiring into Mrs. Smith's death, sirs? How may I be of help to you?" Miss Tolerance asked.

The shorter of the Runners stepped forward and took a notebook from his pocket. He flicked through the pages and read from words he had obviously written there himself. He had a strong West Country accent: hard esses and tormented vowels. "Zeems as you was the last person to see the deceased Mrs. Smith alive."

Miss Tolerance responded serenely, "I cannot say that I was, Mr. Penryn. She was certainly alive when I left her one day, and as certainly dead when I returned the next. But the last person to see her alive is surely the person who killed her."

From the settle, Sir Walter said, "I take it you disclaim that honor?"

"Utterly." Miss Tolerance did not smile.

"But you did see the deceased two times in two days," Penryn said. "You ain't denying it."

"Not in the least, sir."

"And what call 'ad you to be going out to Leyton twice in two days?" the other Runner broke in. By the evidence of his voice, he was London born and bred, and unlikely upon principle to believe anything Miss Tolerance said.

She sipped at her tea and took that moment to order her thoughts. "On the first day, I visited Mrs. Smith on the suggestion

of Mrs. Cockbun of that town, to whom I was referred by the tapster at the Queen's Arms. I was in hopes she could assist me in
an inquiry I was making. We spoke briefly and then I left. On
my second visit, I had made the trip to retrieve something of
mine I had left there by accident."

"And the nature of that property?" Sir Walter regarded her
blandly. He might have been discussing fishing, or the price of
wax candles.

"A riding crop." Responding to the magistrate's expression of
polite doubt, she added, "It was a gift from a dear friend, now
deceased; I have it here if you would like to see it. I rode straight
to Mrs. Smith's, found her dead, and reported it immediately to
the justice of the peace."

Sir Walter referred to his notebook and nodded. "A Mr. James
Gilkes. He tells me that you seemed uncommon interested in
searching the deceased's household."

Miss Tolerance smiled with a blandness to match Sir Walter's.
"Does he say so, sir? Perhaps that was only in comparison with
his own lack of interest in the matter. I hoped to find evidence.
Mr. Gilkes appeared to be in hope of his dinner."

For the first time in the interview, Sir Walter Mandif's smile
conveyed sympathy. "He struck me very much the same way,
Miss Tolerance. Did you also detect a certain distaste for the
victim, based upon his notion of what she had been?"

And for myself, based upon what he believed I was, she thought,
but said only, "I did indeed, sir."

Sir Walter nodded but did not pursue the matter of Mr. Gilkes
further. "You waited upon Mrs. Smith on Tuesday morning, and
returned the next day at about the same hour?"

"A little earlier the next day, I believe."

"And in the time between, what were you doing?"

Miss Tolerance thought back. "I stopped first at the Queen's
Arms to send some wine and food to Mrs. Smith and Mrs. Cockbun, to thank them for their help. I returned to this house, did
some shopping in Bond Street in the afternoon, had a brief interview with a client that evening, and went to bed. It was not

until the next morning I realized where my crop was, and then I returned to Leyton."

"There are people who saw you during this time?"

"There is a woman in my aunt's employ with whom I went shopping; I am sure she will tell you we spent the afternoon together. I cannot give you the name of my client, sir, but there are servants here who can tell you that I had a visitor."

Mandif nodded. "That will do for now. One last thing, Miss Tolerance. May I inquire about your business with the late Mrs. Smith?"

"In a general way I can tell you I was hoping she would help me to locate another person, a retired woman like herself."

"You cannot tell me more specifically?"

Miss Tolerance shook her head and did her best to indicate her heartfelt regret. "It was upon a matter of business, and I undertake to preserve the confidentiality of all the inquiries I make, sir. To tell you more about my business with Mrs. Smith would be to risk breaking my word."

Sir Walter closed his notebook and regarded Miss Tolerance squarely. "Yours is an unusual occupation, ma'am. 'Tis not often one hears a woman refusing to tell a secret."

" 'Tis not often a woman's livelihood depends upon her ability to keep counsel, sir," Miss Tolerance said.

Hook and Penryn conferred in whispers by the door, but did not share their conclusions with the magistrate. Without turning, Sir Walter asked Penryn if he had taken down the witness's statement in the entire, and when the Runner said that he had, Sir Walter rose to his feet.

"This matter is not yet closed, ma'am. You should hold yourself available for further questioning, should the need arise."

At the same time that she was assuring Sir Walter Mandif that she would happily do so, Miss Tolerance marveled at the brevity of the interview and its relative civility. "You may always find me here, or through my club, Tarsio's. Sir Walter, is a murder in Leyton not outside of Bow Street's jurisdiction?"

"We were retained to look into it by a neighbor of Mrs. Smith who dislikes the notion of robbery and murder upon his doorstep. I cannot say that I blame him."

"And did this neighbor direct you to me?"

"Indirectly, Miss Tolerance. You spoke to the captain's wife, who directed you to Mr. Gilkes. It was Mr. Gilkes who gave us your name."

"Not the Viscount Balobridge?" she asked.

"Balobridge?" Sir Walter seemed genuinely surprised. "The politician? No, why would he? I have not the honor of Lord Balobridge's acquaintance."

Now it was Miss Tolerance's turn to smile blandly. "I am delighted to hear it, sir. The viscount had asked me for information which I could not provide to him, and he threatened to lay information with Bow Street about my involvement in the matter of Mrs. Smith's death."

"And how the devil did he know of it? Well, permit me to put your mind at ease upon this point, Miss Tolerance. Bow Street is not in the custom of fulfilling threats, even for such notable peers as Lord Balobridge." Sir Walter bowed again and left, with the Runners falling into step behind him, a quite military parade through Mrs. Brereton's quiet garden.

The morning mail brought a letter from Versellion which enclosed the note she had given to Mrs. Virtue to guarantee the purchase of the fan. Across it the words *Obligazion Redeemed* had been written in small black capitals, and the initials *F.V.* Miss Tolerance was shocked to realize that in the turmoil of the last several days, she had completely forgotten the marker; being reminded of the obligation by its redemption was pleasant indeed. Also in Versellion's letter were banknotes—"against the expenses of further inquiry." Miss Tolerance at once sat down with her counts-book, wrote the sum in, and struck off a number of expenditures against it. That done, she sent a note to the stables to arrange for the hire of a horse, changed her clothes, and set off for Greenwich and Mrs. Deborah Cook, once Deborah

Cunning, to authenticate the Italian fan for good and all.

As Miss Tolerance had expected, Mrs. Cook was not only at home, but delighted to see her. Her round face beamed as she sent the maid for tea and cakes. They waited, talking of unexceptional things. When the tea had been brought and poured out and partly consumed, Miss Tolerance took the fan from her pocket and presented it to Mrs. Cook. The older woman opened the fan and smoothed its silk with tender fingers before she looked up, her eyes bright with sentimental tears, to announce that it was indeed the fan she had been given by Versellion's father five-and-twenty years before.

Miss Tolerance thanked the woman, slipped the fan back into her pocket, and asked casually if there had ever been any secret history attaching to the fan. Mrs. Cook denied it, although her romantic soul clearly longed to be able to answer in the affirmative.

At last Miss Tolerance took out her pocketbook and extracted several of Versellion's banknotes from it.

"But my dear—" Mrs. Cook's pretty, broad face flushed, and the frills on her head rustled as she shook her head. "This is *twenty pounds.* I cannot accept such a sum for the very little assistance I have given you."

Miss Tolerance smiled. "And I cannot give less," she replied. "It was my client's expressed desire." She told the lie without hesitation. "To compensate you for any pain these recollections might cause you. But you must promise me that you will not spend it all on cakes and novels."

Mrs. Cook shook her head, briefly speechless. She offered again to share the largesse with Miss Tolerance, who refused with thanks. Shortly afterward, Miss Tolerance made her adieus and left.

She rode back to London, meditating upon the fan in her pocket. What was it about that gaudy, pretty thing that could cause two deaths and such turmoil? It was an expensive toy, to be sure: silk, gold, and diamonds. But she had found no secret other than that odd Italian note, and that was certainly of a more recent vintage than Versellion's family mystery. Miss Tolerance realized now that she had been hoping that Mrs. Cook would deny that this was her fan—then at least they would have known that the mystery was still soluble, that the real fan, if found, would yield up the secrets for which Mrs. Smith and Matt Etan had died.

The fan in her pocket bounced gently against her thigh with each step her horse took. Was the secret only a fever dream of Lady Versellion's? Had Mrs. Smith and Matt died to secure that secret or to keep it hidden? Had she and Versellion, in three days of scrutiny, missed some clue in the fan itself, some code or secret writing? That smacked entirely too much of the overblown romances Mrs. Cook favored, and Miss Tolerance could not bring herself to believe it. Had a secret been removed from the fan by one of its owners—Humphrey Blackbottle or the redoubtable Mrs. Virtue? Had that secret been exchanged for the extraordinary letter on Italian horticulture that she and Versellion had found hidden in the hollow stick?

Miss Tolerance looked up and realized that she had not yet crossed the Thames. She was within easy distance of the apartments where she had once met Humphrey Blackbottle. With a frown of distaste for the neighborhood, the house, and the gentleman himself, Miss Tolerance turned her horse toward Blackbottle's rooms and Clink Street.

Thirteen

Daylight made no improvement to the environs of Clink Street. The streets which by moonlight had been pitch-dark and empty were, in the light of day, still shadowy, but packed with people and their works. If the bills that plastered every wall were any indication, the citizens of Southwark were martyrs to dangerous ills of every sort, for which cures were urgently advertised. Local amusement was not limited to drink and venery; Miss Tolerance sidestepped an argument between the owners of two cocks set to peck each other's eyes out later for the gratification of the crowd. The scent of food from the cook shops mingled unpleasantly with the smells of offal and ripening garbage. The door to Blackbottle's Clink Street establishment stood open, presumably to let in any breeze. Miss Tolerance could not but wonder what effect the smells admitted thereby had upon custom.

When she entered the house, she found little evidence that anyone but herself minded the stench. A few girls sat in the parlor, fanning themselves wanly. The doorkeeper—a different person from the fellow who had attempted to rob her on her last visit—sat just inside the door, balanced so far back on the legs of his chair that Miss Tolerance expected to see him fly backward, arms pinwheeling, at any moment. When he saw her, he immediately straightened up, glowering.

"We don't serve *your* sort," he said.

Miss Tolerance smiled politely. "What sort is that?" she asked.

His eyebrows drew together and he frowned more fiercely. "She-mollies. Bully girls." Where the other doorkeepers at Blackbottle's establishments had by moonlight seen no harm in Miss Tolerance's man's dress, this fellow clearly thought it an abomination of the deepest stripe. "The girls here are *good* girls," he growled.

"I cannot tell you how relieved I am to hear it, sir," Miss Tolerance said. "You set my mind greatly at ease. If Mr. Blackbottle is available, I have some business with him."

The doorkeeper hesitated, clearly unsure of what to do.

"Please do not let my dress deceive you. I have not come seeking employment, nor have I come—if I understand your objections—to seduce any of the women employed here." Miss Tolerance smiled precisely the smile she would have given a hansom driver who had taken the longest route and expected to be paid for it.

The doorkeeper leaned back.

"There is a coin in it for you if you give your master my message *now*," she added.

The man stared at her a moment longer, then stood and started heavily up the stairs. Miss Tolerance called after him, "Tell him that Miss Tolerance, who found him in Heeble Lane a few nights ago, requests the pleasure of a few moments of his time." The man trudged up the stairs without pause, his square back hunched up to his ears. He gave no sign of hearing.

Miss Tolerance took the chair the doorkeeper had lately vacated and sat down to wait. A few minutes later, a heavy woman in a yellow dress came to the head of the stairs and asked if Miss Tolerance was the lady waiting to see Sir Humphrey. When

Miss Tolerance replied that she was, the woman jerked her head to direct her to the third door on the left.

Had anything been required to draw Sir Humphrey Blackbottle to her memory, the violet dressing gown he wore would have done it. Sir Humphrey wore the garment over a shirt with exquisitely starched collar points and a lavishly folded cravat, the dandified effect somewhat spoiled by the old-fashioned half wig that sat sloppily on his head, and a thin stain of red—Miss Tolerance suspected claret—that ran across the belly of his shirt. He was sitting at a desk with a number of papers and a counting book ranged around him, but when he saw his visitor, he rose to greet her with every evidence of gladness.

"There, and I thought I'd never see your pretty phyz again, dear lady. Come and take a glass of wine with me!" He reached across to a table where a decanter sat, and several imperfectly cleaned glasses. Miss Tolerance had no difficulty in refusing the libation.

"Well, what can I do for you?" The whoremaster stared at his visitor with bright, bloodshot eyes.

"You were very helpful to me the other evening, sir, but I wonder if you could answer one more question in the matter we discussed. You bought Mrs. Cunning's jewelry from her, including the fan I mentioned. Did you buy any other fans at that time?"

Blackbottle drained the claret from his glass in one gulp. Several new, tiny red spots joined the earlier stain on his shirtfront. "I was buying up jewelry in those days—a business investment, you could call it, my dear. I had in mind to open a new house, an elegant, high-class affair like the one your auntie runs in Manchester Square—you thought I didn't know you was Mrs. Brereton's niece, did you? I have my ways." His grin was full of blackened teeth. "I thought to deck out my girls in silk and trumpery and make the custom pay according."

"You did not open the brothel of which you speak?"

The man rolled the stem of his glass between two fingers as if it had some oracular value. "In the end I didn't, no. Seemed a better idea when I was thinking than when I started in. Too much capital outlay, you know. Couldn't find girls of the sort I wanted. You'd have done nicely, now." He grinned. "I'd have given you a brooch or two, my love."

"It's kind of you to say so, sir," Miss Tolerance said. "May I ask to whom you gave the fan when you bought it, sir?"

Blackbottle shrugged heavily. "Thought I'd told you that. Fanny—Mrs. Virtue. I gave her a mortal lot of pretties over time. Sweet piece of business Fan was in her prime, half a dozen lordlings and worshipfuls weeping for a bit of her."

"But the fan was in her hands all these years?"

"I imagine so; not like Fanny to let a gewgaw out of her hands. But you'd do best to ask her. She might even tell you true." He grinned, leaned back, and eyed Miss Tolerance up and down. "I don't ken what you're playing at, my darling. Pretty girl like you should be in keeping with some rich gent. You think me a vain old Beau Nasty, but I've connections. I could do you good."

Miss Tolerance shook her head. "I appreciate your concern, sir, but I'm afraid that would not suit me."

"You'd come used to it. Must have been once, to be what you are."

"What I am is no whore, sir."

"Halfway to one, sweet." Blackbottle's hand shot out to grab her wrist. "Stay and talk. I'd be a fool to let a pretty one like you out of my hands."

Miss Tolerance reached down and disengaged his hand. Blackbottle was strong, but he was also, despite the hour, half drunk. He rocked backward, holding his wrist, scowling at her.

"I'll call Bobby upstairs to civilize you. He'd like that; he come over all moral about the way you're dressed."

"I shall remember to wear sprigged muslin and kid slippers the next time I call." Miss Tolerance was pleased that her tone was unruffled; she did not feel so calm. "For now, please believe that civilizing me would require far too much—what did you call it?—capital outlay. I'm sorry to have disturbed you."

Miss Tolerance bowed slightly and took her leave. At the head of the stairs she looked down and saw Bobby, the doorman, sitting on the last step, his beefy back to her. She had her foot on the riser to descend when something, perhaps the sound of a breath taken sharply inward, made her turn. At the end of the hallway a slender man, too well dressed to be a local, stared at her for a moment before he went into a room. The door closed behind him and Miss Tolerance heard a woman's voice, raised in greeting. Miss Tolerance turned and went down the stairs.

It was not until she had gained the street and reclaimed her horse from the boys she had paid to watch it that she realized who the man had been. Sir Randal Pre, whom she had recently stopped from cutting the throat of one of her aunt's whores. It was unsettling to encounter a man whom last she had seen swearing and vowing vengeance. Miss Tolerance did not regard it as more than coincidence; there were many brothels in London, but not so many as to render impossible an encounter with a familiar face.

It was now midafternoon. Mrs. Cook had confirmed that the fan she sought was the fan she had received from Mrs. Virtue. Now it seemed she must speak to Mrs. Virtue again. Once she had crossed the Thames, Miss Tolerance turned in the direction of Cheapside. On this third visit to Blackbottle's brothel, the doorman, Joe, greeted her with a bob of his head and told her with polite regret that Mrs. Virtue was out of the house, shopping for gloves. Even the offer of sixpence did not change the doorman's story, and given that he offered her a chair to wait in, and even suggested that she might be more comfortable in Mrs. Virtue's own rooms, Miss Tolerance surmised that the bawd was truly out of the house. She left her card, with a note to the effect that, as it had been before, a meeting would be to Mrs. Virtue's advantage, and went home to Manchester Square.

Miss Tolerance returned her hack to the stable, where she was advised that the horse she had taken to Richmond and thence to Oxford had been returned by Versellion's groom, and the bill discharged. Pleased by this news, she returned to her cottage, changed her dress, and, having an errand to do, went out to Bond Street, accompanied by Marianne and Chloe and the required maid. Chloe had forgotten both her gratitude and her irritation with Miss Tolerance, and chatted about bonnet patterns until Marianne rolled her eyes at Miss Tolerance in mock horror. She was near Miss Tolerance in age, a fair, plump, pleasant-looking woman with a brisk, friendly manner. Miss Tolerance found it difficult to imagine her as an object of passion, but Mrs. Brereton had assured her before that Marianne had a small army of faithful followers. They reached Bond Street, bought gloves and stockings at a shop on a side street, and turned back to Manchester Square. As they approached the corner of the Square, Miss Tolerance noted several men in deep discussion at the corner of the street nearest her aunt's doorway, a very unexceptional thing until one of them broke away from his fellows and called to her.

She stepped away from her companions and waited. The man who approached seemed familiar to her, but she was sure she had never spoken to him. _I must be tired,_ she thought. _That's twice today I've failed to put a name to a face._ The man came possessed of a neat brown coat, light pantaloons, and Hessian boots. His hair was dark, his face long and well shaped, and his eyes very blue. He walked slowly, examining her. His expression was not pleasant.

"Well," he drawled, when he was a few feet from her. "My cousin's whore."

Miss Tolerance felt her face flush, and her hand tightened on the bundle she held. "I'm sorry, sir. I think you mistake me for someone else." She nodded her head and turned back to Marianne and Chloe.

"I say you are my cousin's whore." The voice was louder this time. Miss Tolerance glanced over her shoulder at the man. She knew now where she had seen him before, quarreling in the street with Versellion. "He has you poking through all the stews in London on his business, I hear." The man, whom Miss Tolerance now believed to be Sir Henry Folle, stepped closer, lowering his voice to tones almost intimate. "As you're a businesswoman, I'll make you an offer for more pleasant work than interviewing Southwark bawds. You come home with me and I'll pay treble what my cousin Edward has; you can whisper me his secrets while I'm—"

"My dear sir," Miss Tolerance interrupted. " 'Twould be a generous offer if I had any idea of what you meant. But even were I the woman you believe me to be, I doubt I would like to have my business noised about in the public street."

Folle pressed forward as if to intimidate her. "If you weren't doing my cousin's business, why were you there? I hear you don't do your whoring here; do you give Blackbottle's the benefit of your—"

Miss Tolerance stepped in and laid a gloved finger across his lips to stop him. The gesture was gentle, almost as if they were conspirators. Behind Folle she sensed, rather than saw, the men who had been talking to him as she came home, watching the contretemps with interest. She raised her voice a little to reach that audience.

"Sir Henry, you are drunk with anger. I suggest you let your friends take you home, that you might sleep it off. And next time try a more wholesome brew, or I shall be tempted to fetch my smallsword and answer you with it." She kept her eyes on Folle's face, but heard his companions in agitated conference. She took her finger from the man's lips. "May I bid you good afternoon?"

As she stepped back, Folle raised his hand—and his walking stick—as if to strike her. Miss Tolerance had already moved in her mind through the steps she must take to stop the blow and use the man's weight and height to throw him to the ground. She was not put to these straits. Two of Folle's companions joined them, restraining Folle, murmuring good counsel about the disagreeable consequences attending public brawls and scandal. One man, an unremarkable fellow of middle years, took Folle away with him; this left Miss Tolerance standing with the other: Lord Trux.

In the wake of the confrontation, Miss Tolerance felt suddenly exhausted. Her heart was racing, her face flushed, and her hands were not entirely steady. She stood looking blankly at the cobbles at her feet; there was a sparse scatter of color across a few of them: dried flowers. *Folle must have had the stuff in his pocket,* she thought. Lavender and verbena drifted across the polished toes of Trux's boots and disappeared down the street. Miss Tolerance cleared her throat and clasped her hands together to force them to steady.

Trux seemed unaware of all this, or perhaps too much aware of his own discomfort to mind hers. Sweat beaded his upper lip, and he was wheezing, whether from exertion or the heat, Miss Tolerance could not tell.

"Must make my apologies for Folle," Trux muttered. "Had a bad day, ain't like him to . . ." Words appeared to desert him. "Ain't like him, beg you to believe it," he repeated. Then, as if remembering that a business relationship was supposed to be existing between them, he adopted his more usual tone of irate condescension. "I have not received any report from you in days, Miss Tolerance. Have you nothing to say to me?"

Miss Tolerance looked around her. "When I last saw you in Oxford, my lord, you were in no situation to receive such a report; I hope your head is feeling better? As for this moment, Sir Henry has drawn a good deal of attention to my aunt's doorstep. Surely you do not wish to have a discussion here?"

Trux nodded importantly. "Of course not, I never meant—perhaps—"

"If you would be so good as to call upon me at Tarsio's in an hour, sir? I shall be very happy to discuss the matter with you then."

"An hour? Better make it an hour and a half." Trux inclined

his head in lieu of a bow. "Again, apologies for Folle. Not like him in the least."

Miss Tolerance turned back to the house. Chloe and the maid had already gone inside, but Marianne still stood upon the step.

"I was about to call Keefe," she said. "I imagine you can hold your own with words, but blows?"

Miss Tolerance smiled grimly. "Do you know the gentleman? Would he actually descend to brawling in broad day with an unarmed woman? I can hold my own with blows well enough. But thank you, all the same," she added more kindly. "My aunt would not be happy if I started a brawl upon her doorstep."

Marianne shook her head. "That she would not. But it was he who came a-purpose to start a fight, and he didn't much like that you wouldn't take his bait." She paused, her hand upon the knocker of the door. "It bothered you, though, I saw that right enough. That he called you a whore."

Miss Tolerance considered with whom she was speaking and measured her words. "It bothered me that he thought I could be bribed to tell a client's business."

"Oh, yes, no one likes to be accused of that," Marianne said matter-of-factly. The door opened and she stepped inside. "It's as Mrs. Brereton says: even a whore has her reputation to think of, and her perhaps more than other folk." She smiled, handed her parcel to Cole, and started up the stairs. Miss Tolerance was left with the uncomfortable feeling that there was more to be said upon the subject.

M iss Tolerance took a chair to Tarsio's an hour later, a more anonymous and thus safer conveyance for a woman in London alone. She was deposited at the door under the watchful eyes of Steen, the doorman, and went directly to the Ladies' Parlor, which, at this hour, was somewhat deserted, the hour being too early for the actresses who frequented the club after the theaters had let out. She ordered a bottle of claret and two glasses, and sat reading the *Gazette*.

Trux arrived well past their appointed time. Miss Tolerance, hearing the whispered conference with which he was directed to her, raised her head and watched him advance through the empty room as if he were the center of all attention. His *amour-propre* had been firmly reinstated, and he appeared as ready to condescend to Miss Tolerance as ever he had done. Miss Tolerance noted now what she had not seen that afternoon: a blotch of purple bruising near Trux's left ear, which she imagined extended well up into the scalp.

"Good evening, sir. Will you take a glass of wine?"

Trux stood over her for a moment, bowed curtly, and spread the tails of his coat to take his seat. He took no wine until he had inspected the bottle and nodded sagely.

When both of them had sampled the claret and found it drinkable, Miss Tolerance broke the silence which had fallen between them.

"Can *you* give me any idea, my lord, why Sir Henry Folle believes that I have been investigating in the Southwark stews?"

She had expected Trux to become defensive. Instead, "That was Pre; he swore he saw you there and came to Folle to tell him—"

Miss Tolerance raised her eyebrows. "Sir Randal is another of Folle's creatures?"

"Another? Do you imply that I am one?"

"Why should you think so, sir? I have had occasion in the last week to encounter persons who appear to be working against my client; I had come to the conclusion that Sir Henry might be one of those opponents, just as you, of course, are my client's friend."

She placed no satirical emphasis upon the statement, yet Lord Trux appeared more uneasy than ever. He changed the subject.

"I am surprised to see you do not wear black gloves—I had understood that your house was in mourning. A very sad thing, from what I hear."

Miss Tolerance wondered how Trux would have heard of Matt's death.

"I only learned of it in a chance way," Trux went on. "Had I not known the name, I doubt I would have attended to what I did hear."

Now she permitted herself a little surprise. "Did you know Matt, my lord? Then you will remember he was a very sweet, good-natured fellow. I cannot imagine why anyone would kill him—and such a savage death, beaten as he was. His face was nearly unrecognizable."

Trux blanched. "I had not heard he was beaten." He swallowed. "But you do not wear mourning for him?"

"The events of the last week have kept me very occupied, my lord. All my ribbons are being changed to black, but that's at the convenience of my aunt's seamstress; I mean no disrespect to my friend. But now—you had called for a report upon *your* friend's business."

"Then there is progress to report?"

"There has been, but as your client made himself known to me—as you will have realized from our meeting in Oxford—is there really any sense in reporting to you rather than him?"

Trux looked nonplussed. Had he not understood, in meeting the two of them together, that she and Versellion were in each other's confidence? As Miss Tolerance awaited his response, a disquieting thought occurred to her. Was it possible that Versellion had never been the "friend" for whom Trux acted? That the person for whom Trux had acted had been Balobridge or Folle, and that Versellion had neatly inserted himself into the tale and won her to his service? *Stupid, stupid, stupid,* she thought. *Was I blinded by his charm and those damned dark eyes? Or—*

"I suppose you are correct," Trux said. "But as I had engaged you to find the fan, and as, when I encountered you and Versellion in Oxford, he said nothing upon the subject, I could not be certain that he had revealed himself to you. And I must admit"—he smiled unpleasantly—"to a certain amount of curiosity in the matter."

Miss Tolerance closed her eyes upon her relief, then opened them again and stared directly at Lord Trux. "I understand completely. But I hope you will have the justice to acknowledge that satisfying the curiosity of a man so deeply in the confidence of Lord Balobridge and Sir Henry Folle would hardly reflect the discretion which so pleased you when you hired me."

There was sweat again on Trux's upper lip. His pinch-nosed condescension had changed almost comically to bewilderment.

"I know that the gentlemen with whom we had our disagreement in the Physick Garden were your hirelings," Miss Tolerance ventured. "But were the others yours? The men who attacked us on the Richmond road, and the ones who pursued us? No?"

Trux shook his head. He looked as if he were entranced, staring at Miss Tolerance with the fixed expression of a rat regarding a snake. "No. That was . . ."

"Balobridge or Folle?"

There was no subtlety in Trux. He sighed heavily. "I suppose Versellion must have realized sooner or later."

"That you had left his camp? I rather think so; a drastic conversion, if you will forgive my saying so, Lord Trux. Not only have you attempted to have a man murdered—"

"Not murder! I would never condone murder, even for—it was only to—"

"Not only have you attempted to have your former patron murdered, but you have turned cat in pan, switched parties entire—a chance step at such a time, and one that might see you labeled as an opportunist, even if you escaped hanging as murderer."

"*They were not hired to murder him!*" The words rang loud in the empty room. Trux looked around him, then continued more quietly but with some intensity. "Just to stop him returning to London. Balobridge persuaded me that changing parties was to my best advantage—"

Comprehension dawned on Miss Tolerance. "By which I apprehend he used the threat of some bit of old scandal to motivate you. I think that must be one of my Lord Balobridge's favored tricks. But you did not hesitate long or hard—nor did you ask for Versellion's help."

"That's an easy thing to say, but I had no idea where Versellion was, and less faith that he would assist me. Things are at a delicate place with me, and the wrong gossip could ruin me. Versellion never valued me as he ought, let me be his errand boy, waiting until he should have a bone—or a pocket borough—to throw at me."

"And Lord Balobridge has been more immediately satisfying? Was it he who hired the men who attacked Versellion in Richmond?"

Trux pursed his lips. "You're not the only one can keep a secret to advantage."

"I see. Then it was Folle?" Trux's expression gave nothing away. Miss Tolerance tried one more shot drawn at random. "My lord," she asked gently, "was it a . . . friendship . . . with Matt Etan that Lord Balobridge used against you?"

Three women, laughing, entered the room at that moment. Trux lurched forward in his seat, and his head swiveled around to see who the noisemakers were. Then he turned back to Miss Tolerance, plainly exerting himself to regain countenance. When he spoke, it was as employer to a hireling.

"You will tell me nothing of the matter for which I hired you?"

"As I am already in contact with Lord Versellion, for whom you were acting, such a report is redundant, my lord. But please: will you not let me help you in dealing with pressure from Lord Balobridge?"

"I am convinced that my future lies with the Crown party, Miss Tolerance. If you can be of no real assistance to me, I will take my leave."

He rose from his chair, trembling perceptibly. Miss Tolerance rose also, and they exchanged courtesies. Her dislike of the man was as firmly established as ever, but now she was aware as well of a strong sense of pity for a man whose ambitions so far outstripped his ability to attain them.

Fourteen

After Lord Trux's departure, Miss Tolerance called for paper, pen, and ink. Her first thought was merely to write a report to Versellion, but upon consideration she decided it would be safer to meet with him. That her spirits lifted at the thought was, she reminded herself, nothing to the point. She wrote a brief note to request an appointment, couched in businesslike terms. Her only concession to romance was to subscribe herself Sarah rather than her usual ST. The note completed, she left Tarsio's long enough to find an idle street-sweep and dispatch him to Versellion House with the note, sixpence, and the promise of another sixpence should he return to Tarsio's with a reply for her. This accomplished, she returned to the Ladies' Salon and took up the *Times* and her claret glass.

To an observer, Miss Tolerance appeared wholly absorbed in her perusal of the *Times*, but this was not true. Her eyes passed over the pages unseeing, her mind occupied in unsettled meditation. She read the text of the Shipping News twice before realizing that it was not the Dueling Notices. The arrival of a footman with the news that an unsuitably grubby boy had appeared at the service door asking for Miss Tolerance was a welcome distraction. She followed through the back halls and found her messenger waiting in the torchlit mews, one hand extended for the promised sixpence, the other clutching a grubby paper. Miss Tolerance exchanged coin for paper and ordered the boy to wait; stepping back into the house, she requested the cook to give the boy a plate of food and lay the charge to her account. This done, she returned to the Ladies' Salon.

Come tonight. I will wait for you here. The note was unsigned and there was no crest to identify its sender, but she recognized Versellion's brisk writing.

Miss Tolerance took up her bonnet, asked Steen to order a chair for her, and left the club. The hour was now close upon nine; crested carriages thronged the streets carrying girls attending parties, men off to their clubs to reduce their fortunes playing at whist and faro, dowagers superintending the mating dances of their daughters and sons. There were also, as she knew, pickpockets, dollies, and elbow shakers moving among the crowds. She was struck with a sense of moving through two worlds and belonging to neither.

The chair arrived at Versellion House.

She was not made to wait for Versellion; indeed, she was barely in the house when he appeared on the stairs and took her into his custody. His smile, more than his words, bespoke his pleasure in seeing her.

"You have made some progress in my inquiry?" he asked for the benefit of the listening servants. He brought her up to a small saloon on the first floor, saw her seated, and offered her wine. "Have you eaten? Will you dine with me? Excellent." He rang for the butler, gave orders for covers to be laid in half an hour, and saw the door closed behind the man. Then he stepped back to her and drew her up, into his arms. The kiss was long.

"I had begun to think you regretted this," Versellion said lightly. His breath stirred her hair. "I should hate to think you'd had your way with me and now meant to abandon me to my fate!" Miss Tolerance heard the tease in his voice and, a moment later, as if he had only just parsed the meaning of his words, the dismay. "My God, I did not intend, I only—"

She laid a finger across his lips. "You were joking. I take no offense. Indeed, it has been a day for such comments, most not nearly so sweetly meant."

"What, has someone said something to hurt you?"

"Would you dash to my defense?" She laughed and let her head rest on his shoulder. "I hope you will not. Making our liaison public would only make matters worse."

"Worse for whom? Sarah, of all people in the world, I should have thought such conventionalities were beyond you. Are you afraid to ruin my reputation?"

"Say rather that I am afraid to ruin my own." Despite her inclination to linger in his embrace, Miss Tolerance freed herself gently and took her seat again. "I have been reminded more often than I like of how little separates me from the great number of Fallen Women. Humphrey Blackbottle offered to find me a wealthy gent to keep me; your cousin Folle greeted me loudly in Manchester Square, calling me whore. You will pardon me if I am easily moved on the subject of my reputation today."

At the mention of his cousin, Versellion's smile vanished. His expression became fixed and icy, and Miss Tolerance was aware, suddenly, of a resemblance between him and Sir Henry Folle. Then, in a breath, the rage dissipated and his expression became one of concern.

"Christ, Sarah, I'm sorry. Had you spoken to him? Balked him in some way?"

"I cannot say there was any logic to it. He approached *me*; he appeared angry, but I don't know what he thought to gain. Perhaps to frighten me into some compromising admission? He did not." Turning away from the unpleasant memory of Folle's rage, Miss Tolerance noted, "I have also had a remarkable interview with Lord Trux this evening."

"Trux? What did he say for himself?" Versellion poured out claret for both of them and sat beside her.

"He owned—after some prodding—that he has indeed gone over to Lord Balobridge's camp—and not reluctantly, I gather. He fancies himself ill used by you."

"Ill used? How?" Versellion appeared as surprised as he might upon learning that his neckcloth considered itself ill treated by his wearing of it.

"It appears he had lost faith that you would ever do anything to further his ambitions. He and Lord Balobridge—"

"That idiot! I'd have found a place for him in the government once this crisis was over."

"Well, either Trux's faith in your assistance was not strong enough, or he was not satisfied that the crisis will be resolved to the benefit of the Whigs. I am strongly of the impression that money is an issue for him—"

Versellion scowled, impatient. "Of course it is, he's hip-deep in creditors. But he's landed himself a neat little heiress; I had supposed he was delaying the duns while the banns were posted."

"What a happy match for the woman who is providing the money," Miss Tolerance murmured. "Whatever his ambitions, I'm not certain Trux would have arranged the attack in Oxford without something greater at stake, some pressure, perhaps. I suspect Lord Balobridge has got hold of some ancient scandal about Trux and threatens to brew a new broth of it. If he—" She stopped.

"What?"

"I apprehend that Trux was acquainted with Matt."

"Matt?"

"Matthew Etan, one of my aunt's . . . workers. The man who was killed when I sent him to you with a message."

"I wasn't aware that your aunt ran a molly-house," Versellion said. He frowned. "Are you saying that Trux and this gussie were—"

"Stop," Miss Tolerance said loudly. Versellion looked at her, obviously startled by the force of the word. She went on a little more gently. "I won't hear such names, not even from you.

Whatever Matt was, he hurt no one. And he was my friend. As for the rest: Trux knew his name, and that he had been killed; everything else is but supposition. For a moment I wondered if he might have been complicit in Matt's death, but . . ." She shook her head. "He was too upset when I spoke of the manner of it. And you saw him in Oxford; Trux could no more beat a man to death than he could fly. He says the men he hired were told only to see you did not return to London."

"You believe that?"

Miss Tolerance sipped her wine. "*He* believes it. He would not tell me who hired the toughs who attacked us on the Richmond road. I suspect it was Balobridge; Trux would have peached on someone he feared less. But I have no evidence, and evidence is what we need."

Versellion reached across to push a curling strand of hair off Miss Tolerance's forehead. "You have been hard at work. I am afraid you have had little time to think of the fan." The hair tucked back, he continued to stroke the skin and hair by her temple. Miss Tolerance felt her cheeks flush.

"You underestimate me." She reached up, captured his hand, and returned it to his knee. The smile she gave him was, she hoped, both sympathetic and businesslike. She described her trip to see Mrs. Cook in Greenwich, and the subsequent visit to Blackbottle's Clink Street brothel. "It appears that the fan in our possession is the one we sought, and that it went almost directly from Mrs. Cunning's possession to Mrs. Virtue's. Whether it ever held a message or token that would be a threat to you or your family, I cannot say. Mrs. Cook swore she knew of no secrets to the fan when your father gave it to her; she is not the most astute observer, but I think she tells the truth as far as she knows it. As for Blackbottle—"

"Can you trust his word?"

"I had to tread delicately, as I did not want him to infer more from the questions than he gave me in answer. I don't doubt he'd try to turn matters to his own advantage if he could. He directed me back to Mrs. Virtue, the bawd from whom we bought the fan. Tomorrow I'll see her. I wonder too . . ." She paused to think.

"What?"

"If I should not seek out Mr. Hawley, who seems so absorbed by the topic of peas. The *Times* portrays his correspondence as a code designed to overthrow the government, if not support a French invasion; as he is not yet in prison, either the actual evidence is weak or he has powerful friends. I must say that the letter we saw did not appear to be coded—but whatever the message's meaning, I'd like to know how it came to be in your fan."

Further conversation was halted when dinner was announced. Miss Tolerance went in to dinner on Versellion's arm, imagining the conjecture their meeting must be subject to in the servants' hall. The meal was very fine, overample for two diners; the remains of the sole and mutton were carried off to be finished belowstairs. Miss Tolerance had little appetite and, confronted at dinner's end by an elaborate pastry and a tray of fruit and cheese, took a pear and began to peel it. She felt tired and a little melancholy.

Their conversation had been pleasantly general, suited to the ears of the footmen who waited upon them. With the servants gone from the room, "How does the Queen?" she asked.

"The same. Dying, I think, but slowly. A group has risen within the Crown party that wants to make the Duke of *Clarence* Regent, despite the bad blood between him and the Queen, and his irregular household. Balobridge will have a mutiny on his hands led by Perceval, who stands Clarence's friend. I've spoken to Wales again—he is determined that the Regency should not go to his brother, and asks me to act his friend."

"You will do so?"

"Of course. I only wish I were certain that he would commit to dissolve the Tory government once he is made Regent, and order a new one. He's playing it politically, smiling upon Whig and Tory alike. I have hope—he's always been a friend to the Whigs. It remains to see if he will be a friend to *me*."

"You have worked so hard for this. I'm sure..." Miss Tolerance began. Exhaustion seemed to lower itself upon her like a veil, and assurance deserted her. What did she know of politics and princes? "And you have hired the man from Oxford to watch after you?"

Versellion smiled. "He and another. One is in the house with me at all times—and damned irritating it is, I must say. I thought I had done with nursemaids years ago."

"I beg you will continue to take the threat seriously, Versellion. I'm glad to hear you are guarded." She sighed. "Well, it is late. I must go."

"I was hoping you would stay."

She shook her head.

"Sarah, if the things my cousin said upset you—is that why you're so cool to me?"

"I dislike the name he gave me, but ... no. I should go home tonight."

"Why?" Versellion challenged her. "What waits for you there?"

"A quiet bed and a disturbed sleep," she admitted ruefully. "I miss my friend; Matt would have teased me out of my funk at your cousin's name-calling."

"Will you not let me be your friend?" Versellion asked quietly. He moved to sit beside her, head tilted to one side to regard her seriously. Miss Tolerance longed to do what he suggested: abandon common sense and take the comfort offered her. "Sarah, stay with me."

"Tonight?"

"Tonight. Tomorrow. Always."

"Are you offering to put me under your protection, Versellion?" Miss Tolerance smiled sadly. "Your generosity does you credit, but you forget where and how I have lived. I have seen too much of what happens to women who rely upon the men who keep them outside of marriage. I am not meant to be kept that way."

"You think I would use you so badly?"

Miss Tolerance bit her lip and shook her head. "That's not the point. It would ruin me all over again. I've lost my reputation once; I cannot afford to lose . . ." She sought the words to explain. "My *professional* reputation. If I am your acknowledged mistress, moneyed women will think the better of hiring me for fear I will seduce the men they want me to follow, and men who engage me may fear I'll let your interests come before their own. Some men will believe that my services compass the use of my body. The work I have done in the last few years to create my odd profession would be for naught. I would either starve—or prove your cousin right in the name he called me."

"Your liaison with Charles Connell did not ruin you *professionally*." His emphasis on the last word was bitter.

"My liaison with Connell was over when I returned to London. I was as good as a widow—and years distant from my elopement. And to be fair, if I were the mistress of a coachman or a farmer, no one would remark it. But to be the present mistress of that notable politician, that marital prize the Earl of Versellion? How could I ply my trade and play that role? And I *must* ply my trade. Sooner or later you will want a son—a legitimate son who could inherit the title and be groomed to the political life—and you and I would part."

"If we married—"

Miss Tolerance laughed tiredly. "After two nights together, am I so irresistible you would offer marriage? For pity's sake, Versellion, you were raised to be a political force! A kingmaker! You need a political wife, rich, expedient, well connected, and well spoke—"

"You are—"

"*Not* rich. *Not* well connected, as you saw in Briarton—I could not even get us a room at the inn! *Not* expedient, for while I do know some shocking things about society's best families, I will never tell them. I'm *Fallen*, Versellion. *Ruined*. Good for none of the commonplace uses of well-bred young ladies."

"Are we to part, then?" Versellion asked at last.

Miss Tolerance closed her eyes and leaned back in her chair.

"Sarah? Do you honestly tell me you don't wish to be with me?"

Eyes still closed, she shook her head. "I cannot say that . . . honestly."

He took her hand again. "Is there nothing we may give each other, then?" he asked.

Miss Tolerance opened her eyes to regard the hand which clasped her own. She thought for a long moment, as desire warred with common sense. At last she raised his hand to her lips. "Comfort, I suppose," she said. For the second time in their acquaintance, she felt as if she had stepped out into a void with nothing more than hope to buoy her up.

Versellion smiled. "Comfort is no little thing." He turned her hand in his and raised it to his lips as he might a glass to toast with. "Wait but a few moments."

He rose, went to the door of the dining room, and spoke with someone in low-voiced conference for several minutes. Miss Tolerance closed her eyes again.

"Most everyone but my valet and Murrett, the guard you had me hire, have gone to bed. I have sent word up to Park that I will valet myself tonight. Which leaves only Murrett, and like you, discretion is part of the service he undertakes to provide for me. I cannot swear that no one will know or imagine that you are here with me, but I will promise not to blazon it about—however much I might like to do."

Miss Tolerance smiled. "I suppose your cousin may have my aunt's house watched to see if I return," she teased.

If mention of Folle disturbed him, Versellion did not let her see it. "I thought all you required was that it *not* be seen that you were stopping here—I did not think to establish that you were sleeping elsewhere." He sat next to her again and took her hand, as easily as if they had been lovers for a score of years. Miss Tolerance smiled. For half an hour they sat, handfast, talking easily of very little. At last they went upstairs.

A t some point long after they slept, Miss Tolerance woke, disoriented by her surroundings. She lay quietly for a few moments, taking in the warm fall of velvet curtains around the bed, the gleam of moonlight on the silver candlesticks on the table near to hand, and Versellion sleeping soundly beside her. It occurred to her that all these things might once have been hers by right. She mused upon this until she felt a danger of self-pity; then she turned, shaped herself to Versellion's body, and closed her eyes to sleep again.

T he sun was only barely risen when she woke again. This time Miss Tolerance rose and dressed, intending to leave the house before her inevitable discovery by Versellion's servants. She permitted herself to sit beside Versellion, still sleeping, for a few moments before going; there was a writing table across the room and she considered leaving him a note, but in the end could not think of anything to say that would not be sentimental or pathetic. Instead, she pushed his dark hair from his face, as if she could communicate by touch those sentiments which she could not voice.

" 'Wilt thou be gone? It is not yet near dawn,' " he murmured. His dark eyes opened and he looked up at her with evident pleasure.

"It's some time past dawn," Miss Tolerance replied matter-of-factly. "I ought to have gone half an hour ago."

He laughed at her. "Literalist! Will you not stay to take a cup of chocolate?"

Miss Tolerance shook her head. "And undo all your discretion? Two cups of chocolate delivered to one room will earn you a reputation for gluttony, or tempt more conjecture on the part of the kitchen staff. I must go." She meant to brush her lips against his in farewell, but he caught her face between his two hands and kissed her thoroughly.

"Come tonight," he urged her.

She threw caution to the winds. "If I can," she agreed. Then, because to stay longer at his side seemed to invite disaster, she left him and slipped from the room, and out of the house unnoticed.

M iss Tolerance was aware, walking back to Manchester Square, well wrapped in her cloak, that she was more tired than she liked. It had not been late when they retired, but in the natural order of things, it had been some time before they slept. Her sleep had been disordered by dreams and waking. All the exertions of the last ten days seemed now to be making themselves felt; she ached, her head felt gluey, and the bustling dawn streets of London seemed vague to her. *A cup of tea*, she thought.

She let herself into the garden through the gate on Spanish Place. The notion of a cup of tea was so enticing that it seemed she could not wait until her own water was drawn and heated. A kettle would be on the hob in Mrs. Brereton's kitchen; she went there first. Cook was making scones and overseeing the slicing of bacon; one of the sculleriers was hulling berries, another stirring something in a bowl, and another readying dishes to receive all this food. Cook, who had looked up from her labors, commented that Miss Tolerance looked like death and prescribed tea and scones.

"I'll have Jess bring 'em round to you if you like, miss."

Miss Tolerance shook her head. "I'll take a cup of tea back with me, and thanks. You've all enough to do, I see."

Jess, the youngest of the scullery maids and the most recently in Mrs. Brereton's employ, grinned. "Ma'am's got that great old lordship this morning, and the ol' man likes to be out and about before the neighbors know what's what. I already took up her tray—"

Cook boxed the girl's ear in a flurry of flour. "An't I tol you enough times, there's to be none talking about the guests?" she scolded over Jess's wails. "Specially *Ma'am's* guests. You'll wind up on the streets, girl."

Jess nodded penitently, one shoulder raised to ward off a second blow, but Cook had gone back to her scones, having made her point. The girl sidled away from Cook and poured a mug of tea for Miss Tolerance from the warming pot by the fire.

"I'll bring you round a pot and some scones if you'd like," she offered.

Miss Tolerance thanked her and, hands wrapped around the mug she held, made her way through the garden to her house. She was shivering by the time she got in, despite the rising warmth of the day. She settled herself on a chair at the cold hearth, her cloak still wrapped around her, and nursed the tea, savoring the warm spill of liquid down her throat. Jess, arriving with teapot and a plate of scones, looked at her with comical dismay and laid one rough hand upon Miss Tolerance's forehead.

"Not burning up, but you've a fever, miss. An' you look like a hundredweight of misery in a bushel basket, if you'll pardon me. D'you want the doctor? Shall I send word to Ma'am you're sick?" The girl bustled around the room making up the fire, drawing curtains, looking for blankets. "You should be abed," she scolded.

Miss Tolerance, thinking of the program of work she had mapped out for the day, shook her head and started to rise. "Too much to do," she began. But she felt weak and off balance when she gained her feet, and sat down hard. "Damn," she muttered. It took effort to think clearly and consider how much work she could reasonably accomplish with a feverish cold. At last, bowing to the inevitable, she sent Jess upstairs to bring down her dressing gown and several blankets—and the invaluable *Art of the Small Sword*, should she need some soporific. When Jess at last returned to the kitchen, Miss Tolerance was well bundled, set up before the fire with her tea, the scones she had no desire to eat, and her writing desk and books to hand.

She drowsed off and on, wakened fully several hours later by a rap on the door. Marianne had brought a nearly undrinkable tisane and a copy of *Tom Jones* from the house.

"I don't think I can read just now," Miss Tolerance protested, sipping miserably at the infusion Marianne pressed upon her.

"I'd no intention to let you," the other woman said comfortably. She was dressed in a round gown and shawl and looked like a prosperous farmer's wife. "You drink that all while it's warm, and then you may have more tea to wash the taste away." She opened the book, squinted at it nearsightedly, and began to read aloud. Miss Tolerance, who had known nothing of the author except that he had been instrumental in founding the Bow Street Runners, found herself engaged, then chuckling as she listened. After an hour or so, Marianne closed the book. "That's enough for now," she said firmly, as if Miss Tolerance had been in the nursery. "You rest."

She rose and started for the door, but Miss Tolerance stopped her.

"You've been very kind. Did my aunt send you?"

Marianne shook her head. "Though she had the tisane brewed up for you. But Mrs. B is always busy with affairs in the house; it's a great lot to manage, that. I just thought . . . you seem to need a friend."

Miss Tolerance straightened in her seat and regarded Marianne with a mixture of affront and curiosity. "Why do you say that?"

"Don't know. It's just the way it seems to me. P'raps I thought you'd be missing Matt. We all do," she added. "But he was specially fond of you."

"And I of him," Miss Tolerance said. "And perhaps you're right. Thank you, Marianne."

The other woman smiled. "You rest. Someone will be over in a few hours to see to you." She took the tray with her and left Miss Tolerance to dreams in which the histories of Tom and Jenny Jones, the Allworthys and Westerns, Lords Trux, Balobridge, and Versellion, Sir Henry Folle, and various modern-day prostitutes mixed freely.

Miss Tolerance was wakened twice more to drink the horrid infusion her aunt had prepared for her; after the second time, it now being well after dark, she made her way rather unsteadily up to her bed and fell soundly asleep. When she woke again, the room sparkled with sunlight and it was after noon. She sat up, relieved to discover the room no longer danced around with her every movement. Downstairs she heard a bustling which proved, upon inquiry, to be the scullery maid, Jess, with more tea and a plate of bread and butter.

She rose and dressed and went downstairs to break her fast. Her head was clear, and while Miss Tolerance was aware of a sensation of fatigue, she could at least entertain the thought of venturing out to see Mrs. Virtue. Cole had left her mail, and she opened it without much attention until one note turned up, written in Versellion's hand. He had somehow discovered an address in London for Dr. Charles Hawley, not much more than a dozen streets distant from Manchester Square. This gave her cause to reconsider her plans for the day: Luton Street was a more prudent destination than Cheapside.

"I had hoped to see you tonight," Versellion's note finished. Miss Tolerance read this ruefully, then took up pen and paper to inform the earl that she had been indisposed, and to thank him for his assistance. This done, she gathered up her reticule, bonnet, and shawl and left the house.

She had not walked two streets away from Manchester Square before she concluded that she was not fully recovered. Miss Tolerance was not in the habit of indulging weakness, and feverish colds—associated in her mind with Connell's death—were her particular abhorrence. However, she could see no purpose in exhausting herself with the walk to Hawley's address; she hailed a hackney carriage and was taken up immediatley.

Luton Street was tidy, prosperous, but not elegant. Number Four was an older house than its neighbors, and rather shabby. The door-knocker was well polished, but the shutters and door wanted painting. The door was opened by a very young maid with freckles and an air of importance; the homely scents of mutton broth and baking bread rose from within. Miss Tolerance inquired for Mr. Hawley.

"I'll ask if he's to home," the girl offered, began to close the door, then eyed Miss Tolerance seriously and added, "You know he an't a *real* doctor, do you?"

Miss Tolerance blinked. "I beg your pardon?"

"Miss Hawley calls him the Doctor, but he can't physick you, if that's what you're wanting. He's only a teacher," she added, as if this must be a great disappointment.

Miss Tolerance smiled. "Thank you, but I don't want physicking just now. I only need a few minutes of Dr. Hawley's time upon business."

The girl nodded and closed the door; evidently the rules of the household did not specify admitting visitors to wait in the front hallway. Miss Tolerance regretted the opportunity to sit for a few moments, but composed herself to wait.

The maid returned, flushed and agitated. "Miss Hawley says the doctor ain't to home," she said rapidly, and started to close the door.

Miss Tolerance put a hand out to stop her. "Will you give him my card?" she asked. "I only need a few moments of his time." She was aware of a woman's voice scolding from the upper floors; the maid looked over her shoulder with some apprehension.

Miss Tolerance pressed her card, and a sixpence, into the maid's hand. "Please see that Dr. Hawley gets my card. Thank you."

She saw the girl pocket her card and the coin before she turned away from the door. She stood at the gate for a moment, considering where she might best find a hackney to return her to Manchester Square, when a stentorian voice behind her cried out for her to stop where she was.

Fifteen

The woman who stood on the steps of Number Four was stocky and plain-dressed, with a square, high-colored face and dark hair pulled back taut, as if to make herself as unattractive as possible. She appeared to be about five-and-forty; her manner suggested she had been bullying the household for many of those years.

She called again. "You! Stop, young woman!" As Miss Tolerance had already stopped and turned back, the command was purely for effect. "What business have you with my brother?"

Miss Tolerance stepped closer to the doorway and said quietly, "It is a matter of business, ma'am."

"I can imagine the sort of business you mean!" Miss Hawley said loudly. Apparently she had no reluctance to carry on an interview at her doorstep for any of her neighbors to hear. "A female alone, calling upon an unmarried man? This is not—this *is* a respectable household, whatever you may have encountered elsewhere. If you've come down from Oxford expecting to pick up some sort of acquaintance you had with Dr. Hawley there, you're to be disappointed. My purpose is to keep my brother safe from the likes of you. My brother is a *scientist*." She used the term as she might have said *archbishop*. "He cannot be bothered by every dubious female who presents herself at our door."

By the end of this remarkable speech, delivered in dramatic tones, Miss Hawley was very nearly shaking her fist at Miss Tolerance, who kept her own demeanor as mild as possible. It was on her tongue to inquire whether other dubious females had already called in Luton Street, but she judged it would be inappropriate at the moment: the woman clearly preferred melodrama to plain dealing.

"I am very sorry to disturb you, ma'am. I have no acquaintance at all with Dr. Hawley yet; I need only a very few minutes of his time, and in fact, the matter upon which I come relates to his scientific inquiries."

The older woman examined her visitor coolly, then turned back to the house. Miss Tolerance, already impressed by the shabbiness of the house and Miss Hawley's dress and considering the likely stipend made to a professor of ancient history, said quietly that a reward might be forthcoming for Mr. Hawley's assistance. The large woman looked back over her shoulder.

"I will not discuss the matter on my doorstep for any passing idiot to hear. Walk in, if you please."

Miss Tolerance did so, and was seated in a narrow, fussy parlor.

It appeared that the mention of money had wholly changed the tenor of their conversation. Far from protecting her brother from Miss Tolerance, Miss Hawley was now moved to confide in her, speaking rapidly.

"My brother has been so troubled of late. All manner of false accusations and charges made against him—I doubt he has the first idea what is happening on the continent these days; he may not even know that we're at war! I protect him, as I have since we were children. He lives for his work, Miss . . ."

"Tolerance."

"Miss Tolerance. Lives for his work, and I am the one who

attends to the daily matters of life, at least when he is here in London with me."

"I will not take up your time, Miss Hawley, as I am sure you are busy—"

But Miss Hawley, having found an audience, could not be stopped. She would air her grievances; Miss Tolerance could do nothing but assume a sympathetic expression and wait for the torrent to stop. "My father used to tell Charles he would never make his fortune as a scholar, and about that he was very right, I may tell you. When the King was well, things were very different, very promising, but after he was stricken—well! I'll be frank: Her Majesty's an indifferent patron, appointments are hard to come by. It's only my management has kept the household going—and my little income. Charles has no thought of money!"

The Queen's patronage, however unsatisfactory, might explain how Dr. Hawley had thus far avoided prison, Miss Tolerance thought. With that patronage in jeopardy, matters must be doubly anxietous with accusations of treason hanging over his head.

Miss Hawley had continued onward. ". . . and to say that he is even capable of treason is slander; he has never had any sense at all since we were children. If he had, he'd have been a member of the Royal Society, with everything handsome about him by now. But no, he broke with Banks and Marsden, lost his best patron, all for the sake of these experiments he finds so compelling, and that has been the end of preferment for him, let me tell you. All my saving and management? Charles spends most of *his* stipend on plants and earth and books—all very well for him, of course, but how am I to manage?"

She did not extend her hand for payment, but the action was implicit. If Miss Tolerance intended to see Dr. Hawley, she would pay for the privilege.

"I think I may be of a little assistance there, ma'am. But my time is limited," Miss Tolerance said. A pervasive smell of boiling mutton, and the pitch of Miss Hawley's voice, were making

Miss Tolerance's head ache. "I must speak to your brother now."

Miss Hawley looked mildly affronted by this uncivil hurry. She had clearly counted upon a few more minutes of unleashing her grievances before she permitted her guest to see her brother. But she rose and left the room. When she returned a few minutes later, it was to gesture Miss Tolerance to follow. They wound through the narrow hallway, down a flight of stairs, and out into a crowded kitchen garden, in the midst of which a stocky man, coatless and aproned, squatted before a vine dabbing at flowers with a fine paintbrush.

Miss Tolerance stepped forward, but was restrained for a moment by Miss Hawley, who whispered, "I beg you will not give any funds to Charles—he is so improvident! Come see me when you have done." When Miss Tolerance nodded, Miss Hawley turned and left them.

"Dr. Hawley?" Miss Tolerance surveyed the garden, which was narrow but deep. What appeared at first to be a great mass of vines resolved itself, upon inspection, into two rows of six growing beds separated by narrow trenches. The vines themselves had been secured to poles and trellised across the length of each bed. The most curious feature of the garden was that all of the plants in the left-hand beds, and nearly all of those on the right, wore small muslin bags at intervals along their branches. In the last of the growing beds, Charles Hawley finished dabbing with a paintbrush at the flower on the vine, and from a pocket in his apron drew a muslin bag and tied it around the flower to which he had been ministering. He did not turn to acknowledge Miss Tolerance's presence, but took up his brush again, dabbed it carefully in a jar, and began painting away at a new flower. Miss Tolerance observed that his face was as red as his sister's, his head almost entirely bald, with a blow-away fringe of dark hair brushing his collar. Fine-tipped brushes bristled from one pocket of his apron, a ball of twine trailed a long end from another, and the ground around his knees was littered with notebooks, pencils, and gardening tools.

Mr. Hawley did not look up when he spoke. "I beg you will

pardon me. This requires the utmost concentration, and I cannot stop what I do. Miranda says you had some business with me. Is there any hope you come from the Society?"

"The Royal Society? No, sir, I am afraid not." She tried to remember if Banks had been mentioned in the letter she held.

"Don't like to be uncivil, but why are you here, then?" Hawley looked down his nose at the flower under his brush, dabbed again, then groped in his pocket for something. "I am not much in the habit of entertaining young ladies." He held his paintbrush high, as one might a dueling pistol, rose to his feet, and retrieved a pile of muslin bags from a gardening table near the kitchen door.

Miss Tolerance decided to be direct. "I am in need to determine how a piece of correspondence mentioning your name could have found its way into a fan belonging to a friend of mine."

"Into a fan? What do you mean, into a fan?"

Miss Tolerance explained the circumstances under which the letter had been discovered. Dr. Hawley spared his visitor a glance of incredulity before he knelt and tied a bag around a flower.

"What is the sense in that?" he asked.

"I was hoping you might tell me, sir,"

The man appeared to think for a moment. "You'll forgive me, miss. I've heard more than my fill of nonsense about letters these days—idiots don't seem to understand that science cannot flourish without free exchange between— Is that the letter?"

Miss Tolerance had taken from her reticule the translation Mr. Deale had made in Oxford.

"It is a copy made in English. The letter was written in Italian, sir."

"Was it writ to Ippolito, Miracoli, or DiPassi?"

Miss Tolerance unfolded the letter. "The salutation is to a friar—"

"Ah, Ippolito. Very sound fellow, Linnaean taxonomist. May I see?" Hawley dusted off his paintbrush on the hem of his apron, where it left a pale residue, and held out his hand for the paper. Miss Tolerance handed it to him.

He scanned it through, nodding and several times making little noises of agreement or dismay, or comments to himself. "Hah! Hah! Of course the flower's color is useful datum! Patience indeed! Hmm. Hah! Question Miracoli? Soundest notion in the— Hmm. Well, yes, of course. Ah."

Miss Tolerance watched this performance with interest. Whatever information Dr. Hawley had, he would plainly have to address the contents of the letter before she could get anything more useful from him.

"But this is *old*," he said at last. "This must have been writ nearly a year ago? We've determined so much since then! Do you know plants, miss? No, no, of course not. Young women only know posies from their suitors, eh? But you must let me show you—" He jabbed the letter back at her absently, stepped over the twine barrier to her side. The sun was hot above them, but the air was fresh and blessedly free of the scent of mutton. Miss Tolerance's headache had lessened. She was prepared to listen while Dr. Hawley explained his work to her.

He was breeding peas. As he took her from bed to bed, he explained the characteristics for which he was breeding. "A pattern emerges, you see? A pattern emerges from which we may predict results, predict which trait will trump another. Tall trumps short, you see? Yellow seed trumps green. Mate a yellow seed with a yellow and what do you get?" He turned to peer at her as if she were his student.

"Ah, yellow?" Miss Tolerance hazarded.

"Precisely! Mate a yellow with a green?"

"Pale green?"

Hawley shook his head emphatically. The fringe of hair over his collar fluttered behind him. "This isn't a watercolor lesson! We seek rules here, scientific constants! The answer in both cases is yellow, do you see? Now mate that plant with a fellow of its generation!" he urged eagerly. "What do you get?"

"Yellow?" Miss Tolerance's headache was beginning to return again.

"Yes and no. A certain number will be yellow, a certain number green. But the point is that you can predict a ratio, and I swear to you, that ratio will be constant! You can predict! *Consider the applications!* Davenant still dismisses Miracoli, but *consider the applications!*" Hawley's pleasant red face grew redder still, and he was nearly shouting. "For plants, for cattle and all manner of animal breeding. Why, were we able to breed men the way we do peas, we might establish with accuracy which human traits trump which: brown hair over blond, tall over short, or—what color eyes did your parents have?"

Miss Tolerance blinked. It had been years since she had considered the matter. "My father's were blue, my mother's were brown."

Hawley nodded enthusiastically. "And your eyes are blue. Have you brothers? Sisters? What of them?"

"I have a brother. His eyes are . . ." She strove to recall. "Brown. His eyes are brown."

"So you see!" Hawley beamed.

Miss Tolerance sighed. "No, sir, I do not."

Hawley shook his head. "No more does Davenant, I fear. But he is a scientist and should know better." He shook his head. "But have you never wondered if it might be possible to determine such things?"

Miss Tolerance frowned. "I regret that I've never given the matter any thought."

"Of course you haven't. We may posit, we may have anecdotes which support Miracoli's contentions, but until we can control breeding under scientific conditions, ensure that no possibility of pollution exists, we may not draw reliable conclusions upon the subject of human traits. . . ."

As the enormity of what Hawley was suggesting occurred to her, Miss Tolerance was hard put to keep her composure. She imagined rows of beds partitioned by twine, containing blue-

and brown-eyed human subjects paired snugly in muslin bags, preparing to breed true. It put anything in her aunt's profession to shame.

Some sound must have escaped from her, for Hawley's expression changed.

"This must sound very foolish to you, my dear. But to those of us who have been discussing the matter for so many years—and you see that peas are so easily controlled. Not at all like cattle—"

"Or ladies and gentlemen," Miss Tolerance agreed. The comment missed its mark.

"Interest in science has fallen off sadly in this country. The King was intrigued by our scientific husbandry, but Her Majesty does not understand, and all her interest has been for the King's sake. But when this theory is proved, it will mean fellowship in the Royal Society at last, and . . ." He paused thoughtfully. "And this was not what you came here to learn, was it?"

"I'm afraid not." Miss Tolerance smiled; it was not difficult to be affected by Dr. Hawley's ardor. "Although you do reassure me that the letter is what it seems on its face, and not some code or cipher—"

"Of course not. We have no time for schoolboy games."

"Just so. But if you cannot tell me how the letter came to be hidden in my friend's fan, can you tell me anything else about it? When it was written, perhaps, or by whom?"

Hawley appeared to give the matter some thought. "By the comments, I'd have to say it was written no more than two years ago, and no less than a year. As to the author . . ." For the first time, Dr. Hawley appeared cautious. "I don't know who sent you."

"The fan's owner did, sir. I am not hunting out treason, if that's what worries you. Was it Mr. Davenant—"

"How do you know that name?" Hawley barked.

"You used it yourself not five minutes ago, discussing the letter."

Hawley put his hand to his head. "My tongue runs away with

me. Miranda says I must control my enthusiasm. I have no desire to call down upon my colleagues the unpleasant scrutiny to which I have been subjected."

Miss Tolerance assured him that she had no desire to create trouble for Davenant or any other of Hawley's botanical colleagues, but Dr. Hawley would not give her Davenant's full name or direction.

"Can you tell me how these letters were sent abroad?" she asked.

"We each found our own way. I sent mine to a colleague in Austria, who smuggled them from there. It's still legal to send letters," he added irritably.

"I believe it is the nature of the letters that has drawn attention," Miss Tolerance observed. "Letters to papist clerics in Bonaparte's countries—about peas! Perhaps the government may be forgiven for wondering whether they are quite what they seem."

Hawley glared at her. "What else could they be? I am as patriotic as any man living, miss, but the squabbles of nations cannot be permitted to interfere with the progress of science!"

"Oh, yes, quite so," Miss Tolerance murmured. Sensing that she had extracted as much useful information from this source as she was likely to get, she thanked Dr. Hawley for his assistance and left him bent once more over a vine, paintbrush in hand. She made her way back from the garden through the house and met Miss Hawley hovering in the hallway.

"Was my brother helpful?" she asked.

Miss Tolerance had already drawn a banknote from her reticule. She pressed it, folded, into the other woman's hand, made her farewell, and had left the house before the amount of the note could be determined and exclaimed over. Miss Tolerance fervently hoped that Miss Hawley would invest the money in poultry and beef and toss out the dismal mutton that scented the house.

Out on the street again, Miss Tolerance was immediately aware that something was wrong. She was on the verge of putting it down to headache, and perhaps too early rising from her sickbed, but something at the end of the street—the movement of a man vanishing into the mews—caught her eye and persuaded her that something truly was amiss. She walked to the corner, considering. She wore a gown, Norwich shawl, and walking boots—hardly the costume for active movement—and her sword and pistols were at home. She would have to improvise.

At the end of the street she turned onto Penfold Street and walked slowly along as if enjoying the air. There were a few more pedestrians on Penfold Street, which was not an important enough thoroughfare to teem with pickpockets and crossing-sweeps, but was not so inconsiderable as to be entirely devoid of tradesmen or casual traffic. Still, by the prickling between her shoulder blades and the less ambiguous evidence of a small mirror she had withdrawn from her reticule and used to survey the street behind her, she knew that the shadowed man had indeed followed her out of Luton Street.

This neighborhood, not far distant from her own, was not well known to Miss Tolerance. She kept watch for a mews or court-yard into which she could vanish, but it took several minutes' walking before she spied one suited to her purpose, and in the meantime, she had to keep checking the position of her unde-sired escort. When she found an arched gate which gave onto a small courtyard, she availed herself of the chance to enter it. She took a position tucked behind the stonework to the left of the gate, and waited.

Her follower arrived a minute later, paused under the arch as if to ascertain that the courtyard was empty, then stepped through. Miss Tolerance immediately stepped behind him and drew the edge of her mirror against his throat as if it were a dagger. She knew the man: he was one of the fellows who had chased her and Versellion from the inn only a week before. She had left him tied and gagged in the stable.

"I should think you would know by now how very little I care to be followed," Miss Tolerance noted coolly.

The man said nothing. He rolled his eyes until the whites

showed, trying to see what weapon she held at his throat.

"I did not have the opportunity, last time we met, to ask you why you were taking such an interest in me. But now—I really think I must inquire for whom you are working."

The man spat out a profane litany which included a considerable commentary upon Miss Tolerance's antecedents. She pulled the mirror's edge rather tighter to his throat.

"I may be all that you say, sir, but you will pardon me if I point out that this is hardly the politic moment to mention it. What is your name and the name of your employer?"

"Go to hell."

"*Your name.*" Miss Tolerance tightened the mirror's edge against his throat. He choked and relented.

"Hart," he growled.

"I presume *you* are Hart? Your employer's name?" The man writhed, trying to shake her loose. He was short and stocky, and from the way he moved, she deduced that he was the sort who relied upon brute power rather than any skill at fighting. So long as he believed she had a dagger to his throat—as she had had, the last time they met—she could keep him subdued.

"I ask again, sir. Who has set you on to me?" She pulled the mirror's edge very tight against his windpipe.

"Folle!" The man choked and gasped.

"Sir Henry Folle? And in the country, when I had the pleasure of leaving you in the stable?"

Hart flinched at the reminder, but nodded. Miss Tolerance lessened the pressure of the mirror against his throat a trifle.

"And did Folle give you any instructions today? Was I to be killed, or merely followed?"

"Followed. Though I'd kill you myself, and welcome," he muttered.

Miss Tolerance pulled the mirror up tightly again. "You persist in mistaking your situation," she said mildly. "If no one has ever advised you that it's very bad policy to antagonize someone who is in a position to cut your throat, please allow me to do so. Now: Folle merely wishes to know where I go? Well, you may tell him, if you wish. But please remember that if anything happens to any of the persons I speak to, in Luton Street or elsewhere, today or next week or next year, I shall lay information with Bow Street against you, and Sir Henry Folle, and as many of your confederates as I can. I hope that is clear to you."

The man grimaced, nodded.

Miss Tolerance, having taken the tiger by his tail, considered the best way to rid herself of the beast and go about her business. "Good afternoon, then," she murmured, and gave him a tremendous shove between the shoulder blades which sent him staggering farther into the courtyard. She turned and ran into the street, screaming for help. In the few seconds it took for Hart to turn and pursue her, half a dozen people had clustered around Miss Tolerance, who cast herself upon the bosom of a fat, elderly gentleman and wept, in a very good imitation of her old governess. Several men in the crowd started after her presumptive attacker, but Miss Tolerance called them back, moaning that if only someone would find her a hackney and ensure that that monster did not assail her again, she would be all right. In a moment or so, the hackney had been procured and the fat gentleman was handing her into it, while another man inquired again whether the lady didn't want him to blacken her attacker's eye for him. Miss Tolerance shook her head, thanked her rescuers, and implored that there would be no further violence. She then sat back and directed the driver to take her to Manchester Square. The mirror she returned to her reticule; she was interested to note that her hand was trembling, and decided that she had had all the exercise she required for one day.

W hen she rose the next morning, Miss Tolerance felt more herself than she had done for many days. She had arrived home from Luton Street, taken another dose of her aunt's vile tisane, and fallen into a heavy, dreamless slumber which lasted until the middle of the night. Waking in darkness and unable to sleep, she settled herself in with *Art of the Small Sword,* regretting *Tom Jones,* which Marianne had taken back to the house, and regretting Versellion's absence even more—until sleep overcame her again. Sleep, it now appeared, had been the medicine she most needed.

It was near noon when she woke, clear-headed and very hungry. She dressed in breeches, shirt, and waistcoat, and went across to the house to break her fast. Cook gave her a mountainous plate of food and instructed her to eat every bite, and Miss Tolerance retired with it back to her cottage to go through the mail Cole had brought her. There was a note from Versellion wishing her better health and hoping she would feel able to make a report on her progress to him shortly—into this she could be pardoned for reading a degree of warmer feeling than the words expressed. There was also, she saw, a note from Lord Balobridge, dated the day before. He had requested a meeting with Miss Tolerance on a matter of mutual interest.

Conscious of some apprehension, Miss Tolerance wrote to Balobridge regretting that she had not seen his letter earlier, and suggesting a meeting that evening at seven at Tarsio's. She sent it off with great curiosity; she had not thought Balobridge likely to make direct contact with her again after their first meeting. She was frankly curious to know what he thought he might gain now that he had not before.

At last Miss Tolerance left the house for Cheapside to call again on Fanny Virtue. The sun was very hot; she began to regret she had not decided upon a light muslin gown instead of men's clothes. The midday streets were crowded and odorous; she was happy to hire a hackney and draw the curtains to shut out the noise and smell a little. Once she stepped out of the coach in Cheapside, the heat and stench had redoubled force. She picked her way along Bow Lane to Blackbottle's house and inquired for Mrs. Virtue. The doorman, not Joe whom she had met before but some other fellow, saw the color of Miss Tolerance's coin, inquired for his employer, and was back to usher Miss Tolerance up the stairs within a minute.

Recalling her meeting with Sir Randal Pre in Clink Street, and the consequent scene with Sir Henry Folle, Miss Tolerance looked about her as she climbed the stairs to Mrs. Virtue's apartment. She saw nothing and no one of note, but heard rather more of the household's activities than she wished to. When she rapped on Mrs. Virtue's door, she was admitted at once.

Mrs. Virtue was seated at a desk this afternoon; several piles of coin and paper, and an imposing ledger, indicated that she was settling accounts. The curtains had been drawn to let in the sunlight, which flattered neither the gaudy-cheap furnishings nor their owner. There was no fire in the grate, but Miss Tolerance had the impression of smoke on the air, a sweet, earthy smell that clung to the upholstery and drapes. Mrs. Virtue's smile was brilliant as she waved Miss Tolerance to a seat and offered her refreshment.

"I begin to think you enjoy your visits here, Miss Tolerance." She let the accent fall musically on each syllable of Miss Tolerance's name. "Is there another piece of jewelry you wish to acquire?"

Miss Tolerance took the chair and refused the tea.

Mrs. Virtue smiled. "It is not drugged, I promise you. See, I drink it myself!" She poured out a cup of tea and sipped at it delicately. Her gestures had been honed, Miss Tolerance observed, so that any simple act—taking up a pen, drinking tea, or turning the page of a ledger book—appeared as a promise of carnal pleasure. That it had not the desired effect upon her visitor did not appear to bother the madam at all. She replaced her cup in her saucer.

"I only come to ask a question or two. Your assistance would be greatly valued."

Mrs. Virtue smiled and noted that she had thus far been most gratified at the value put on her assistance. "You have a most openhanded . . . employer."

"Where his interest is involved, I believe I have. Ma'am, in one of the sticks of the fan I received from you, I found a letter, and was hoping you could explain it to me."

For the first time in their brief acquaintance, Mrs. Virtue's ripe smile faltered. The artful rose of rouge upon her cheeks suddenly stood out as her skin paled. "I know nothing of such a letter," she said.

"And yet it was there, ma'am. And written within the last year or so, when the fan was in your hands." Miss Tolerance softened her tone a little. "I don't mean to alarm you, ma'am. Neither my employer nor I particularly care about the contents of the letter; my only concern is how it came to be there."

"What sort of a letter?" Mrs. Virtue asked. "How could I explain such a thing?" Her color was returning; her brown eyes were flinty, and Miss Tolerance had the impression of much rapid thought taking place behind them. The continental accent Miss Tolerance had noted on prior visits was more marked.

"It is a note between horticulturists," Miss Tolerance said. "Regarding vines. The letter is writ in Italian, and destined for a monk somewhere in that country. All I need to know, ma'am, is how that letter came to be secreted in the sticks of—of my employer's fan, which I had thought was in a box, quite forgotten, for nearly twenty years."

"Did I tell you that?" The older woman looked troubled. "I have sometimes a weakness for certain diversions which can affect the memory—"

"Opium?" Miss Tolerance asked. "I thought I recognized the scent of it. Did you forget the letter had been placed in the fan, ma'am?"

For a moment, it seemed Mrs. Virtue would respond to the sympathy in her visitor's voice. Then the madam collected herself. "What if I tell you I have no idea how this letter comes to be in the fan?"

"I will, of course, believe you," Miss Tolerance lied. "But perhaps I needn't ask about the Italian letter at all. Perhaps I need only ask if the fan remained in your hands for all the years after Humphrey Blackbottle gave it to you."

"In my hands?" Mrs. Virtue faltered for a moment, then smiled. "Ah, in my possession. Yes, it was."

"So no other correspondence could have made its way into—or out of—the fan without your knowledge?" Miss Tolerance watched the other woman closely. "It is an excellent hiding place, after all."

"You are pleased to joke with me, Miss Tolerance." The woman regarded Miss Tolerance with hauteur, her soft chin raised defiantly. The music of her voice had become a growl of displeasure, making of Miss Tolerance's name *Tolla-ranze.*

Miss Tolerance was struck with inspiration.

"As you are, I believe, Italian, I thought you might be acquainted with *Frate* Ippolito."

The cup which Mrs. Virtue held shook. She looked down at the drops of tea which marred the gauze of her gown.

"Why should you think me Italian?"

"Your accent is not strong, and your command of English is excellent, ma'am. But when you are distressed, it has a distinctly Italianate lilt. May I assume *Frate* Ippolito is not unknown to you?"

Mrs. Virtue regarded her visitor with dislike. She looked, now, years older than Miss Tolerance had previously believed. "What is it you want, Miss Tolerance?"

"I believe I have been clear on that point, Mrs. Virtue. Information, which will go no farther than to my employer's ear, I promise. You put the letter destined for Friar Ippolito in the fan?"

"If I did?"

"Was there anything else hidden in the fan before you put the · letter there?"

"What sort of thing are you looking for, Miss Tolerance? An elephant? A diamond of great worth? There was nothing in the damned fan until I placed that cursed letter there."

"Why *did* you place it there? Why didn't you send it on?"

"When it came to me, I could not—the one to whom I was to give it was delayed on the continent. Later, the risk was too great! Have you not heard some other scientist is being questioned about the letters? He has not yet been arrested, perhaps he has powerful friends. But I am a woman, a whore, and a Catholic. What do you think would happen to me?"

Miss Tolerance could imagine all too easily.

"I was very young when I came to this country, but I have prospered in my way. I have no wish to leave, and still less wish to be hanged for treason. So I hid the letter. Later, when you inquired for it, I was . . . out of myself. I take the opium for headaches. I heard the offer of sterling and forgot about the note—the habit of selling things is a hard one to break off." She shrugged.

"But if I may ask—what is your interest in all this? Why send the letters at all? You are not a botanist, surely."

"My cousin, the friar you spoke of, asked me to help him. I am very fond of my cousin, Miss Tolerance. He came between us: my father, my brothers—"

"Interceded?"

"Yes. After I was ruined, he interceded so they did not come after me when I ran away."

Without thought, Miss Tolerance said, "At least *your* father wished to bring you back."

Mrs. Virtue laughed. Her dark eyes glittered. "My father wished to *kill* me. To remove the stain on his honor, you understand. Were it not for my cousin, I would have been dead before you were born. My family—I was renamed Fanny Virtue before I was twenty, but I was born Francesca d'Ippolito." She spoke the name as if claiming a dignity long lost.

"I was Sarah Brereton," Miss Tolerance said quietly. "*My* father only *wished* me dead."

"There you see the difference between your nation and mine, Miss Tolerance." Mrs. Virtue stood up. "Whatever your master thinks to find in that fan, I give you my word of honor . . ." She paused as if the humor in the phrase had just made itself felt. "I give you the word of Francesca d'Ippolito that there was nothing in the fan I received from Sir Humphrey."

Miss Tolerance stood also. "Then I thank you. I am sorry if my questions have called up painful memories, ma'am." She bowed and started for the door.

"But Miss Tolerance, you said earlier that your openhanded employer would be grateful."

Mrs. Virtue was clearly not about to let a moment of shared feeling interfere with prosperity. Miss Tolerance sighed and took out her pocketbook. "I trust this will be sufficient?" She offered a few coins to the madam.

Mrs. Virtue examined them philosophically. "I suppose I cannot expect more for the little I have told you," she said. "Thank you, Miss Tolerance. As I do not think you will call again, it has been a pleasure making your acquaintance. And if you ever find your current profession no longer suits you, I beg you will come to me for advice."

"I thank you for your consideration, ma'am, but I am not likely to do so."

Miss Tolerance bowed and left.

Sixteen

Returned to Manchester Square, Miss Tolerance spent a useful several hours thinking and darning stockings. Her visit to Dr. Hawley she regarded as an intriguing cul-de-sac. Had she been hired to establish the criminality of that suspicious correspondence, she was confident she could have assured the Home Office that Dr. Charles Hawley, of Oxford and London, posed no threat to the nation. She had also gained a new appreciation of the extraordinary fervor with which some persons approached botany. From Hart, the tough she had waylaid, she had testimony that the attacks upon Versellion derived from his cousin Folle—some of the attacks; she was not yet prepared to acquit Lord Balobridge of involvement. And from Mrs. Virtue—née Ippolito—assurance that no correspondence other than the peculiar letter to her cousin had ever been hidden in the fan.

Of course, she thought, one must ponder the veracity of Hart, and Mrs. Virtue, and even Dr. Hawley.

At length Miss Tolerance put aside her darning, changed her dress, and asked Cole to procure a chair to take her to Tarsio's.

Despite, or perhaps because of, its raffish reputation, Tarsio's included among its members a fair number of men of good family who were drawn there by the eclectic nature of its membership and the scent of adventure that hung about the place. At a little before six in the afternoon, however, the respectable membership were at home, dressing for dinner and the evening's diversions. At this hour the actresses who held court here were gathering themselves for their departure to the theaters; the gamers nodded over gazettes and pints of ale, resting their eyes until the deep players arrived at the tables rather later in the evening. Wishing for more privacy and more discretion than this crowd was likely to afford her, Miss Tolerance took the precaution of securing a private parlor, and of warning Steen that Lord Balobridge was likely to ask for her. She then—since the hour was considerably removed from the time set for their meeting—settled down to stare at the paper and think.

Versellion would have to be told about his cousin, and Folle himself would have to be confronted. If Hart had told the truth and Folle had hired the attacks on Versellion, did it follow that he was behind the deaths of Matt Etan and poor Mrs. Smith? If Lord Balobridge featured in any of this—and he must, else why had he sent the swordsmen out after her the evening she returned from Versellion House?—why had he asked for this evening's meeting?

And the fan. That small, pretty, useless trinket. What had Versellion set in motion by looking for it, by hiring her? What would the end be?

A footman entered and announced that Miss had a visitor asking for a moment of her time. Something in the footman's manner implied that the visitor was not up to the standards of the establishment, so when Miss Tolerance asked the visitor's name, she was surprised by the answer. She looked at the mantel clock: her meeting with Balobridge was almost an hour away. "You may desire him to come in," she said. "But I have only a little time to give him."

Lord Trux was shown into the room, but it was Trux as she

had never seen him, nor imagined he could appear. It had been three days since she had spoken with him downstairs in Tarsio's Ladies' Parlor; it appeared as though Trux might have slept in an alley that whole time. The man was unshaven, his eyes bloodshot, and his hair rumpled; his clothes were creased, wilted, and begrimed. Recalling the modish peacock who had first spoken to her on the matter of the fan, Miss Tolerance could barely believe this was the same man.

Trux waited until the door closed on the salon, marched forward unsteadily, and planted himself before Miss Tolerance. He did not trouble himself to bow or even greet her. Instead, he stood and examined her, weaving slightly as he did so. He smelled of drink, and Miss Tolerance observed wine blots on his crumpled neckcloth.

"Were you a man, I'd demand satisfaction," he said at last. His voice was pitched so low, the words so slurred and sloppy with rage and drink, that it was hard to understand what he was saying. "I'd heard you was better than most of your sex, you pretend as if it's so, but it's lies. Don't even know what you are—not a woman nor a man. Just the lying whore that's ruined me."

He turned to leave. Miss Tolerance, more startled than if his attack had been physical, rose and called after him to explain what he meant. But Trux would not stop, except at the door, where he turned and spat the word "Bitch" at her before he left.

What was she to make of this? Miss Tolerance sat down again, agitated and amazed, as much by the degree of rage Lord Trux had shown her as by his words. She went over her recollection of their last meeting; she had let him know that she believed him to have switched allegiance from Versellion, and she had speculated—to her mind, rather gently—that Trux had had a connection to Matt Etan which some other party was using against him. She had made no threats. She had done nothing to ruin him.

At a few minutes past seven, Lord Balobridge was announced. Miss Tolerance, reasonably composed again, rose and made her curtsy to the old man. He wore handsome evening dress of dark blue which made her glad she had taken pains to make her own appearance as ladylike as possible. As Balobridge advanced toward her, leaning heavily on an ebony stick, Miss Tolerance realized that his countenance, which on their last meeting had been one of agreeable condescension, was grim. Pardonably sensitive in the wake of Trux's abrupt visit, Miss Tolerance could not determine whether Balobridge's expression was due to the discomfort which made his ebony stick a necessary assistance, or some other matter. With a sense of disquiet, she composed her own expression to a hospitable smile, curtsied, and bade Balobridge to take a seat by the fire.

"Will you take some wine, sir? The club has a passable cellar."

Balobridge shook his head. "I do not intend to stay that long, Miss Tolerance. Nor, frankly, would I care to share wine with you."

Miss Tolerance folded her hands in her lap. "That's plain speaking," she said quietly. "Will you tell me what the matter is, sir?"

"You sit there, bald-faced as a strumpet, and tell me you do not know?" Balobridge stared at her coldly.

"I do more than that, my lord. I ask that you either tell me how I have offended you, or leave. I do not mean disrespect to you, but it would be bad business to permit any further namecalling; I have had quite enough of it for one evening. Lord Trux was here less than an hour ago—"

Balobridge leaned forward. "Trux was here? Where has he been? How did he look?"

"He looked like hell." Miss Tolerance chose her words to shock. "He, like you, seemed to think I should understand why."

Lord Balobridge leaned back in his chair again and examined the gold-chased handle of his walking stick. "You maintain still that you are not aware? You may have heard, then, that Trux was betrothed to a very wealthy young woman of good family— quite a coup for both sides, as she was getting a title of fair antiquity, and he was getting a very considerable fortune. You may also have heard that Trux has been deep in debt for some time and was relying upon that money to mend his credit. And I am sure you must have heard that on Saturday morning a note was sent to the young woman, detailing some features of Trux's past which caused her to cry off from the wedding in disgust. As for Trux, the ink was barely dry upon her letter to him when the bailiffs—somehow apprised of the estrangement—were at his door and he was forced to run to avoid them. It is very unlikely, despite his lineage and good title, that Trux will make another such match, since the matter has become unpleasantly public. It will be . . . difficult . . . for him to repair his fortune."

Miss Tolerance felt a coldness descend upon her.

"You think I did this?" she asked. "Why?"

"That has been the question I have asked myself," Balobridge said silkily. "I confess, at first I did not see the advantage. Mere dislike for Trux—he is not a likable fellow, God knows—seems to me a paltry reason. There's no money in ruining him, unless you were paid to do so—"

"My lord, I think you mistake me. I did not ask your opinion of my motives, but why you accuse *me*. Has there been something in my behavior to you—other than my refusal, upon principle, to help you against the interests of my client—that suggests I would set out to destroy two lives?"

"Your distinctions are too nice," Balobridge said. "Did you not destroy Horace Maugham when you gave evidence to his wife about the wenches he had in keeping?"

Miss Tolerance laughed. "Do you call that ruin? Mrs. Maugham probably railed at him for a fortnight. In a six-month he'll have another set of rooms and another set of girls waiting for him. He will not starve, or lose his home. He will not be jailed, or pilloried and subject to the abuse of the mob, and I doubt that anyone but the high-sticklers at Almack's will long remember the matter. Mr. Maugham might have avoided censure by moderating his behavior before I was brought in to uncover it. But this—I would not expose anyone to the disgust of society on a rumor, a whisper—and out of sheer malice or pique.

Nor would I ruin the expectations of a woman who made a misalliance all unwary." Miss Tolerance's voice was cold and hard. "My own ruin has left me with little appetite for the ruin of others."

"I should have thought it would be just the opposite," Balobridge said.

"Then you do not understand *me*. My lord, I do not know the name of Trux's affianced wife, nor her direction. I do not know who his creditors are, to alert them to the loss of his expectations. On Saturday morning, when you say this letter was sent, I was home in bed with a feverish cold; any of the staff of my aunt's establishment could tell you so. None of this proves anything—I could easily have found out the woman's name, I could have written a letter before I took to my bed. I have no way to clear my name, except to tell you, sir, that I did not write that letter. I would give you my oath, but what is the oath of a ruined woman?"

Balobridge pursed his lips, his eyes still downcast, apparently studying his cane. "You're very hot upon the subject, Miss Tolerance."

She gave a short choke of bitter laughter. "My lord, I have paid enough for the things that I *have* done. I refuse to pay for things I did not do. You must look elsewhere for your culprit."

Now Balobridge looked at Miss Tolerance directly.

"Almost, you convince me, Miss Tolerance. I should like to believe what you say."

Miss Tolerance shook her head. "You will believe what you wish, sir. I have no reason to ruin Lord Trux. The worst I knew of him was that he was complicit in an attack upon my client and was therefore not to be trusted. He is a dandy and, I suspect, a spendthrift. His manner is often haughty and unpleasant and his understanding is at best inferior. He has ambition, but I doubt he has talent; his only chance lay in the sponsorship of a more powerful man. Frankly, my lord, I was strongly under the impression that that man was you. None of these things would give me any reason to contrive Trux's ruin." Miss Tolerance was horrified to hear her voice shake. "But you will believe what you wish. I know that all too well."

In the quiet that fell, the hiss of the fire, the murmur of voices, and the rattle of bottles in the hall outside seemed shockingly loud.

"If it was not you, then who?" Balobridge asked at last.

"If the information given to the young lady was what I imagine it was—I had rather thought that was *your* weapon, my lord."

"*Mine?*"

Miss Tolerance smiled. "When last I spoke to him, Lord Trux certainly thought you were capable of using it, sir. He was quite terrified; it was not only the hope of preferment which persuaded him to cast his lot with you." She watched as Balobridge's cheeks reddened with rage, small precise patches of color in his pale face. "You see how unpleasant a false assumption is, sir. So: you did not expose Trux, and it's plain you have as little admiration for him as I. Why are you here, then?"

He gave thought before he answered. " 'Tis a matter of appearance. I made certain assurances to Trux. He was, as you say, under my patronage. I cannot suffer an attack upon one of my protégés." Lord Balobridge leaned heavily upon his stick and stood up. "If I have done you an injustice, Miss Tolerance, you have my sincerest apologies. I do not know who else might have done this. Unless the whisper was true, and someone else, his . . ." It appeared that words failed him.

"His catamite?" Miss Tolerance prompted.

Balobridge pursed his lips. "Such a person would not balk at blackmail, I imagine."

"Sexual perversion does not absolutely require that one be a liar, my lord."

"You appear to have a broad and varied acquaintance, Miss Tolerance," Lord Balobridge said thoughtfully. "I wish—I wish you were not so firmly allied with the opposition. I think that you might have been a valuable friend."

Miss Tolerance rose and curtsied. "Thank you, sir." A question came to her. "My lord, may I hope that you do not plan to make a show of vengeance upon me for appearance's sake, perhaps send more of your messengers?"

"Messengers?" Balobridge did not pretend to be perplexed. "The gentlemen you bested in Spanish Place? No, Miss Tolerance, I do not. Upon that"—he smiled slowly—"I would give you my oath, but what is the oath of a politician?"

When Balobridge was gone and she was left alone in the salon, Miss Tolerance sat heavily in her chair again, upset beyond reason at the interview just past. There was no reason for Balobridge to believe her protestations of innocence—except that she knew she had not done it. She had no illusions about the sort of business she undertook: her trade was most often in information, and she could not afford to be overnice about how that information would be used. *But there is a difference*, she insisted to herself. There was a difference between finding out for Hermione Maugham the particulars of an infidelity she already suspected, and taking an episode of Trux's past which, when brought to light, could do nothing but ruin Trux and the prospects of the innocent woman to whom he had been betrothed.

And had she been hired to learn Trux's secret? She might well have learnt it and told her client, but—how easy it was to distance herself—she would never have sent the note to his fiancée, never have called down the bailiffs upon the man.

From his manner, Miss Tolerance believed Lord Balobridge's denial of involvement. It made sense. Balobridge was better served by keeping Trux's past as a threat to motivate his tool. What other reason could there be to expose him? Concern for the bride? Miss Tolerance rejected the thought immediately: while the girl might be better off without Trux, publishing the details of the scandal was not to her benefit. The only other reason to have done this, she thought, was to punish Trux.

Miss Tolerance rose, left the salon, and desired Steen to fetch a chair for her.

The servant who admitted her was plainly flustered by the appearance of a woman dressed handsomely for a dinner or card party, at a house where neither was taking place. It became apparent, after a moment or so, that the house did have guests, and guests of some importance, but that this was an exclusively male gathering. The footman stammered a few words, then left Miss Tolerance waiting at the door and went to take counsel with the butler.

The butler appeared after a moment, apologizing for his subordinate's stupidity and guiding Miss Tolerance up the stairs to a salon on the first floor. It was a pleasant room, not large but handsomely appointed, and despite the fact that it had been empty, it was well lit and inviting. She walked idly about the room as she waited, stopping to examine the cluster of paintings on one wall and to peer out the window into the shadowy street below.

"Sarah!" Versellion stood in the doorway. "My dear, I wish you had come any night but tonight. The Prince and Grenville are below, and His Highness has been talking about the war—I am trying to talk him away from the belief that all Whigs hope for is a negotiated peace with Bonaparte, and—"

"I have only a question to ask, and then I will leave you to the Prince." Miss Tolerance stood by the doorway, not trusting herself to go too close, as if she might fall under the spell of his smile, or be stirred to rage by it. "Did you ruin Trux?"

"Ruin Trux?" the earl repeated.

"I must have the truth, Edward, if we are to continue together in any fashion at all."

Versellion frowned slightly. "I prefer to think that I saved Miss Ash from marriage to a man of unfortunate tendencies."

Miss Tolerance felt faint for a moment, as if the enormity of her emotions would overwhelm her. "Miss Ash? Trux's betrothed? Are you so solicitous of her welfare?" She kept her eyes on Versellion, trying to read his expression, and sat heavily upon the nearest chair.

Versellion shrugged. "She is probably hurt now, but I doubt there was great love on either side. With her fortune, she'll find another suitor in short order."

"What a comfort that must be to her," Miss Tolerance said coldly. It seemed to her that Versellion was having difficulty knowing what face to put upon the matter. "Let us agree that you did not do it for Miss Ash's benefit. Why *did* you?"

"Necessity," Versellion said simply. He was clearly more upset by her distress than at the thought of Trux's ruin. "'Tis the way politics are played, Sarah. Trux betrayed me. I had to punish him; I could not let myself be seen so weak. And I needed several persons in my own party and among the Tories to understand that I have the will to use a weapon if I must."

"And so you did."

"I did." He was coming toward her now, hand outstretched.

"All politics. But I don't fathom why you are so distressed, Sarah. Your dislike of Trux—"

"Where did you learn about Trux's past?" she asked dully.

"You said—"

"I told you what I *wondered*. I had not come as close as to suppose anything, and I knew nothing for fact. You have made me complicit in this . . ." Words failed her. She clenched her teeth together, rose from the chair, and went to the window, avoiding him.

When she looked back, she saw Versellion standing in the middle of the room, watching her warily as if he feared a great hurt at her hands. Despite her anger and distrust, she was moved by the vulnerability of that gaze. One hand was still open at his side, as if at any moment he might reach out to implore her understanding.

"I did not think," he said at last. "It was a stupid, thoughtless, political thing to do. I did not think of you or Miss Ash or— *Damn!*" This last was in response to a knock on the door. A footman entered warily, looked from the earl to Miss Tolerance, then murmured something in a low voice to Versellion. "I will come," Versellion said. "It is the Prince, I must go down. Sarah, for the love of God, wait for me. I will not be long, I promise. Please."

He turned and followed the footman from the room with a backward glance. Miss Tolerance watched him go, then resumed her restless prowling of the room, stopping by the window to watch a crowd of drunken revelers, young dandies with more money than sense by the look of them, baiting the Watch. She saw the Watch raise his rattle threateningly, saw the drunkards make faces of mock terror and reel away from the corner into the unlit street, and then she turned back, blinking in the light. She returned to the paintings.

She knew little of art; she recognized some of the important names of an earlier day, but knew nothing of their styles or schools. There was an unappealing collection of apples in a silver bowl next to a dead pheasant: all, even the bowl, looked as if they might have been carved from wood. She rather liked one landscape, a scene looking over fields as the mist was clearing to reveal a fine rising sun. The painting reminded her of the country where she had grown up; for a moment she imagined herself as a girl, riding over such fields and returning to her lessons late, breathless, flushed, and wind-tossed, filled with uncomplicated joy.

She looked away.

There were several portraits on the same wall. Judging from the clothes their subjects wore, the oldest was more than a hundred years old, the most recent somewhat less than thirty. In the oldest, a fine-looking older man in the steepled wig and full-skirted coat of Queen Anne's day stared reprovingly at her; there was no trace of humor about the face, only a simper of rectitude. There was a pretty portrait of a young woman with a rosy, dimpled face and powdered hair; her eyes were pale blue and round. The eyes seemed familiar to Miss Tolerance. They were not Versellion's color or shape; with surprise she realized that Sir Henry Folle's eyes were very like this unknown girl's.

The last painting she stared at the longest, seeking some clue, something that might help her to understand her lover better. The figures in the painting were clearly Versellion and his parents. The boy looked to be six or seven, his parents both appeared to be well into middle age. The father had the same dark hair and long, well-sculpted face as his son; his eyes were of a gray-blue which appeared to match the blue coat he wore and the glinting blue of the intaglio signet he wore on one hand. He smiled, his expression a blend of intelligence and confidence; Miss Tolerance recognized the expression from the Versellion she knew, but with rather more kindness. Versellion's mother was slender, almost emaciated, the bones of her collar visible even through the fichu that crossed her bosom. She wore a pretty lace cap on hair that was an indeterminate color between yellow and gray, her eyes were watery blue, and her fine-boned countenance was curiously insubstantial, so that even the hint of color in her cheeks could not save her from looking ghostly. Her expression rather affirmed the impression of insubstantiality: her lips were pressed in a tight, anxious smile as she looked at a point halfway between her husband and son.

The boy Versellion was seated between his parents. His hair was long, in the fashion of the day, and spilled over the collar of his coat. Like his father, the boy wore blue and buff, the Whig colors, and his placement in the foreground, as much as his dark hair and dark eyes, made him the focus of the painting, drawing the eye from his parents. The artist had captured something of the boy's charm, and his reluctance to sit still for so long. His resemblance to his father was truly striking, but there was vulnerability there as well, as if his mother's expression of uncertainty were the only thing he had inherited from her. Miss Tolerance noted that one of his hands lay open in his lap, as if he might raise it at any moment to ask for something.

She turned away, blinking. If she meant to keep her resolve and deal dispassionately with Versellion, it would not do to examine this boy too closely. Again she walked a circuit of the room, stopping to look out on the empty street. Finally she took her chair again and closed her eyes, waiting.

She became aware, after an indeterminate period, of noise downstairs, the noise of guests departing, voices raised to thank the host, the scurry of servants restoring hats and other property to the visitors, and then the door closing. A few more murmurs in the hallway and then Versellion had entered, closing the door quietly behind him. Miss Tolerance kept her eyes closed, acutely aware of him in the room, listening for him, feeling his warmth as he passed behind her chair and came to sit next to her. He reached to take her hand.

"I am not asleep," she said, and opened her eyes.

He drew back, regarding her with confusion. There were a few minutes of quiet in which it was clear to Miss Tolerance that he was struggling to find the right thing to say to her. At last, "I'm sorry it took so long. The Prince . . . I meant to return to you immediately. Sarah, I have been thinking all this while of what to say to you. It comes to this. I'm sorry. I acted wholly with my head—that part of my head that thinks politically, in terms of getting and maintaining power."

Miss Tolerance looked away from him, fearing that in the repentant earl she would see too much of the vulnerable boy in the painting, and give way too easily.

"You are a politician," she agreed. "But if we are to continue together in any way—if I am to pursue the fan, if we are to be lovers—you cannot play the politician with me. Can I trust *you*? You hired me for my discretion, but discretion must flow two ways. Without that . . ."

He nodded and reached again for her hand. "There has never been a reason to do it before, to keep the politician in check. You see that I need you." His smile was rueful and wholly charming. "At the moment, in fact, I can think of far more reasons why I need you than you me."

She was not prepared to acquit him yet. "I am serious, Versellion. Trux believes that I sent Miss Ash that note. My reputation is my livelihood, and this tarnishes it."

His smile vanished. His grip upon her hand tightened. "I see that now, Sarah. I am not sorry for Trux—he played his game and got caught, and was punished for it. I am sorry for Miss Ash, although I think she's well shut of a bad bargain. And I am heartily sorry if you were harmed by any action of mine. I will not allow rumors of your involvement to stand." He raised her hand, unresisting, to his lips.

Miss Tolerance sighed.

"And this will never happen again," he promised.

She sighed again. He believed what he said, but she would take care to watch what she said to him from now on. Versellion must have sensed a giving-way in her, for he smiled again.

"I have missed you. Are you quite recovered?"

"I have been busy on your business. I met with Dr. Hawley," she said. "And Mrs. Virtue." She began to explain the little she had learned from Hawley and the Cheapside madam. Versellion stopped her.

"We may dispense with Dr. Hawley and his associates, I gather. And Mrs. Virtue?"

"I believe we may dispense of her as well. She was anxious that her involvement in forwarding the letter not come to light— she has even less chance than Hawley of defending herself. She says she did not remove anything from the fan in order to hide the letter there, and while there are many things she might be concealing, I think she is dealing plain with us upon this subject."

"Can you be certain? If she is hiding something—"

"I have her word of honor. I believe her." Miss Tolerance shook her head at Versellion's expression of disbelief. "There is something else, Edward. I want you to promise not to act upon this information until we have thought the matter through."

Versellion promised.

She explained what her attacker in the alley had told her. Versellion listened thoughtfully. "My cousin hired the men who attacked me. Was Trux working with him?"

"I am not perfectly sure of it. 'Tis another reason I wish you had not written that letter to Miss Ash, for I certainly cannot ask Trux about the matter. I still believe he was working with Balobridge, which argues either that Balobridge and Folle are in league, or Trux was working both sides of a game I doubt he had the wit to understand."

"Christ." Versellion loosed her hand and leaned back in his chair, running his hands through his hair. "You're right, I must think about this before I act. I know my cousin hates me—but have me killed? My God. He'd have the title from it, I suppose that's motive enough. But even our fathers at their worst never contemplated anything like . . ."

"Like murder? You will need rather more evidence than the word of a footpad to catch him out. Just be on your guard for now." Miss Tolerance sat up in her chair. "My God, what o'clock is it? And how did your meeting with the Prince?"

"Well, I think." With apparent effort, Versellion turned his attention from his own thoughts. "As well as I can expect. He was noncommittal but friendly. And he has agreed to come to the party my aunt Julia is holding here. It will be seen as a sign that he is declaring himself a friend to the Whigs." He stood and looked at the ormolu clock on the mantel. "It is late. Will you stay?"

Miss Tolerance bit at her lip, considering.

"Sarah, please. We need to make a new beginning, you and I."

She had no more energy to resist him or herself, and what he said was true. "I am a great believer in new beginnings," she said at last, and took his arm.

Seventeen

After a pleasantly restless night, Miss Tolerance was wakened by her lover's kiss. Versellion, in the wake of their argument, was disposed to passion. Miss Tolerance put her wariness aside to return his embraces with her whole heart—but still insisted upon leaving early, shortly after sunrise, and making her way to Manchester Square as quietly as an unaccompanied woman might do at such an hour. Before she had left his house, noting the slenderness of her pocketbook, she had presented Versellion with a reckoning of all the monies she had advanced in his behalf, and of the time she had spent upon his business. Versellion had settled the account with only a mild tweak for her insistence upon mixing business with pleasure.

"Indulge me," Miss Tolerance said. "I work far more effectively when I know I shall not have to scramble for my supper. Now, you will promise me to keep your bodyguards about you when you leave the house?"

He assured her he would do so, although he owned the accompaniment bothersome.

"Death would be more bothersome still," she reminded him, and with a kiss, and then a second, she left him.

She went first to her own cottage, where she stripped off her evening dress, dozed, bathed, and finally dressed and took herself across the garden to her aunt's establishment. She found Mrs. Brereton presiding over a pot of chocolate in a parlor overlooking Manchester Square, deep in conversation with one of the girls. The older woman's dress indicated that she had not yet been to bed. Half past eight in the morning seemed a harsh time for so serious a talk, and Miss Tolerance kept herself out of the way until, at last, the young woman left looking chastened, and Mrs. Brereton signaled to her niece to approach.

"I am not certain at all that Clara is meant for this establishment," Mrs. Brereton said coolly, and handed her niece a small gilded cup. "She exhibits very little ability to adapt herself to the requirements of her callers. I expect my girls to exhibit a little range, or at the very least not to subject me to displays of fastidious vapors." She shrugged. "Clara plays the pianoforte and sings beautifully, and her manners are exquisite, but in matters of love, I begin to think her better suited to a bread-and-butter place in Southwark where all she would be expected to do was lie on her back and moan convincingly."

Miss Tolerance raised her eyebrow.

Mrs. Brereton regarded her niece without irony. "My love, not everyone is up to the standard I set here. Your acquaintance at Blackbottle's establishments—"

"*Acquaintance* is a generous word for it. How did you hear I had been at one of Blackbottle's houses?"

Mrs. Brereton made a vague gesture with one hand, as though brushing away a fly. "Here or there, my love. Perhaps poor Matt told me before— You know how talk flies about."

Since it was Mrs. Brereton's expressed policy that talk not fly about, at least not on her premises, and since Miss Tolerance's recent experience with idle speculation had been painful, it was now on the tip of her tongue to say that she did *not* know. She was saved from making this observation by the appearance in the doorway of a departing client. The morning sun which filled the hallway lit the gentleman from behind; when she had blinked the dazzle from her eyes, Miss Tolerance was dismayed to see that it was Sir Henry Folle.

Miss Tolerance composed her face into tranquil lines and prepared to study the bottom of her chocolate cup. She had no wish to disturb the early morning peace of her aunt's parlor, and hoped Sir Henry would feel likewise. At first, it seemed that he did. His swagger, and the disorder of his clothes, suggested that he had just risen from one of Mrs. Brereton's well-appointed beds. His hair was tousled, and his neckcloth was creased and would not hold the shape of the knot he had attempted. Miss Tolerance particularly noticed the gold-headed walking stick she had observed before; there was, she saw now, an intaglio jewel set on one face of the knob, deeply graven with the lines of a family crest. A glimmer of unpleasant suspicion occurred to her.

"Good morning, madam," Folle said to Mrs. Brereton. He evidently awaited Mrs. Brereton's signal to join her, which she gave with an inclination of her head toward the sofa. Folle advanced easily into the room and turned to discover who Mrs. Brereton's companion was. When he recognized Miss Tolerance, his demeanor changed remarkably. His back straightened, his eyes darkened, and his affable expression became hard and brazen. Mrs. Brereton, perhaps willfully, appeared to note nothing of the change.

"Good morning, Sir Henry. Will you take a cup of chocolate?" She indicated that he might sit. Folle bowed crisply and took, not the sofa, but the chair opposite Mrs. Brereton, nearest Miss Tolerance. "I trust you passed a pleasant night?" Mrs. Brereton continued. She passed a cup to Folle.

"Oh, very pleasant, very pleasant indeed." Folle sprawled, one arm draped across the back of his chair, and eyed Miss Tolerance. "Interviewing new talent, Mrs. B? I swear, you whores work the damnedest hours!"

Mrs. Brereton's smile cooled. "You are pleased to be provocative, Sir Henry. You will kindly recall that this is not a tuppenny stew, and moderate your manner accordingly."

"Beg pardon, Mrs. B," Folle said. "But let me just tell you—that one there is already employed at some mean business in Southwark. God only knows what poxes she carries about with her." He eyed Miss Tolerance. "Though *some* men might think her worth the risk."

Mrs. Brereton frowned. "This is not one of my employees, but my niece. But perhaps you already knew that? You have been warned, Sir Henry. I shan't think twice about refusing you entry if you continue—"

"Exiled from the finest quim in England? That would be a sad thing." Folle put his chocolate cup aside and inclined his head to Miss Tolerance in a mockery of politeness. "I am sorry I mistook your niece for something she ain't. That leaves, of course, the question of what she *is*."

Miss Tolerance smiled brightly. "I know well what I am, sir. And curiously, I have been hearing a good deal of what *you* are."

Folle's brow lowered. "From my noble cousin?"

"From a Mr. Hart, sir."

Folle sat back with a lurch, as if the name had struck him a blow. If the hostility with which he treated Miss Tolerance had heretofore come from her perceived alliance with Versellion, it was obvious with the introduction of Mr. Hart's name that Folle was ready to detest her for her own sake.

"He recommended that I ask *Mrs. Smith* for more details." Miss Tolerance watched to see if the lie hit home. "Sadly, that is not possible."

"Why is that?" Folle's grip on his walking stick tightened.

"Mrs. Smith is unavailable, having been murdered."

At the last word, Folle lifted his stick several inches from the ground. Then, with a gesture bespeaking conscious will, he let it drop again. Miss Tolerance was aware that one of the footmen was hovering in the doorway, sensing trouble.

"What would an old dead whore know about me?"

"I believe Mr. Hart thought you would know something about *her*, Sir Henry. Did I say that she was either old or a whore?" Miss Tolerance's voice was low and mild.

"You can't trap me. And who cares what a lying blackguard like Hart says?"

"Oh, I found him compelling when he had a knife to his throat," Miss Tolerance said mildly. "He spun me a tale that he was hired to pursue a noble lord and bring him down. He seemed to think his employer would stop at nothing to get what he wanted. And I'm certain Bow Street would take an interest, sir. Attempted murder is a grave matter, far graver for ordinary mortals like ourselves." She returned his look of malice, smiling. "A peer might 'scape prosecution where a commoner would certainly hang. . . ." Miss Tolerance watched the effect her words had been having, and at the last let her words trail as she might have run her fingers through a still pond.

Folle rose to his feet, red-faced and unable to speak for his rage. Again he lifted his stick, but higher this time, nearly over his head. He would have brought it down upon Miss Tolerance except that the footmen, Cole and Keefe, had appeared on either side of Folle to restrain him.

Mrs. Brereton rose from her chair and observed that Sir Henry might find it more commensurate with his dignity to leave under his own power. Folle, still furious but under control again, shrugged off the footmen and stalked out of the salon. Cole and Keefe followed him purposefully. Miss Tolerance put a hand to her head, as if to be sure that no blow had fallen. Mrs. Brereton sat again and poured more chocolate. The expression with which she regarded her niece was not a pleasant one.

"I will thank you not to bring your business into my salon, to the detriment of *my* business, Sarah," she said coldly.

"I beg your pardon, Aunt," Miss Tolerance said meekly. "Although, if you recall, the business brought itself to me."

"*He started it*? Spare me your nursery excuses. Was that an argument I just witnessed, or some peculiar sort of interrogation?"

"Both, I suppose. Folle has confirmed for me the two things I believed, Aunt Thea. That he killed Mrs. Smith—the old woman in Leyton I told you about—and that he hired another murder done. He may even have been behind Matt's death."

Mrs. Brereton put her cup down; the saucer rattled. "Matt?" She was silent for a moment, privy to a range of thought and grief Miss Tolerance could only guess at. Then, "Why would Folle kill Matt?" she argued. "His tastes do not run that way, it's only ever been girls—"

"Not all reasons for murder revolve around sex, Aunt Thea. Money, politics, family—all those can be excellent motivations for murder, and in Folle's case, I think they were. But for now, whatever I believe, I have little evidence to lay before the magistrate."

Mrs. Brereton shook her head. This was the first time her niece's business had so nearly coincided with her own, and she clearly did not like it. "But where did Folle learn you had been interviewing in Southwark?" she asked.

"Here or there, Aunt. You know how talk flies about."

This sally failed to amuse Mrs. Brereton, who asked coolly if Miss Tolerance had learned anything useful from Humphrey Blackbottle. Miss Tolerance admitted that Blackbottle himself had been of indifferent assistance. "One of his . . . people . . . provided a good deal of help, however."

"I'm surprised to hear it. I should have thought that sort of person to be close as a clam and twice as suspicious." Mrs. Brereton refreshed the chocolate in her cup and added sugar. "I cannot imagine that Blackbottle attracts a superior quality of help as a general rule, although—is there an Italian woman still manages his Cheapside house? I remember her from when I first came to London. She peacocked it around on the arm of her lover so boldly we almost thought he'd put his wife aside for her. It came to nothing in the end, though. The earl lost his interest in her and took up with that Deb Cunning, whom you say is now in Chelsea."

Miss Tolerance stared at her aunt in fixed amazement. "Do

you mean Mrs. Virtue, ma'am? There was a connection between her and Mrs. Cunning?"

"Only a man, my dear, and several years separated them, I think. Fanny Virtue, I believe she called herself. She was a few year older than I, very pretty, and new to London. Gave herself great airs, which made it sadder, I suppose, when her earl shifted his affections—"

"And that earl was the late Earl of Versellion?" Miss Tolerance asked.

"Of course. Within a year, I think, he had dropped her. He went through a string of light-o'-loves before he settled on the pretty, silly one."

"Mrs. Cunning." A vista of possibility had suddenly opened before Miss Tolerance.

"Yes. And La Virtue did not manage herself at all well. I put that down in part to old Versellion, for it was he introduced her to the Chinese vice—poor thing, she could barely remember her own name for a time after their parting, quite drowned her sorrows in opium, if one could say that. But as she's still alive, and still managing Blackbottle's business for him, I daresay she recovered herself from the habit."

Miss Tolerance rose to her feet, staring at her aunt. "Why did you not tell me these things earlier?" she asked. "My God."

"You never asked me," Mrs. Brereton said mildly. "You asked about Deb Cunning, but not La Virtue. Sarah, will you not finish your chocolate?"

"I'm sorry, ma'am, but I cannot. I regret to leave so abruptly, but—"

She did not stop to finish the sentence. Mrs. Brereton was left to drink her chocolate in silence.

Anticipating another trip into Cheapside, Miss Tolerance returned to her cottage and changed into men's clothes. The morning was bright and warm; in the garden a breeze murmured through the leaves with a green scent on it. Miss Toler-

Madeleine E. Robins

ance started out on foot. The ideas forming in her head were so loose and yet so compelling that she required the walk in order to focus upon them and attempt to draw them into some whole and reasonable form.

Mrs. Virtue had been the lover of the old Earl of Versellion. Had Mrs. Cook known this? Had Humphrey Blackbottle acquired the fan for Mrs. Virtue particularly because of its connection to the old earl? It seemed logical to believe that Mrs. Virtue must know more of Versellion's history—and of the fan—than she had permitted Miss Tolerance to learn, despite the word of honor given as Francesca d'Ippolito. For a few minutes Miss Tolerance's anger—at Mrs. Virtue for her deception, and at herself for not catching her at it—burned very brightly. But the exercise of walking was as beneficial to rational thought as she had hoped; within a few streets of Manchester Square, Miss Tolerance recalled that she had never mentioned Versellion's name to Mrs. Virtue. It was possible that the footman Versellion had sent with his payment had been indiscreet, and that Mrs. Virtue had deduced the identity of his employer, but after another street's worth of consideration, Miss Tolerance discarded this idea as unlikely. She had heard Versellion order the footman's discretion, and did not believe the order would have been lightly disobeyed.

It was as likely as not, then, that Mrs. Virtue had told the truth. Miss Tolerance began to compose a plan whereby she would confront Mrs. Virtue and in some way extract any information the madam had about Versellion's family without drawing a line to the matter of the fan.

" 'Old up, miss."

A hand with blackened nails had gripped her arm strongly. Looking up, Miss Tolerance recognized the Bow Street Runner Penryn. "Zor Walter Mandif's compliments, and he's been wanting a word, if it's convenient."

Miss Tolerance, stopped in her tracks, said nothing but looked pointedly at the hand on her arm. It was removed.

"And if it is not convenient?" she asked.

Penryn smiled. He was in need of a razor, and his dark hair fell, overlong, over his forehead; from his odor Miss Tolerance deduced that he was not affecting the Romantic, but merely of slovenly habits. In his grin she saw a frank pleasure in the power of his office, compounded with some curiosity about herself.

"Mozt people find it convenient, miss. Zor Walter's two streets over, at a coffeehouse, and begs you'll join 'im there."

Miss Tolerance considered for a moment and revised her plans. There was no point in antagonizing the Runners or their tame magistrate, and it was unlikely that Mrs. Virtue would disappear during an hour's delay. She would follow Penryn, but she found it impossible to go without at least a token show of reluctance.

"I do not know if it's wise for me to follow a man I barely know into a side street," she murmured.

The Runner looked affronted. "Are you implying that Bow Street cannot take care of its witnesses, miss? Or of doing them 'arm itself?"

Miss Tolerance lowered her eyes demurely. "I would not think of doing so, Mr. Penryn."

After a moment the man seemed to take the joke. One side of his mouth crooked up, and he muttered something about women. "Come along of me, then, miss." He wheeled around, clearly anticipating that Miss Tolerance would follow, and strode off. She caught up in a few swift steps, adjusted her pace to match his, and they went off to find Sir Walter Mandif.

The Radical Coffeehouse was either a very unpopular place, or one whose denizens were not generally abroad until later in the day. Miss Tolerance stepped into the coffee room, which was large, shadowy, but banded with glittering stripes of sunlight from the windows, in which she could see the dust of ages stirred up by the sullen efforts of a girl scrubbing down tables. The place smelled of damp wood and mold, tobacco smoke and wood smoke, and very faintly of coffee. Miss Tolerance found Sir Walter Mandif sitting against the far wall, bleached by a shaft of sunlight, with a newspaper open on the table and a tankard to hand. He rose when he saw his visitor approaching and thanked her for attending him with the same courtesy he might have extended to a woman more regularly attired and situated than she was. Mr. Penryn, having provided the prize, withdrew to the bar and left Miss Tolerance with Sir Walter.

"You choose an interesting venue for this meeting, Sir Walter. Would it not have been better done to meet with me at my cottage, or perhaps at Tarsio's, if not at Bow Street itself?"

Sir Walter offered her coffee, which she declined. "I thought, perhaps, a neutral meeting place," he said. "This business appears to be more complicated than it first looked, and discussing it in a brothel did not seem prudent."

"My home is not a brothel, Sir Walter."

"No, indeed, Miss Tolerance. But it is situated awfully close by one, is it not?"

Miss Tolerance admitted the justice of this. "But which business is it that you wish to discuss?"

"The death of Mrs. Smith, of Leyton."

"Are you still interested in it? Not many would be so solicitous of justice for a poor old Fallen Woman."

"It is the murder of just such as Mrs. Smith, the poorest and most helpless, which does the greatest harm to our society, do not you think?" Mandif raised his tankard to his lips, tasted its contents, made a face, and set it down.

"I do, as it happens. But not many of your rank share that view, I think."

"The poor, the working folk, are the plinth on which society stands. England could survive without the peerage, but without farmers or millers or weavers? Not likely."

"And so you pursue criminals to protect the poor and working classes?" Miss Tolerance was fascinated. "Do I still number among your suspects?"

Sir Walter's expression was thoughtful. "Until Fortune presents me with a more likely one, or you present me with absolute evidence that you could not have done it, I must with regret consider you so. In point of fact, I have no other."

"What a very uncomfortable position I am in." Miss Tolerance considered what she might safely say. To accuse Folle without proof—and presently she had almost none—was dangerous. But she did not relish the thought of being called to meet with Bow Street at every turn.

"I have learned a few things which might be of help to you," she said finally. "I suspect you and your assistants would do well to find and speak to a Mr. Hart." She described him. "I have reason to believe that he knows something of this business. You might also set one of your dogs upon the trail of Sir Henry Folle, to see what he can sniff up."

Sir Walter's eyebrows raised and his bland fox-face became suddenly sharp. Miss Tolerance found the change unnerving.

"Aiming rather high in your suspicions, ma'am. Have you evidence to back your accusation?"

Miss Tolerance was aware that she was in danger. She was a woman alone, Fallen, known to live by the sword, making vague accusations about a member of a distinguished political family. She saw the chasm open at her feet and stepped across it as carefully as she could.

"I have not accused anyone of anything, Sir Walter. But this morning, at my aunt's house, Folle said something which led me to believe that he knew Mr. Hart and was not unacquainted with the matter of Mrs. Smith. Pray believe me, if I had anything more specific to offer you, I would."

Sir Walter leaned back in his chair.

"Are you certain I cannot procure a cup of coffee for you, Miss Tolerance?" he asked at last. "Or perhaps some ale? They brew their own." He looked into his tankard without pleasure. "Very badly."

Miss Tolerance was startled into a laugh. "You make an inviting offer, sir, but thank you, no."

"As you wish." Sir Walter leaned forward again, elbows upon his newspaper. "Miss Tolerance, I realize that you feel some sort of professional obligation to be discreet, but I urge you—do *not* pit yourself against me, or against Bow Street. If you know anything that will help me in finding the killer of Mrs. Smith, please tell me."

He seemed entirely sincere. Miss Tolerance could only match his sincerity with her own. "Sir Walter, what I could offer you now is only supposition and vague notions. I have given you the little I can; I know what I believe, but I cannot prove it."

Mandif nodded. "I do not mean to bully you. Indeed, you do not strike me as the sort of woman who can be bullied."

"Perhaps not, sir, but I am fully sensible of how little position I have to defend in this business. Sir Walter, if you will take my word, I will promise you that when I can demonstrate any of my suspicions to you, I will do so. It will be considerably easier if I do not need to fear tripping over Mr. Penryn and his partner at every turn."

The magistrate nodded. He raised a finger and Penryn, watching over the rim of his tankard, nodded and joined them.

"See if you and Hook can turn up a Mr. Hart," Mandif ordered. "A spice and cracksman, from the sound of him. Miss Tolerance, where did you last encounter Mr. Hart?"

Miss Tolerance grinned. "In Penfold Street." She explained the circumstances of their meeting.

Penryn was incredulous. "You 'eld a rapparee like that up w' a mirror?"

Sir Walter waved that question away. "And the last you saw of him?"

"Running from a crowd of gentlemen who intended to teach him a lesson for setting upon a helpless female."

Mr. Penryn shook his head in appreciation, running his grubby hand from nose to chin and back again. " 'Elpless!"

"Mr. Penryn, if you find this Mr. Hart, I would suggest that you take anything he says with regard to this lady with a grain of salt," Sir Walter said mildly. "I commend your resourcefulness, Miss Tolerance, but I suspect you have made an enemy."

Miss Tolerance concurred. "My object at the time was to extract information while securing my own safety, Sir Walter. I confess I was not thinking of Mr. Hart's dignity."

"You will understand, Miss Tolerance, that until such time as Mr. Hart's role in the death of Mrs. Smith is confirmed, I must, with regret, continue to regard you a possible suspect."

"I never doubted that would be the case, sir. Now, if you need nothing more from me, I was about business when Mr. Penryn found me. May I go?"

Sir Walter rose and bowed over her hand. "Thank you for your assistance, Miss Tolerance. We will doubtless meet again."

Miss Tolerance said all that was polite and took her leave. While she liked the magistrate, it was not difficult to hope that such a meeting would never take place.

She had lost the train of thought which had occupied her earlier. Miss Tolerance hired a hackney and directed it to Cheapside, then leaned back, revisiting her plans for Mrs. Virtue. It was hot and stuffy in the carriage, and she felt a headache growing in the back of her head, likely because she had broken her fast with nothing more than her aunt's chocolate several hours earlier. When she dismounted at Cheapside, she first stopped at a pie shop and bought a pork pie, eating it quickly, taking time only to swat away the hand of a child pickpocket.

Feeling better for her luncheon, Miss Tolerance picked her way through the crowd and turned in to the familiar, unpleasant precincts of Bow Lane. Drunkards of both sexes slept in the doorways, but the narrow street was otherwise almost empty. From somewhere above her head came the sound of a child weeping. Miss Tolerance found the door to Blackbottle's and rapped upon it smartly. Joe, the porter, appeared at once with a face that said she was not whom he had expected.

"You!" The man looked worried; no, more than worried. His skin was ashy, his brows drawn together in a grimace of anxiety, and his voice was hoarse. "What the hell do you want?"

Miss Tolerance stepped carefully. "Good afternoon. I need to speak to Mrs. Virtue. I know it may be early for her, but—"

"You can't. Shove away." He started to close the door, but

Miss Tolerance shouldered in just far enough to keep him from doing so.

"Wait!" Miss Tolerance reached for her wallet. "She will want to see me, I promise. And I can make you—"

"Push off, you quean!" The doorman's face was congested with rage. "Keep your fuckin' money! Won't buy your way in 'ere no more."

Warily, Miss Tolerance tried one more time. "Mrs. Virtue will want—"

"Nothing!" the man roared. "She's dead. For all I know, it's a-counta you coming and going 'ere. Christ knows what's going to happen now!"

At the news, Miss Tolerance took a step back and stared at Joe. Of all the things she might have expected, she had not imagined this. "Dead how?" she asked. "When?"

Perhaps seeing the effect his news had upon her helped the porter to regain himself. Joe took a breath and said, somewhat more calmly, that the body had been found perhaps two hours earlier, when the maid went up to bring Mrs. Virtue her chocolate.

"How did she die?" Recalling her aunt's comment that morning about the Chinese vice, and her own vague impressions of sweet smoke on the air, she imagined the woman drifting away on a cloud of opium.

"Beaten." Joe dropped the word as if it were a weight he could not bear to carry. "Some bastard got past me somehow. Beat 'er brains out proper—maid had right hysterics at the sight. I sent a man to Blackbottle to tell 'em, 'e'll know what to do. But Christ Jesus, the bastard got past me—"

Miss Tolerance stood very still. "Beaten? I must see her."

The corner of Joe's mouth turned down. "I told you, she—"

"No, let me look at her now."

"Why? You going to gawk at the poor ol' thing? What call you got—"

"Let me see her," Miss Tolerance repeated. She was suddenly

filled with impatience. "For the love of God, I may see something that will help find the killer."

" 'Zat what you do, miss? Catch killers? Rather uncommon line a work for a female." Joe stood, arms crossed, filling the doorway. "You was catching killers the last time you come, too?" The doorman smiled unpleasantly. "Or maybe you brung 'em along of you, showed 'em right to the door, like—"

She could not knock the man down and force her way past him; Miss Tolerance held on to her temper and spoke so quietly she knew Joe would have to strain to hear her. "I no more led killers to your mistress's door than you let a killer in that door. If we have both been used, then let me do what I can to right the wrong and find Mrs. Virtue's killer."

Joe bowed his head, as if the effort of thinking all of this through were very great. Finally he stood aside, wordlessly, and let her pass. Miss Tolerance passed the little salon, where a half dozen women in grubby robes and dresses sat weeping; only as she ascended the stair did Joe call after her, "Make sure you're gone before Blackbottle gets here!"

The first floor was uncharacteristically quiet. Most of the doors, including the one to Mrs. Virtue's apartment, stood open. Miss Tolerance was struck, as she entered the room, by how undisturbed it first seemed; the furniture and knickknacks were in their accustomed places, the door to the farther chamber was ajar. The fire had burnt to embers, the candles had guttered out, and as neither the maid nor Mrs. Virtue had drawn the drapes to admit sunlight, it was quite dark. Miss Tolerance went at once to the windows and pulled the drapes back, the better to examine the body that lay in an unnatural attitude on the sofa.

The pie she had eaten earlier rose in Miss Tolerance's throat. It was an effort to perform her examination coolly. Mrs. Virtue lay with her shoulders and head flung over the back of the sofa and her arms splayed backward, almost touching the floor. She wore an elegant dress of red and gold tissue that strained at the awkward position she lay in; one of her breasts had slid half out of the bodice. An embroidered slipper had fallen off, or perhaps been kicked off in an attempt to defend herself, Miss Tolerance thought. She had been struck across the face, but the blows that had killed her were to her head: temple and crown bore the impressions of the blows in blood, skin, and shattered bone. Because of the angle at which she had fallen, blood had flowed downward, matted her fiery hair, and puddled on the floor, where it was half dried now. Looking more closely at the body, Miss Tolerance saw bruises on the woman's neck and shoulder from which she gathered the weapon had been hard, heavy, and wielded with much force. From the bruise that purpled one cheek, she also gathered another thing: whatever had struck the madam across the face had been carved or engraved.

An intaglio signet, perhaps.

Miss Tolerance inspected the vicinity of the sofa, noting the order everywhere except on the person of the victim. Had Mrs. Virtue's assailant put things back after a struggle? She suspected that the killer had taken away his weapon—in the shape, she could not help but think, of a gold-crowned walking stick inset with a carved signet—but perhaps there was evidence of why the struggle had taken place. No, nothing of the sort. But on a second glance she realized that one of the candlesticks by the sofa bore the smears of quick polishing, as if someone had wiped away the marks of gore from its surface. When she lifted the thing, she noticed, with a sickening turn to her stomach, a few long strands of red hair clinging to the bottom of the candlestick.

Two murder weapons? Had Mrs. Virtue been killed by two men?

Miss Tolerance completed her inspection and returned downstairs.

Joe looked up at her. " 'Ad enough?" His tone was bitter.

"I think so. When was she last seen alive?"

The man shrugged as if he could not see the point of the question.

"Dunno. In the course a business, people was always in and

out. It was maybe five of clock this morning. Maid didn't go in until near noon. Mrs. V don't like people coming in to chat, pass the time. *Didn't* like."

"Did you have brisk custom last night? Anyone not known to you? Anyone who seemed to be hiding his identity?"

Joe looked at Miss Tolerance as though she were an idiot. "Half the men come 'ere don't want—"

"If you want the killer found, *think*," Miss Tolerance said. "You have regular custom, I've heard the girls greet them by name. Any men who were not familiar? Did Mrs. Virtue have any callers? Can you give me anything—"

"There was a couple of gents—sort as could buy better but like our girls. But there's always a few of that sort in an evening—or a morning, come to it." The doorman paused. "There was a man wore his hat down low, wore a greatcoat—"

"A greatcoat in June? And you didn't think this remarkable enough to mention?"

"Christ, miss. Some gents come here don't want to be known. Some as don't care, some as think it gives 'em a rep as a hellboy and a goer, but we get some few don't want their precious names linked to Blackbottle's. Anyway, this cove didn't ask for Mrs. V, just went into the parlor and took his choice of the girls."

"What time did this shy fellow arrive?"

Joe's face was red, his mouth working. Clearly his conscience was suggesting a complicity in Mrs. Virtue's death which he could not bear. "Sometime after dawn. But he didn't ask for her. . . ."

Miss Tolerance saw no point in pressing further. She had her own idea of what might have happened. If she pushed the doorman too far, she might lose him. "I'm sorry, Joe," she said at last. "She was a great lady in her way." Again, she took out her pocketbook, and this time extracted a note. "You'll want to put up a hatchment and other mourning gear," she said. "If Mr. Blackbottle forgets, this should pay for them."

Joe nodded, took the note, and crumpled it in his hand. "That's decent of you, miss."

As neither one could think of anything further to say, Miss Tolerance nodded in farewell and left the doorman standing there, rolling the note in his hand absently.

Eighteen

Miss Tolerance returned to her cottage, meditating upon death.

In the several years that she had been an agent of inquiry, she had been called upon to ask questions, skillfully misdirect the truth to her own ends, and on occasion to defend her own life in the pursuit of a client's objective. But in those years death had not accompanied her upon her rounds as it seemed to do now. Mrs. Smith, Matt Etan, now Fanny Virtue, dead. Versellion a likely target for assassination. Miss Tolerance had believed her new-wrought profession would make her independent and spare her the choice of death or whoredom. Apparently it was not to be so simple.

From death and whoredom, her thoughts moved to Mrs. Virtue and Mrs. Cunning, thence to Versellion and Hawley, to Mrs. Virtue again, to Trux, to Balobridge, to Folle. Sir Henry Folle in particular provided her with considerable scope for rumination; she was morally certain that he had killed Mrs. Smith and Mrs. Virtue, and perhaps even Matt. The why of the murders was more difficult for her to imagine, unless all three had frustrated Folle beyond bearing by refusing to reveal what he wanted. She could imagine Mrs. Smith doing so, but fond as she had been of Matt, Miss Tolerance could not imagine him keeping a secret if telling it could save him pain. Likewise, Mrs. Virtue might have easily been bought of any secrets she held. But if Folle had demanded information that Matt or Mrs. Virtue simply did not possess?

Miss Tolerance reminded herself that she really had no evidence of Folle's involvement other than the handful of dried flowers that had fallen from his pocket the first time he tried to strike her, and a bruise on Mrs. Virtue's cheek which might have come from the signet upon his walking stick. She was aware that her strong dislike for the man colored her feelings; hundreds of signets existed in London alone, perhaps dozens like Folle's. Yet she could not escape the belief that Sir Henry Folle had struck that fatal blow.

Folle's great aim, it seemed to her, was to discredit and ruin his cousin Versellion. In her head, Miss Tolerance played scenes between Mrs. Smith and Folle, Matt Etan and Folle, Fanny Virtue and Folle; in each scene that same murderous rage which she had seen briefly turned upon her overwhelmed Folle when he was balked of the information he sought. In each scene he loosed his fury and left, still without the wherewithal to ruin Versellion. Perhaps that was why he had hired Hart and his associates to attack Versellion.

However convincing this logic might seem to her, Miss Tolerance was well aware that it was just now only storytelling. She needed evidence to support her musings. Once home, she sent a note round to the stables to ask that a horse be made ready, and another to Versellion, asking for a few moments of his time later that afternoon. She then spent half an hour cleaning her sword and pistols. She carried them with her when she left for Leyton.

She was not certain what she hoped to find at Mrs. Smith's cottage, or even if there would be anything left to find. She stopped first at the Queen's Arms, long enough to inquire of the barman what the local news was of Mrs. Smith's murder. He recounted the reluctant involvement of the justice, Mr. Gilkes, who had convened the coroner's court right there in the taproom of the Queen's Arms. There had also been considerable local excitement at the visit of two men from Bow Street. Mrs. Smith, it seemed, had had some coin put by to satisfy her legal debts, and a nephew in the north to whom the cottage and her effects had been left. That young man, the barman said in tones of disapproval, was taking his time coming to see his new holdings, and thus denying the local merchants their share of his custom. Miss Tolerance heard this gossip with private satisfaction: perhaps the furniture sellers and their ilk might not yet have stripped the place.

In fact, except for a ten days' accumulation of dust and the ripening smell of the river in the summer warmth, Mrs. Smith's cottage was just as Miss Tolerance recalled it. She satisfied the curiosity which had been balked on her last visit with the justice of the peace, and inspected the two tiny upstairs rooms, which yielded nothing of worth. In the kitchen, the neglected foodstuffs had either rotted or been attacked by rats or squirrels. It was in the parlor that Miss Tolerance concentrated her attention. She could not say what she was looking for; a dropped kerchief with Folle's monogram would have been useful, or one of Folle's visiting cards. Since those were unlikely, she began a methodical survey of the dark little room. The honey-colored light of late afternoon seemed hardly to penetrate the foliage without and the lacy curtains within; still, Miss Tolerance was loath to push the curtains aside and make the neighbors a gift of her presence. She had no ambition to be found, by some curious servant, on her hands and knees, combing the rug with her fingertips.

A quarter hour yielded one of Mrs. Smith's flowered candles and some wax dripping, and a handful of the potpourri that still scattered the rug. When she stepped out of the cottage, the late afternoon light was dazzling; she took a moment to let her eyes adjust, looking about her on the chance that an assailant might

have followed her. Unchallenged, she returned to Manchester
Square.

V ersellion had replied to her note, asking her to meet at Versellion House. After returning the horse to the stable, securing her discoveries in a locked box in her cottage, and
changing into feminine attire, Miss Tolerance made her way toward St. James's Square. It was now that hour of the early evening when riders and carriages had returned from the
promenades, and pedestrians from forays to Bond Street and
Piccadilly. In many houses women were beginning the process
of dressing for dinner and the evening's entertainments. All of
haute London was in retreat, moving away from each other to
prepare for their next encounter. The rest of London, however,
was still at work, delivering parcels, sweeping crossings, and
picking pockets. It seemed as if those two worlds, of work and
diversion, moved past each other with barely a contact. *Unless,
of course, they meet in me,* Miss Tolerance thought.

Versellion House was in a state of alarming turmoil; every
door on the ground and first floors had been thrown open, and
a press of maids and under-footmen seemed to be polishing
every visible inch of the public rooms. The ball, Miss Tolerance
recalled. The ball at which Versellion hoped to finally sway the
Prince of Wales to the Whig cause. With surprise she realized
that the party was to be the next night. She felt curiously distant
from the hectic activity around her; the effect of too much death,
she thought.

Miss Tolerance was shown to the same salon on the first floor
where she had argued with Versellion about Trux. The evidence
of super-polishing made her loath to sit lest she wrinkle the
brushed and shining perfection around her. Instead, she walked
about the room, examining the paintings again.

"Lost among my ancestors?"

Miss Tolerance nodded and turned away from the paintings.
Versellion was dressed for riding, and the disorder of his hair

suggested that he had just returned from that exercise. He had a flush of excitement about him, as if the preparations for the ball had infected him. Even his movements seemed quick and staccato.

"I regret I am so caught up here I cannot ask you to stay this evening," he said. "But tomorrow night—"

"You will have a house filled with people until dawn." Miss Tolerance shook her head. "I thought it best to tell you certain things before then."

"You have news?" He drew her to a sofa and sat down with her.

"Not the sort of news that will rejoice you, I hope. Mrs. Virtue, the woman from whom I bought the fan? She is dead."

Versellion went very still. "Christ, is there no end to it?" He looked down, running his hands over his face as if he could scrub the news away. "You must think it to do with the fan, or you wouldn't tell me."

"I think . . ." Miss Tolerance paused, took a long breath. "I think your cousin Folle is the killer. Of Mrs. Virtue and my friend Matt, and of Mrs. Smith of Leyton."

The earl drew his hand down to cover his mouth. "My God," he said at last. "Why?"

"Why do I believe it to be so? Or why would he do such things?"

The earl did not answer. He sat, eyes closed, hand still covering his mouth, as if to contain the words and feelings which filled it. At last he said, "You think he is capable of it? I know Henry has a temper . . ."

Miss Tolerance raised a hand to her head as if remembering where his blow might have struck her. "I have been on the wrong end of his temper, Versellion. Where you are concerned, I truly think your cousin is not in his right mind. But there is more. A tough I encountered the other day gave your cousin Folle up as the author of the attacks on you, and Mrs. Virtue . . ." She paused, trying to find a delicate way to say what she must. There was none. "Mrs. Virtue wears a bruise in the shape of your family's crest, doubtless from that damned stick your cousin wields so freely."

Versellion's hand clenched on his jaw until the knuckles whitened. Then, quite suddenly, he relaxed his hand and sat back on the sofa, regarding Miss Tolerance sadly. "What must be done, then?"

Miss Tolerance shook her head. "I have not sufficient evidence to give Bow Street—who do not scruple to tell me how interested they are in my part in these deaths. Without evidence, or direct confession, 'twill be difficult indeed to have the matter taken seriously."

"He'll be here tomorrow," Versellion said thoughtfully.

"At the ball? Is that wise, Versellion?"

"My aunt invited him, and Balobridge—that whole Tory lot, long before I knew that Wales would honor us with his presence. I cannot revoke the invitations, after all. It is Aunt Julia's party far more than it is mine."

"Will it serve your aunt's purposes to have you assassinated at her ball?" Miss Tolerance asked irritably.

"My concern has been how to keep them from queering my game—approaching Wales while I am trying my party's case with him. But perhaps you could serve a double purpose: keep me safe and surprise a confession from Henry."

Miss Tolerance eyed her lover with doubt. "At your party? What do you imagine I would do? Confront him at a contredanse and, at the change, have him drop to his knees and confess all? He's more likely to add me to the happy ranks of his victims."

"At my party?" Versellion echoed. "I only say that if you could engage him for half an hour, it would give me time to speak with Wales privately. And something useful might come of it—my God, if Balobridge catches wind of what you suspect and believes my cousin endangers his own safety, he'll give Folle up fast enough."

"Edward, what you propose plays out very like the last act of a farce. Truly, what do you think would happen?"

"You would distract my cousin and Balobridge and permit me to carry on my discussion with the Prince uninterrupted. And"—he smiled—"I would have the pleasure of seeing you dressed for a ball."

"I have no such dress. A few evening dresses, some round gowns—you have seen pretty nearly the full extent of my wardrobe, in fact—and nothing appropriate to this sort of occasion. And it is far too late—"

"I will take care of it," Versellion promised. "Sarah, I believe this is the best possible thing. The mere fact of the setting—my cousin will never expect to see you, will never expect you to approach him. He will be entirely unprepared for a confrontation. Perhaps you *will* wring something from him."

"And do you mean to invite Bow Street as well, to hear the confession you imagine your cousin will make? Masters Penryn and Hook would make a charming addition to your aunt's guest list. No, Edward, it won't do, not any of it."

She took back her hand, which he had taken in his own at some point, and sat without further comment. After a few minutes, Versellion sighed. "I won't press you. And as I should have almost no time to give you, I suppose it is foolish of me to feel that you *should* be there."

"I shall take that as a compliment," Miss Tolerance said. "But listen: I do think that you should instruct your bodyguards to increase their caution in the next few days."

The earl looked chagrined. "You will scold me when I tell you I dismissed them—nothing has happened since we returned to London and I dislike being followed around wherever I go. After all this time—"

"If I am right and your cousin is the killer, the thought of you solidifying your position with the Prince of Wales may be enough to drive him beyond caution. Particularly in light of Mrs. Virtue's death, I would say the time of greatest jeopardy is probably now. Please, Versellion, promise me you will hire them back."

"I do not plan to leave the house between now and the ball,

and I am quite adequately guarded by my people here—not to mention the legion of servants my aunt has retained to assist with the ball. I haven't the time to give to the matter—if it will make you feel better, I promise I shall hire them back."

Miss Tolerance felt moved to scream, but bit down on her anger. Versellion had never been able to fully believe in a threat to his person. Why should she expect he would change now? "I shall not see you, then, until after the ball," she said at last. "I hope all goes well for you."

He took her hand again and raised it to his lips; it was both a caress and a farewell. Already, she felt sure, his mind was upon politics again, massing arguments to sway the Prince of Wales. "It shall. It must," he said.

She took it, quite rightly, as her dismissal.

M rs. Brereton was hosting a musical evening that night. In Miss Tolerance's experience, this modest term did not adequately express the extravagance of Mrs. Brereton's entertainments, which featured songs, tableaux, and performances of a distinctly carnal nature played out by employees of the house, most clad only in vague draperies of gauze and spangles. The music itself was excellently performed and generally ignored. As on these evenings the wine flowed even more freely and expensively than usual, and the behavior of the patrons was generally outrageous, Miss Tolerance preferred to avoid the house. She let herself into the garden by way of Spanish Place and went straight to her cottage. The evening was warm and humid, but she stirred up the fire and put the kettle on for tea. Later, she thought, she would go across to the kitchen long enough to beg her dinner. For now, she took up her counts-book to tend to her bookkeeping.

Half an hour later, as she added up a column of figures for the fourth time, someone knocked on Miss Tolerance's door. She put down her pen with some relief and went to answer it; she was surprised to find Marianne, with a tray of covered dishes.

"I had thought all of you were employed with the entertainment," Miss Tolerance said. She stood aside to let the other woman enter.

"I can't sing, won't act, and don't much care to stand about in a spangled slip to be pawed at by the boys," Marianne said matter-of-factly. "I generally ask for these evenings off. Thought you might like a bite of something."

Miss Tolerance discovered her appetite in the presence of food, and the two women ate cold beef, cheese, fruit, and pastries while waiting for the kettle to boil again.

"I'm glad you thought of it," Miss Tolerance said when they had finished their meal. "I've wanted to thank you again for your care when I was sick."

Marianne shook her head; her brown curls swayed with the motion, and one dropped over her eye. "You needed a friend," she said simply. "Should have brought that book again, *Tom Jones*. Thought you liked it."

"I did. Perhaps you can bring it another time."

They did not talk much; the stretches of silence were companionable, broken by an observation or query from one to the other. Marianne had brought her workbag, and as she darned, she gave comical descriptions of Mrs. Brereton's staff in rehearsal for the evening's dissipation.

"All day Chloe's been rehearsing; she must have started at dawn. Keefe and Daisy were hard put not to laugh at her when they came upon her in the green salon this afternoon, dragging silk scarves across her chest and flinging them to the floor—"

"Good heaven, in service of what?"

"The dance of Salome. Thank God, someone talked her out of having Cook make a savory to look like the head of John the Baptist! And Chloe's balance is none too good, so half the time she waves the scarves, it wasn't what she meant to do at all, but only a sign she was trying not to fall over!"

"I'm sorry I missed this," Miss Tolerance said. "It would have been far more diverting than most of my activities today."

"I heard about your brangle this morning. I'm sorry."

Miss Tolerance poured more tea. "Sir Henry Folle? That's certainly nothing to your account."

Marianne shrugged. "I don't know. He was in a foul temper when he arrived last evening, but I thought I'd gentled him out of it."

"Sir Henry is your . . . visitor?" Miss Tolerance struggled to imagine Marianne, placid and sensible, with the volatile Folle.

"He came regularly; I suited him better than any of the other girls, and he is the sort that requires an even hand. Well, that's a thing of the past, now. Mrs. B has forbidden him the house."

Miss Tolerance felt herself torn. She liked Marianne very well; would any purpose be served in telling her what she suspected of Folle, now that the man could not return to Mrs. Brereton's? "I'm sorry if I cost you custom," she said at last.

"Bless you, dear. There will be another one to take his place," Marianne said comfortably. "I'm only sorry he was in such a tear this morning. Politics and family always seemed to provoke him, and lately he's been wild."

Miss Tolerance sipped at her tea. "Had he been calling upon you long?" She could not have said why she asked, except that a sort of politeness seemed to require it.

Marianne smiled. "A year, perhaps."

"I can't think why I did not know it," Miss Tolerance said.

"Can't you?" Marianne seemed genuinely surprised. "Mrs. B don't want us advertising who our followers are. And you've always held yourself rather apart from those of us who worked the house; no reason why you would know who my callers were—or anyone's."

Miss Tolerance blushed, feeling as if a charge of incivility had been leveled at her. "I didn't mean—" she began.

"Of course you didn't." Marianne poured more tea. "Some of the girls have said, from time to time, that you thought you were too good for the rest of us. It was Matt who used to say it was more likely that you were afraid you were no better. I confess it took me a little while to understand what he meant by it."

The pocket watch upon the mantel ticked loudly, its steady rhythm punctuated by the snapping of the fire. Miss Tolerance felt as if she had been shown a mirror's view of herself, and had to study it carefully to confirm that it was indeed a true one.

At last she said, "Matt was a clever fellow."

The breeze carried applause and a sudden roar of appreciation from the house. Marianne looked up from her darning. "That will be Chloe's turn. She'll be waving her scarves and tinkling the bells on her fingers, wrapping her legs round the gentlemen—" Another roar seemed to confirm Marianne's guess. "I shall have to go back presently, or I shall have no chance at all of getting to my room undisturbed."

"Will you be able to sleep with all that din?"

Marianne grinned. "If I couldn't sleep through noises of all sort, I would never have survived a month in your aunt's house." She folded the stocking upon which she had been working and put it and her pincushion and needle case back in her workbag.

"You will be safe, going back in?"

"Safe? Safe enough, anyway. Keefe and the staff watch over us—particularly at the entertainments, when the blood runs very hot. I don't fear anything like little Chloe's adventure with Sir Randal that you stopped. But if I'm spied, they'll want to drag me in to the business—"

"And you cannot sing and will not act." Miss Tolerance rose to her feet. "I'll walk you cross the garden, then."

At the doorway, Marianne stared across at the house, brilliantly lit and noisy. "A fine, rollicking party," she noted. " 'Twill be a great mess in the morning."

E merging from her cottage the next morning, Miss Tolerance found a large bandbox upon her doorstep. At first she thought it might be a bit of debris from the entertainment across the garden; however, it was whole, neatly tied, and clearly contained something. She brought the box in and opened it curiously. On the folds of tissue paper a card rested; in Versellion's characteristic hand, it said, *In case of need. —V.*

The item to be used at need was a dress, suited to the most formal party or ball saving only a Court function. It was of silk so dark blue as to look purplish in the sunlight, over a slip of eggshell *mousseline de soie*. The bosom was cut low and edged round with gold embroidery and beads; the sleeves were slit to reveal the lighter fabric underneath, cuffed with the same embroidery and beads as the bodice. Whoever had selected it had considered her coloring and figure and chosen something which would display both to advantage.

Miss Tolerance sat gingerly beside the dress and ran her fingertips over its silky surface, admiring the way that it caught the light and held it in its depths. She was no less moved by beautiful fabric and exquisite stitchery than any of her sex, and for a few moments she entertained delicious fantasies of wearing the dress and appearing at the ball. Then she folded it back into the tissue paper which had wrapped it, and returned the dress to its box. When she learned the direction of the dressmaker from whom it had come, she would return it; she did not imagine she would have a use for the dress, and keeping it would only make her wistful for privileges she had forfeited a decade before.

Then she went across the garden and requested Cole to hire a hackney coach; she was bound for Chelsea.

Nineteen

The day was hot, the sun high overhead; the stink of sewage and fish rose up from the Thames as her hackney crossed the river, and followed some good way on as they drove south and east. Miss Tolerance had given directions to the Great Charlotte Inn and settled herself in a corner of the hackney with her eyes closed. She did not doze, however; when the driver pulled up before the inn, she had his fare ready and stepped lightly from the carriage. She wore a walking dress of steel-blue linen and a bonnet with a matching feather, and made a picture of such astonishing respectability that no casual observer would have dreamed of her true estate; the girl who met her at the door of the inn did not appear to recognize this visitor as one who had come before.

"Mrs. Cook? Aye, ma'am, she lives upstairs. Do you want me to ask after her?"

Miss Tolerance nodded and gave her name. The girl—Nan, or Nancy, Miss Tolerance recalled—stopped midway up the stairs and looked back sharply at her guest. "You was here before. But—"

"Not so finely dressed." Miss Tolerance smiled.

The girl grinned and started up the stairs again. "Looks fine on *you*, miss," she called down. "No one'd ever know you was—" Whatever she believed Miss Tolerance to be was lost as the girl rounded the landing and started up the next flight of stairs. A moment later the girl called down without ceremony: Mrs. Cook was in and Miss Tolerance should walk up, please.

As before, Mrs. Cook would not talk seriously until she had offered her visitor tea and cakes. By this visit the older woman clearly felt Miss Tolerance to be an old friend; she complimented her upon the cut of her dress, suggested that a neck frill might look handsome with it, and went so far as to offer to make one, embroidered in whitework, as a gift. "You've been so kind to me, my dear," the older woman said comfortably.

They chatted for a few minutes, but once the tea had arrived, Miss Tolerance felt free to begin her inquiries.

"The late earl's mistress before me . . ." Mrs. Cook frowned. "There were some girls, I think, but they were a here-and-there business. The woman who came before—do you know, young as I was, and in love as I was, I was so jealous of that girl! Particularly . . ." She faltered, as one caught in the throes of memory.

Miss Tolerance quirked her eyebrow encouragingly.

"Oh, because she was so very pretty, and Versellion had brought her from Italy. Of course, by the time he and I met, the affair was some time over, but still I fretted about it, the way girls do, and since he never wholly broke the connection—" She stopped. "You don't want to hear my sentimental nonsense."

"Indeed I do. It is of the greatest interest to me. Do you happen to remember the name of the Italian woman?"

"Oh, yes. Francesca de—something Italian. Versellion called her his Italian Fan. He used to make a very coarse joke about snapping her open. . . ." Mrs. Cook pursed her lips and her rounded chins quivered. "He never said such things about me."

Miss Tolerance stared at the old woman. Her thoughts were briefly in cascading disarray. "Do you know," she said at last, "if this was the same woman who was known as Fanny Virtue?"

Mrs. Cook nodded. "She took that name, yes. You know, despite Versellion's interest in her, she did not prosper." She leaned forward confidingly; her stays creaked. "I believe she went to work in a brothel! A very sad come-down for a woman who had been mistress to an earl." It was evident from her tone that Mrs. Cook was comparing Mrs. Virtue's florid career with her own impoverished but respectable end.

"I believe," Miss Tolerance said, "that she worked for Humphrey Blackbottle, and through him came to own that fan which the old earl once gave you."

Outrage, then hurt, and at last a smile of satisfaction chased across Mrs. Cook's moon-shaped, guileless face. "But you have the fan back again," she said finally. "I suppose it's of no matter. I should not have sold it, but I was in such straits. And now Versellion's son has it?"

Miss Tolerance agreed. If Mrs. Virtue was the Italian Fan, then the matter of what had happened to the pretty, gaudy trinket she had chased was not a secret worth guarding. But if Mrs. Virtue was the Fan that Lady Versellion had warned her son about—what was the secret she had carried? The madam herself was no longer capable of telling, and while it might be that the secret went with her to her grave, it might not. Would Versellion be satisfied to let the matter go so unresolved?

Something occurred to her. "Why did the earl not sever connection to Mrs. Virtue if it so distressed you?"

Mrs. Cook pursed her mouth, drawing up her chin so that it appeared to be one soft, gibbous column from collar to lower lip. "It is not my secret to divulge. I promised—"

"Was it the opium?" Miss Tolerance threw the question out at random; her aunt had implied that Mrs. Virtue had learnt the Chinese habit from the earl. Perhaps that had created an unwilling bond between them.

"Opium?" Mrs. Cook looked utterly confused, her eyes as

large and blue as cornflowers. Their very blueness reminded Miss Tolerance of Fanny Virtue's dark, liquid, brown eyes. An echo of something ran through her mind, and Miss Tolerance was struck with an idea, or the outline of one, so forceful it rendered her speechless.

Finally, "Is there nothing else you can tell me about the link between Mrs. Virtue and the late earl, ma'am?" She asked without emphasis, not wanting to betray the excitement she was feeling.

"No, nothing. I gave my word," Mrs. Cook answered. There was a suggestion of melodrama in her tone.

"I understand." Far from being disappointed, Miss Tolerance felt the old woman's refusal to say more was as near to a confirmation of her own ideas as she was like to get from this quarter.

She rose, leaned down, and kissed the older woman on her soft cheek. "You have kept your word, and behaved with great honor, ma'am. Many of your sisterhood would not have been so discreet."

"Well, they ought to be," Mrs. Cook said. She took Miss Tolerance's hand in her own. "I think *you* would have."

It was on the tip of her tongue to disabuse Mrs. Cook of this romantic notion, but Miss Tolerance found she could not; the older woman regarded her with such sentimental admiration that it seemed unkind. She took her leave of Mrs. Cook, who looked at her sadly and remarked that she did not imagine she would see Miss Tolerance again. Moved by sudden affection as much as pity, Miss Tolerance promised that she would visit.

"We shall have cakes and tea, and talk about the war, and not the past. It's best to let the past stay buried, my dear. You'll find that as you grow older." Mrs. Cook rose to show her visitor to the door; she wheezed with the exertion, and gave Miss Tolerance a kiss smelling of peppermint lozenges. "Do be careful, my dear. This is a harsh world."

Miss Tolerance said something in reply, although she was not certain what. Her mind was very full of what she had learned; she now had a motive for Sir Henry Folle in Mrs. Virtue's death—only, to prove him a murderer, she risked making public the old whore's secret. She needed urgently to speak to Versellion, but could not do so until tomorrow, when his cursed ball, and his appointment with the Prince, would be over, and he could hear the revelations she had to share with him with a ready mind.

The ride back to Mayfair was no more pleasant than the ride to Greenwich had been; the hackney carriage was badly sprung, and the heat, if anything, more oppressive than it had been earlier. Miss Tolerance, lost in thoughts that knit the whole of Versellion's case together, barely noticed her discomfort. It was midafternoon when she arrived in Manchester Square; with the notion of occupying herself, she changed into breeches, shirt, and waistcoat, and took to the garden to do fencing drills until she was exhausted. The heat, rather than lessening as the hour grew later, was greater; her shirt stuck to her arms and shoulders, the hair she had tied at the nape of her neck was sweat-soaked. She advanced and retreated upon a target, thrusting in *tierce*, in *quarte*, feinting and beating—as much as she could do without a partner to work with—in hopes that the activity would quiet the thoughts that milled through her busy mind.

She had completed a complicated pattern that ended in the boar's thrust, a lunge so deep she finished it on one knee, her point up and under the breastbone of her imagined opponent.

"Bravo, Miss Tolerance." Lord Balobridge's voice was as dry as the whispering of the ivy along the garden wall. "I see now how you vanquished my men."

Miss Tolerance was at once on her feet, sword sheathed. "I don't believe I had to resort to anything so elaborate, sir," she said pleasantly. "How may I be of service to you?" She drew her sleeve across her forehead, very much aware of the picture she presented, hair tangled, clothes sweaty and disarrayed.

Balobridge appeared to be as discomfited as Miss Tolerance.

"Mrs.—your aunt said I might find you here," he began. "Ordinarily I would have sent a letter."

"I collect that your business is urgent, then?" Miss Tolerance invited him with a gesture to enter her cottage, and led the way. "May I offer you tea, or a glass of wine?"

Balobridge shook his head. Either he was genuinely upset, Miss Tolerance thought, or it suited his purposes to appear so. He did not immediately tell her what the matter was; Miss Tolerance decided to wait until he was ready to say. She sat quietly.

"This is difficult," Balobridge said at last. "I am concerned; indeed, I think I must be in part to blame for what has happened, and I pray God that I am not too late." He looked about the room. "Have you no clock? Do you know what time it is?"

"There is a watch upon the mantel," Miss Tolerance informed him. "Is the time so important to you?"

"I don't know. It may all be nothing, but I fear—I fear—" Balobridge took a handkerchief from his pocket and dabbed carefully at his upper lip. "Miss Tolerance, I may have loosed a tiger into your patron's ball."

"I collect you mean Sir Henry Folle?"

Balobridge nodded. He folded the handkerchief neatly and returned it to his pocket before he spoke; when he did, his voice was low and uncharacteristically agitated.

"I make no excuse for my aims. To change governments while we are at war would be disastrous. But my tools—it made sense to ally with Folle; he's always had the devil's own temper, particularly where his cousin was concerned, but the squabbling of the Folles has been a matter of gossip for generations. How could I not turn him to my party's advantage? And to give the devil his due, Versellion has always tried to maintain a cordial face with his cousin—which only made Folle angrier, of course, any fool could have—I am running on."

"Yes, sir, you are."

Again Balobridge took the kerchief out and blotted his upper lip. " 'Tis hot today, is it not?"

"My lord, Sir Henry Folle's temper is known to me also. What has happened today to bring you to my door in such a state of alarm?"

"Miss Tolerance, I beg you will believe how difficult this is. A man in my position makes compromises, decisions others not steeped in political life might find . . ."

"Vile?" Miss Tolerance suggested pleasantly.

"Questionable." Balobridge gave her a look of dislike. "I never intended an innocent's death; all I have done I have done for the good of my country and my party." He paused heavily, as if waiting.

"And what *have* you done, sir?"

"Not an hour ago Folle and I were walking in Bond Street. We encountered His Highness."

"The Prince of Wales? Was this a chance meeting or by design?"

"Accident, a damned unfortunate chance. His Highness spoke with us for a few minutes—polite piffle, you know the sort of thing. But in the course of the conversation, he nudged Folle as one who is in on the joke, and asked if he would see Folle at Versellion's ball tonight. 'Your cousin means to speak to me—means to cut your party quite out, hey?'" Lord Balobridge pinched his nose. "I have known the Prince since he was a boy, and still I am not certain if he is a clever man who sometimes plays the fool, or a fool who makes inspired moves. Had he thought for a month, he could not have said anything better calculated to cause trouble."

"I take it Sir Henry did not take kindly to the Prince's comment?"

"I thank God Wales moved on soon after—Christ knows what Folle might have said in his presence else. Miss Tolerance, the man was mad. He was crazed with rage, shaking with it, walking along Bond Street with his hands fisted, muttering to himself like a Bedlamite. If I could make plain to you—he paced along, his voice first low, then loud, and what he said to me made so little sense I am almost afraid to credit it—muttering of Versellion, and you, and The Old Woman. Then—and this was the more frightening—he stopped. As suddenly as one might snuff a candle! He smiled at me and said he would see me at Versellion House, and that he was quite looking forward to it."

For a moment Miss Tolerance and Lord Balobridge sat quiet, each considering what this might mean. A bird sang outside in the garden, and distantly Miss Tolerance could hear a woman's voice on the street, hawking violets.

"Clearly, my lord, you believe Folle to be dangerous," Miss Tolerance said at last.

The old man looked Miss Tolerance squarely in the eye, an edge of anger replacing the fear in his voice. "Do not you, Miss Tolerance? I think he means to do something to keep Versellion from cementing his interest with the Prince tonight."

"What could he do that would not do his cause more damage than Versellion's?"

"Kill Versellion," Balobridge said baldly.

Miss Tolerance looked at him in dismay. "At a ball, in full sight of hundreds of people—including His Royal Highness? What does he think he would gain?"

"He is not thinking. It's gone far beyond that. Now he does not care that our party takes the prize, so long as he can keep his cousin from it. Not all my persuasions could calm him, and then he was gone, before I thought to have him restrained."

Miss Tolerance imagined Sir Henry Folle walking the streets of London like a rabid dog, waiting for the moment when he could tear out the throat of his hated cousin. Indeed, the image fit easily with her idea of Folle and his crimes, but she considered the source and frowned.

"My lord, you have all my admiration, but I think that altruism has no great part of your nature. Why are you here? If Folle killed Versellion, would not your party be that much closer to fixing its interest with the Prince?"

Balobridge attempted a shocked demur, then stopped. " 'Twould be a false benefit, Miss Tolerance. Folle kills Versellion, and the sympathy of the people, and very likely Prince and Parliament, will be with the Whigs. It would be as well to turn the nation over to Bonaparte—the result would be the same, ruled by the whim of tradesmen and farmers—"

"Better to let the tradesmen and farmers starve at the whim of the peerage?"

Lord Balobridge spoke through his teeth. "Argue philosophy with me another time, Miss Tolerance. Whatever my politics, I do not want to see your *employer* slain."

Miss Tolerance caught her temper. "No more do I, sir. But I learned from Lord Trux that you were behind an attack on the Richmond road that purposed to kill him. Perhaps you would explain why you wanted Versellion dead on the Richmond road, but do not want him dead tonight?"

Balobridge smiled unpleasantly. "Dead tonight, at the feet of the Prince of Wales, with half of London privy to the details? At the hands of a man known everywhere to be my protégé? Miss Tolerance, lowering as it is to admit, I have set something in motion that it seems I no longer control."

This admission Miss Tolerance found more compelling than any demur that had gone before. "You have no idea where Folle is?"

Balobridge shook his head. "I have men watching his house— I am quite willing to hold him there, should he return—but he has not appeared yet. I may be able to stop him, Miss Tolerance; I am not without resources. But should he elude me—I do not like to think what will happen."

"Tell Versellion not to let him be admitted," Miss Tolerance suggested.

"I have sent a note to his aunt, who acts as hostess for the party. But Julia Geddes has always had a soft spot for Folle; I fear she will not listen. Miss Tolerance, your credit with Versellion is greater than mine. I tell you all this in hope that you will persuade him to be on his guard—"

"Deny his cousin the party, only to find there was no danger and he has given Folle a grievance in London's eyes? Or better still, delay his conference with the Prince so that you might speak with him first?"

Balobridge rose from his chair, leaning heavily on his walking stick. His doggish face was pale, his lips compressed into a line; the tip of his nose was red and there were small, feverish patches of color on either cheek. "I had thought better of you, Miss Tolerance. I have explained my motives as much as I care to do; regardless of whether you believe me or not, Versellion is in danger. You may act as you see fit." The old man turned on his heel and went to the door. Miss Tolerance watched him start across the garden and called to him.

"My lord—I will do all that I may."

M iss Tolerance wrote out a note, outlining Balobridge's story for Versellion, and took it across for Cole to bring to Versellion House. "Go yourself, please, and give it to no one other than the earl himself," she instructed. Then she wrote out another note, directed to Sir Walter Mandif, and sent it off, too.

At seven o'clock Miss Tolerance inquired if Cole had returned from Versellion House yet, and was surprised to learn that he had not. Keefe brought her a note, a reply from Sir Walter in which he thanked her for her information, but noted that as Folle had as yet committed no crime for which there was ready evidence, his own hands were neatly tied as to action. *But should you think of a way in which I may assist you*—Miss Tolerance balled the note up in her fist and tossed it into the fire.

At half past seven Cole appeared, wearing the look of dejection common to hirelings who have defaulted of a command. "I never did see the earl, Miss Sarah. Waited all this time, and finally Lady Julia's maid come in to say that my lord was very busy, and if I had a message, I'd best give it to her. I didn't think I should do that, so home I come. I'm that sorry, miss."

As Miss Tolerance assured Cole that it was not his fault, she was already calculating what was best to be done. Possibly there was no danger. Balobridge might have overreacted or, worse, schemed to force her or Versellion into overreacting. Folle might well have rethought his anger, perhaps decided to avoid the party altogether. Versellion *had* sworn to rehire the bodyguards he had let go; they would see to him.

But if not?

"Wait a moment, Cole," she said, and wrote out another note.

> Sir:
> *If you wish to assist me, will you serve as my escort to the ball at Versellion House this evening? I shall be ready to leave Manchester Square by 9 p.m., if you will call upon me then. I realize this is short notice, but I hope you will believe me that I do not make this request lightly. Your very humble servant . . .*

Miss Tolerance read it over, deploring the melodrama of the request, but sanded it, sealed it, and sent Cole off with it to Sir Walter Mandif. That done, she went upstairs to her chamber to take the blue ball gown out of its bandbox and approximate the appearance of a woman of virtue and means.

At a quarter after nine o'clock, Keefe returned to announce the arrival of Sir Walter Mandif. The magistrate wore evening dress and an inquiring quirk to his eyebrow, but bowed politely over Miss Tolerance's hand and presented his compliments upon her appearance. With little time, no hairdresser, no more jewelry than a chain and locket for her neck, and gloves and a pair of slippers, she had borrowed from her aunt Miss Tolerance had managed to create a version of herself that was demure yet presentable. She thanked Sir Walter for his help and explained more fulsomely what the situation with Folle was.

"How do you imagine we will gain entry to the last great party of the season? I was not invited; those are not the circles in which I move," Mandif said.

Miss Tolerance smiled. "I am known to Versellion's staff; unless he has specifically forbidden me the place, which I do not believe to be the case, I think they will admit me."

"Well, then." Sir Walter helped her to arrange a scarf over her shoulders and offered his arm. "My carriage is waiting in the street. We will arrive unfashionably early. . . ."

" 'Tis my first ball," Miss Tolerance said. "I do not wish to miss anything."

The ballroom at Versellion House was not large, and might have passed under other circumstances for a large gallery or salon; but it easily supported musicians, tucked in a corner below ornamental galleries, and could hold two dozen couples— if they did not mind scraping elbows as they moved through the sets. There were as well a profusion of smaller public rooms on the ground and first floors, all brightly lit and slowly filling with guests. The gardens behind the house had, as well, been opened for the ball. Miss Tolerance, despite a note of pleasure deep within her—eight-and-twenty and it was her first ball!— still damned the party for having so many rooms in which Sir Henry Folle might have secreted himself.

Sir Walter Mandif had given their names—Miss Tolerance had, for the evening, reclaimed the name Brereton—and the footman bowed them in with a raised eyebrow but no hesitation. Lady Julia Geddes, receiving guests at Versellion's side, smiled vaguely at these people she did not recognize, but asked no questions. Versellion had heard her name announced; any surprise he felt at her arrival was well in hand by the time she and Sir Walter reached the earl to make their bows.

"My lord, may I present Sir Walter Mandif, the magistrate of whom I have spoken?" Miss Tolerance put as much meaning as she decently could into her words. Versellion bowed and thanked Sir Walter for bringing Miss . . . he hesitated, then brought out the name Brereton instead of Tolerance.

"To what do I owe this charming surprise?" he murmured.

"I was warned that there might b—"

Miss Tolerance's warning was cut short as Lady Julia demanded Versellion's attention. "Edward, see who is come!" Miss Tolerance and Sir Walter moved away.

She had planned to watch Versellion herself; she proposed that Sir Walter make a round through the public rooms to see if

Folle was anywhere among them. When Sir Walter pointed out that he did not know what Folle looked like and was thus useless for the purpose, Miss Tolerance sighed, took his place, and began to wander seeming casually through the refreshments room, the card room, and the other chambers where an enterprising murderer might be waiting. The competing needs for thoroughness and speed warred in her, complicated by the need to play the part of a woman wandering aimlessly through a party seeking acquaintance.

At the end of an hour, having persuaded herself that Folle had not yet arrived, Miss Tolerance returned to the ballroom, which by now was crowded and stickily hot. Sir Walter lounged against one wall watching the dancers, among whom the Earl of Versellion numbered.

"No sign of Folle, I take it."

She shook her head agian.

"Would you like to dance?"

Miss Tolerance shook her head again. "You're very kind to ask, sir, but I doubt I remember how. My last dancing lesson was rather more than ten years ago. Safer to remain a wall-flower."

"Not at your first ball!"

She smiled. "If they are all as hot as this one, 'tis likely to be my last, as well."

He laughed at that, and for a little time they chatted as they watched, in an attitude so very casual that an observer might have deduced that they were lovers seeking to disguise the fact. Miss Tolerance was enough entertained that she did not at first notice when Sir Henry Folle entered the room. The footman's voice pronouncing his name brought her to full alert.

Seeing him, Miss Tolerance was immediately convinced of the justice of Lord Balobridge's concern. Folle, tonight, appeared both intense and precariously balanced; his eyes burned as he looked around the room. Indeed, he appeared so agitated to her that she wondered that Lady Julia could greet him with a placid smile and a kiss on the cheek.

"That is Folle," she murmured to Sir Walter.

"Then at last we know where we are: your man is here, Versellion has not yet been assassinated. How are we to proceed now? Follow Folle about? Wait until he produces a pistol or takes a sword down from the wall, or—" Sir Walter did not finish the thought. The footman was announcing the Prince of Wales and his party.

The musicians ceased their playing. The dancers stopped, all eyes turned to the doorway. A tall, fat man with several orders pinned to his coat appeared in the doorway and there was a burst of applause, which he waved away amiably. The Prince made his way across the room to Lady Julia through a line of curtseys; by the time Wales had reached his hostess, Versellion had joined them. In watching the Prince, Miss Tolerance had briefly lost sight of Folle. Now she saw him, edging toward the Prince and Versellion through the crowd.

Miss Tolerance began to move, too, calculating at what point she would intersect Folle's path, and how fast she would have to go. They were only a dozen paces from Folle's target when she caught his arm. He turned to her blankly, as if he didn't recognize her. By now the crowd had resumed their conversations and the musicians their playing; there was nothing remarkable to see about Miss Tolerance and Folle—except for his expression when he recognized her.

"Take your hands off me, you bitch," he said, deep in his throat. "You will not stop me."

Miss Tolerance, just as cold, tightened her grip. "Someone must stop you, Sir Henry, before you do something stupid." She relaxed her features and moderated her tone to a slight whine. *Give him something to believe*, she thought. *Greed or betrayal. Better yet, both.* She would play the part Folle expected of her.

"You want to hurt your cousin? Fine. I'm none too fond of him myself right now. But rather than the violence you plainly intend, I can give you a weapon far more elegant."

"What weapon? What are you talking about?" Folle asked.

Miss Tolerance pulled Folle about so his back was to Wales and Versellion. "I know the secret of the fan," she told him. "And it will bring him down. But I will not tell you here, where Versellion can see. He will know I gave it to you if he sees us speaking. There is a row of withdrawing rooms along the conservatory hall; I will be in one of them in a few minutes' time. Bring your pocketbook."

She permitted him no time to argue; if he was going to take her bait and permit her to lure him from his quarry, she must be as mysterious as possible. She returned to Sir Walter, explained what she was attempting, and asked that he keep Folle under his eye until the man had joined her in the withdrawing room.

"And then?"

"Pray for me. I have not the slightest idea what I shall tell him." Miss Tolerance smiled. "If your dignity will admit of listening at doors, you can hear what I do—perhaps Folle will say something useful."

On the ground floor, a hallway ran between the salons and led to a conservatory which, in its turn, led to the gardens. Nearest the conservatory there were several small rooms suited to close conference, each no more than a dozen feet square, furnished with a divan, a pair of gilded chairs, a side table, and a branch or two of candles. The first of these was occupied, by the sound of it, by a man and woman engaged in a quarrel. The door to the second appeared to be locked; no sounds issued from it. The third room was unoccupied; Miss Tolerance entered, seated herself, and waited an anxious few minutes until the door opened again. It was Folle, and Lord Balobridge was directly behind him.

"You see, there she is. Now, what have you to tell me? If I find this is all a trick—"

"Why would I trick you? Your cousin owes me my fee and some other considerations as well, and shows no sign of paying. A woman in my position must tend to herself first." Miss Tolerance pushed the note of hurt and anger back into her voice. "If you can guarantee my fee—"

"Anything you like," Folle snapped. "Was there correspondence in the fan? Was it treason?"

"Treason? No, there was nothing about treason in that fan—whyever should you think so?" She went to the door and locked it. "There. Now we shan't be interrupted. May I inquire how you came to learn of the fan in the first place?"

Lord Balobridge spoke: "I should think you knew that already, Miss Tolerance. Trux told me about your hiring, and about the fan."

She nodded. "And, of course, you knew only what Trux told you. Well, as it turns out, it was never a fan we sought. It was a woman."

Folle was pacing the short length of the room, hands clenched behind his back as though he feared them capable of independent action. "A woman?" He set his teeth together and looked toward the door.

"Before you return to assassinate your cousin, sir, will you permit me to explain?"

Perhaps it was the bald statement of his intention that stopped him; Folle turned back, rocked on his heels, and nodded. Miss Tolerance began her recitation, hoping to God that Sir Walter Mandif was where she had told him to be.

"I began as you did, believing what we sought was a fan. I started, upon information, in Leyton, where I spoke with two women, hoping for assistance in finding Deborah Cunning, to whom the fan was given thirty years ago. By diligent investigation—I really am quite good at my work, Sir Henry—I was able to discover Mrs. Cunning's—now Mrs. Cook's—address, and spoke with her, only to find that she did not have the fan, that she had sold it years before to Mr. Humphrey Blackbottle, of whose establishments you have spoken to me several times." Miss Tolerance smiled. "I did, at last, procure the fan—at which point the men sent by Lord Balobridge to assassinate Versellion"—she nodded politely at Balobridge—"drove him, and me, out of the city for a time. Try as we might, we could not discover anything about the fan which explained its importance, and I began to wonder if we had, indeed, the correct fan.

"By this time, of course, I was also much concerned by the death of Mrs. Smith, in Leyton, and of Matt Etan, late of my aunt's establishment, and my friend. I wondered for a time why you killed Mrs. Smith and not Mrs. Cockbun, Sir Henry." She did not pause to enjoy Folle's wild-eyed start. "But then I realized that Mrs. Cockbun would have told you anything for the pleasure of your company, where Mrs. Smith was likely to be less forthcoming. Did you bully her, Sir Henry? I don't think she would have helped a bully. Raised your temper, didn't she?"

Folle's face was red, his lips tightly closed. He looked away from her.

Miss Tolerance opened her reticule and took out a piece of wax and a twist of paper. "Did you note the candles in Mrs. Smith's parlor, Sir Henry? They had dried flowers pressed into them. Like the bowls of dried flowers Mrs. Smith kept about, I suspect they were meant to mask the smell of the river behind the house. And of course, wax takes a fine impression." She held her palm flat so that Folle and Balobridge could both see the bits of wax, one of which clearly bore enough of the lion crowned with flames—the Folle crest—to be recognizable. "I suppose Mrs. Smith sent you about your business and you struck at her the way you twice made to strike at me—and when you tried to strike me in the street, Sir Henry, you dropped some of the dried flowers from Mrs. Smith's parlor—I suppose they got into your pocket or cuff. You really ought not to carry that stick if you cannot control your temper."

She closed her fingers around the pieces of wax before Folle could snatch them away, but Folle seemed incapable of movement.

"As you do not appear to have visited Mrs. Cook, I presume you could not find her. That must have maddened you. And when you encountered poor Matt, who was only my messenger to Versellion, you beat h—"

"That was Hart began it! Hart struck first, to loosen your friend's tongue, but the filthy mongrel wouldn't speak. We would not even have pulled him aside, but we thought that it was *you*! And then we took the note from him—it was useless! Hart swore the sodomite must know more and hit him again. Then that little piece of filth turned to me, ran at me, threw himself at me begging for help! Tried to work his—his wiles on me," Folle spat. His hand closed convulsively on nothing; Miss Tolerance privily thanked God he was not carrying his walking stick that evening.

"He asked for your help, so you beat him to death, sir?" Miss Tolerance kept her voice cool, but it shook a little nonetheless. "What I do not understand is how you knew to find him—or that I had given him a message to deliver."

A look passed between Balobridge and Folle. "I was told you'd gone out with a note to my cousin."

"Who told you?"

Folle looked at Balobridge. Balobridge studied the backs of his hands. In the silence, Miss Tolerance was aware of music from the ballroom: a waltz.

"Well, let me finish. I only found the last piece of the puzzle this morning: the identity of the Fan."

Balobridge spoke. "I don't suppose you would care to unravel the mystery for us, Miss Tolerance? What is there about this woman to threaten Versellion?"

"I have my suspicions, my lord. Unfortunately, I cannot ask the lady herself. She was an abbess at one of Mr. Humphrey Blackbottle's establishments, as Sir Henry knows, and she was beaten to death two nights ago."

Balobridge turned to regard Folle with horror, as if this final death had tipped the scales against him.

Folle laughed. "You traipse around London for a fortnight and all you can come up with is a dead whore?"

Miss Tolerance reminded Sir Henry that she had not been traipsing around London for his benefit. "And for my client's benefit, I suppose it works out very well. If the woman knew any secrets, she can no longer divulge them. If you had not killed her, sir, you might have persuaded her to sell her secret to you."

Folle stopped his pacing.

Balobridge rapped his cane on the floor. "What in God's name are you talking about?"

"Sir Henry knows, sir. The old woman you heard him raving about earlier today was the madam in a Cheapside brothel, brought from Italy to be the mistress of the current earl's father. The Italian Fan. I have excellent reason to believe that Sir Henry visited her two nights ago and beat her to death with that cane he wields so freely."

Sir Henry Folle took a step forward; the immobility of a moment before had clearly passed off in a new cloud of rage and panic.

"You bitch! You cannot accuse me of that—whoever this Cheapside whore is, I never set eyes upon her. Two nights ago—you know where I was. You damned quean, if Versellion thinks he can hang me upon this evidence—" He sprang at her.

Miss Tolerance took up one of the gilded chairs in both hands and held Folle off with it. The chair was remarkably heavy for such a spindly looking thing, she thought irritably. She was not certain how long she could continue to hold Folle off. "Get help!" she spat at Balobridge, but the old man sat stock-still, as if he were dazed or mesmerized by the brawl breaking out before him.

Folle had grabbed one leg of the chair and attempted to pull it out of Miss Tolerance's hands, while sweeping his other fist at her viciously, just out of range to make his blows land. Again he pulled, and Miss Tolerance let the chair go, sending him reeling backward, still upon his feet. She saw her way past Folle to the door; if she could reach it, Sir Walter Mandif or a passing footman or—anyone—might come to her aid. Miss Tolerance took two steps to her left, another back around the end of the sofa, and then her heel caught in the trailing elegance of her skirt and she fell heavily to her knees.

Before she could recover herself, Folle was on her, his face snarling into hers and his hands around her throat. Miss Tolerance was briefly aware that Lord Balobridge had recovered from his paralysis and was clinging uselessly to Folle's arm, attempting to prise him loose; she tried her own strength against Folle, but this close, without weapons, and with her dress pinned to the floor by her own weight and Folle's, she was not his match. *Damn,* she thought. She tried to pull his hands from her throat, but the leverage was wrong; she tried to tear at his face, but her hands were curiously weak. *Damn it, somebody come!* Her thoughts grew more disordered; she knew she must not stop fighting, but she was tired. Her ears were ringing and she saw sparks before her eyes. *My first ball, and I cannot hear the music anymore.*

When Folle was pulled off her, Miss Tolerance fell backward against the wall, taking gulps of air. For a moment it was all she could do to realize that she was not dead, nor likely to be; Folle's arms were pinned behind his back by one of Versellion's footmen, with Sir Walter Mandif just behind. In the doorway Miss Tolerance saw Versellion himself, and beyond him, the Prince of Wales. Sir Walter was saying something.

"... of the Crown, in the murders of Mrs. Charlotte Smith, Matthew Etan, and ..." He paused and looked at Miss Tolerance. "Mrs. Fanny Virtue?"

Miss Tolerance nodded. She saw that Balobridge had effaced himself against the wall. Mandif followed her gaze and stated that Lord Balobridge must be taken into custody as well, upon suspicion of complicity in an attempt upon the life of the Earl of Versellion. The old man nodded tiredly.

Sir Walter looked from Miss Tolerance to Versellion. "Perhaps, my lord, you have another chamber in which Miss Tolerance can recover herself? I should like, if it is convenient, to hold these gentlemen here until the Runners arrive to take them into custody."

Everything seemed out of her hands now, and Miss Tolerance was content to have it so. As she started for the door, she heard Folle burst into accusations and recriminations: Balobridge had masterminded all, that bitch—by which she assumed she was meant—was putting him up for a murder he had not committed, she was in Balobridge's pay as well as Versellion's, his cousin had connived with Balobridge . . . the rest of Folle's ravings were lost to her.

In the doorway Miss Tolerance found herself flanked by Versellion on one side and the Prince of Wales on the other. The Prince said something about bravery and gallantry, and bowed over her hand. Miss Tolerance attempted a curtsy from which she could barely rise; her knees were weak.

"You will excuse me, sir?" Versellion said hurriedly to the Prince. When Wales nodded his dismissal, the earl led Miss Tolerance through the crowd of the curious which had inevitably gathered in the hallway, and up the stairs to the salon she had waited in before. He hovered over her as if she were enfeebled and barely able to walk; at the door to the salon, he dispatched a maid to bring back wine.

"Not wine, please. Tea?" Miss Tolerance said.

The maid went at once. Versellion settled Miss Tolerance upon a sofa and sat beside her. After a few minutes, she looked up at him.

"You must return to your party," she said.

"Not while you are—"

"Just tired, Edward. The tea will help. But the Prince is still below; ought you go back to him?" She had seen his sideways glance at the door and understood the pull between love and politics.

"I should not stay away long," he promised.

"Go. I shall do as Sir Walter suggests and recover myself. I have much to think about. *Go.*"

Versellion's smile bespoke his appreciation, and the kiss he placed upon her palm suggested something rather warmer, but he did not linger. As he passed from the room, the music and the low murmur of the crowd sounded from the ballroom downstairs—the party was going on, doubtless as a tactful cover for the evening's events. Miss Tolerance leaned back on the sofa and looked down at her hands, which, she noted, were still trembling quite badly.

Twenty

After a time, Miss Tolerance got up and examined herself in the mirror to see what damage Folle had done. Her hair hung about her head and bruises were already ringing her throat. Thankful there was no need to pass under the eyes of the respectable crowd below, Miss Tolerance settled in a deep chair and sat for a time with her eyes closed. She was aware that the maid returned with the tea and a plate of cakes from the buffet downstairs; after the girl left, she roused herself sufficiently to pour a cup of tea, but she did not remember to drink it. Slumped in the corner of the chair and lulled by the distant sound of the music, she dozed.

When she woke, it was well past one. The music still played, buoyed by the pleasant murmur of many voices. There would be dancing until four or so, she thought, leavened with excited murmurs about an incident in one of Lord Versellion's withdrawing rooms that very night. Then the remaining guests would be fed breakfast before they went home. Thinking of breakfast, she realized how hungry she was: she drank a cup of cold tea and ate the cakes. Then, unable to sleep again, she began to pace the room. She spent a long time examining the portrait of Versellion and his parents, and then a small print of the Folle crest with *impavidus fiducia* inscribed below it: *terrible responsibility*. She thought about her own position in her aunt's house. And she thought about Sir Henry Folle's confessions that evening.

After an hour or so, she tidied her hair and stole along the corridor to the back stairs and down to the servants' hall, where she pressed a note, and a coin, upon one of the kitchen boys, instructing him to deliver it without delay. To his protests about the time, she replied that it was urgent—and that she would give him another shilling when he came back. That sent him off at a run, and Miss Tolerance returned to the room upstairs, noting that the party was thinning as to company, but by no means over.

She dozed again. When she woke, the music had stopped, and the light through the windows was the gray that comes before dawn. She stepped to the window to observe carriages drawing up, collecting passengers, and departing in a dozy line. She watched for a long time, and so saw a hackney carriage draw up, leave several passengers, and depart again. Miss Tolerance nodded to herself but stayed by the window.

The door opened behind her. "You are awake," Versellion said. "How do you feel? I'm sorry I was kept away so long. . . ."

"I shall have some bruises, but bruises fade."

"I'm glad you did not go. I was afraid you would."

Still watching the carriages, Miss Tolerance shook her head. "What happened at your conference with the Prince?"

The earl had come to stand behind her, not quite touching. "We had just begun when one of the footmen arrived to tell me that Cousin Henry was strangling a lady, and a magistrate was attempting to break the door down," Versellion said. "You may imagine how this intrigued the Prince. He insisted upon accompanying me, as you saw. After that, of course, mere politics paled in comparison with your adventures."

"But you returned to him," Miss Tolerance said. "You spoke further."

"You might say so," Versellion said, a little bitterly. "I do not know that anything we said was to the purpose. His Highness is playing a deep game, and I'm not sure he will commit himself to anyone until he has the Regency in his pocket. I thought to play the Prince to my party's ends, but it appears he may have thought to play me, too."

"Lord Balobridge said he could never make out whether Wales was a smart man playing a deep part, or an inspired fool," Miss Tolerance said.

"Lord Balobridge's view is colored by his party; Wales is no fool. And Balobridge now has a good deal more to worry about than the Prince's moods. You neatly took two rivals out of the game tonight, and I don't think that will hurt my cause."

"Your cause?" Miss Tolerance asked.

"My party's cause. The same thing."

"Ah, yes. Of course."

Versellion looked at her quizzically. "Do you doubt me? I don't seek power for myself, Sarah. But without power, nothing can be accomplished. With power—"

"With power, the object becomes maintaining or amassing more power, I believe. Ask the Prince of Wales; I suspect he understands that far better than you think." She stepped away from him and turned back into the room. "I discovered the secret of the fan yesterday."

"My God!" Versellion held a chair for her, then took one for himself. "My God, after all that has happened? What is it?"

"Not an it. A who. I was waiting to tell you until after the ball: the fan was a woman. Mrs. Virtue, Fanny Virtue."

"What, the old whore?"

"*Whore* is a hard word, Edward. Particularly a hard word to use for your mother."

V ersellion began a thunderstruck protest, but Miss Tolerance put up a hand to stop him. Her voice was cool and thoughtful, meant to soothe rather than excite.

"In a sense, you might say that the letter in the fan indeed led me to the secret you sought. When I met with the botanist Dr. Hawley, he said something about eye color, had I ever seen two blue-eyed parents produce a brown-eyed child. I don't know if I have or not—Dr. Hawley is in dead earnest about his botanical experiments, but I saw nothing to demonstrate that he's correct. But his question lodged with me, and every time I saw this picture"—she gestured at the family portrait on the far wall—"it nagged. It was not until yesterday, when I learned that your father's pleasant name for Mrs. Virtue was his 'Italian Fan,' that it began to fall into place. You look like your father, Edward, but your eyes are exactly like your mother's in their shape and their color. Did you know the secret when you hired me?"

Now Versellion leaned forward, elbows on his knees, and looked at her with intensity. "You're sure of this? I can't believe— *Why*? Why raise me as his son when— And my mother! Lady Versellion. How she must have felt, raising me as her own. . . ." He ran his hands over his face. "My father . . ."

"I imagine he determined to keep his brother from inheriting the title, even if it meant passing his bastard son off as legitimate get," Miss Tolerance finished. "Politics and family, the two great passions of the Folles. And the family temper makes it easy for those passions to overrule all other concerns. I should like to think you killed Mrs. Virtue in passion, not cold blood."

"Good God, what are you saying?" Versellion dropped his hands and sat upright. "What are you saying?"

Miss Tolerance frowned. "Please do not be coy, Edward. I think there can only be honesty between us now, no matter how used to prevarication your political life has made you. I admit I thought it was Folle. He killed Mrs. Smith and poor Matt—and I don't like him. It was easy for me to believe he killed your mother as well." Versellion twitched away from the word *mother* as Miss Tolerance went on.

"But he swore—when he was in custody, and had nothing to gain by it—that he knew nothing of Mrs. Virtue's death. He didn't know her name until I told him. And I remembered later that . . . a friend of mine at Mrs. Brereton's house had been with him at the time he would otherwise have been killing Mrs. Virtue."

Versellion appeared to collect himself. He smiled forgivingly. "If it is not my cousin, it could still be anyone else. It might have been one of Folle's agents, the man who attacked you."

"Hart? Would he have had access to your signet? When you struck her, you left a mark on her cheek with your ring."

"You cannot tell me a signet left a clear enough mark to convict me! And you seem very eager to believe me capable—"

"The mark was not as clear as the one your cousin left in the wax at Mrs. Smith's, but it was highly suggestive of your ring. When I put that together with motive, and once I knew he could not have done it, I realized that your cousin had no reason to want Mrs. Virtue dead. Indeed, had he imagined her existence, do you not think he would have guarded her life with his own? She had the secret he could use to undo you." She asked again, "Edward, how did you come to kill your mother?"

"Don't call her that! Sarah . . ." Versellion reached out a hand to her, but Miss Tolerance regarded him with a cool eye and did not extend her own. After a moment he let his hand drop. When he spoke again, it was quietly, his eyes fixed upon the floor as if seeing the whole played out before him there.

"All right, if you will have it. It was an accident. I went there—you said she knew nothing of the fan, and then I got a note from her bidding me come. We were looking for a secret about my family, and she knew one. There was no danger from the secret, she said, but I should know what it was. She told me to come to the house disguised, ask for a girl, then excuse myself and find her. I swear to you, Sarah, I had no idea. I found her lounging on her sofa, for all the world as if she were a goddess receiving on Olympus. She told me to take off my hat and scarf and let her see me. Then she said I looked just like *him*. The longer she looked at me, the more agitated she became, murmuring to herself. She began to weep a little, then came at me. I swear, I felt as though she were attacking me. Threw her arms about my neck."

Miss Tolerance nodded sadly.

"I pushed her away—she was drunk or sick, sloppy with it. Disgusting. I asked her why she'd summoned me . . . and she told me. She wept all over me. *Figlio mio*, she kept saying. She wanted to kiss me, embrace me. She wanted me to kiss her. I couldn't even draw a breath, she would not give me a moment to think."

Miss Tolerance looked at her lover pityingly. In a few words his world, his self, had unraveled, and the clever Mrs. Virtue had been too addled with opium and sentiment to see it.

"She told you she was your mother."

"She told me I was her son. She kept pressing in on me. I had to push her away, she kept grabbing at me until I finally struck her. Only once, I swear it. Then she sat down again and told me the whole story. At the end she looked at me as if this must be welcome news. She tried to embrace me again, this raddled old woman pawing at me, claiming me over and over— My God." His voice shook. "She wouldn't stop! I was in such a rage and she wouldn't stop and there was a candlestick—"

"And you struck her down and left the house."

He nodded. "I was in such a panic I could not think what to do."

"A panic. And yet, you thought to wipe the candlestick. And when I came to tell you that she was dead, you pretended astonishment."

"I was afraid to tell you what I had done—Christ, I was afraid to think of it myself."

"You would have let your cousin hang for your mother's death as well as for the others."

"*Don't*—" He broke off. He studied her for a moment. Then

the line etched between his brows smoothed, and he gazed at Miss Tolerance with great reasonableness. "Would it truly do good to confess myself a murderer? I stand poised to do such good, Sarah. Henry was always volatile, he could never brook opposition—indeed, to be honest, he had long ago passed the point where his rages could be excused. He killed your friend, and that old woman—"

"Mrs. Virtue was an old woman, too," Miss Tolerance reminded him.

"Sarah, I acted in the shock of the moment. Surely you must see that."

"I do."

"My cousin is a dangerous man, Sarah. I am not. Sarah." His tone was gentle, not wheedling but persuasive. "You know me. You know what I want. If I win my point with the Prince, my party can accomplish so much good. Perhaps then"—he spoke as if he were changing the subject—"you will overcome your scruples and be with me. When I consider the crop of insipid maidens paraded before me tonight, and how much finer a politician's wife you would make than any of—"

"Please, Edward." Miss Tolerance laid a finger over her lover's lips to stop the words. "You misread my character. I cannot be bought by the suggestion of marriage."

He looked genuinely astonished. "It is no suggestion. Sarah, if you love me . . ." He took her hand in his own; this time she permitted the gesture, but did not return the clasp.

"I do love you," she said sadly.

"Then listen to reason. Accept that this is the best outcome for everyone. And think of what we might do together. To have you with me would make a better man, a better politician of me. I love you, Sarah. Can we not find a way to make ourselves happy?"

"What way?" Miss Tolerance withdrew her hand. For an unsettling moment, she felt as if she had been taken to the top of a mountain and offered all the kingdoms laid before her. "What way? Even if I told you yes now, I could not forget, or deny, what I know. You would never forget that I knew it. I love you, Edward, but you killed that woman, your mother, and I cannot forget that."

She could not tell if it was anger or sorrow that straightened Versellion's shoulders. He looked away from her. "Then we must part?"

Miss Tolerance nodded. "Yes."

"As easily as that?" He raised one hand to her, open-palmed.

"Nothing in this is easy." She turned to the door. "Sir Walter, are you there?"

Versellion pulled his hand away as if she had burnt him.

"I'm sorry, Edward. There are some things I cannot do. Should I scruple to let a matricide rise to the prime ministry?"

The door opened and Sir Walter Mandif entered, with his two Runners behind.

"You're giving me to Bow Street?" Versellion stared at her in horror.

Miss Tolerance pursed her lips and nodded. Anything she could think to say would sound cold, she thought, and the tumble of feelings behind her impassive expression was not cold in the least.

"That is what is generally done with murderers," Sir Walter Mandif commented mildly. "Mr. Hook, if you please?"

The shorter of the two Runners had already advanced upon Versellion. "Edward Folle, I arrest you in the name of the Crown. . . ."

Miss Tolerance turned to Mandif. "You heard it all?"

"I believe so." Mandif's long, foxy face was drawn with fatigue, but he looked upon her sympathetically.

"Then you heard that there were . . . extenuating circumstances. He had had a shock—"

"It will all come out at trial," Sir Walter said. "I shall make sure the entire circumstance is laid before the court."

Versellion had gone from immobility to a rage which rivaled anything Miss Tolerance had seen on his cousin's face.

"In court? *If* I'm tried, I can only be tried by my peers," he spat. "The House of Lords is like to prove more sympathetic than *you*."

"Perhaps they would, sir," Mandif said quietly. "But given the circumstances of your birth, I cannot say for certain that you will be tried by the Lords. It seems you're not a peer but a peer's bastard."

"Sarah!" Versellion appealed to her one more time, in a voice in which outrage and entreaty were mixed. "Sarah, this is all wrong!"

Miss Tolerance nodded mutely.

"Sarah, say something to me," Versellion barked.

"I tried to tell you what happens to a man who thinks his rank will exempt him from pain. I'm sorry. . . ."

Sir Walter Mandif offered his arm to Miss Tolerance. "You need to go home," he suggested. "It has been a long night for all of us, but for you most of all. I shall arrange it."

Miss Tolerance nodded and Sir Walter led her downstairs. He left her on a chair in the front hallway while a hackney was summoned. When Hook and Penryn emerged from the room upstairs and marched down the stairs with Versellion between them, she watched their progress without expression. He would have paused before her, but the Runners urged him forward, past her chair, through the door, and into a waiting carriage.

S he did not cry in the carriage that wheeled through the waking London streets to return her to Manchester Square, nor when she removed the beautiful dress and crawled into her bed. She thought she would weep there, but her feelings were too new for mere weeping. She slept instead, for a long time. Late that day Miss Tolerance awoke and dressed herself. She had left the ball gown draped carelessly over a chair the night before, and as she picked it up now, she noted, sadly, a long rip in the skirt and several smaller rents in the bodice, souvenirs of her struggle with Folle. One more sign, she thought wearily, that she was not meant for ballrooms. Miss Tolerance piled the dress into its bandbox, carried it with her to her aunt's house, and asked the laundress to see that it was mended and cleaned, after which whoever wanted the thing might lay claim to it. Then she climbed up to her aunt's sitting room.

She found Mrs. Brereton in her customary attitude, sitting at her desk with a neat pile of duns before her and her counts-book nearby. Mrs. Brereton rose immediately when she saw her niece and put both arms around her, drawing her to sit beside her on the sofa.

"Rumors are flying all over London, and most of them mention you. How *are* you, my dear?"

Miss Tolerance smiled wearily. "Tired. Hungry."

Mrs. Brereton *tsk*ed comfortably. "You shall have a cup of tea before anything else." She lifted the silver bell at her hand.

In a few minutes Miss Tolerance had been furnished with tea and a bowl of soup. Mrs. Brereton took a sip from her own tea, then put it aside.

"Now, my dear, which of these rumors am I to believe? Versellion and his cousin, both murderers? Versellion a bastard? The Prince of Wales himself intervening to rescue you from death at Sir Henry Folle's hands? What extraordinary melodrama!"

Miss Tolerance nodded. "It is that, ma'am. But I notice you do not mention Lord Balobridge. Has he not sent word to you that he, too, is in custody? Or has he somehow got free?"

Mrs. Brereton's expression did not change. "Balobridge in custody? For what? And why would that old Tory send word to me?"

"Because the old Tory is your lover, and you have been giving him information about my movements since this whole affair began," Miss Tolerance said flatly.

Mrs. Brereton appeared to consider what she might safely say. Miss Tolerance shook her head irritably to forestall any new lies.

"I thought it was one of the girls, or one of the servants. But your rule of discretion is too well known, the punishments too absolute—and your people's loyalty is strong. The only person who might easily get round the rule is the one who made it, Aunt. You. I only wish I understood why."

"It was simply business," Mrs. Brereton said. "Balobridge assured me you would come to no harm. And I really told him very little, Sarah, things which could not hurt you. It kept him happy—and Balobridge, happy, is very generous."

"Are you so desperate for cash, Aunt Thea?"

"I am not getting younger, Sarah. A generous lover is not a thing to dismiss lightly at my age."

"Well, your lover lied. I might have been killed several times."

Mrs. Brereton raised her chin angrily; her eyes narrowed. "But you *weren't*."

Miss Tolerance nodded. "That is true, but only because of my own efforts at survival. Were you so hot to turn a profit on me that you had to sell me to Balobridge?"

"That is unfair. I have respected your unwillingness to work here, however finical—"

"Then I suppose it was finical, or old-fashioned, of me to hope that family loyalty would outweigh the claims of your generous lover."

"Family? Don't be naive, Sarah. What has family ever done for you or me? They cast us both out—"

"The more reason, I should have thought, that *our* familial bond would be inviolable." Miss Tolerance saw the anger in her aunt's eye and looked back unblinking. "Your lover Balobridge sent men to kill Versellion—and me. Balobridge was Sir Henry Folle's accomplice, and Sir Henry Folle himself killed Matt—*beat him to death* upon your information."

Mrs. Brereton paled.

"Had you not realized that? Matt went out in my coat, upon my errand, was mistaken at first by Folle and his man for me—because *someone* told Balobridge that I had gone out again—and Folle flew into a rage when Matt knew nothing of use to him, and killed him."

"That was Folle," Mrs. Brereton whispered at last. She rose

from the sofa and began to pace in front of the fireplace. "I had no way of knowing. Balobridge swore—"

"I don't doubt he did," Miss Tolerance said.

"What was I to do? Say no to him?"

"You might have done. I did."

Her aunt stopped pacing and turned to regard her niece with equal coldness. "*You* did. I am sick of your schoolroom scruples! Particularly when they are so malleable! At least I am selective in my customers—I've never seen you turn someone away because you did not like the cut of his coat!"

Miss Tolerance regarded her aunt with astonishment. "The cut of his coat? God, Aunt, anyone can be bamboozled by his tailor; turn away custom because the client is old, or badly dressed, or lacks wit, and I'd have very little indeed. You can afford to be nice in your clientele: you place so few conditions upon what happens once they have come through your door."

"And you have so many conditions on what you will do?"

"Not so many as I would like, but a few. My reputation—"

"Good heavens, girl, you lost your reputation a decade ago! All this pretense—"

"I lost my virginity. I lost my innocence. The world seems to regard this as the same thing as honor, but I do not. You lost your 'honor' a score of years before I did, but do you steal from your customers, Aunt? Do you sell their secrets? Do you force your . . . employees . . . to take men they detest, or to do things they detest?"

Mrs. Brereton shook her head sadly, as if her niece's incomprehension saddened her. "That's not honor, girl. That's good business sense."

"Then I am lucky I can afford to be a good businesswoman, Aunt."

The two women watched each other warily. It was the older one who spoke first.

"Perhaps it was a mistake, telling Balobridge what he wanted. I did not see the harm, but perhaps I was shortsighted." Mrs.

Brereton looked at her niece apprehensively. "Sarah, what are you going to do now?"

"Do?" Despite the warmth of the day, Miss Tolerance felt cold. She rubbed her hands together briskly. "I don't know. Wait for my next client. Mend my stockings. Why? Do you want me out of the cottage?"

Mrs. Brereton shook her head. "No. Did I say so? Certainly not. I should miss having you here." She smiled. "We are family, after all."

Miss Tolerance laughed softly. "Why, so we are."

"And we may go on as we have before?"

"As before? Not quite. But in terms of *business*"—her emphasis was light but satirical—"this place suits me very well. I will be happy to rent the cottage from you, and take tea with you, and assist you when I can. But we should be clear upon this one point: your business is in selling the sexual favors of your employees; mine is in providing information and discreet errands for my clients. We must agree each to keep to our own businesses. I shall keep my counsel. You will not sell yours." Miss Tolerance meant the words to hurt, but she could not tell if they had hit their mark.

"Well, then." Mrs. Brereton returned to the sofa and sat again. "Let me give you more tea."

D espite the brave words she had used with her aunt, Miss Tolerance returned to her cottage feeling very much alone. She looked at the counts-book on her table but could not bring herself to open it. The *Gazette* and the *Times* lay folded there, but she was unwilling to look at them. She put the kettle on for tea and then decided she wanted none. She was not sleepy, but wanted more than anything else not to sit and brood over the events of the last four-and-twenty hours. She thought of returning to Mrs. Brereton's house to find a book, but could not make herself leave the cottage.

A knock at her door made her jump. It was Marianne.

"I thought you could do with some distracting," she said placidly. "This seemed to help when you were sick." She put *Tom Jones* on the table with a firm thump and looked at Miss Tolerance as if to dare her to say no.

"I was just wishing for something to read," Miss Tolerance said. "Would you like some tea? The kettle is just on."

Marianne took up her seat on the settle and began to read aloud. Miss Tolerance made tea and poured it out. To her surprise, she found, an hour later, that she and Marianne had drunk the pot dry. She took a little water from the kettle, rinsed the pot with it, and put the kettle back on the hob to heat again. Marianne read on through the end of the chapter and finished just as Miss Tolerance was measuring out tea into the pot.

"Well, you've stirred things up properly, haven't you?" Marianne leaned into the corner of the settle and grinned, as if stirring things up were a very good joke upon all concerned. From the calico workbag at her side she took out a piece of knitting and began to work.

"What have you heard?" Miss Tolerance asked.

"Nothing of account from your aunt or anyone in the house except Cook, who said you had a long face when you passed through the kitchen. But some of the guests in the house was buzzing with This One's ruin and That One's scandal. And it seems you caught our Matt's killer after all. I feel bad about that—Folle was one of mine."

"You couldn't have known," Miss Tolerance assured her.

"No, I couldn't," the whore said calmly. "And you, you got your heart broken, did you?" Marianne tilted her head sympathetically. "No, no one has said so, but you've the look of it. If you want to talk, I promise it will go no further."

"I believe you," Miss Tolerance said. "But there's little to talk about. He—I fell in love with a client."

"He didn't love you?"

Miss Tolerance laughed sadly. "Oh, yes, he did, I think."

"Well, then, where's the heartbreak in that?"

"My client was the Earl of Versellion."

Marianne's mouth pursed in an "O" of appreciation. "The one you turned in to Bow Street? That's *hard*. You could have let it slide, couldn't you?"

"Let murder slide?" Miss Tolerance asked incredulously.

"No, I suppose not," Marianne murmured. "There's some as might."

Miss Tolerance shook her head. "You think it was harsh of me to turn him in? The woman he killed was old, Fallen, no great loss to society. Was it not hard for her to die in such a way?"

"Hard for you to make such a choice." Marianne leaned forward to inspect the teapot. "I think it's ready. May I pour you another cup?"

The watch on the mantel ticked. Marianne's knitting needles clacked quietly, and the fire hissed and popped. Miss Tolerance took up *Tom Jones,* and began to read aloud from the point where Marianne had stopped. She leaned closer to the fire; the summer light was fading, and she had not yet lit a lamp.

Miss Tolerance was sufficiently engrossed in reading that she did not at once hear the knock on the door. When she answered, Cole put his head in.

"Miss, a gentleman has brought a message." He offered the letter to her.

Miss Tolerance sighed, marked her place, and put the book down. She needed to work, after all. New business would give her something to think about beyond her own woes. She broke the seal on the letter and read it with increasing surprise.

My dear Miss Tolerance:
The Crown is likely to forget to proffer its thanks for your assistance in the matters lately resolved. I cannot. I realize that your assistance came at no little hazard, and at some personal cost. I would like to call upon you to offer my congratulations, my appreciation, and, perhaps, my sympathy, for the cost you have borne in settling this affair. It is difficult to make such an offer

*without misinterpretation to a woman situated as you are, but
with all respect I beg you will consider me your friend to command.*

> *Your servant, Walter Mandif*

Miss Tolerance was dismayed to find tears welling in her eyes
as she read, and reread, this missive. *I must be very tired indeed,*
she thought.

"Well?" Marianne asked, and at the same moment, Cole said,
"The gentleman is waiting for a reply, miss."

"Is he?" Miss Tolerance looked about her uncertainly.

Marianne rose and gathered up her knitting. "I'll be off. You
have things to do, I'm sure." She was past Cole and out the door
before Miss Tolerance could think of what to say. Miss Tolerance
watched her go, thinking: the business of the fan had cost her,
but she had gained as well. At last she turned back to Cole, still
waiting for an answer. He was plainly curious and concerned.

"Well, Cole. Will you ask my friend Sir Walter if he will take
a cup of tea with me?"

The footman bowed and went back to deliver the message.
Miss Tolerance lit the lamps, put the kettle on again, and waited
for a knock at her door.

A Note on History,
and of Thanks

I t didn't happen like this. As any friend of the English Regency will tell you, George III recovered from his initial bout of madness in 1788. Despite several subsequent periods of derangement, he ruled the country until 1811, when his son, the Prince of Wales, was installed as Regent for the remaining nine years of his father's life. Queen Charlotte was never Regent. Wales *did* secretly marry the Catholic widow Maria Fitzherbert, but the marriage was never publicly acknowledged (an early trial of the "don't ask, don't tell" system, and about as successful) and Wales did not forfeit succession to the throne. He later officially (and bigamously) married Princess Caroline of Brunswick, and the two made each other very miserable indeed; he had many liaisons after Mrs. Fitzherbert, but it is interesting to note that he was buried with a miniature portrait of her tucked close to his heart. In other words, I made a whole bunch of this stuff up, while trying to stay true to much of the history of the era.

There are many things I didn't make up: the vehement anti-

Catholic sentiment of the late 1700s and early 1800s; the vogue for botanical and agricultural research, much sponsored by George III himself; the lack of options open to "Fallen Women" of good family; and the extraordinary number and range of houses of prostitution in London at this time. The reformer Patrick Colquhoun estimated that there were fifty thousand prostitutes at work in London in the late 1700s, some three thousand of them of "good family." I doubt that there was ever so forward-looking and broad-minded a house of joy as Mrs. Dorothea Brereton's, however. Likewise, the custom of *noms d'amour* I made up, as I did the Dueling Notices in the newspapers Sarah Tolerance reads; although the laws against dueling were flouted constantly, it was never on so systematic a basis. And, of course, the anticipation of Gregor Mendel's research by Dr. Charles Hawley's international cabal of scientists is wholly a fabrication.

Playing around with history is a tricky thing. One twitch to the real past and a dozen new questions show up. A generous double handful of people helped before, during, and after the fact to make the book work, and I cannot thank them enough.

A formal salute to my stage combat teachers, Richard Rizk, T. J. Glenn, David Brimmer, and M. Lucie Chin (particularly David, who read over the fight scenes herein and saved me, and thus Sarah Tolerance, from any fatal mistakes). They inspired me with their grace, the wit of their choreography, and their ability to roll with the punches—literally.

I got enormous support and encouragement from a number of sources: the members of my writers' workshop, who were willing to enter a world they knew nothing of while trying to critique the story it contained. My friends on-line and off, particularly Gregory Feeley, Sherwood Smith, Ed and Elena Galliard, Greer Gilman, Susan Shwartz, and eluki bes shahar, all of whom suggested sources or sent along material that helped me build my skewed Regency convincingly. Andrew Sigel loaned me books, read the first draft of the book, and asked many hard questions about issues of royal succession, closing loopholes while opening possibilities. My friends Steven Popkes and Claire Eddy offered both constructive suggestions and their unflagging faith that I could make this book work. Barbara Dicks, my very first editor, got me started as a writer and a fan of the English Regency. I owe more than mere thanks to those friends in Tor editorial who came up with the notion of a "hard-boiled Regency" one rainy afternoon years ago and dropped the plum in my lap; I hope they like the result of their brainstorm. My agent, Valerie Smith, energized me with her faith in me and in the project.

To Patrick Nielsen Hayden, my editor, thanks for his enthusiasm and his patience on those occasions when I broke into auctorial neurosis; Teresa Nielsen Hayden, ditto. Thanks also to the copy editor, Dave Cole, and other production staff who labor unsung, and to Irene Gallo, Empress of Design, who sets the stones to look like jewels. Thanks, too, to the staff of Barnes and Noble's Cafe at the Broadway and 83rd Street store in Manhattan, where most of this book was written!

Merest decency requires that I acknowledge my debt to Jane Austen, one of the sharpest, funniest writers in the English language, whose meticulous examination of her social scene inspired Sarah Tolerance's dilemma; and Dashiell Hammett, whose works inspired the shape of her story.

Finally, thanks to my husband, Danny Caccavo, whose love and support keep my feet on the ground when the story lures me up into the ozone; and our daughters, Julie and Rebecca, who inspire me every day.